image COMICS PRESENTS

SONATA

A *Shadowline* PRODUCTION

FOR
ANOMALY
PRODUCTIONS

STORY
DAVID HINE &
BRIAN HABERLIN

ART
BRIAN HABERLIN

COLORS
GEIRROD VAN DYKE

LETTERS
FRANCIS TAKENAGA

LEAD DEVELOPER
DAVID PENTZ

PRODUCTION
DIANA SANSON &
HANNAH WALL

FOR
Shadowline

MELANIE HACKETT
EDITOR

MARC LOMBARDI
COMMUNICATIONS

JIM VALENTINO
PUBLISHER/BOOK DESIGN

FOR
image

ERIKA SCHNATZ
PRODUCTION

IMAGE COMICS, INC.
Robert Kirkman—Chief Operating Officer
Erik Larsen—Chief Financial Officer
Todd McFarlane—President
Marc Silvestri—Chief Executive Officer
Jim Valentino—Vice President
Eric Stephenson—Publisher/Chief Creative Officer
Jeff Boison—Director of Publishing Planning
& Book Trade Sales
Chris Ross—Director of Digital Sales
Jeff Stang—Director of Direct Market Sales
—Director of PR & Marketing

Get the Companion App to see how the comic
was made, view behind-the-scenes content,
and much more!
Go to: **ExperienceAnomaly.com/sonata**

image

Unused Cover

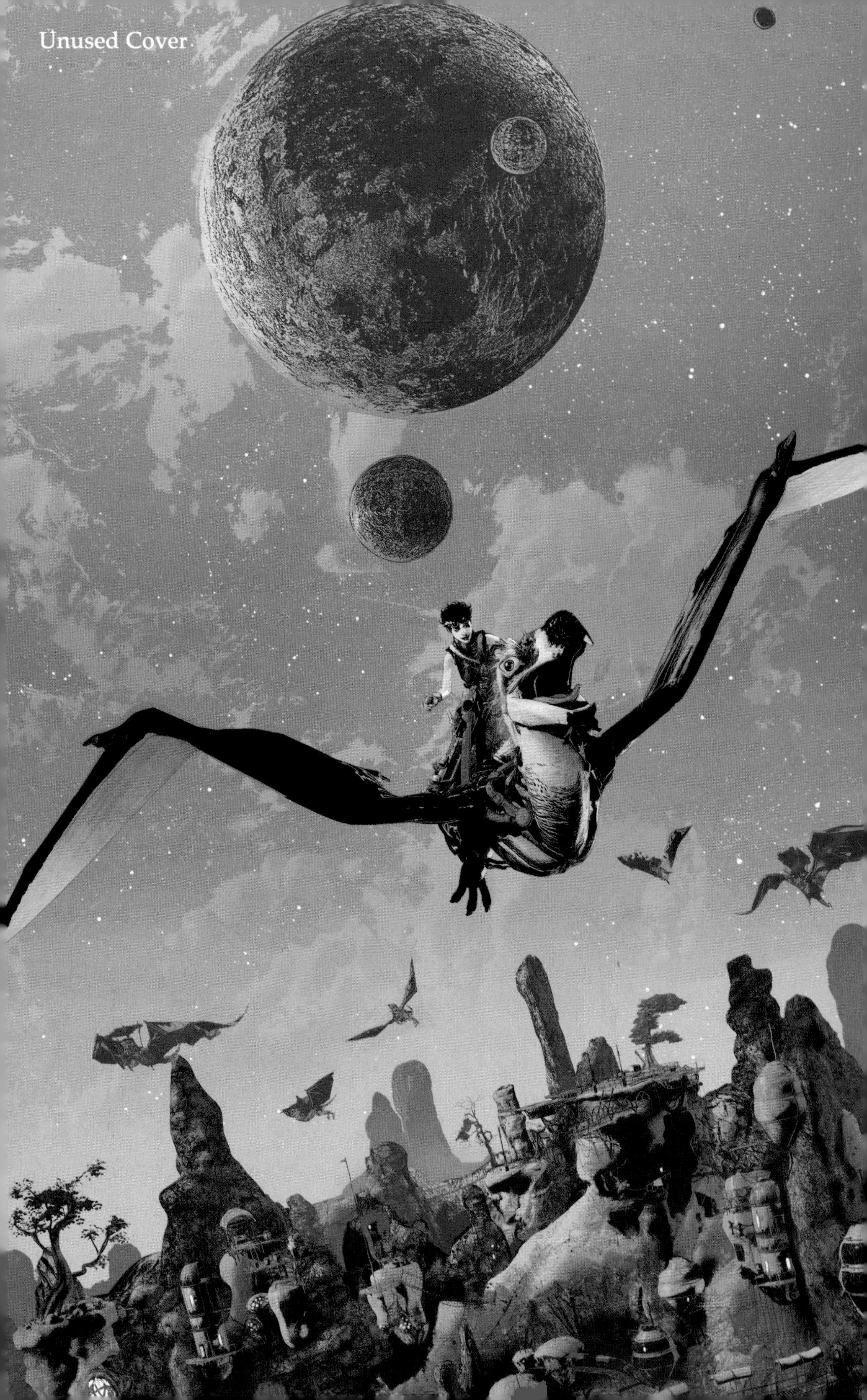

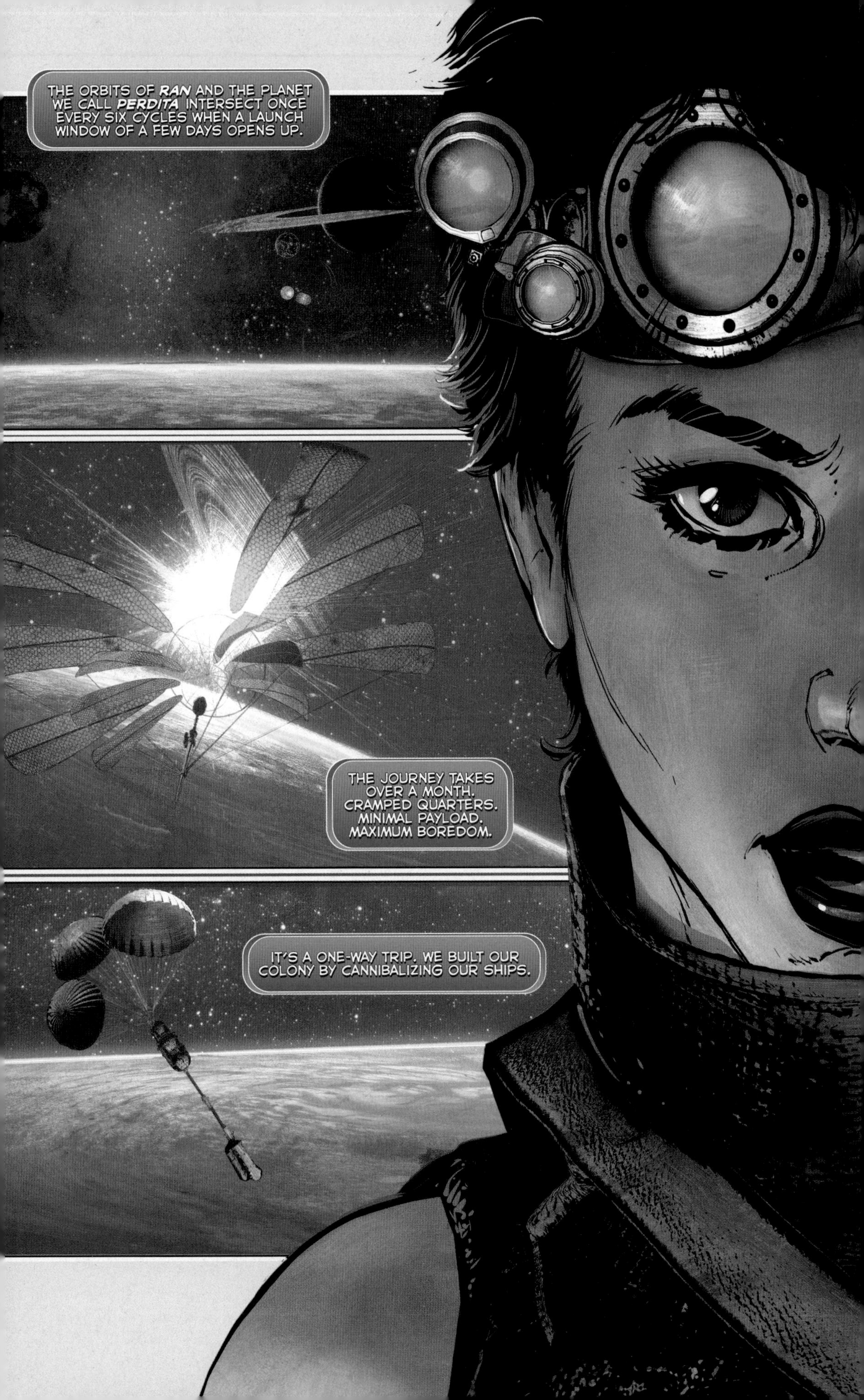
THE ORBITS OF RAN AND THE PLANET WE CALL PERDITA INTERSECT ONCE EVERY SIX CYCLES WHEN A LAUNCH WINDOW OF A FEW DAYS OPENS UP.
THE JOURNEY TAKES OVER A MONTH. CRAMPED QUARTERS. MINIMAL PAYLOAD. MAXIMUM BOREDOM.
IT'S A ONE-WAY TRIP. WE BUILT OUR COLONY BY CANNIBALIZING OUR SHIPS.

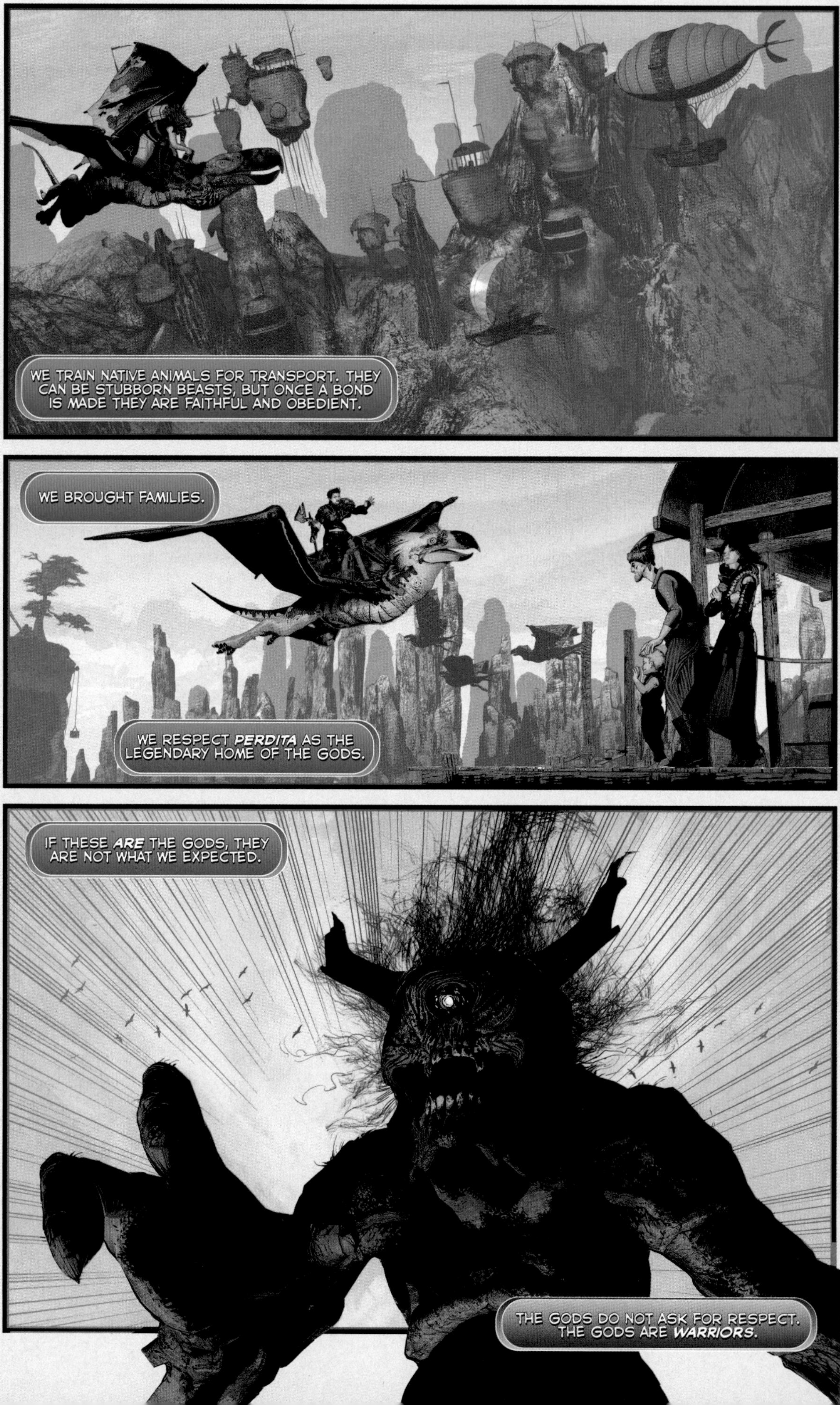
WE TRAIN NATIVE ANIMALS FOR TRANSPORT. THEY CAN BE STUBBORN BEASTS, BUT ONCE A BOND IS MADE THEY ARE FAITHFUL AND OBEDIENT.
WE BROUGHT FAMILIES.
WE RESPECT PERDITA AS THE LEGENDARY HOME OF THE GODS.
IF THESE ARE THE GODS, THEY ARE NOT WHAT WE EXPECTED.
THE GODS DO NOT ASK FOR RESPECT. THE GODS ARE WARRIORS.

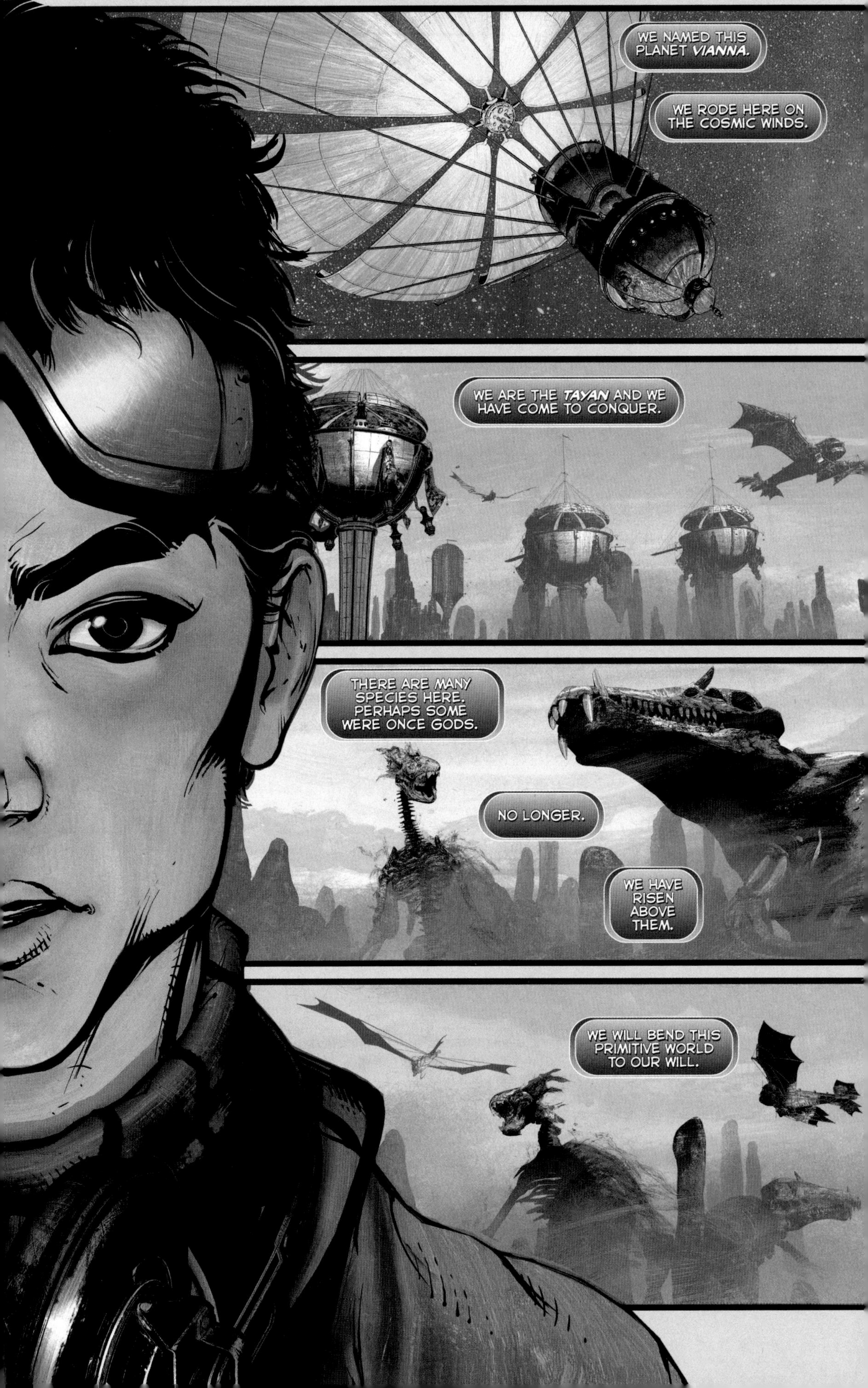

WE NAMED THIS PLANET VIANNA.
WE RODE HERE ON THE COSMIC WINDS.
WE ARE THE TAYAN AND WE HAVE COME TO CONQUER.
THERE ARE MANY SPECIES HERE. PERHAPS SOME WERE ONCE GODS.
NO LONGER.
WE HAVE RISEN ABOVE THEM.
WE WILL BEND THIS PRIMITIVE WORLD TO OUR WILL.

I DID NOT CHOOSE THIS WAY OF LIFE. NONE OF US DO...
...BUT I WILL DO MY DUTY AS A TAYAN...
...EVEN IF I MUST KILL YOU!
WE RANS WANT NOTHING MORE THAN THE RIGHT TO LIVE IN PEACE...
...BUT IF I MUST FIGHT TO PRESERVE THAT RIGHT, THEN I WILL FIGHT...
...EVEN IF I HAVE TO DIE!

Issue #1 Cover A

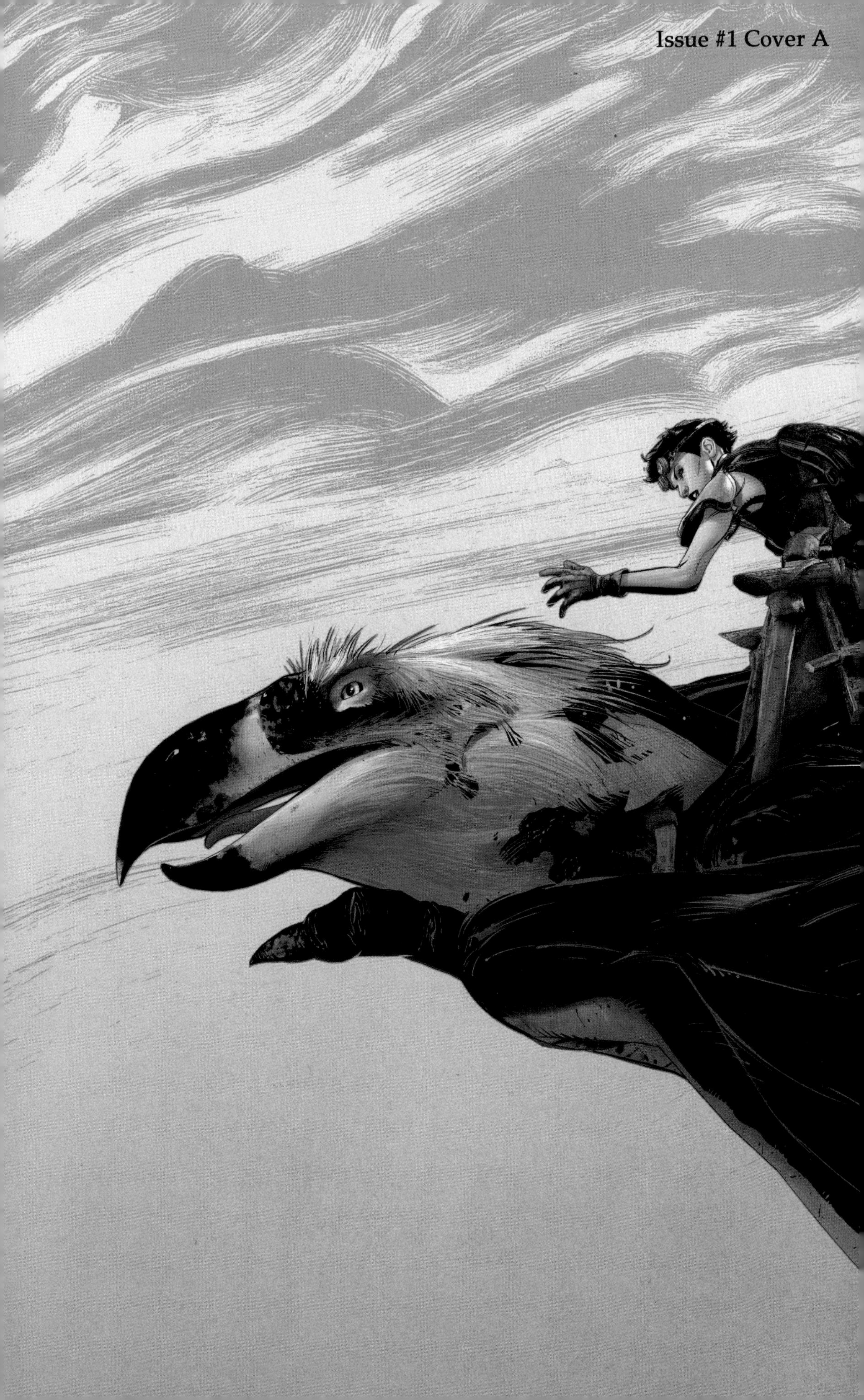

Issue #1 Cover B

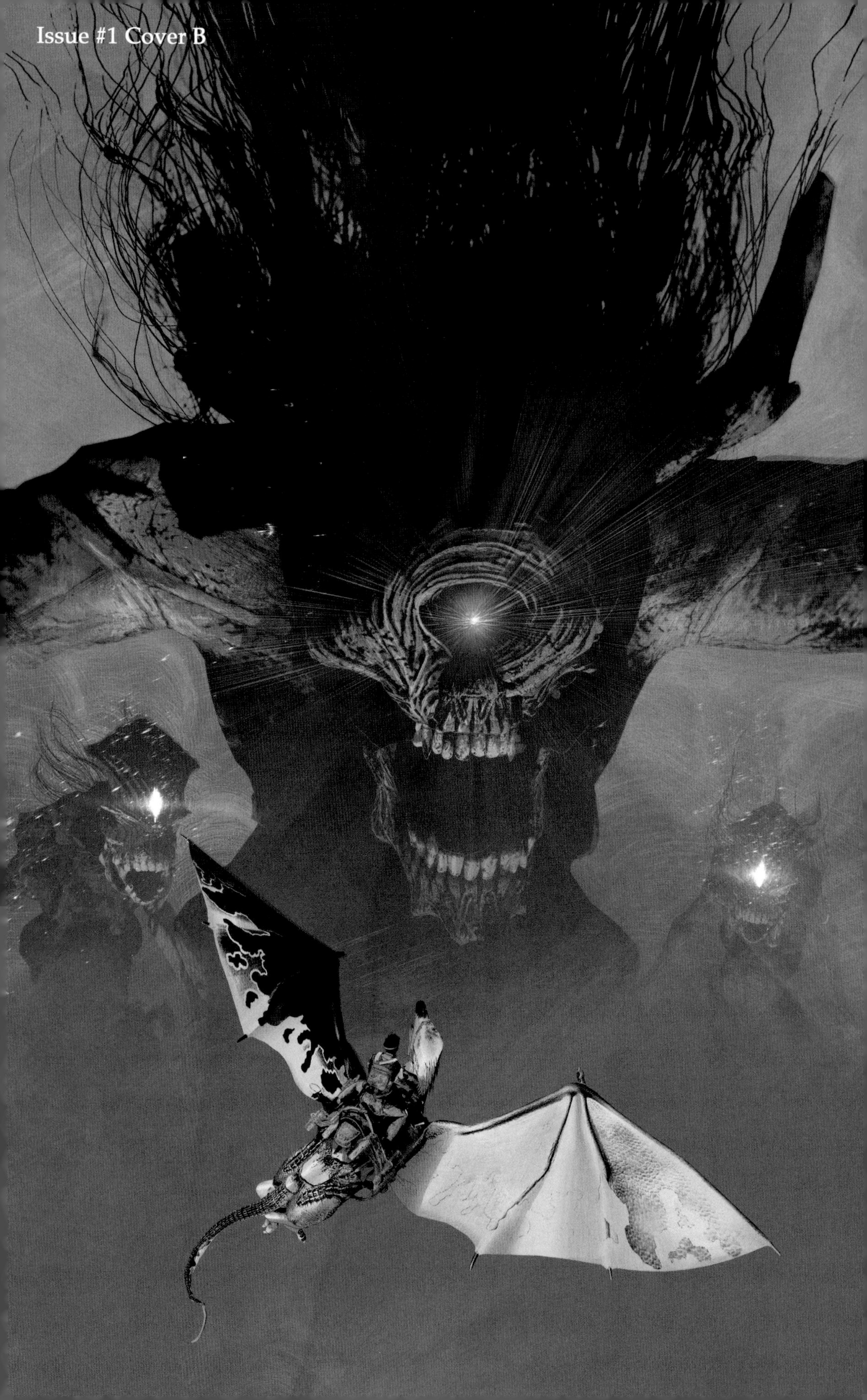

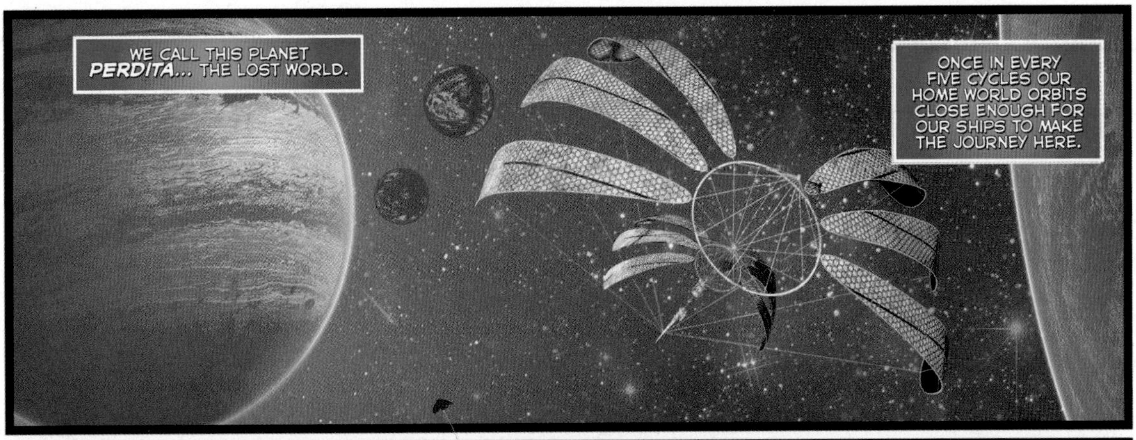
WE CALL THIS PLANET PERDITA... THE LOST WORLD.
ONCE IN EVERY FIVE CYCLES OUR HOME WORLD ORBITS CLOSE ENOUGH FOR OUR SHIPS TO MAKE THE JOURNEY HERE.

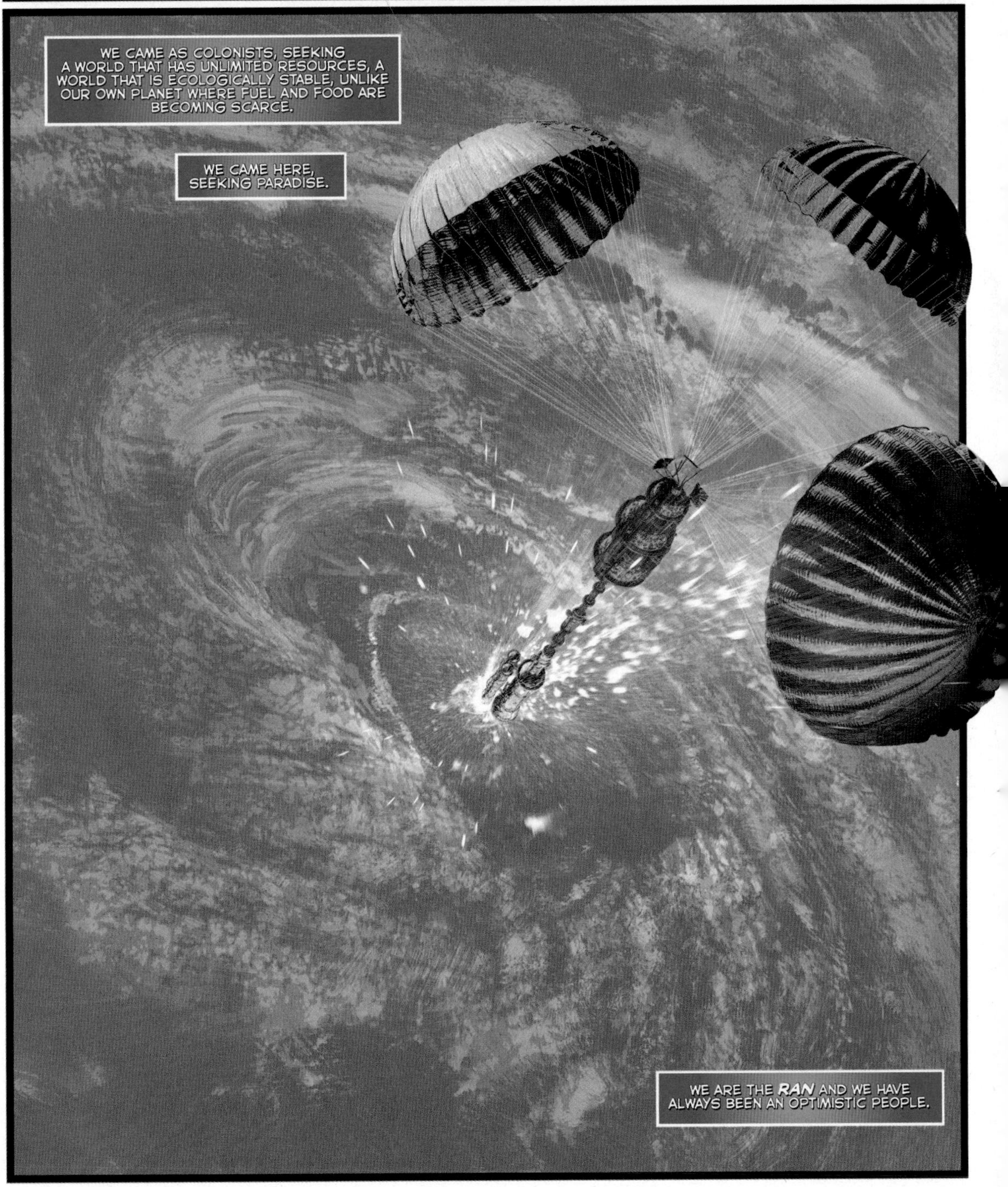
WE CAME AS COLONISTS, SEEKING A WORLD THAT HAS UNLIMITED RESOURCES, A WORLD THAT IS ECOLOGICALLY STABLE, UNLIKE OUR OWN PLANET WHERE FUEL AND FOOD ARE BECOMING SCARCE.
WE CAME HERE, SEEKING PARADISE.
WE ARE THE RAN AND WE HAVE ALWAYS BEEN AN OPTIMISTIC PEOPLE.

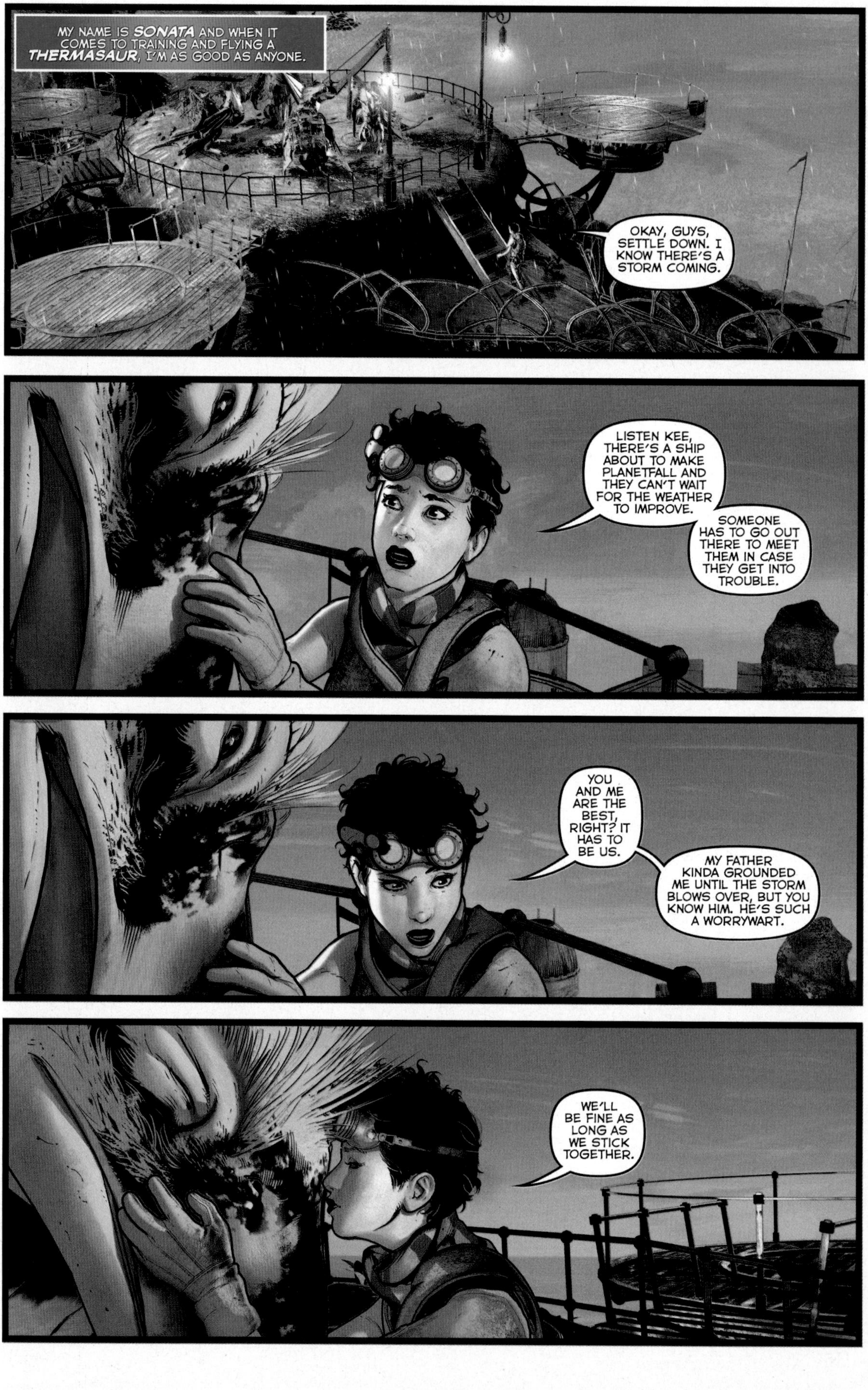
MY NAME IS SONATA AND WHEN IT COMES TO TRAINING AND FLYING A THERMASAUR, I'M AS GOOD AS ANYONE.
OKAY, GUYS, SETTLE DOWN. I KNOW THERE'S A STORM COMING.
LISTEN KEE, THERE'S A SHIP ABOUT TO MAKE PLANETFALL AND THEY CAN'T WAIT FOR THE WEATHER TO IMPROVE.
SOMEONE HAS TO GO OUT THERE TO MEET THEM IN CASE THEY GET INTO TROUBLE.
YOU AND ME ARE THE BEST, RIGHT? IT HAS TO BE US.
MY FATHER KINDA GROUNDED ME UNTIL THE STORM BLOWS OVER, BUT YOU KNOW HIM. HE'S SUCH A WORRYWART.
WE'LL BE FINE AS LONG AS WE STICK TOGETHER.

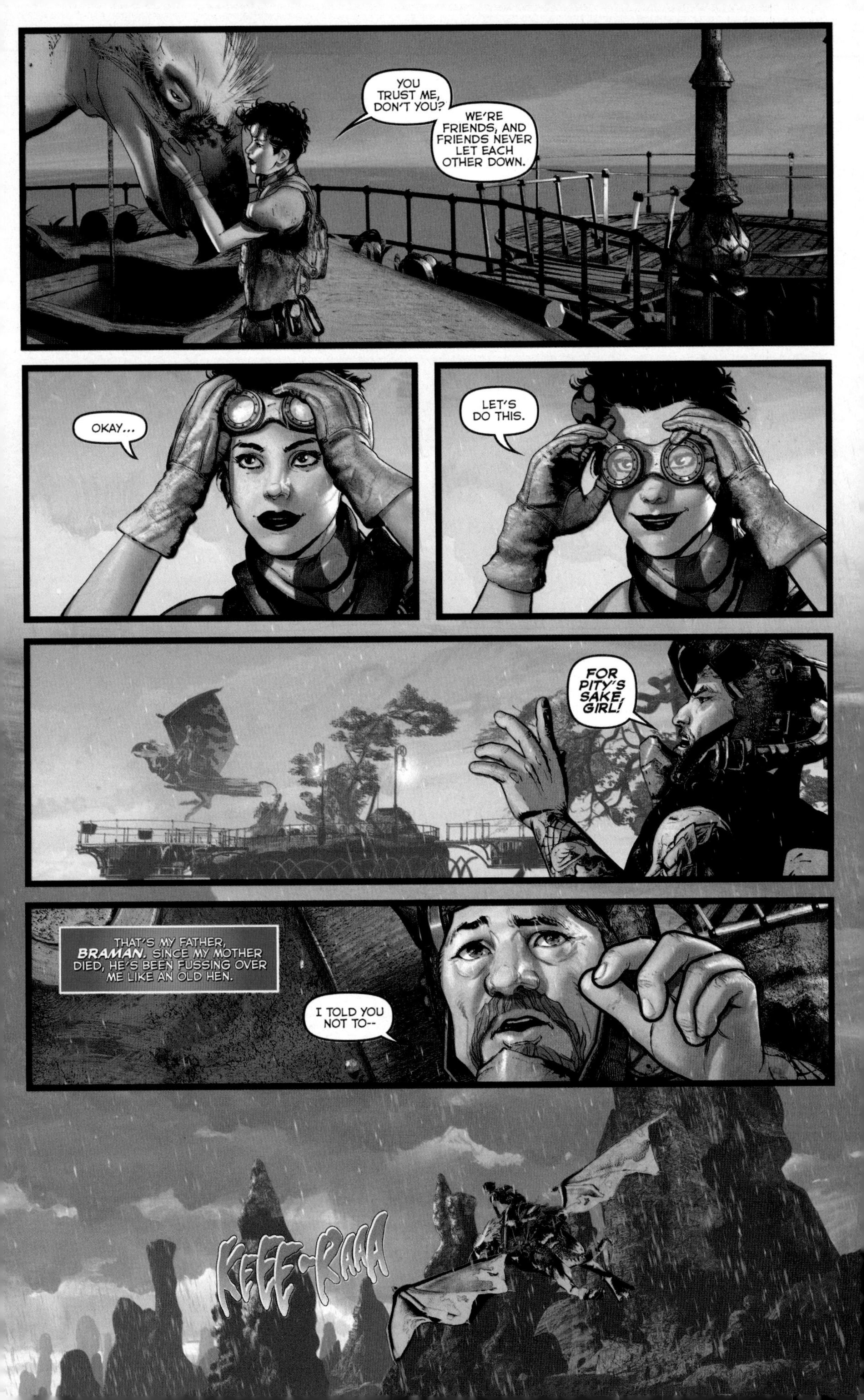
YOU TRUST ME, DON'T YOU?
WE'RE FRIENDS, AND FRIENDS NEVER LET EACH OTHER DOWN.
OKAY...
LET'S DO THIS.
FOR PITY'S SAKE, GIRL!
THAT'S MY FATHER, BRAMAN. SINCE MY MOTHER DIED, HE'S BEEN FUSSING OVER ME LIKE AN OLD HEN.
I TOLD YOU NOT TO--
KEEE-RAAA

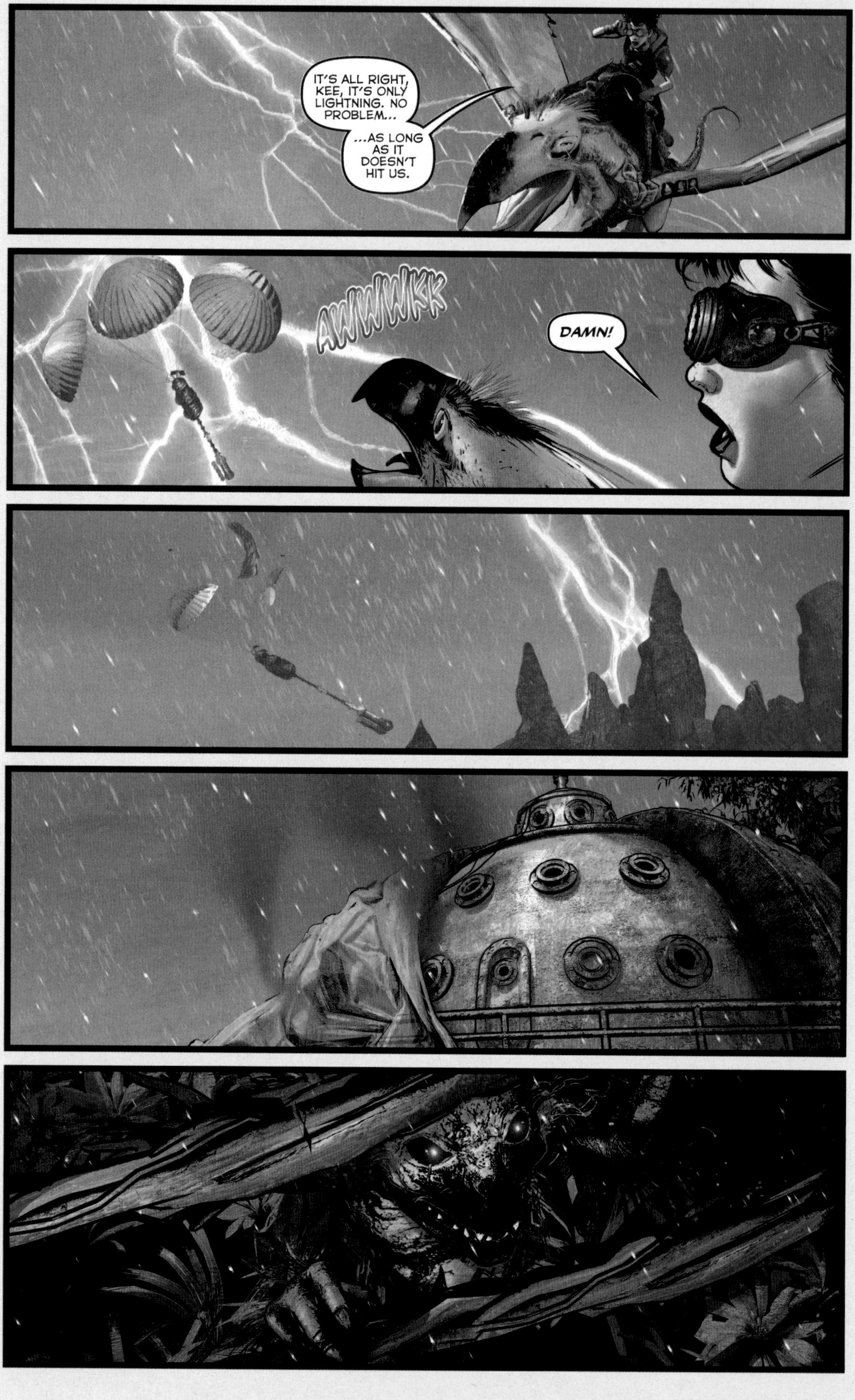
IT'S ALL RIGHT, KEE, IT'S ONLY LIGHTNING. NO PROBLEM...
...AS LONG AS IT DOESN'T HIT US.
AWWWKK
DAMN!

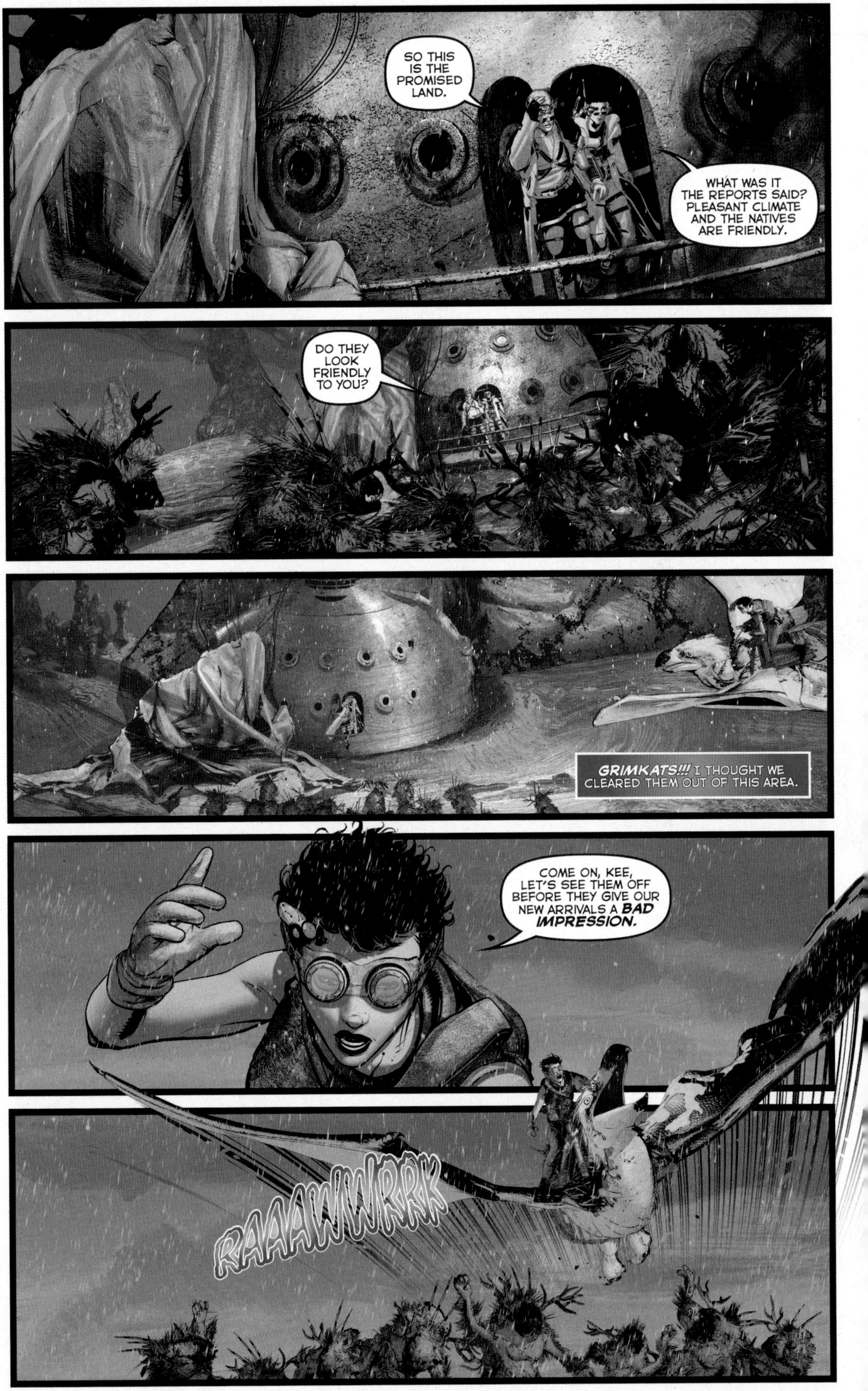
SO THIS IS THE PROMISED LAND.
WHAT WAS IT THE REPORTS SAID? PLEASANT CLIMATE AND THE NATIVES ARE FRIENDLY.
DO THEY LOOK FRIENDLY TO YOU?
GRIMKATS!!! I THOUGHT WE CLEARED THEM OUT OF THIS AREA.
COME ON, KEE, LET'S SEE THEM OFF BEFORE THEY GIVE OUR NEW ARRIVALS A BAD IMPRESSION.
RAAAWWRRK

MY FATHER WOULD SAY I'M GRANDSTANDING. HE THINKS I SHOULD LEARN A LITTLE HUMILITY...

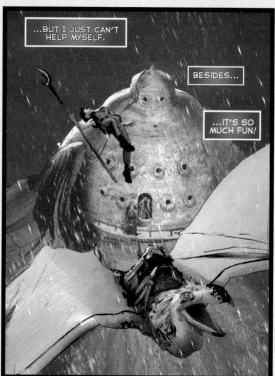

...BUT I JUST CAN'T HELP MYSELF.

BESIDES...

...IT'S SO MUCH FUN!

DON'T WORRY, THEY AREN'T AS TOUGH AS THEY LOOK.

THAT'S IT, *RUN YOU SKABBOUS VERMIN!*

RUN AND--

--OH NO...

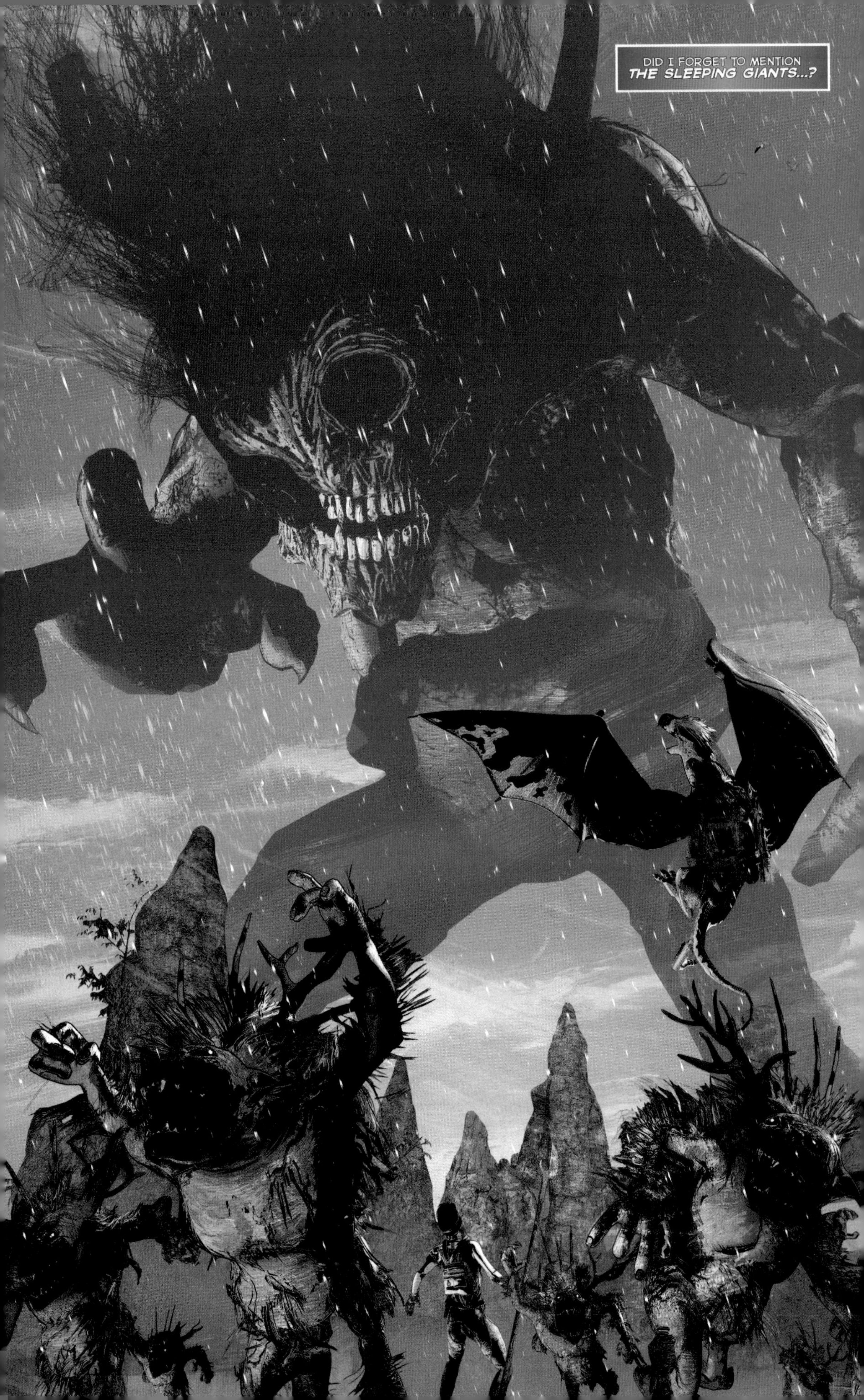
DID I FORGET TO MENTION
THE SLEEPING GIANTS...?

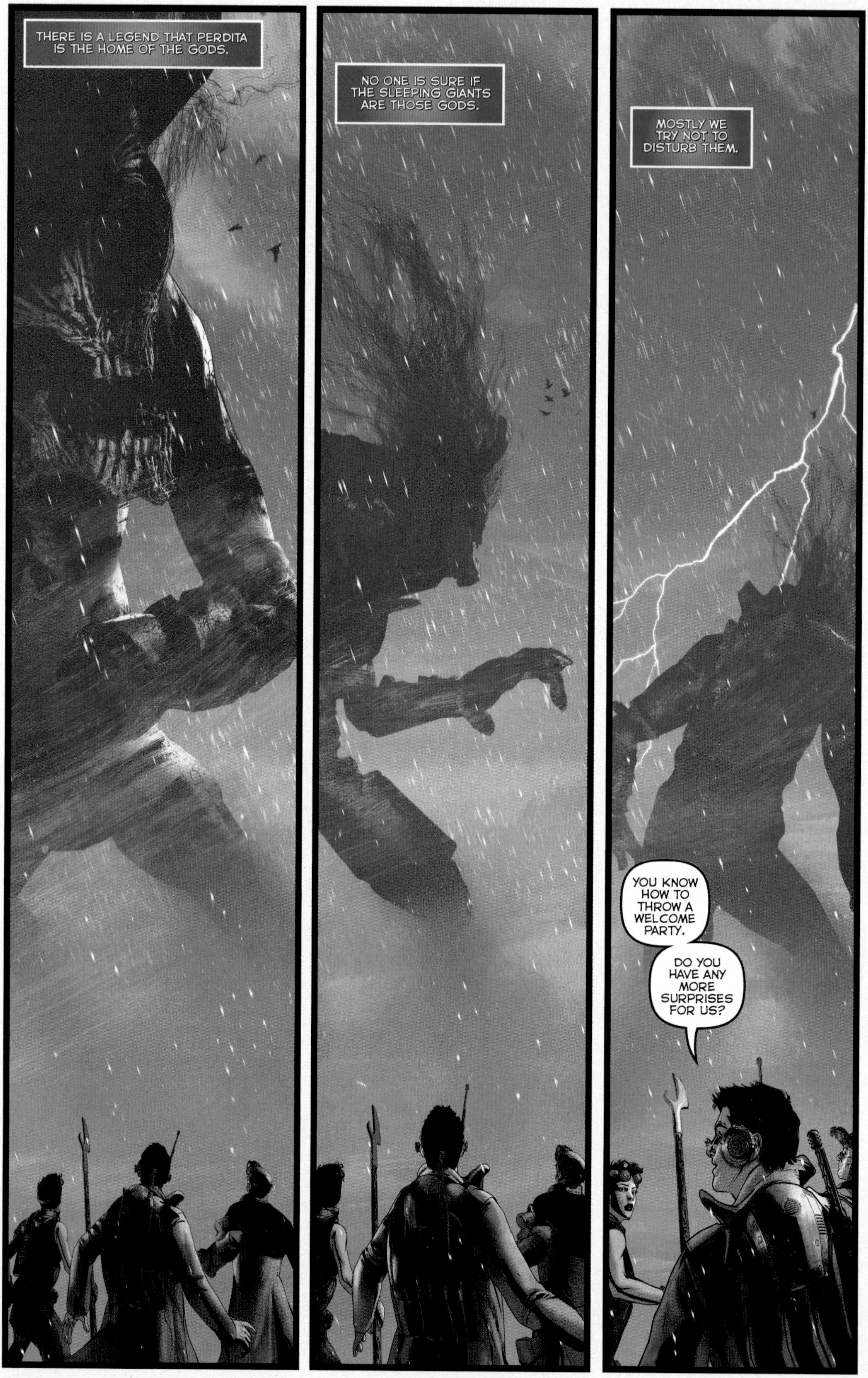
THERE IS A LEGEND THAT PERDITA IS THE HOME OF THE GODS.
NO ONE IS SURE IF THE SLEEPING GIANTS ARE THOSE GODS.
MOSTLY WE TRY NOT TO DISTURB THEM.
YOU KNOW HOW TO THROW A WELCOME PARTY.
DO YOU HAVE ANY MORE SURPRISES FOR US?

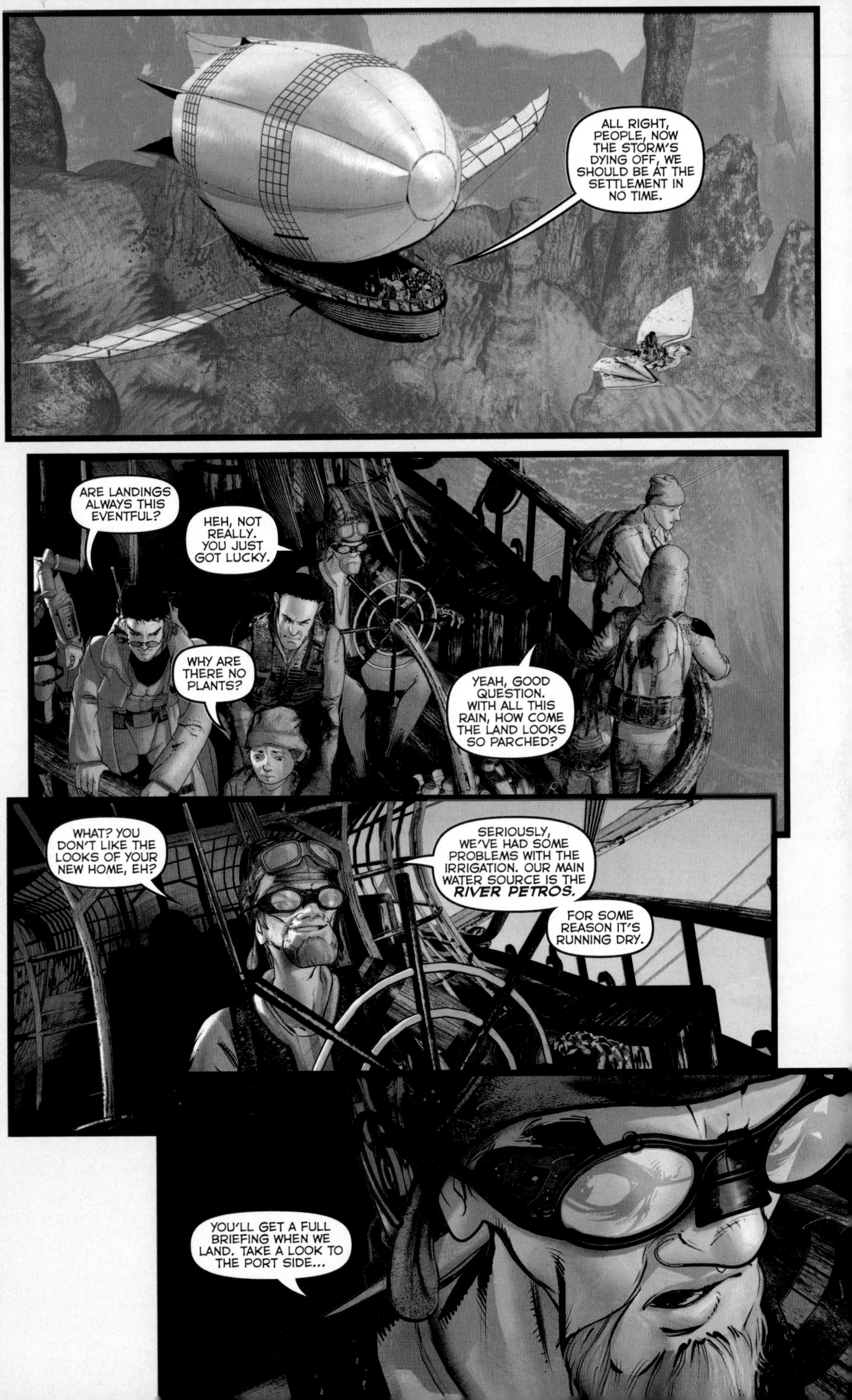
ALL RIGHT, PEOPLE, NOW THE STORM'S DYING OFF, WE SHOULD BE AT THE SETTLEMENT IN NO TIME.
ARE LANDINGS ALWAYS THIS EVENTFUL?
HEH, NOT REALLY. YOU JUST GOT LUCKY.
WHY ARE THERE NO PLANTS?
YEAH, GOOD QUESTION. WITH ALL THIS RAIN, HOW COME THE LAND LOOKS SO PARCHED?
WHAT? YOU DON'T LIKE THE LOOKS OF YOUR NEW HOME, EH?
SERIOUSLY, WE'VE HAD SOME PROBLEMS WITH THE IRRIGATION. OUR MAIN WATER SOURCE IS THE RIVER PETROS.
FOR SOME REASON IT'S RUNNING DRY.
YOU'LL GET A FULL BRIEFING WHEN WE LAND. TAKE A LOOK TO THE PORT SIDE...

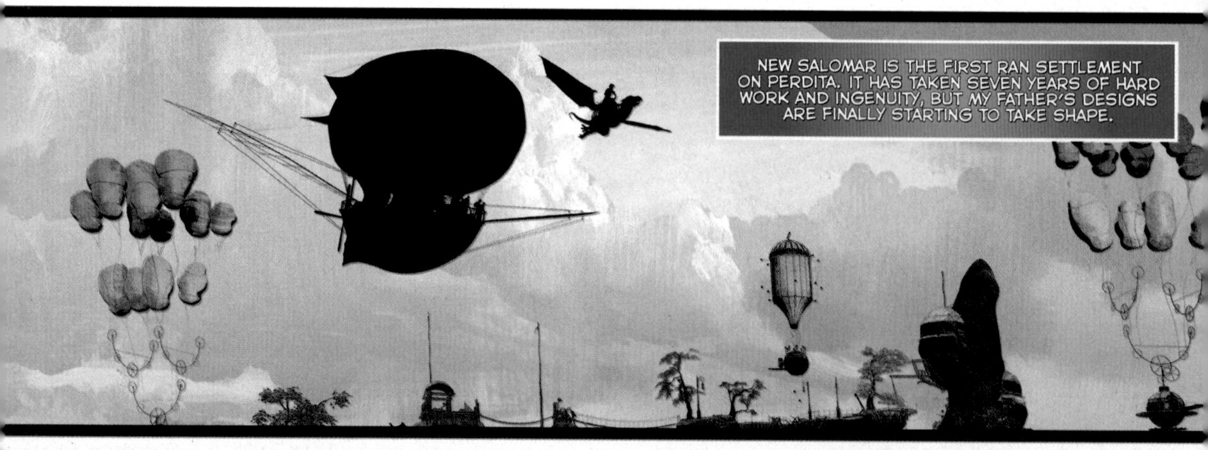
NEW SALOMAR IS THE FIRST RAN SETTLEMENT ON PERDITA. IT HAS TAKEN SEVEN YEARS OF HARD WORK AND INGENUITY, BUT MY FATHER'S DESIGNS ARE FINALLY STARTING TO TAKE SHAPE.

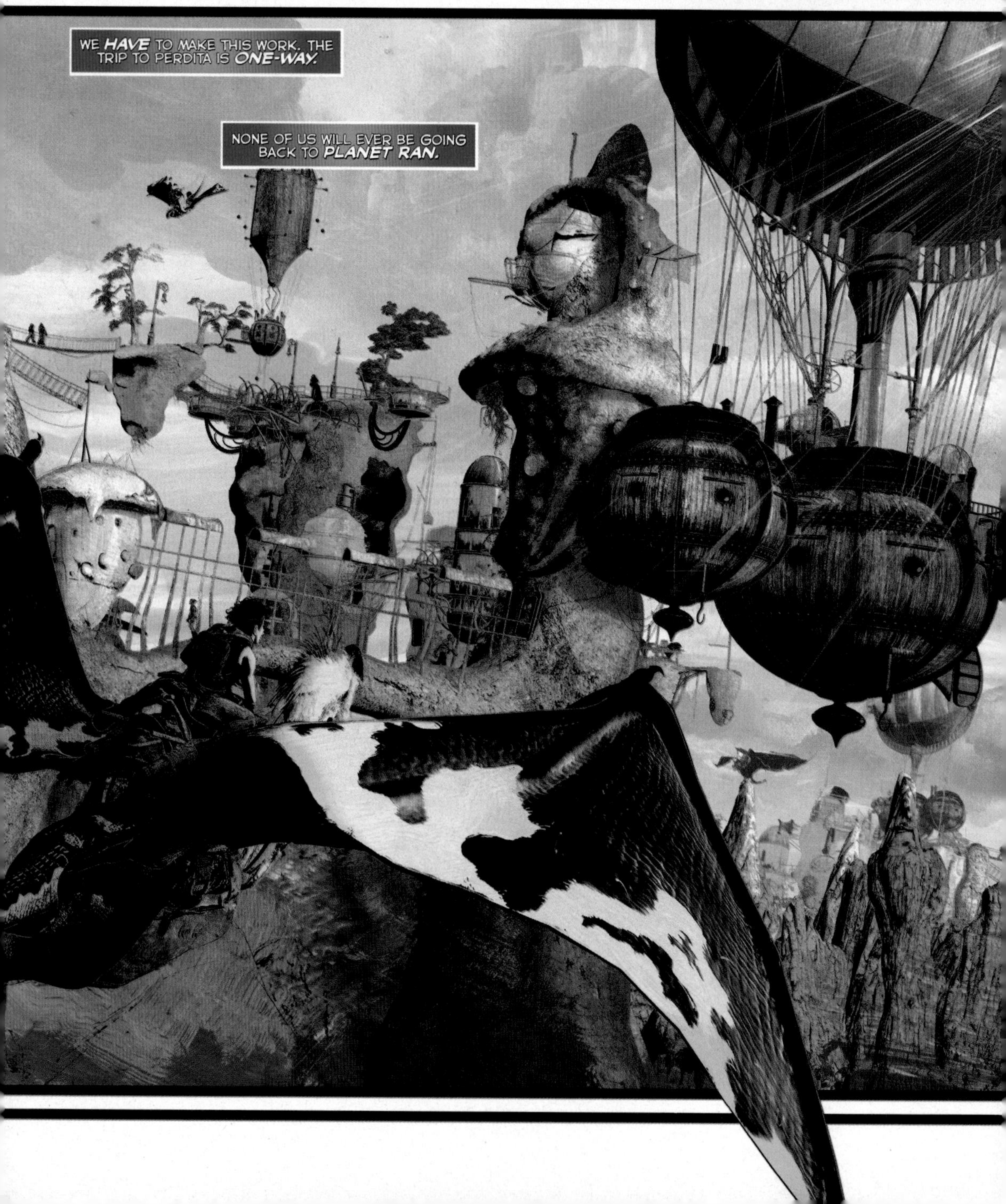
WE HAVE TO MAKE THIS WORK. THE TRIP TO PERDITA IS ONE-WAY.
NONE OF US WILL EVER BE GOING BACK TO PLANET RAN.

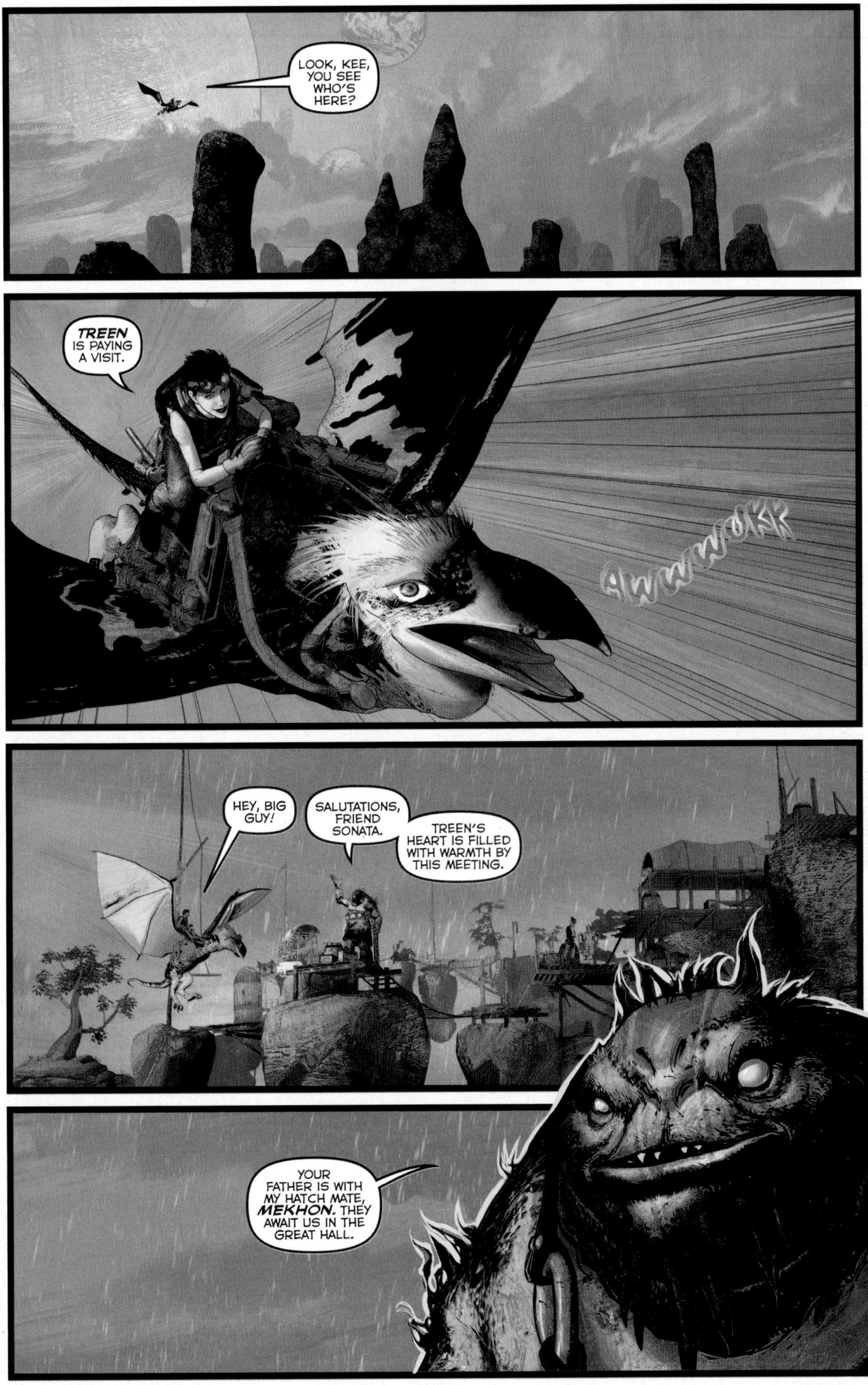
LOOK, KEE, YOU SEE WHO'S HERE?
TREEN IS PAYING A VISIT.
HEY, BIG GUY!
SALUTATIONS, FRIEND SONATA.
TREEN'S HEART IS FILLED WITH WARMTH BY THIS MEETING.
YOUR FATHER IS WITH MY HATCH MATE, MEKHON. THEY AWAIT US IN THE GREAT HALL.

OKAY, THIS' LOOKS SERIOUS.

SONATA, I'M GLAD TO SEE YOU MADE IT BACK IN ONE PIECE...

...IN SPITE OF DISOBEYING MY ORDERS *NOT* TO FLY IN THE STORM.

OUR *LUMANI* FRIENDS HAVE BROUGHT US NEWS.

AS YOU KNOW, INVADERS FROM *PLANET TAYA* HAVE SET UP CAMP IN THE REGION.

NOT STRICTLY 'INVADERS,' BRAMAN. WE HAVE NO ABSOLUTE JURISDICTION HERE.

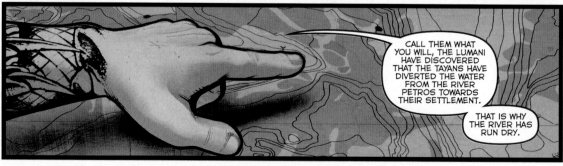

CALL THEM WHAT YOU WILL, THE LUMANI HAVE DISCOVERED THAT THE TAYANS HAVE DIVERTED THE WATER FROM THE RIVER PETROS TOWARDS THEIR SETTLEMENT.

THAT IS WHY THE RIVER HAS RUN DRY.

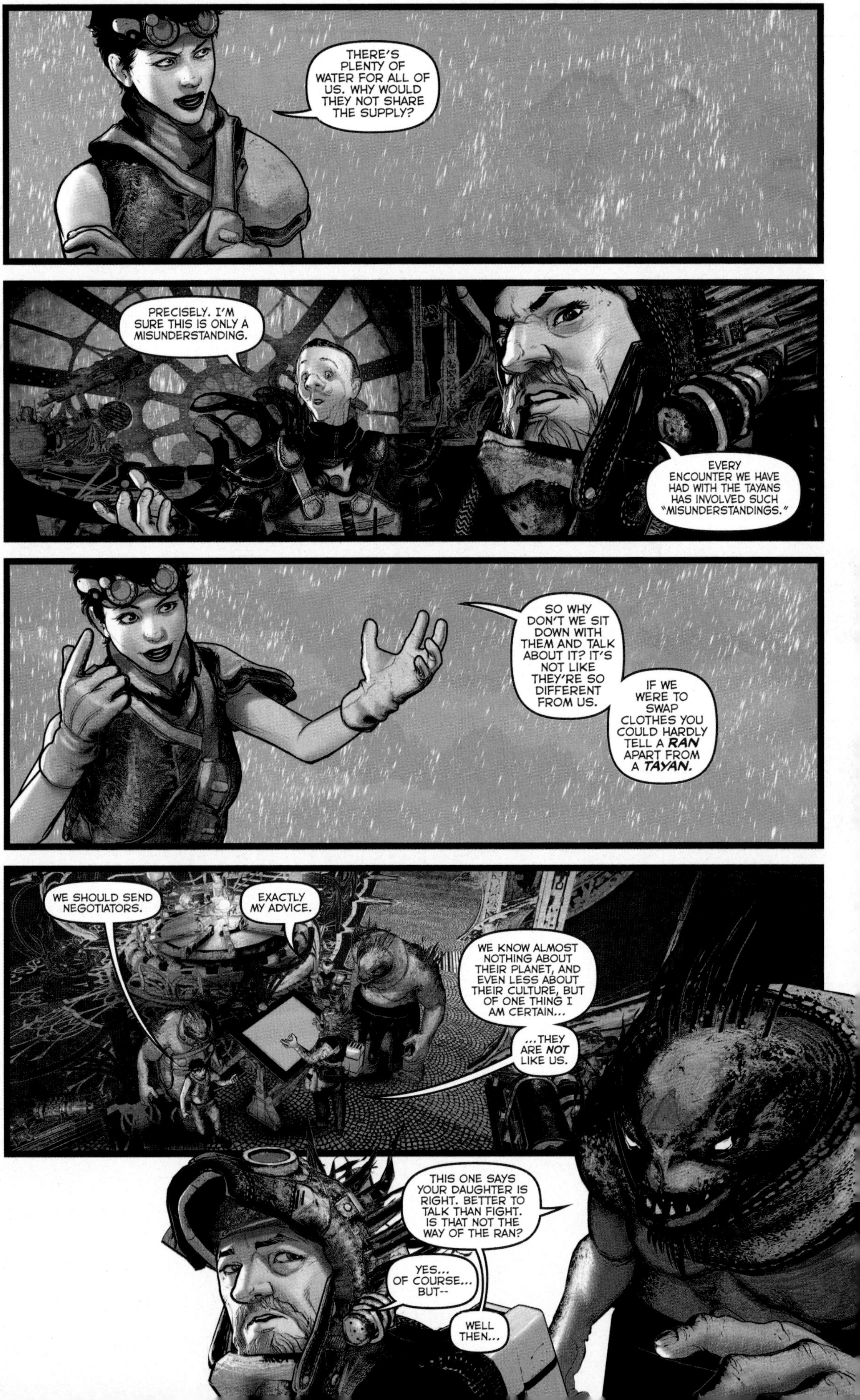
THERE'S PLENTY OF WATER FOR ALL OF US. WHY WOULD THEY NOT SHARE THE SUPPLY?
PRECISELY. I'M SURE THIS IS ONLY A MISUNDERSTANDING.
EVERY ENCOUNTER WE HAVE HAD WITH THE TAYANS HAS INVOLVED SUCH "MISUNDERSTANDINGS."
SO WHY DON'T WE SIT DOWN WITH THEM AND TALK ABOUT IT? IT'S NOT LIKE THEY'RE SO DIFFERENT FROM US.
IF WE WERE TO SWAP CLOTHES YOU COULD HARDLY TELL A ***RAN*** APART FROM A ***TAYAN.***
WE SHOULD SEND NEGOTIATORS.
EXACTLY MY ADVICE.
WE KNOW ALMOST NOTHING ABOUT THEIR PLANET, AND EVEN LESS ABOUT THEIR CULTURE, BUT OF ONE THING I AM CERTAIN...
...THEY ARE ***NOT*** LIKE US.
THIS ONE SAYS YOUR DAUGHTER IS RIGHT. BETTER TO TALK THAN FIGHT. IS THAT NOT THE WAY OF THE RAN?
YES... OF COURSE... BUT--
WELL THEN...

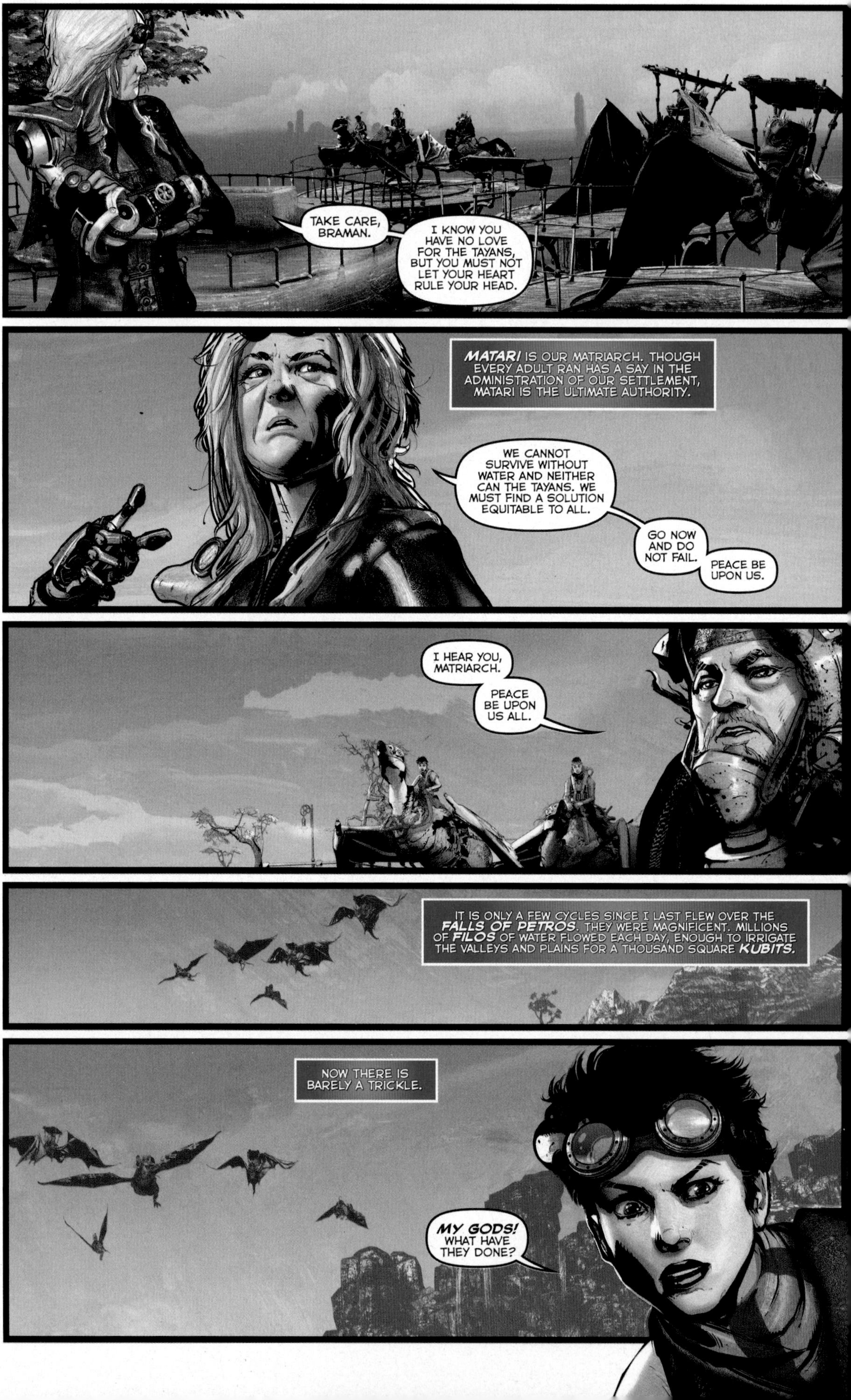

TAKE CARE, BRAMAN.
I KNOW YOU HAVE NO LOVE FOR THE TAYANS, BUT YOU MUST NOT LET YOUR HEART RULE YOUR HEAD.
MATARI IS OUR MATRIARCH. THOUGH EVERY ADULT RAN HAS A SAY IN THE ADMINISTRATION OF OUR SETTLEMENT, MATARI IS THE ULTIMATE AUTHORITY.
WE CANNOT SURVIVE WITHOUT WATER AND NEITHER CAN THE TAYANS. WE MUST FIND A SOLUTION EQUITABLE TO ALL.
GO NOW AND DO NOT FAIL.
PEACE BE UPON US.
I HEAR YOU, MATRIARCH.
PEACE BE UPON US ALL.
IT IS ONLY A FEW CYCLES SINCE I LAST FLEW OVER THE FALLS OF PETROS. THEY WERE MAGNIFICENT. MILLIONS OF FILOS OF WATER FLOWED EACH DAY, ENOUGH TO IRRIGATE THE VALLEYS AND PLAINS FOR A THOUSAND SQUARE KUBITS.
NOW THERE IS BARELY A TRICKLE.
MY GODS! WHAT HAVE THEY DONE?

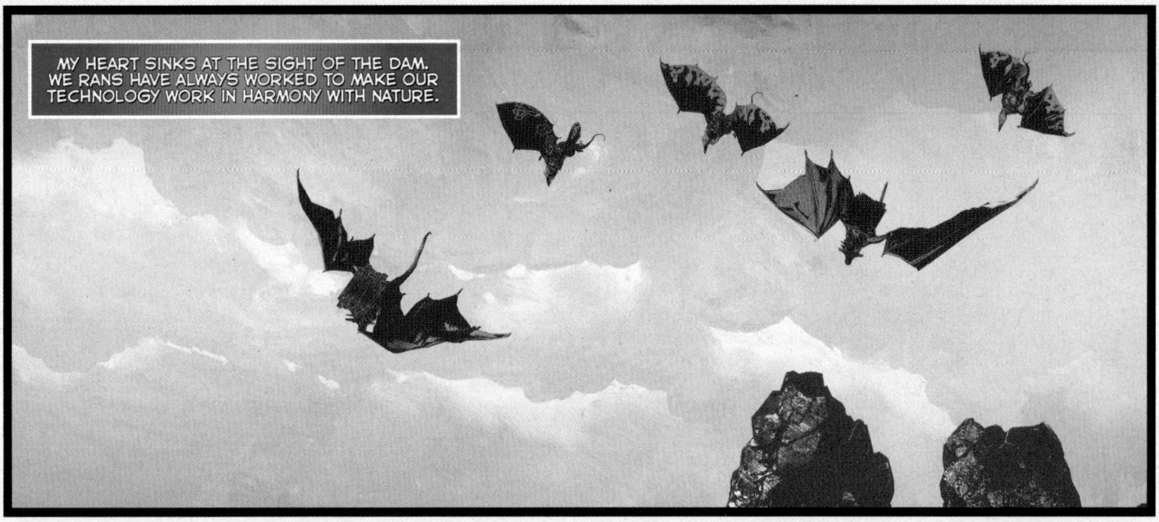
MY HEART SINKS AT THE SIGHT OF THE DAM. WE RANS HAVE ALWAYS WORKED TO MAKE OUR TECHNOLOGY WORK IN HARMONY WITH NATURE.

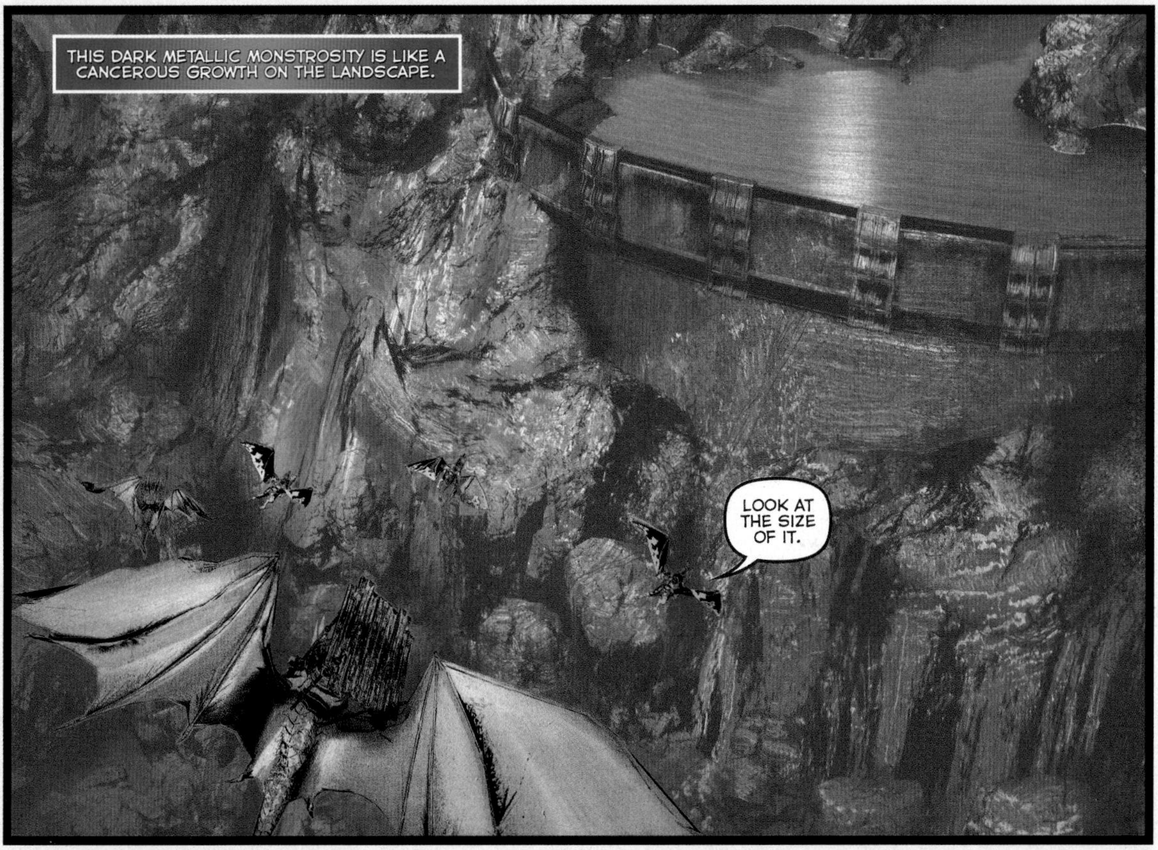
THIS DARK METALLIC MONSTROSITY IS LIKE A CANCEROUS GROWTH ON THE LANDSCAPE.
LOOK AT THE SIZE OF IT.

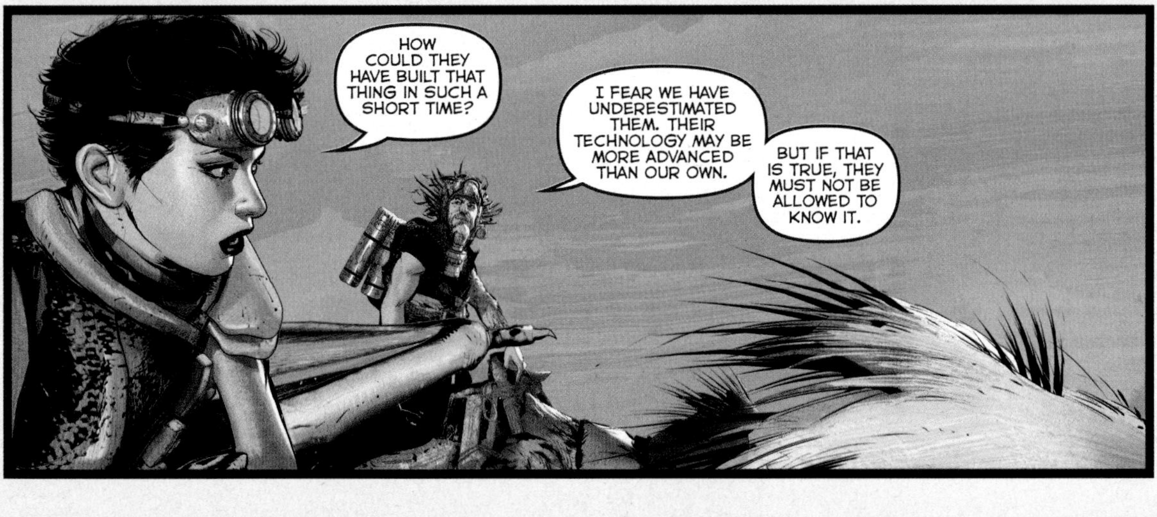
HOW COULD THEY HAVE BUILT THAT THING IN SUCH A SHORT TIME?
I FEAR WE HAVE UNDERESTIMATED THEM. THEIR TECHNOLOGY MAY BE MORE ADVANCED THAN OUR OWN.
BUT IF THAT IS TRUE, THEY MUST NOT BE ALLOWED TO KNOW IT.

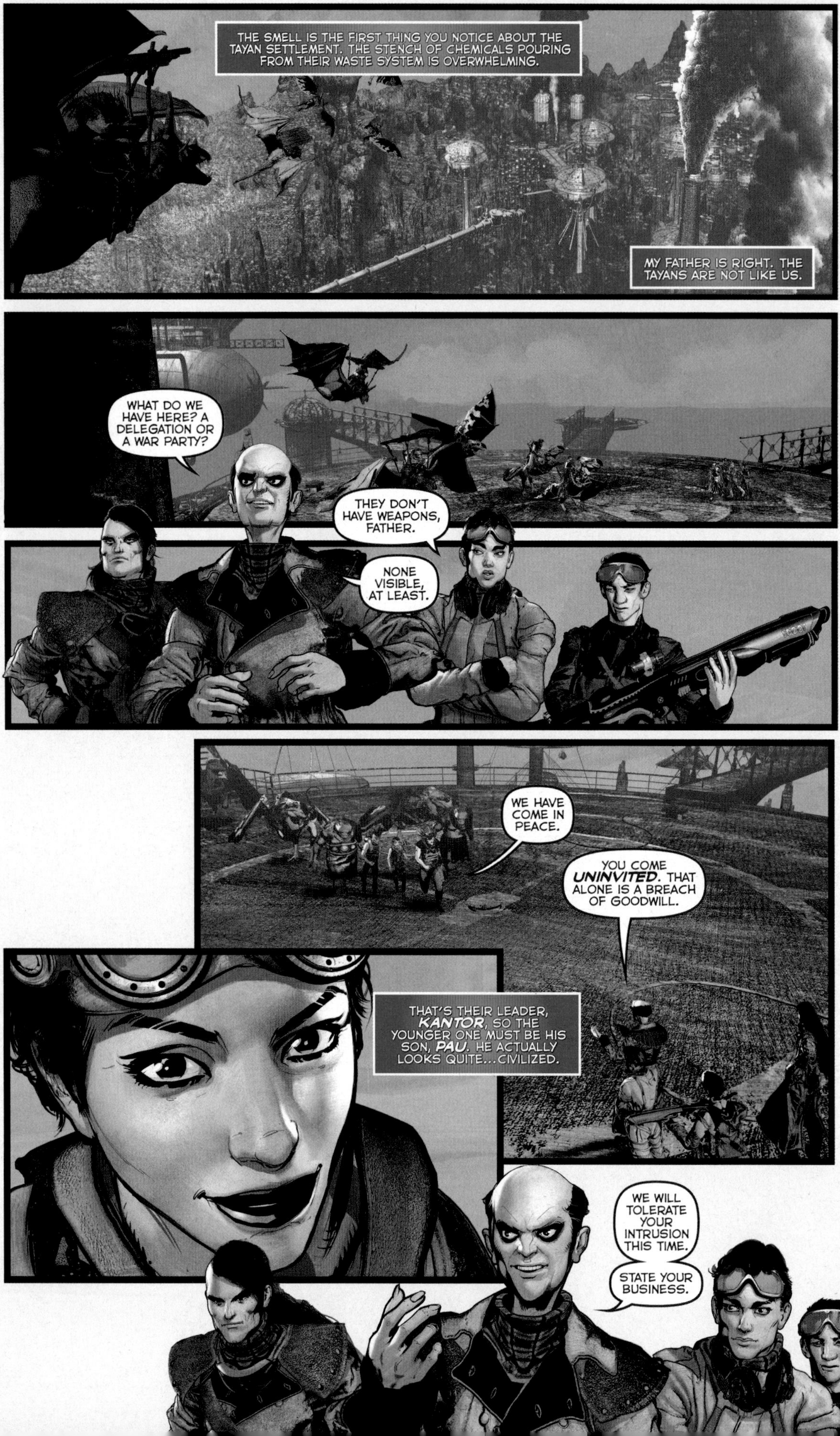
THE SMELL IS THE FIRST THING YOU NOTICE ABOUT THE TAYAN SETTLEMENT. THE STENCH OF CHEMICALS POURING FROM THEIR WASTE SYSTEM IS OVERWHELMING.
MY FATHER IS RIGHT. THE TAYANS ARE NOT LIKE US.
WHAT DO WE HAVE HERE? A DELEGATION OR A WAR PARTY?
THEY DON'T HAVE WEAPONS, FATHER.
NONE VISIBLE, AT LEAST.
WE HAVE COME IN PEACE.
YOU COME *UNINVITED*. THAT ALONE IS A BREACH OF GOODWILL.
THAT'S THEIR LEADER, *KANTOR*, SO THE YOUNGER ONE MUST BE HIS SON, *PAU*. HE ACTUALLY LOOKS QUITE... CIVILIZED.
WE WILL TOLERATE YOUR INTRUSION THIS TIME.
STATE YOUR BUSINESS.

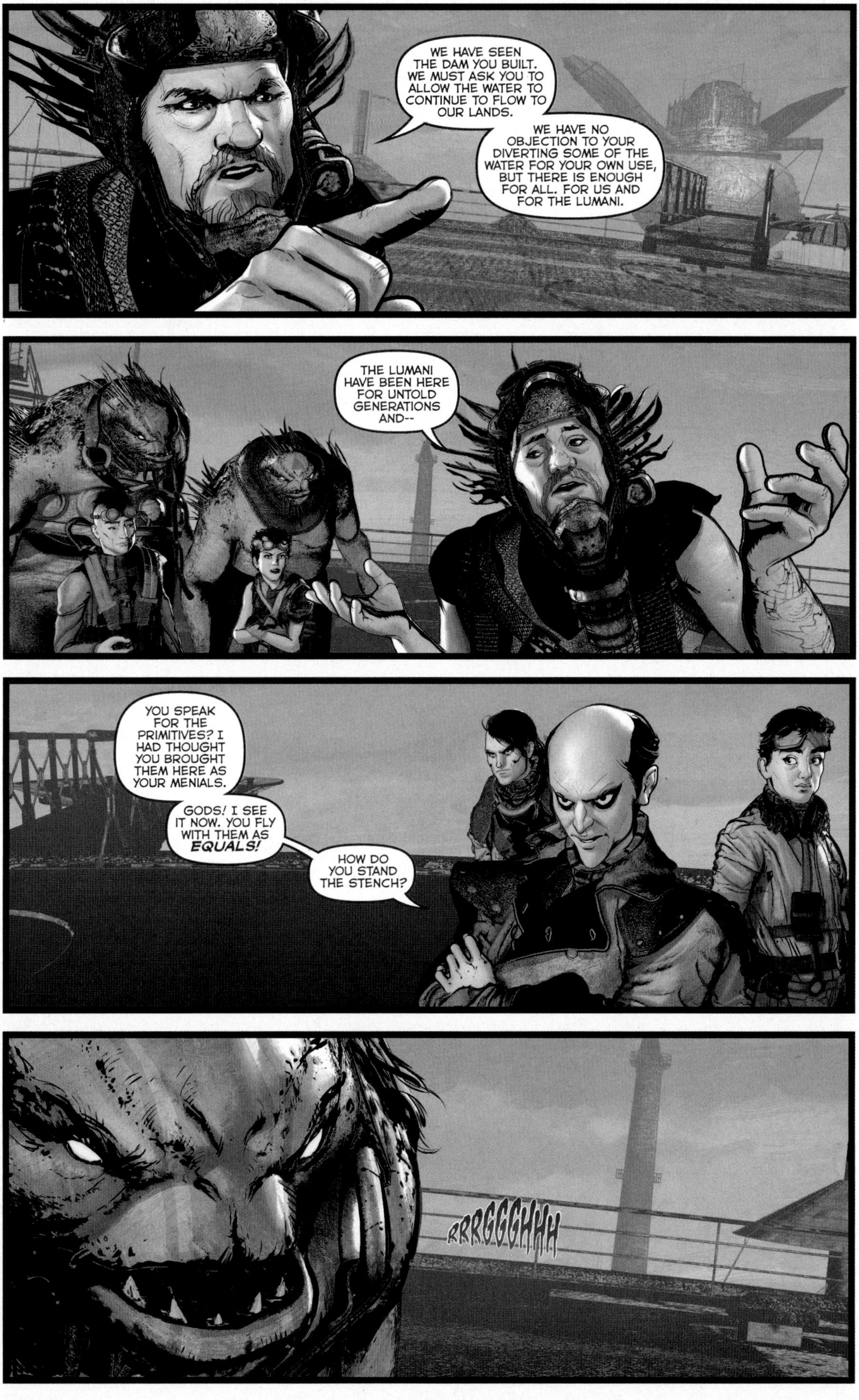
WE HAVE SEEN THE DAM YOU BUILT. WE MUST ASK YOU TO ALLOW THE WATER TO CONTINUE TO FLOW TO OUR LANDS.
WE HAVE NO OBJECTION TO YOUR DIVERTING SOME OF THE WATER FOR YOUR OWN USE, BUT THERE IS ENOUGH FOR ALL. FOR US AND FOR THE LUMANI.
THE LUMANI HAVE BEEN HERE FOR UNTOLD GENERATIONS AND--
YOU SPEAK FOR THE PRIMITIVES? I HAD THOUGHT YOU BROUGHT THEM HERE AS YOUR MENIALS.
GODS! I SEE IT NOW. YOU FLY WITH THEM AS ***EQUALS!***
HOW DO YOU STAND THE STENCH?
RRRGGGHHH

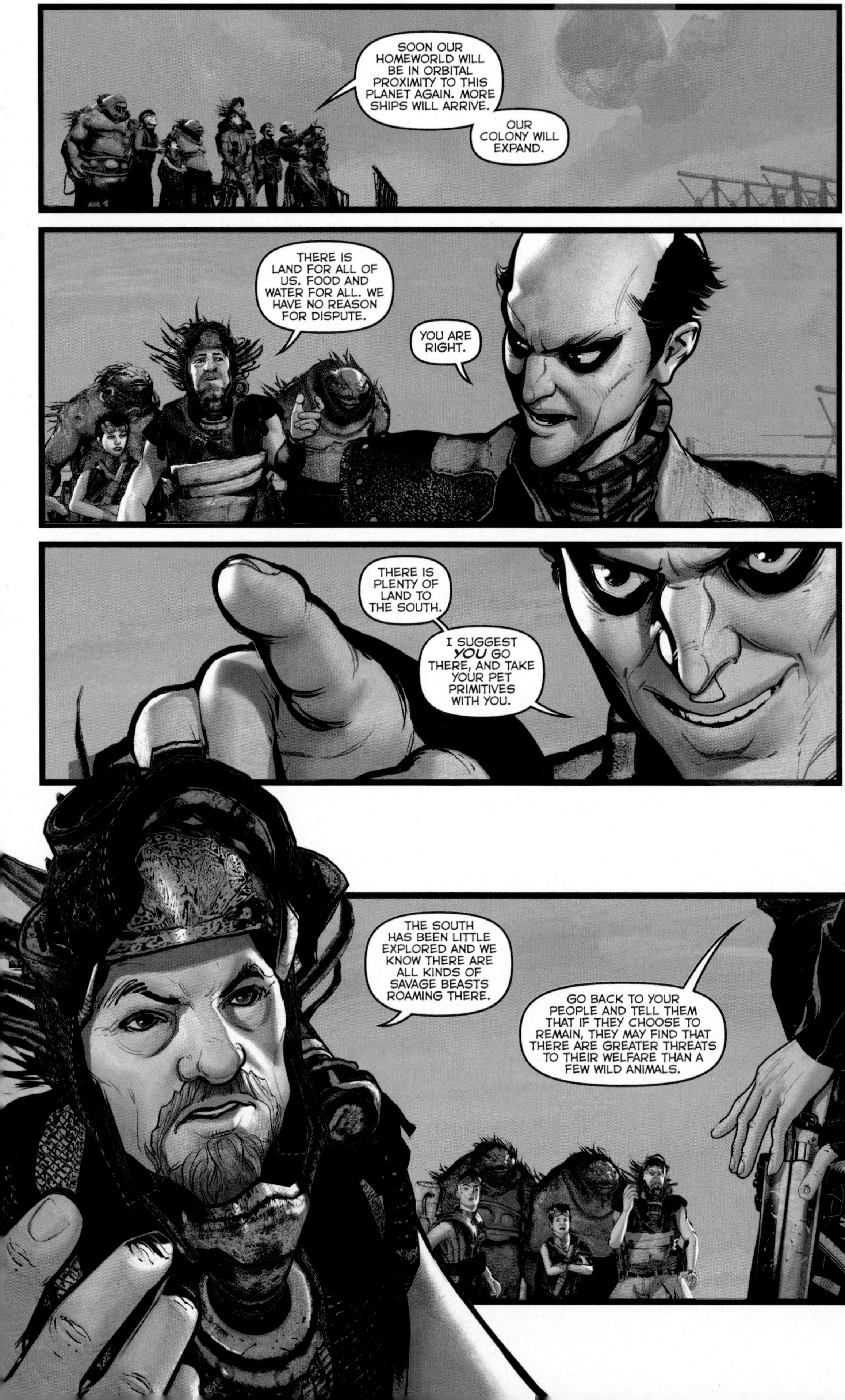
SOON OUR HOMEWORLD WILL BE IN ORBITAL PROXIMITY TO THIS PLANET AGAIN. MORE SHIPS WILL ARRIVE.
OUR COLONY WILL EXPAND.
THERE IS LAND FOR ALL OF US. FOOD AND WATER FOR ALL. WE HAVE NO REASON FOR DISPUTE.
YOU ARE RIGHT.
THERE IS PLENTY OF LAND TO THE SOUTH.
I SUGGEST *YOU* GO THERE, AND TAKE YOUR PET PRIMITIVES WITH YOU.
THE SOUTH HAS BEEN LITTLE EXPLORED AND WE KNOW THERE ARE ALL KINDS OF SAVAGE BEASTS ROAMING THERE.
GO BACK TO YOUR PEOPLE AND TELL THEM THAT IF THEY CHOOSE TO REMAIN, THEY MAY FIND THAT THERE ARE GREATER THREATS TO THEIR WELFARE THAN A FEW WILD ANIMALS.

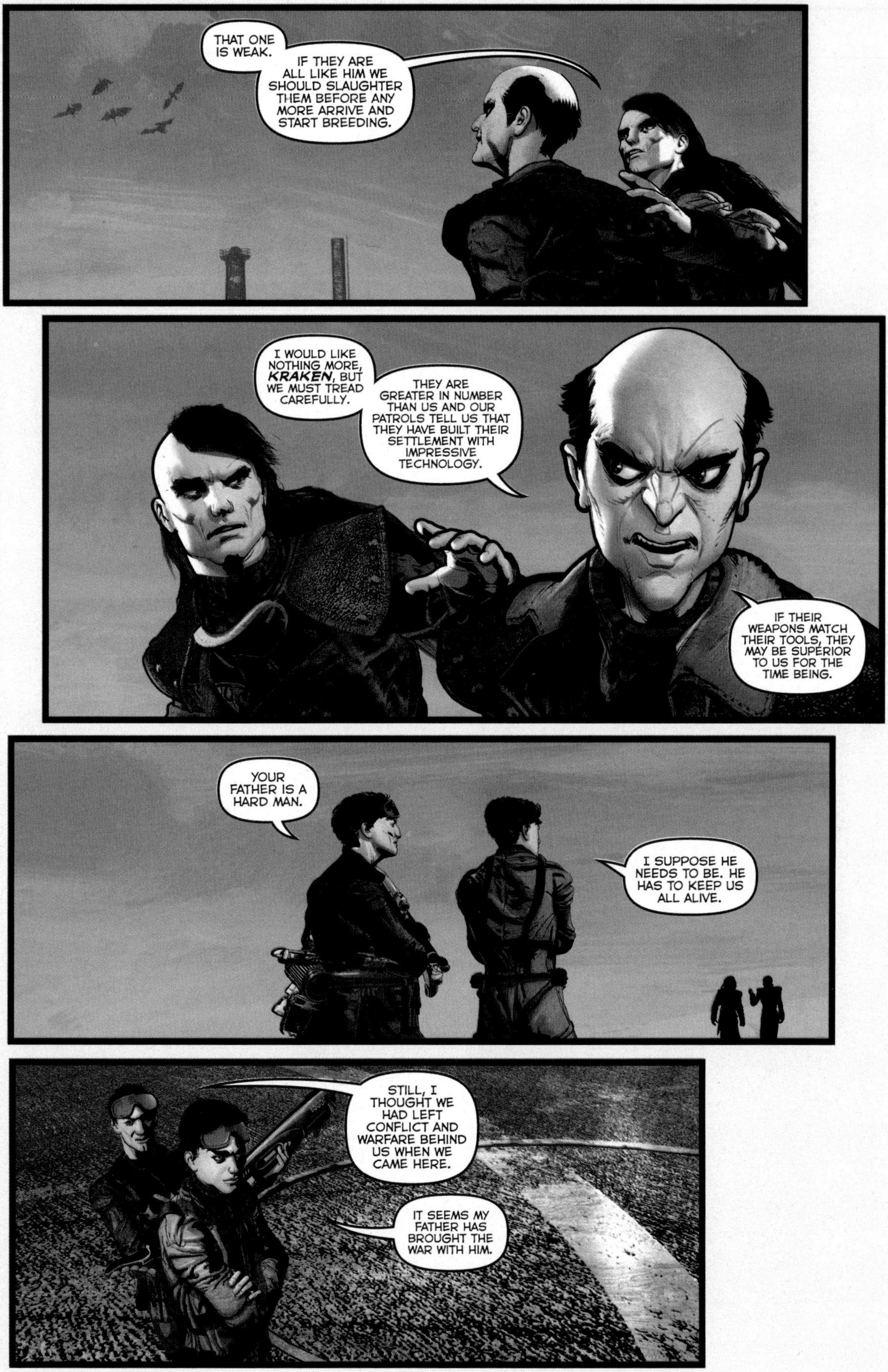
THAT ONE IS WEAK.
IF THEY ARE ALL LIKE HIM WE SHOULD SLAUGHTER THEM BEFORE ANY MORE ARRIVE AND START BREEDING.
I WOULD LIKE NOTHING MORE, KRAKEN, BUT WE MUST TREAD CAREFULLY.
THEY ARE GREATER IN NUMBER THAN US AND OUR PATROLS TELL US THAT THEY HAVE BUILT THEIR SETTLEMENT WITH IMPRESSIVE TECHNOLOGY.
IF THEIR WEAPONS MATCH THEIR TOOLS, THEY MAY BE SUPERIOR TO US FOR THE TIME BEING.
YOUR FATHER IS A HARD MAN.
I SUPPOSE HE NEEDS TO BE. HE HAS TO KEEP US ALL ALIVE.
STILL, I THOUGHT WE HAD LEFT CONFLICT AND WARFARE BEHIND US WHEN WE CAME HERE.
IT SEEMS MY FATHER HAS BROUGHT THE WAR WITH HIM.

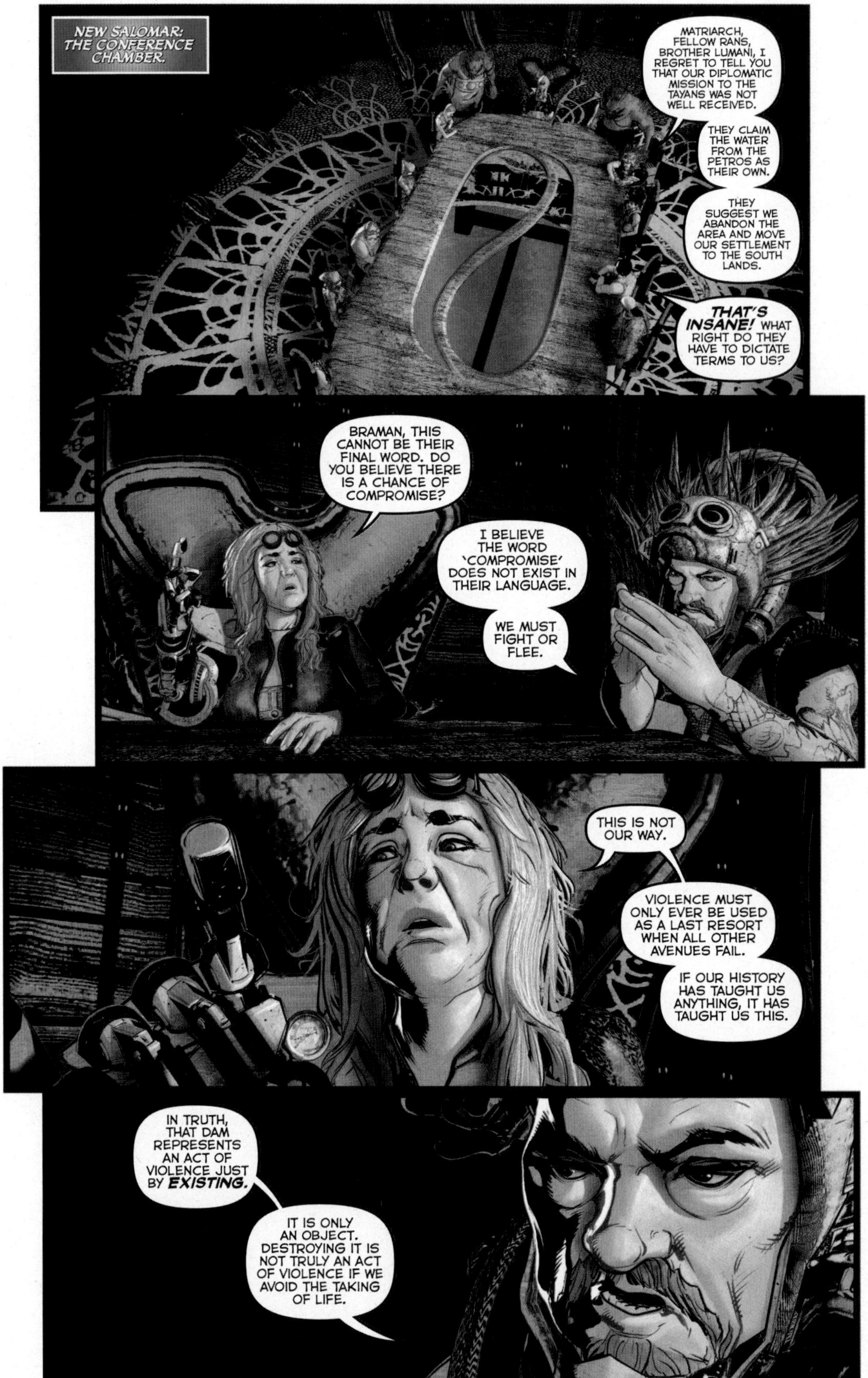
NEW SALOMAR: THE CONFERENCE CHAMBER.
MATRIARCH, FELLOW RANS, BROTHER LUMANI, I REGRET TO TELL YOU THAT OUR DIPLOMATIC MISSION TO THE TAYANS WAS NOT WELL RECEIVED.
THEY CLAIM THE WATER FROM THE PETROS AS THEIR OWN.
THEY SUGGEST WE ABANDON THE AREA AND MOVE OUR SETTLEMENT TO THE SOUTH LANDS.
THAT'S INSANE! WHAT RIGHT DO THEY HAVE TO DICTATE TERMS TO US?
BRAMAN, THIS CANNOT BE THEIR FINAL WORD. DO YOU BELIEVE THERE IS A CHANCE OF COMPROMISE?
I BELIEVE THE WORD 'COMPROMISE' DOES NOT EXIST IN THEIR LANGUAGE.
WE MUST FIGHT OR FLEE.
THIS IS NOT OUR WAY.
VIOLENCE MUST ONLY EVER BE USED AS A LAST RESORT WHEN ALL OTHER AVENUES FAIL.
IF OUR HISTORY HAS TAUGHT US ANYTHING, IT HAS TAUGHT US THIS.
IN TRUTH, THAT DAM REPRESENTS AN ACT OF VIOLENCE JUST BY EXISTING.
IT IS ONLY AN OBJECT. DESTROYING IT IS NOT TRULY AN ACT OF VIOLENCE IF WE AVOID THE TAKING OF LIFE.

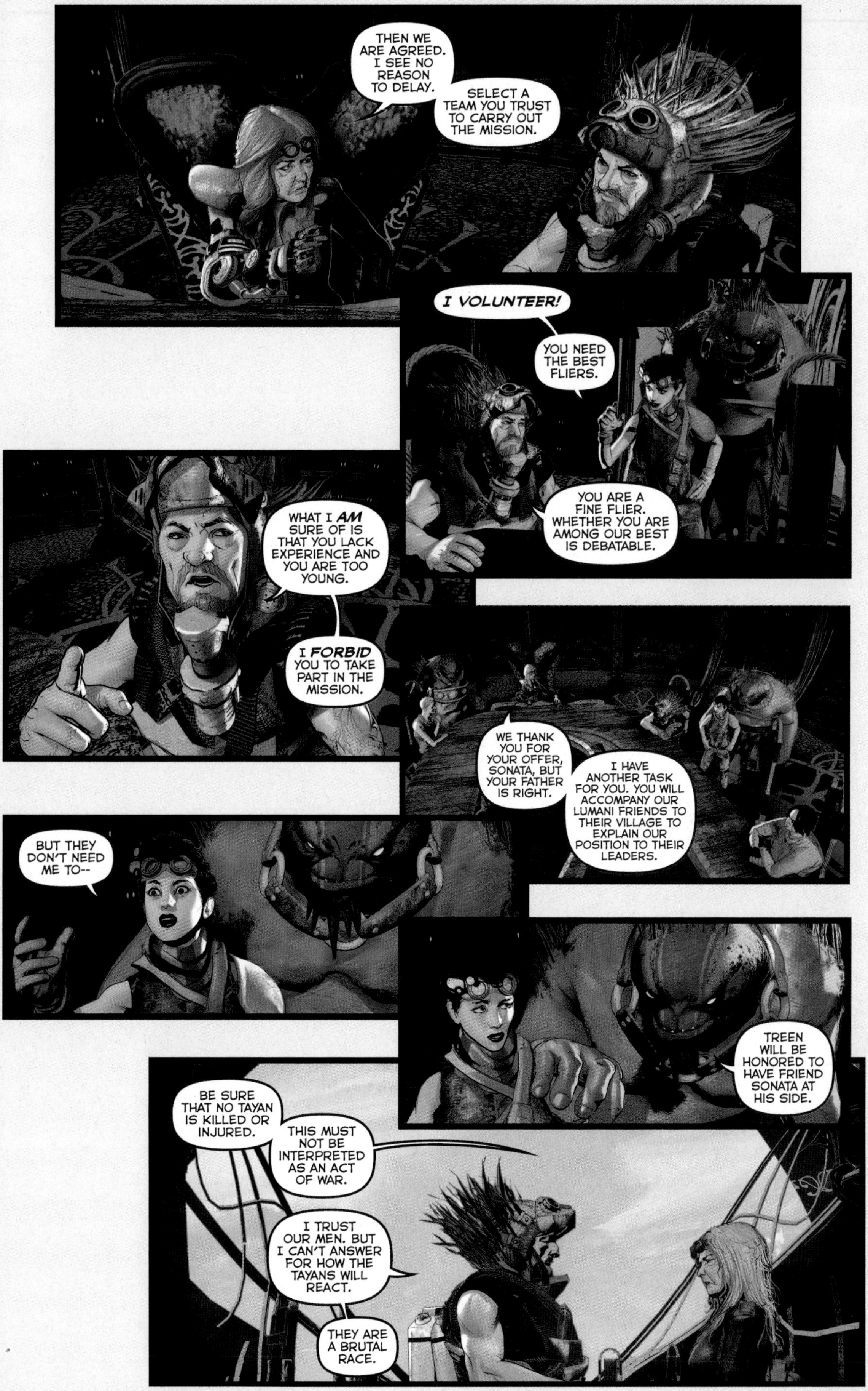
THEN WE ARE AGREED. I SEE NO REASON TO DELAY.
SELECT A TEAM YOU TRUST TO CARRY OUT THE MISSION.
I VOLUNTEER!
YOU NEED THE BEST FLIERS.
YOU ARE A FINE FLIER. WHETHER YOU ARE AMONG OUR BEST IS DEBATABLE.
WHAT I AM SURE OF IS THAT YOU LACK EXPERIENCE AND YOU ARE TOO YOUNG.
I FORBID YOU TO TAKE PART IN THE MISSION.
WE THANK YOU FOR YOUR OFFER, SONATA, BUT YOUR FATHER IS RIGHT.
I HAVE ANOTHER TASK FOR YOU. YOU WILL ACCOMPANY OUR LUMANI FRIENDS TO THEIR VILLAGE TO EXPLAIN OUR POSITION TO THEIR LEADERS.
BUT THEY DON'T NEED ME TO--
TREEN WILL BE HONORED TO HAVE FRIEND SONATA AT HIS SIDE.
BE SURE THAT NO TAYAN IS KILLED OR INJURED.
THIS MUST NOT BE INTERPRETED AS AN ACT OF WAR.
I TRUST OUR MEN. BUT I CAN'T ANSWER FOR HOW THE TAYANS WILL REACT.
THEY ARE A BRUTAL RACE.

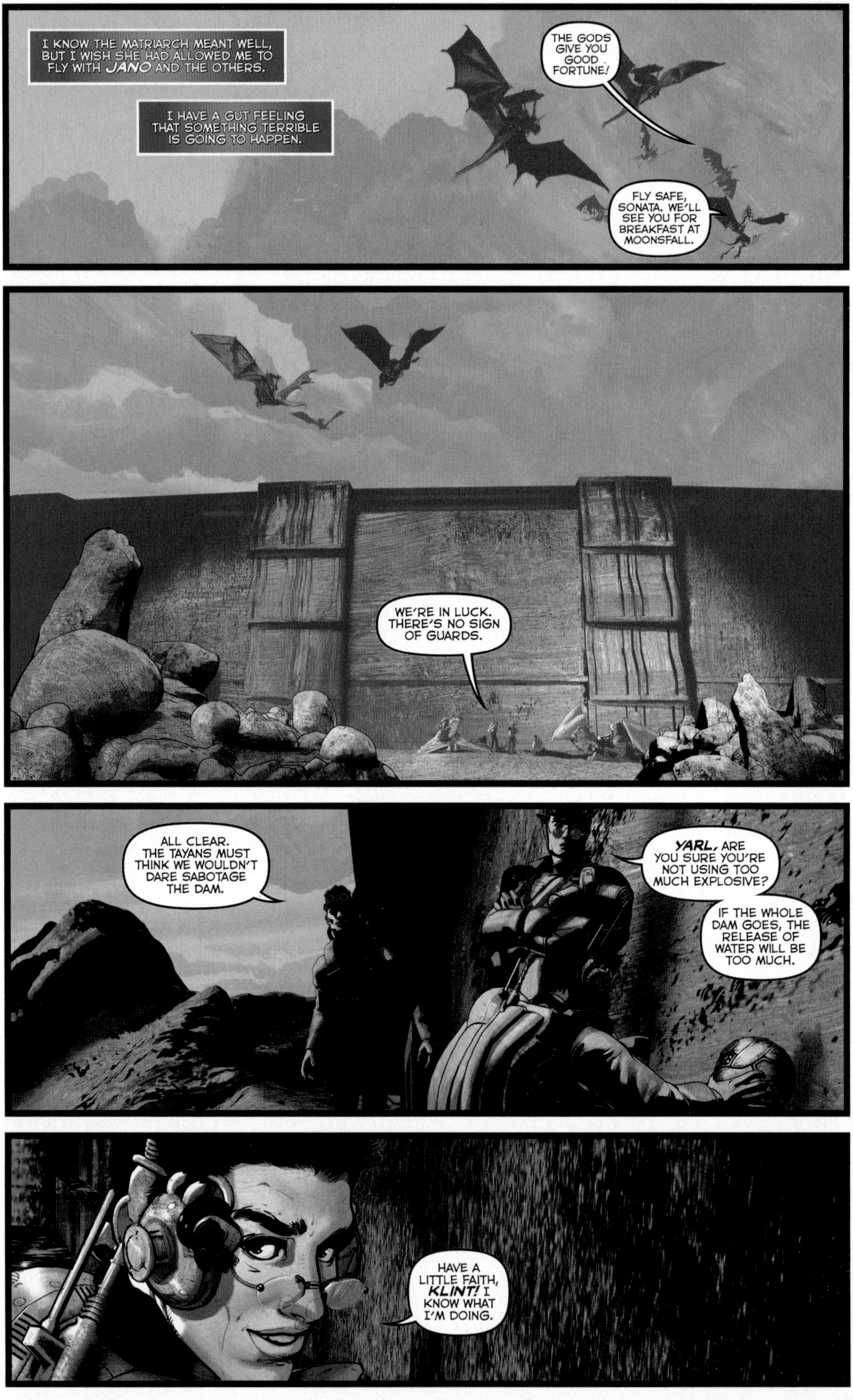
I KNOW THE MATRIARCH MEANT WELL, BUT I WISH SHE HAD ALLOWED ME TO FLY WITH JANO AND THE OTHERS.
I HAVE A GUT FEELING THAT SOMETHING TERRIBLE IS GOING TO HAPPEN.
THE GODS GIVE YOU GOOD FORTUNE!
FLY SAFE, SONATA. WE'LL SEE YOU FOR BREAKFAST AT MOONSFALL.
WE'RE IN LUCK. THERE'S NO SIGN OF GUARDS.
ALL CLEAR. THE TAYANS MUST THINK WE WOULDN'T DARE SABOTAGE THE DAM.
YARL, ARE YOU SURE YOU'RE NOT USING TOO MUCH EXPLOSIVE?
IF THE WHOLE DAM GOES, THE RELEASE OF WATER WILL BE TOO MUCH.
HAVE A LITTLE FAITH, KLINT! I KNOW WHAT I'M DOING.

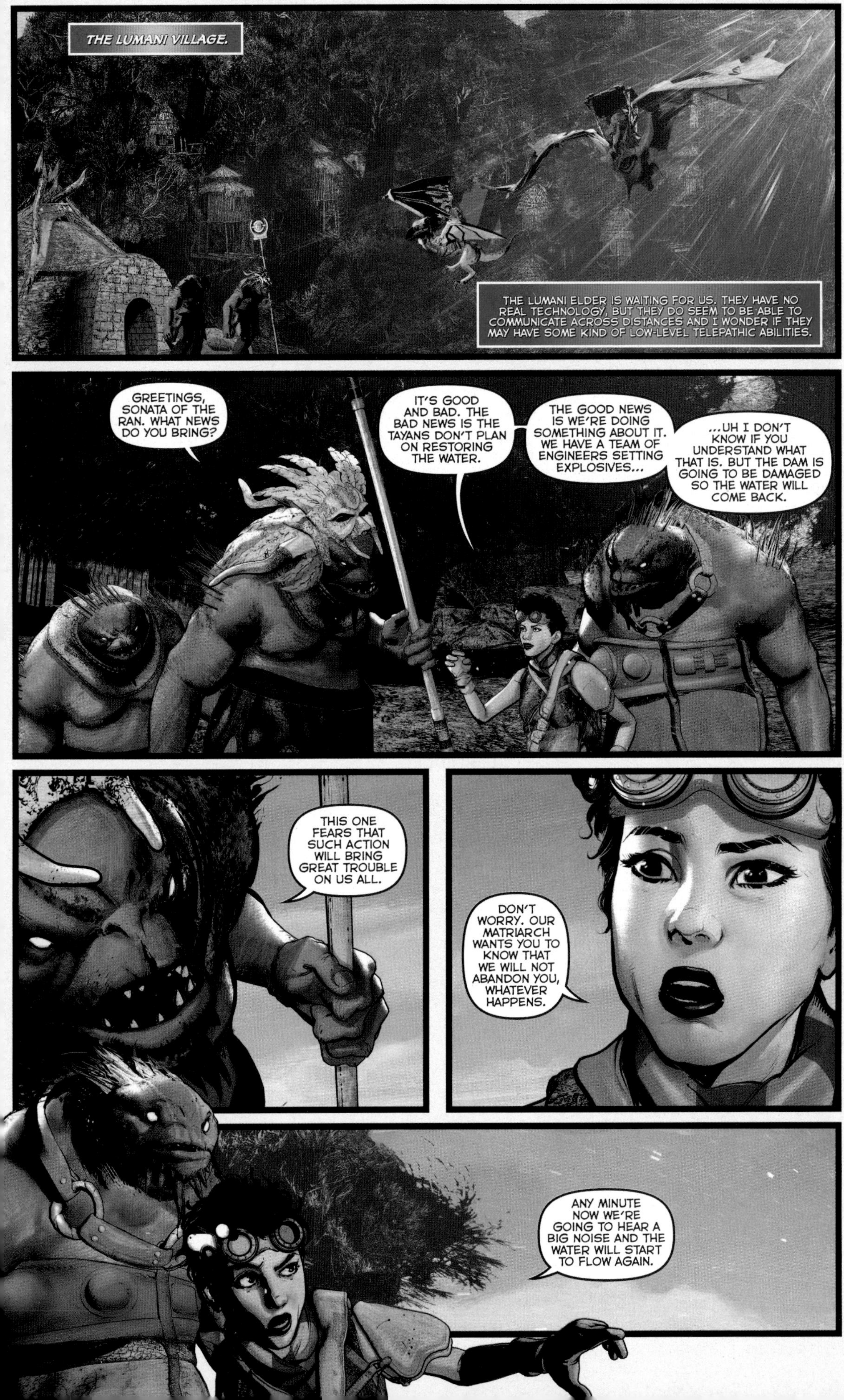
THE LUMANI VILLAGE.
THE LUMANI ELDER IS WAITING FOR US. THEY HAVE NO REAL TECHNOLOGY, BUT THEY DO SEEM TO BE ABLE TO COMMUNICATE ACROSS DISTANCES AND I WONDER IF THEY MAY HAVE SOME KIND OF LOW-LEVEL TELEPATHIC ABILITIES.
GREETINGS, SONATA OF THE RAN. WHAT NEWS DO YOU BRING?
IT'S GOOD AND BAD. THE BAD NEWS IS THE TAYANS DON'T PLAN ON RESTORING THE WATER.
THE GOOD NEWS IS WE'RE DOING SOMETHING ABOUT IT. WE HAVE A TEAM OF ENGINEERS SETTING EXPLOSIVES...
...UH I DON'T KNOW IF YOU UNDERSTAND WHAT THAT IS. BUT THE DAM IS GOING TO BE DAMAGED SO THE WATER WILL COME BACK.
THIS ONE FEARS THAT SUCH ACTION WILL BRING GREAT TROUBLE ON US ALL.
DON'T WORRY. OUR MATRIARCH WANTS YOU TO KNOW THAT WE WILL NOT ABANDON YOU, WHATEVER HAPPENS.
ANY MINUTE NOW WE'RE GOING TO HEAR A BIG NOISE AND THE WATER WILL START TO FLOW AGAIN.

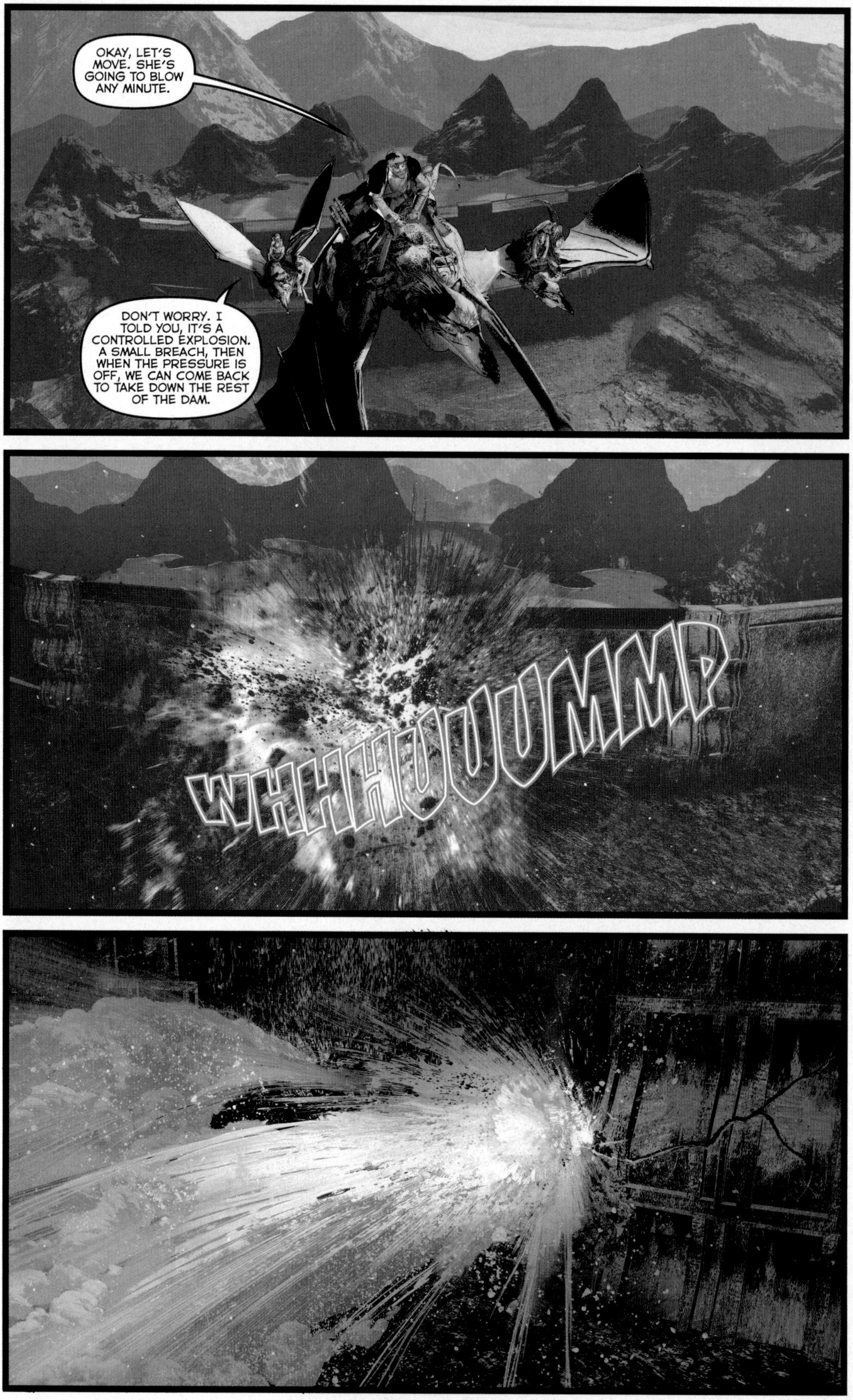
OKAY, LET'S MOVE. SHE'S GOING TO BLOW ANY MINUTE.
DON'T WORRY. I TOLD YOU, IT'S A CONTROLLED EXPLOSION. A SMALL BREACH, THEN WHEN THE PRESSURE IS OFF, WE CAN COME BACK TO TAKE DOWN THE REST OF THE DAM.
WHHHUUUMMP

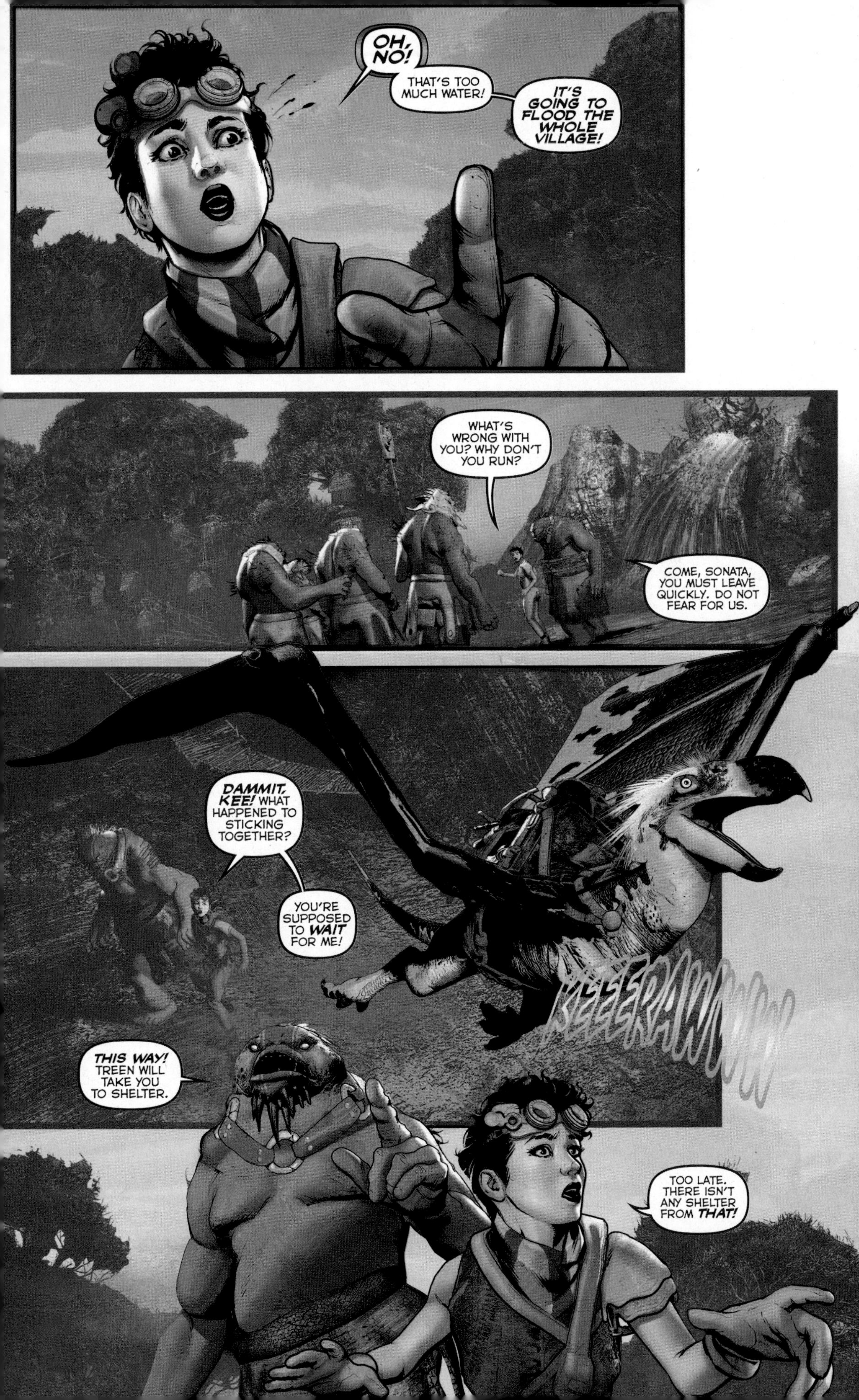
OH, NO!
THAT'S TOO MUCH WATER!
IT'S GOING TO FLOOD THE WHOLE VILLAGE!
WHAT'S WRONG WITH YOU? WHY DON'T YOU RUN?
COME, SONATA, YOU MUST LEAVE QUICKLY. DO NOT FEAR FOR US.
DAMMIT, KEE! WHAT HAPPENED TO STICKING TOGETHER?
YOU'RE SUPPOSED TO WAIT FOR ME!
THIS WAY! TREEN WILL TAKE YOU TO SHELTER.
TOO LATE. THERE ISN'T ANY SHELTER FROM THAT!

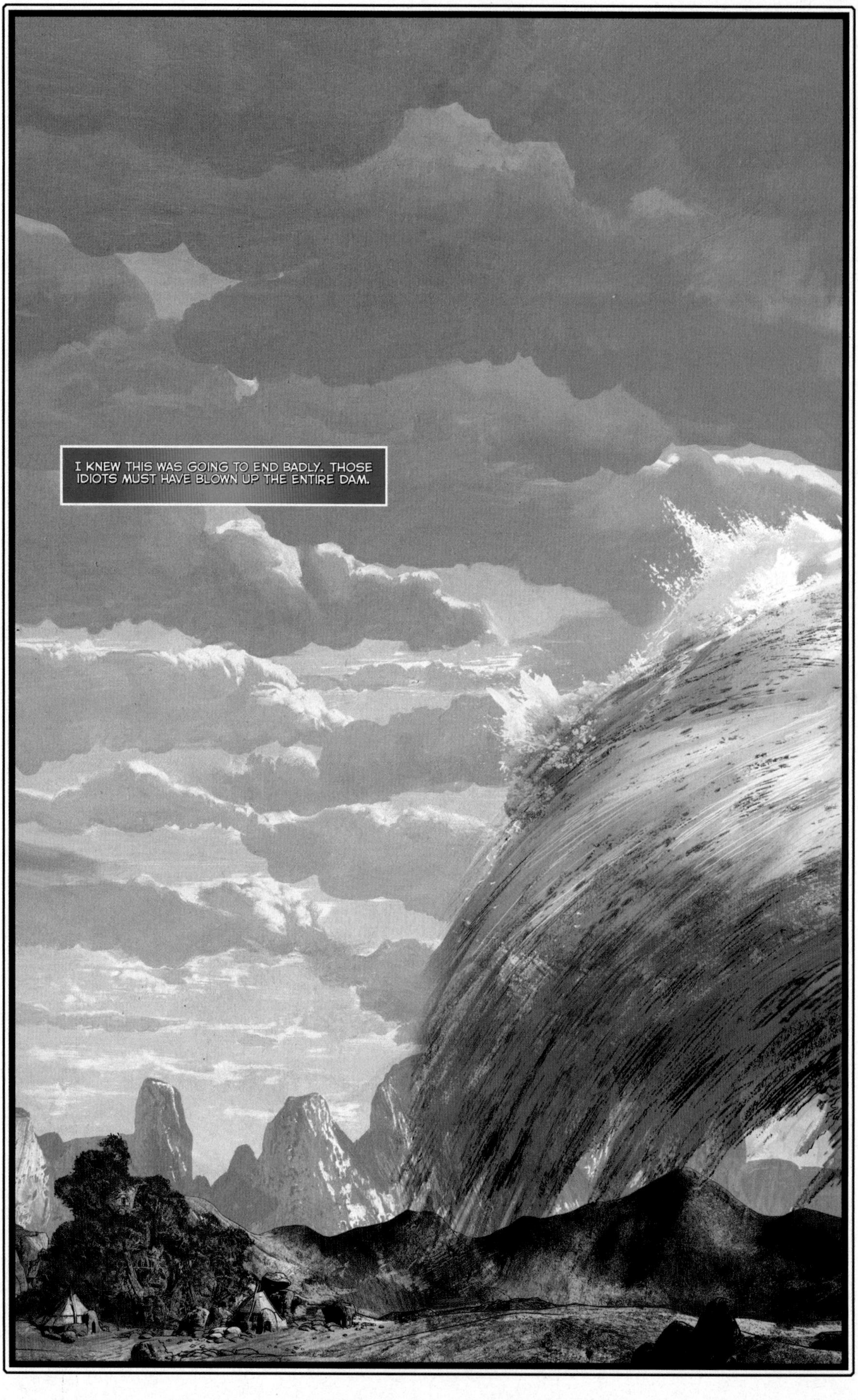
I KNEW THIS WAS GOING TO END BADLY. THOSE IDIOTS MUST HAVE BLOWN UP THE ENTIRE DAM.

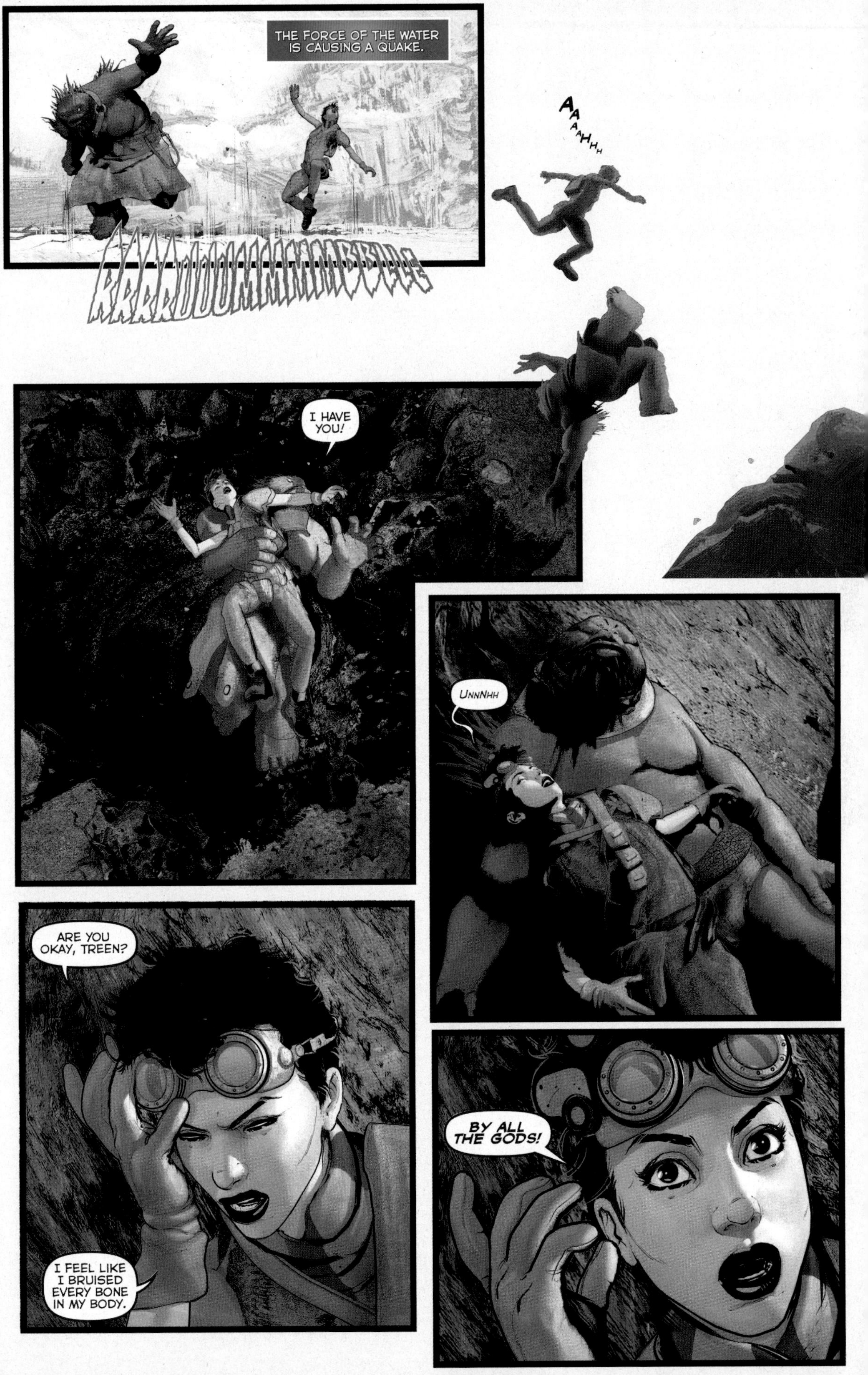
THE FORCE OF THE WATER IS CAUSING A QUAKE.
AAAAHHH
I HAVE YOU!
UNNNHH
ARE YOU OKAY, TREEN?
I FEEL LIKE I BRUISED EVERY BONE IN MY BODY.
BY ALL THE GODS!

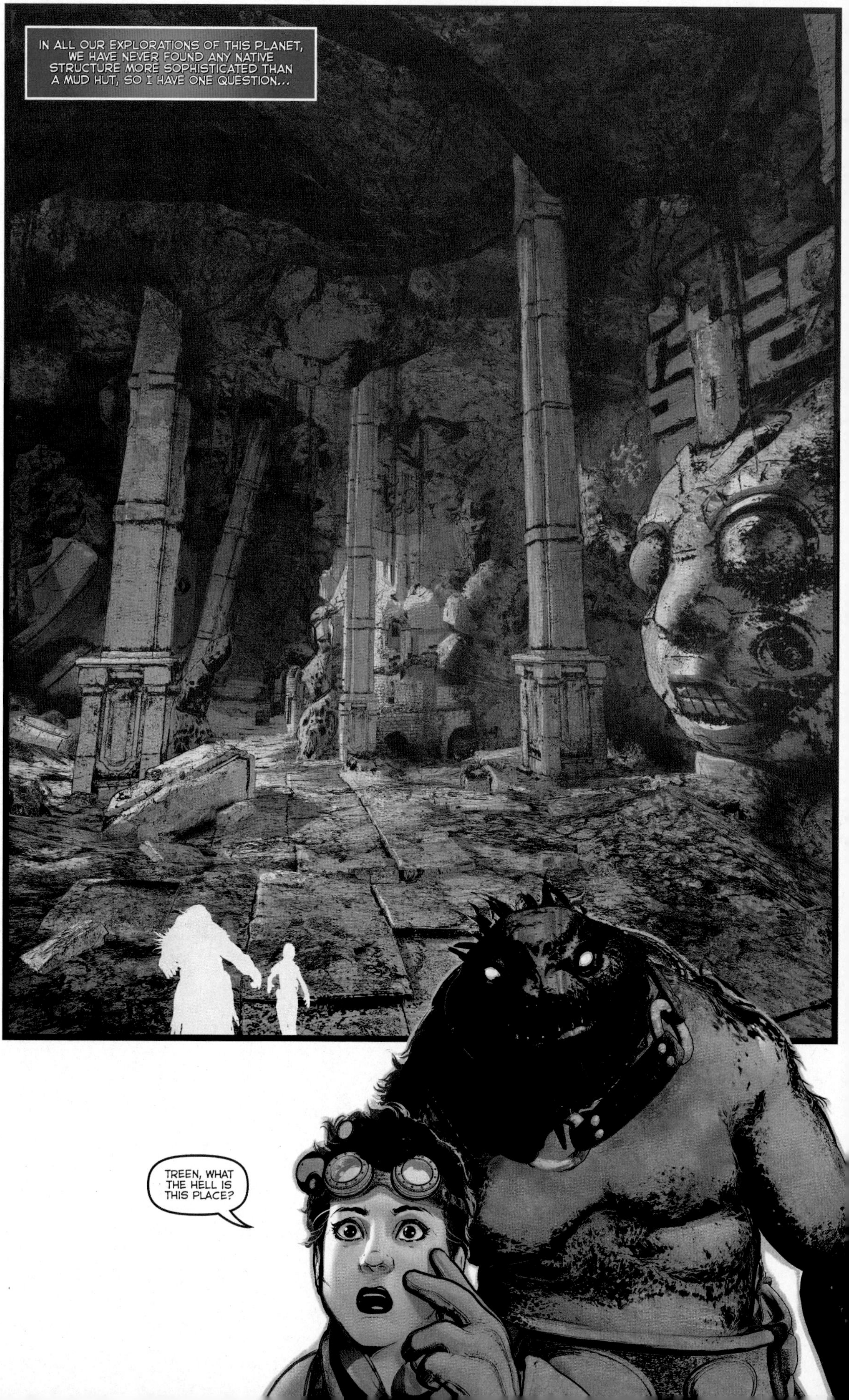
IN ALL OUR EXPLORATIONS OF THIS PLANET, WE HAVE NEVER FOUND ANY NATIVE STRUCTURE MORE SOPHISTICATED THAN A MUD HUT, SO I HAVE ONE QUESTION...
TREEN, WHAT THE HELL IS THIS PLACE?

Issue #2 Cover A

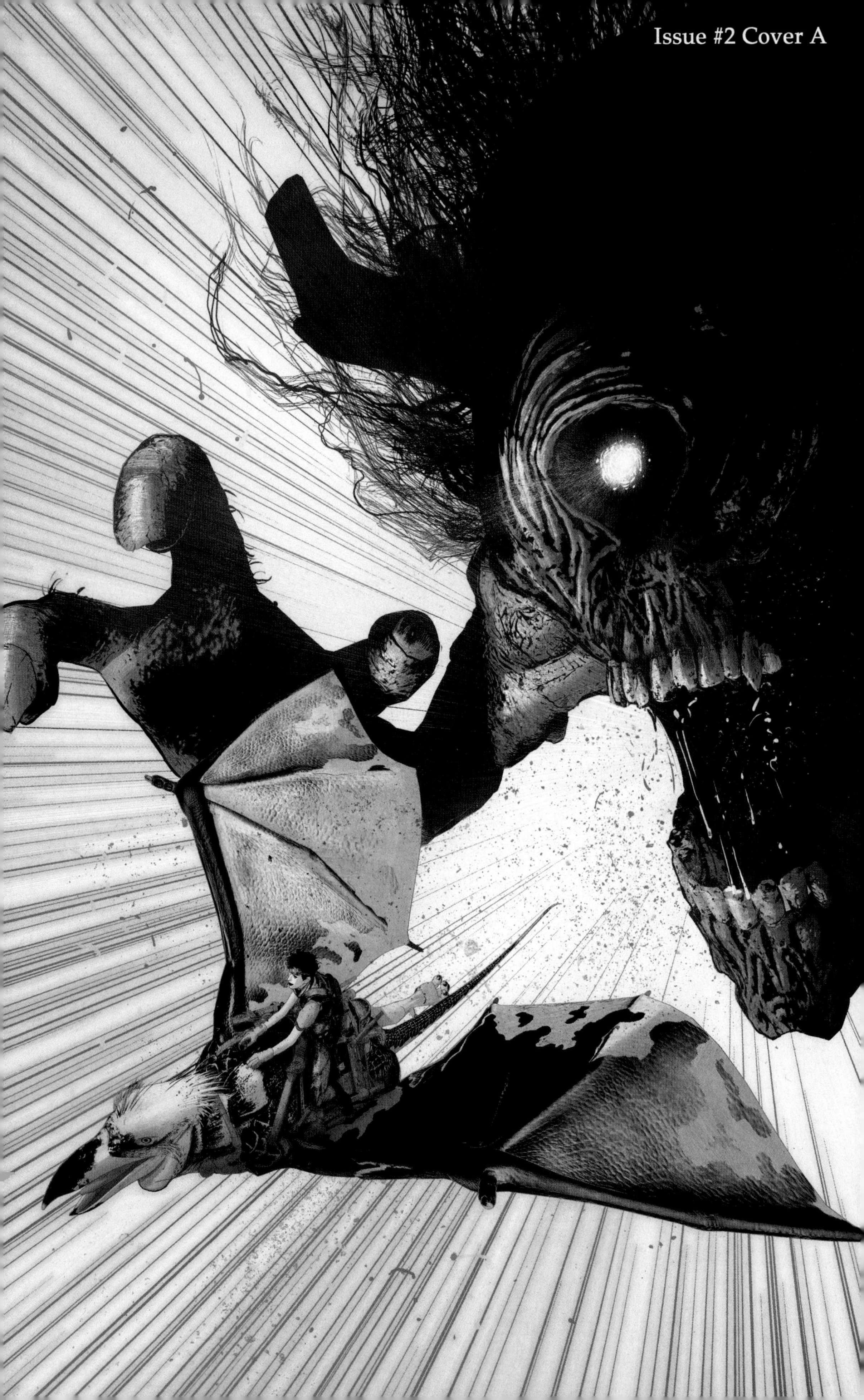

Issue #2 Cover B

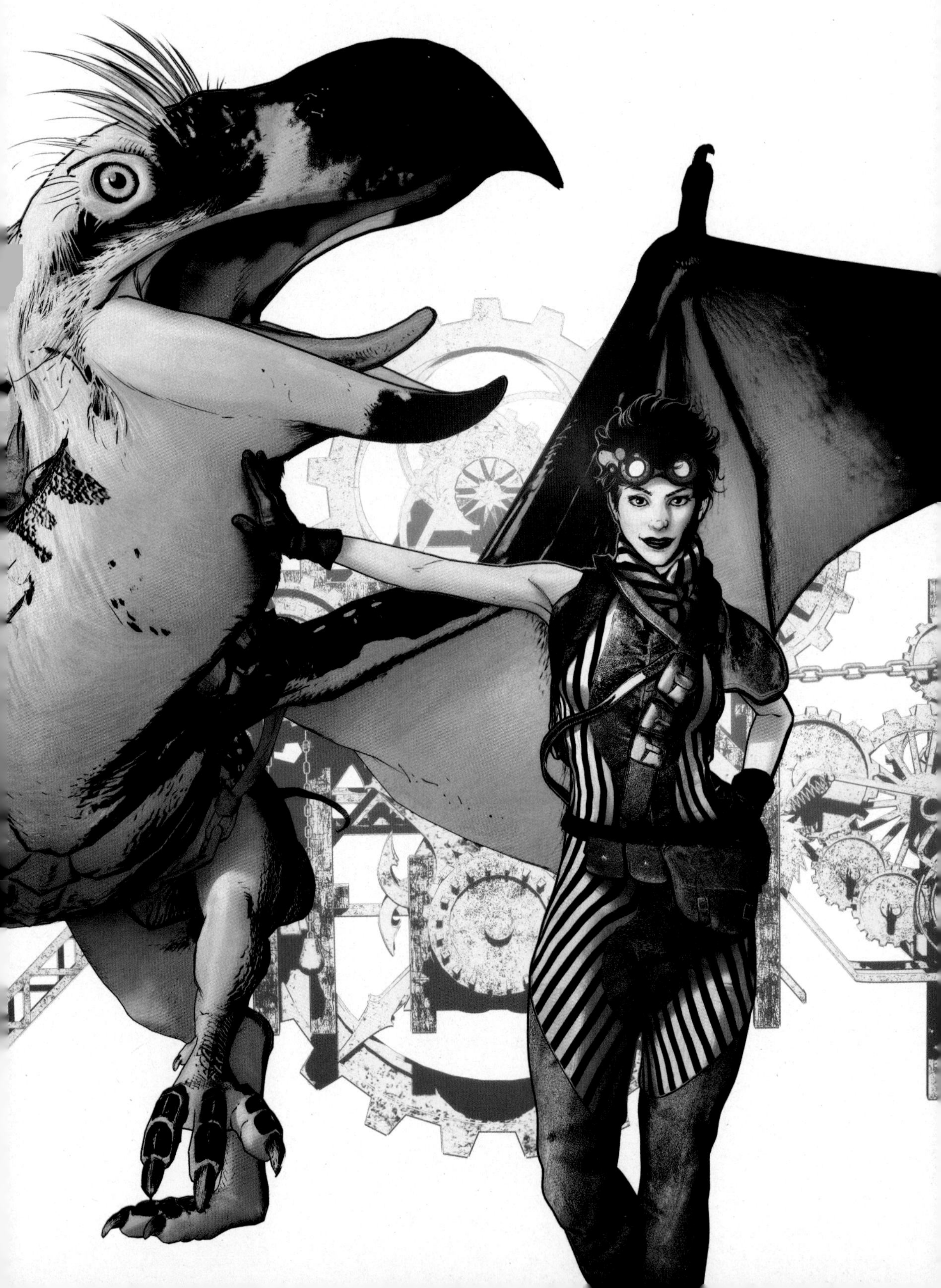

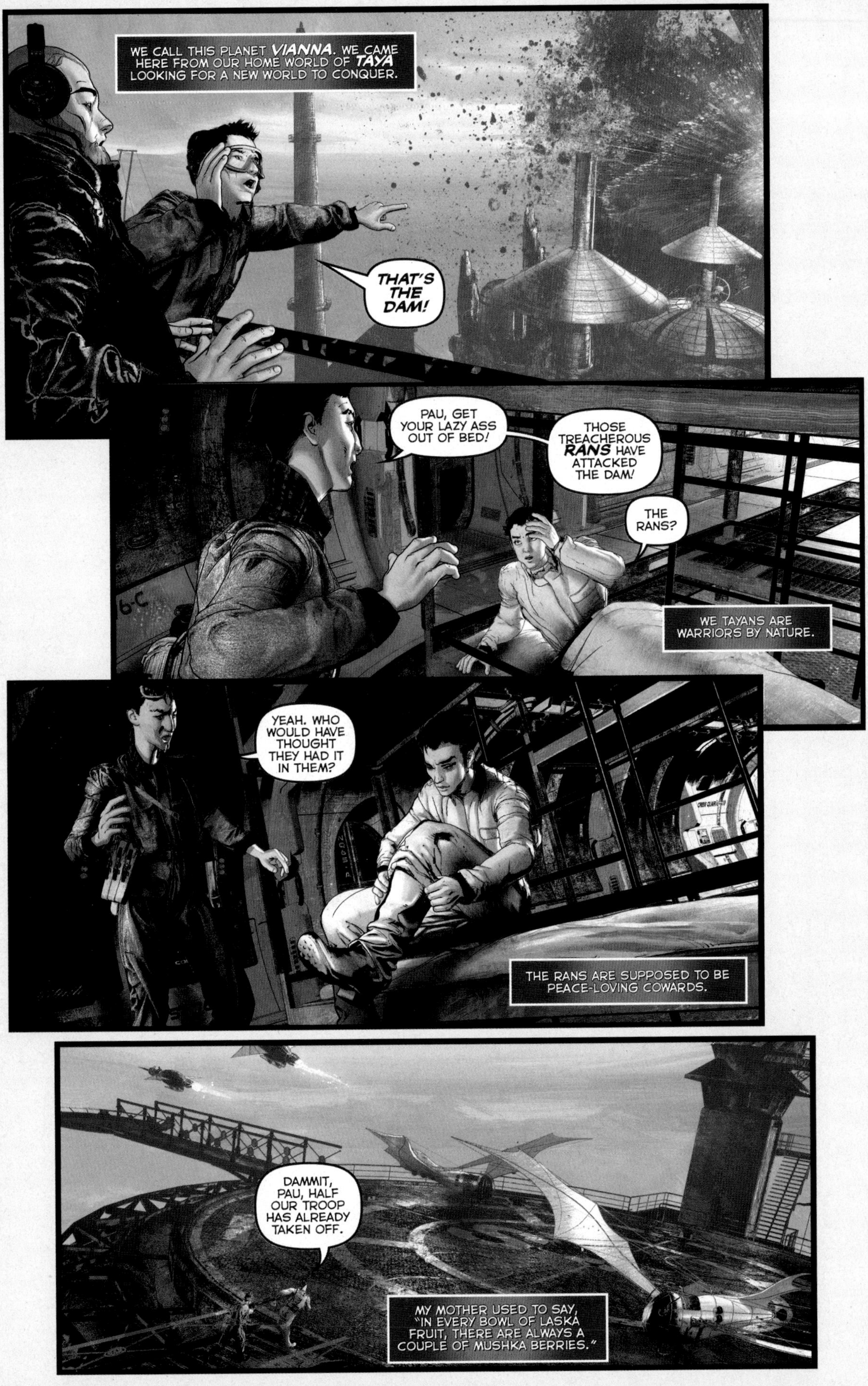
WE CALL THIS PLANET VIANNA. WE CAME HERE FROM OUR HOME WORLD OF TAYA LOOKING FOR A NEW WORLD TO CONQUER.
THAT'S THE DAM!
PAU, GET YOUR LAZY ASS OUT OF BED!
THOSE TREACHEROUS RANS HAVE ATTACKED THE DAM!
THE RANS?
WE TAYANS ARE WARRIORS BY NATURE.
YEAH. WHO WOULD HAVE THOUGHT THEY HAD IT IN THEM?
THE RANS ARE SUPPOSED TO BE PEACE-LOVING COWARDS.
DAMMIT, PAU, HALF OUR TROOP HAS ALREADY TAKEN OFF.
MY MOTHER USED TO SAY, "IN EVERY BOWL OF LASKA FRUIT, THERE ARE ALWAYS A COUPLE OF MUSHKA BERRIES."

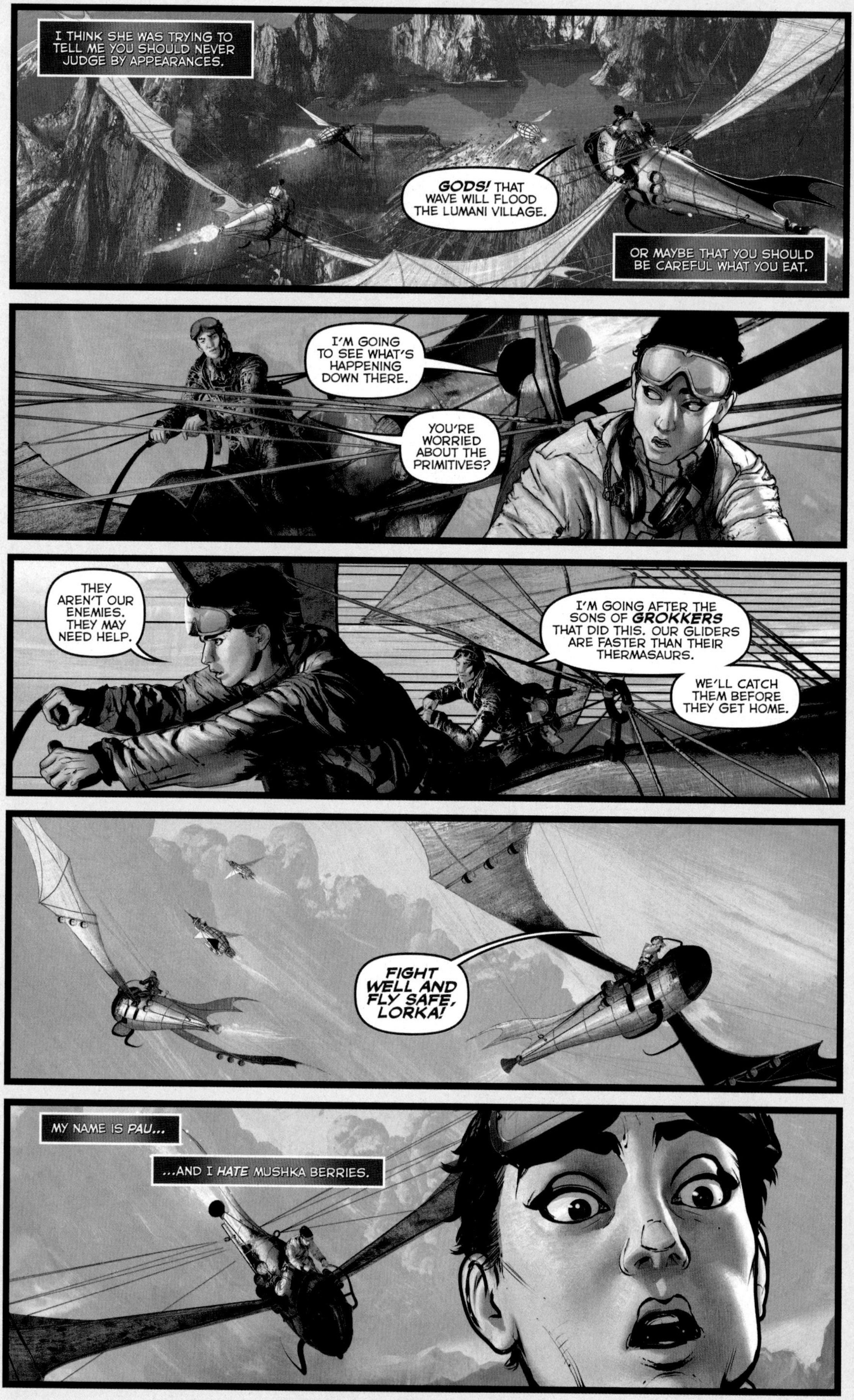
I THINK SHE WAS TRYING TO TELL ME YOU SHOULD NEVER JUDGE BY APPEARANCES.
GODS! THAT WAVE WILL FLOOD THE LUMANI VILLAGE.
OR MAYBE THAT YOU SHOULD BE CAREFUL WHAT YOU EAT.
I'M GOING TO SEE WHAT'S HAPPENING DOWN THERE.
YOU'RE WORRIED ABOUT THE PRIMITIVES?
THEY AREN'T OUR ENEMIES. THEY MAY NEED HELP.
I'M GOING AFTER THE SONS OF GROKKERS THAT DID THIS. OUR GLIDERS ARE FASTER THAN THEIR THERMASAURS.
WE'LL CATCH THEM BEFORE THEY GET HOME.
FIGHT WELL AND FLY SAFE, LORKA!
MY NAME IS PAU...
...AND I HATE MUSHKA BERRIES.

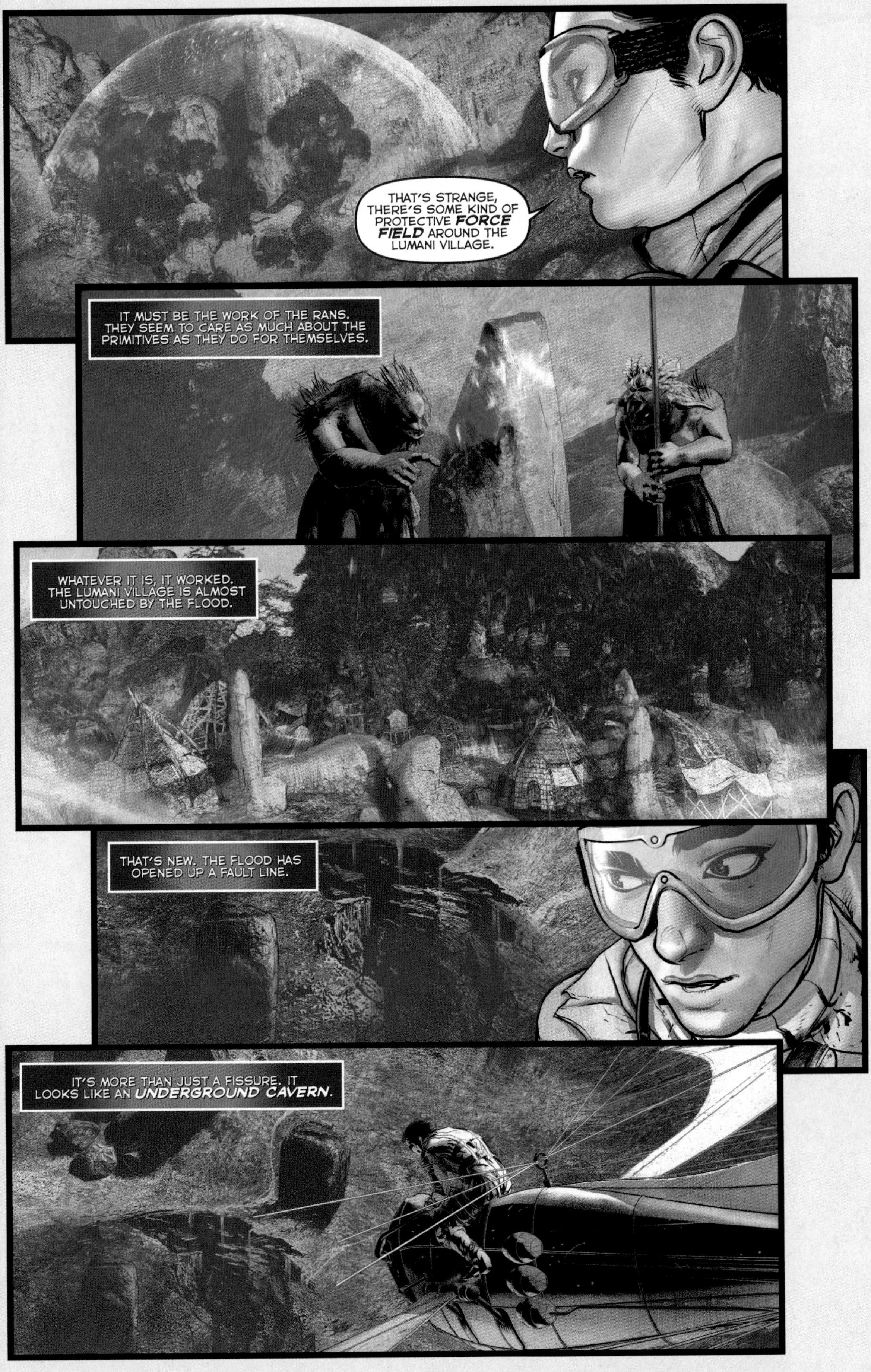
THAT'S STRANGE, THERE'S SOME KIND OF PROTECTIVE FORCE FIELD AROUND THE LUMANI VILLAGE.
IT MUST BE THE WORK OF THE RANS. THEY SEEM TO CARE AS MUCH ABOUT THE PRIMITIVES AS THEY DO FOR THEMSELVES.
WHATEVER IT IS, IT WORKED. THE LUMANI VILLAGE IS ALMOST UNTOUCHED BY THE FLOOD.
THAT'S NEW. THE FLOOD HAS OPENED UP A FAULT LINE.
IT'S MORE THAN JUST A FISSURE. IT LOOKS LIKE AN UNDERGROUND CAVERN.

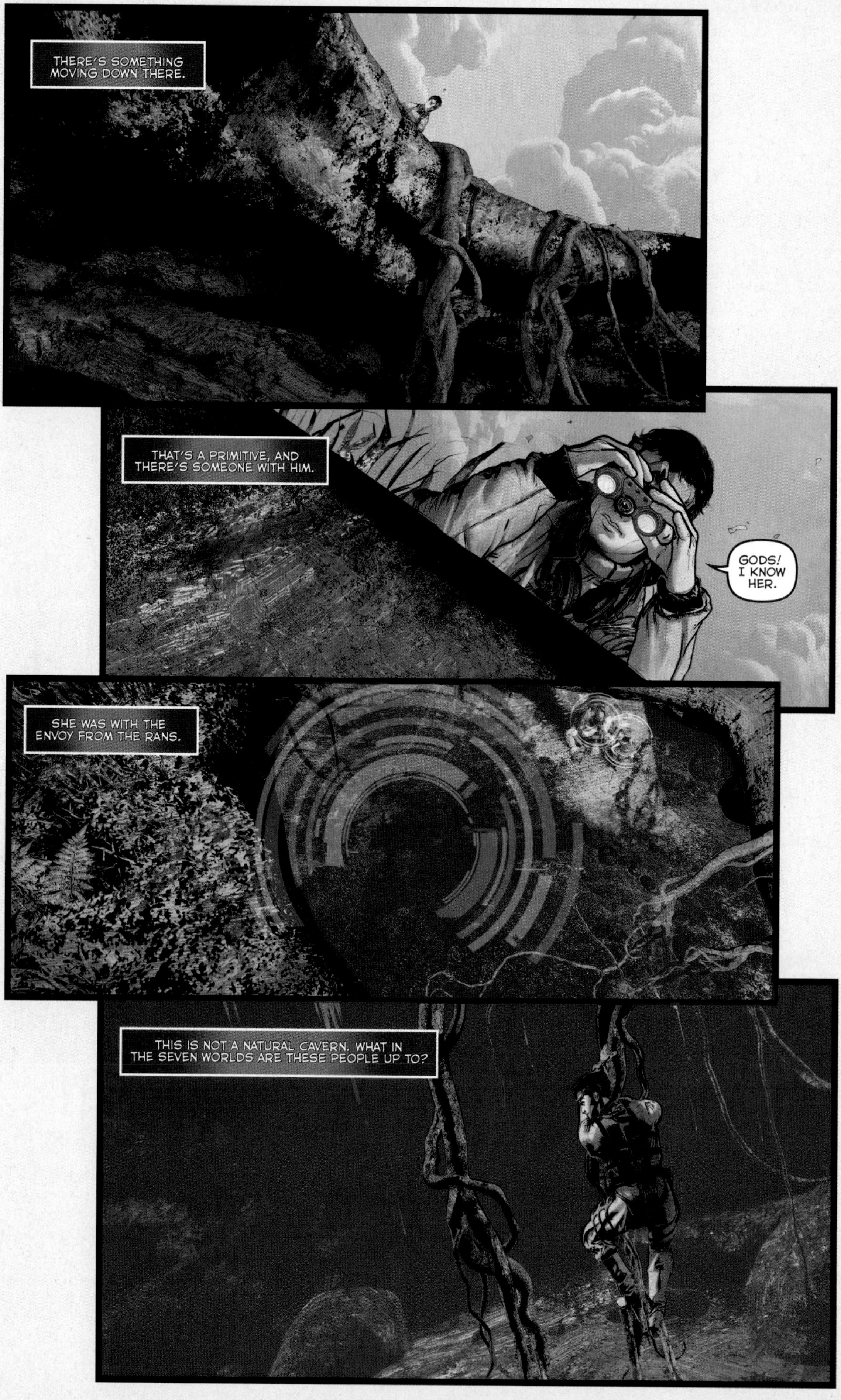
THERE'S SOMETHING MOVING DOWN THERE.
THAT'S A PRIMITIVE, AND THERE'S SOMEONE WITH HIM.
GODS! I KNOW HER.
SHE WAS WITH THE ENVOY FROM THE RANS.
THIS IS NOT A NATURAL CAVERN. WHAT IN THE SEVEN WORLDS ARE THESE PEOPLE UP TO?

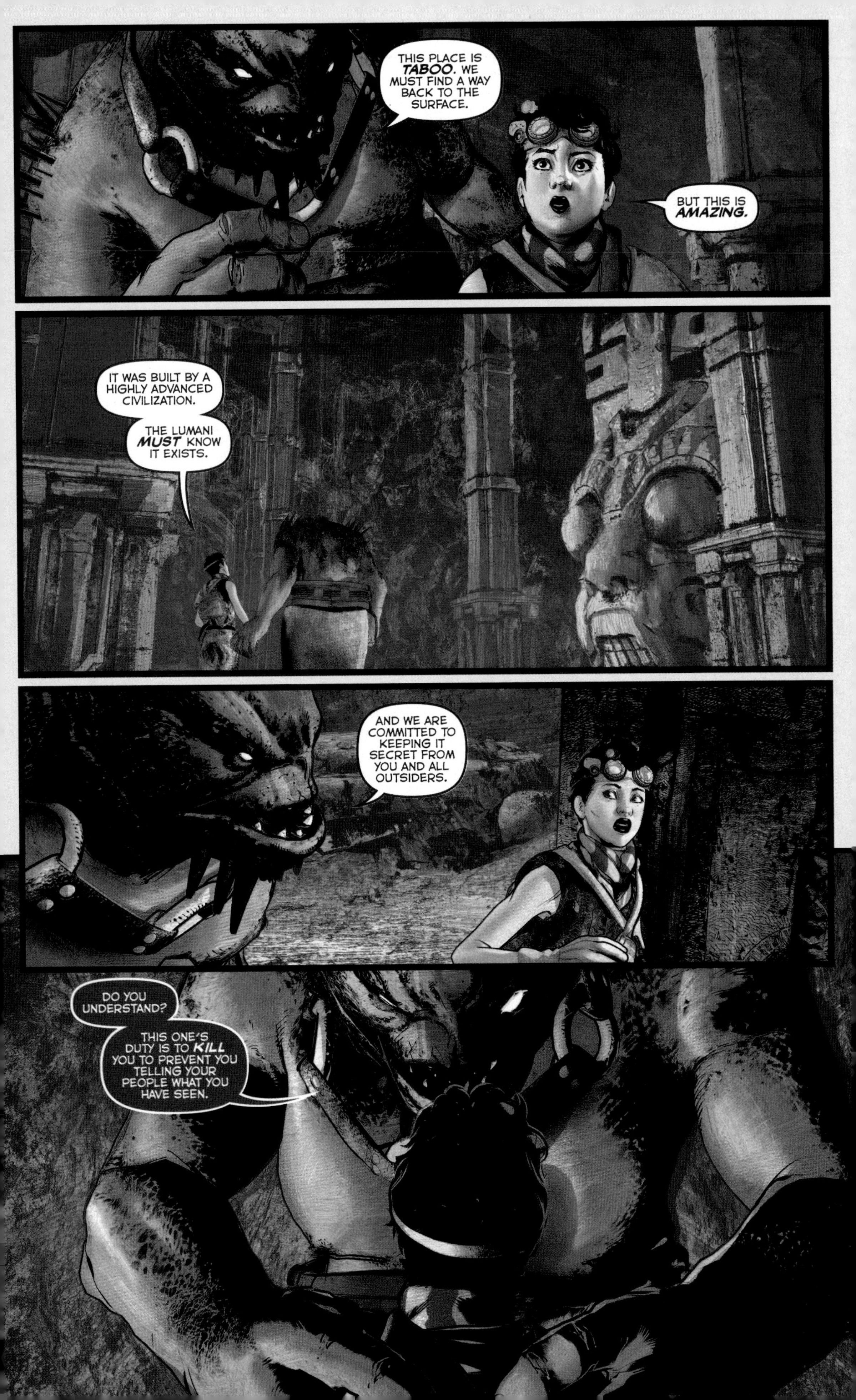
THIS PLACE IS TABOO. WE MUST FIND A WAY BACK TO THE SURFACE.
BUT THIS IS AMAZING.
IT WAS BUILT BY A HIGHLY ADVANCED CIVILIZATION.
THE LUMANI MUST KNOW IT EXISTS.
AND WE ARE COMMITTED TO KEEPING IT SECRET FROM YOU AND ALL OUTSIDERS.
DO YOU UNDERSTAND?
THIS ONE'S DUTY IS TO KILL YOU TO PREVENT YOU TELLING YOUR PEOPLE WHAT YOU HAVE SEEN.

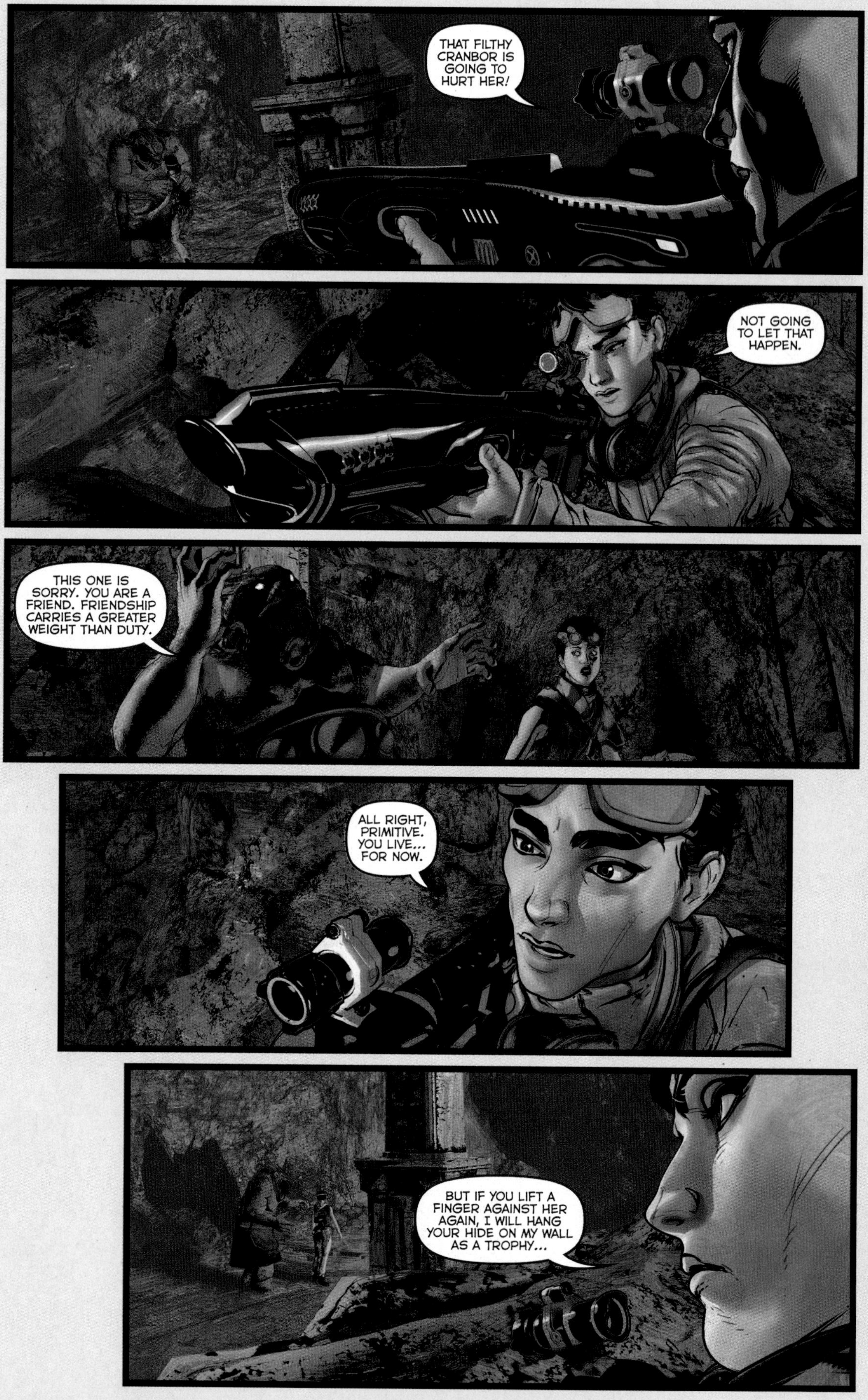
THAT FILTHY CRANBOR IS GOING TO HURT HER!
NOT GOING TO LET THAT HAPPEN.
THIS ONE IS SORRY. YOU ARE A FRIEND. FRIENDSHIP CARRIES A GREATER WEIGHT THAN DUTY.
ALL RIGHT, PRIMITIVE. YOU LIVE... FOR NOW.
BUT IF YOU LIFT A FINGER AGAINST HER AGAIN, I WILL HANG YOUR HIDE ON MY WALL AS A TROPHY...

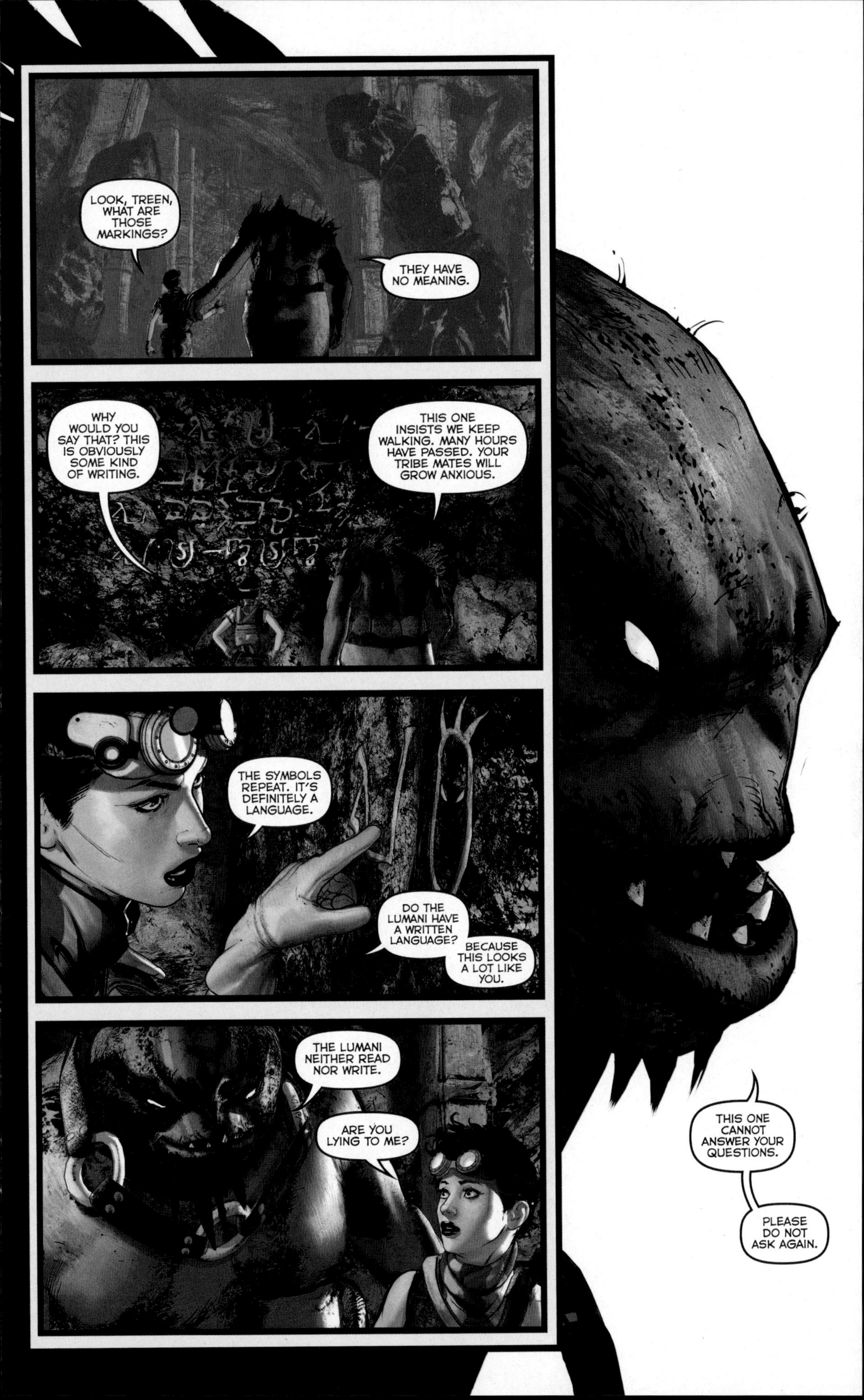

LOOK, TREEN, WHAT ARE THOSE MARKINGS?
THEY HAVE NO MEANING.
WHY WOULD YOU SAY THAT? THIS IS OBVIOUSLY SOME KIND OF WRITING.
THIS ONE INSISTS WE KEEP WALKING. MANY HOURS HAVE PASSED. YOUR TRIBE MATES WILL GROW ANXIOUS.
THE SYMBOLS REPEAT. IT'S DEFINITELY A LANGUAGE.
DO THE LUMANI HAVE A WRITTEN LANGUAGE?
BECAUSE THIS LOOKS A LOT LIKE YOU.
THE LUMANI NEITHER READ NOR WRITE.
ARE YOU LYING TO ME?
THIS ONE CANNOT ANSWER YOUR QUESTIONS.
PLEASE DO NOT ASK AGAIN.

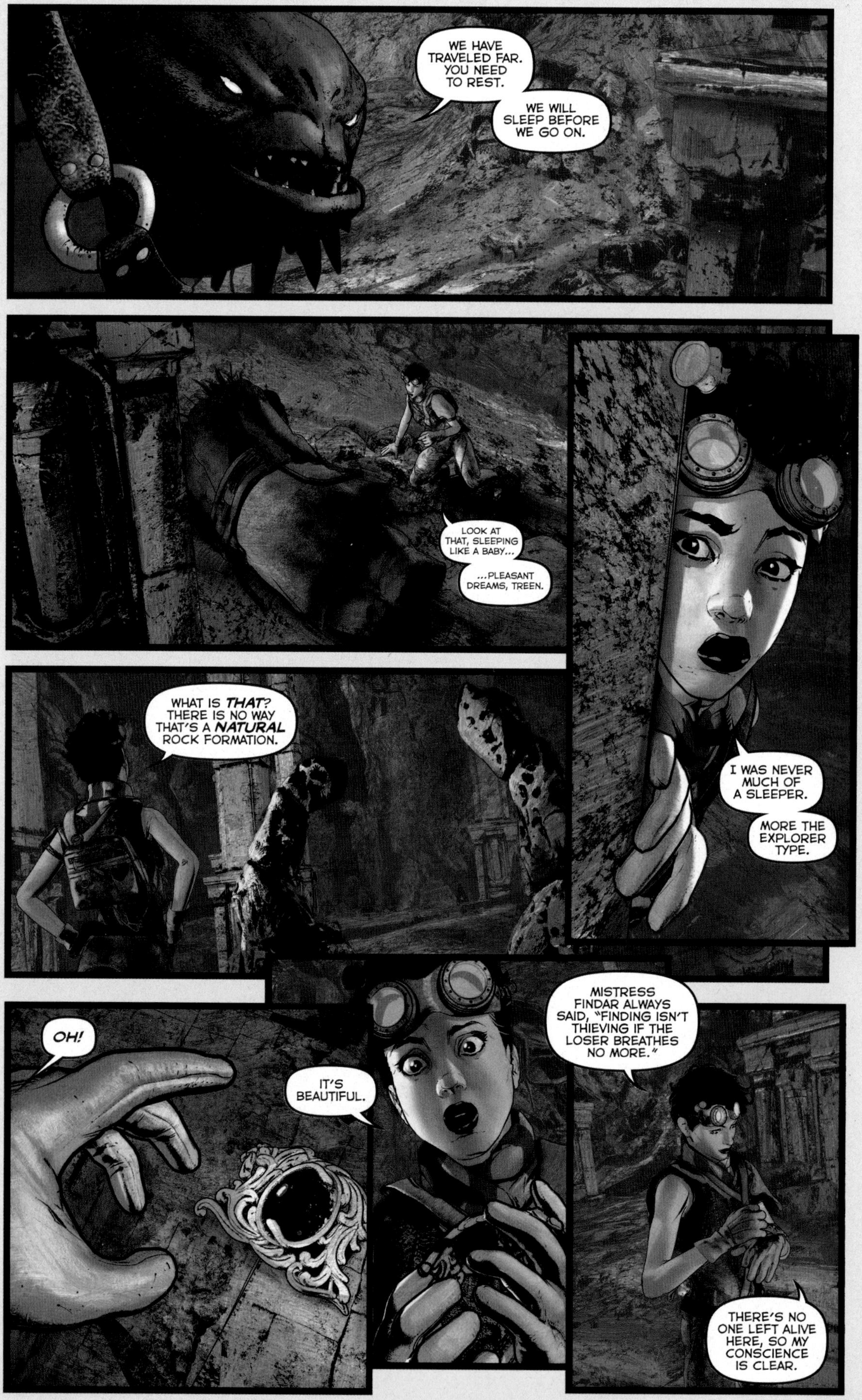
WE HAVE TRAVELED FAR. YOU NEED TO REST.
WE WILL SLEEP BEFORE WE GO ON.
LOOK AT THAT, SLEEPING LIKE A BABY...
...PLEASANT DREAMS, TREEN.
I WAS NEVER MUCH OF A SLEEPER.
MORE THE EXPLORER TYPE.
WHAT IS THAT? THERE IS NO WAY THAT'S A NATURAL ROCK FORMATION.
OH!
IT'S BEAUTIFUL.
MISTRESS FINDAR ALWAYS SAID, "FINDING ISN'T THIEVING IF THE LOSER BREATHES NO MORE."
THERE'S NO ONE LEFT ALIVE HERE, SO MY CONSCIENCE IS CLEAR.

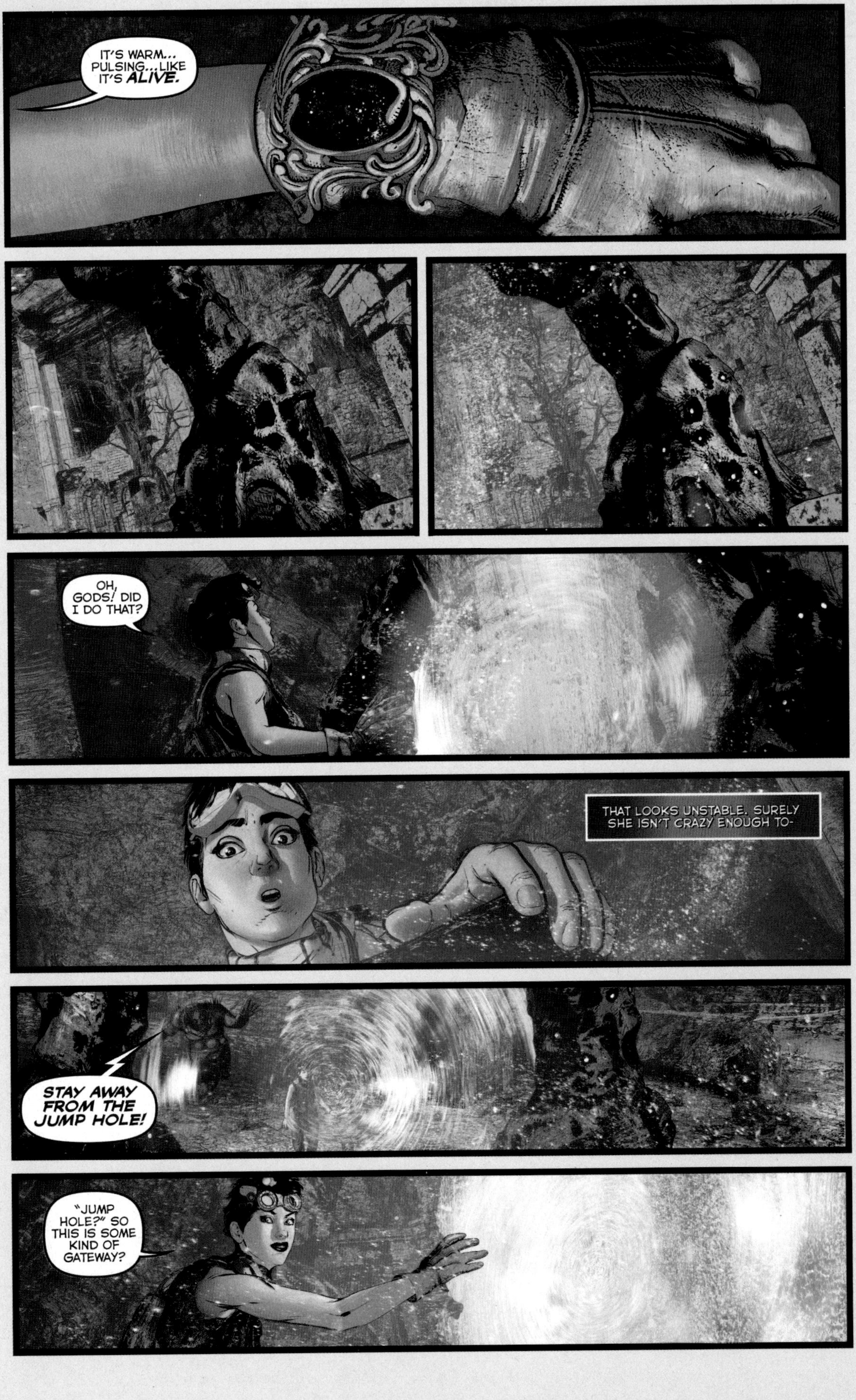

IT'S WARM... PULSING... LIKE IT'S ALIVE.
OH, GODS! DID I DO THAT?
THAT LOOKS UNSTABLE. SURELY SHE ISN'T CRAZY ENOUGH TO-
STAY AWAY FROM THE JUMP HOLE!
"JUMP HOLE?" SO THIS IS SOME KIND OF GATEWAY?

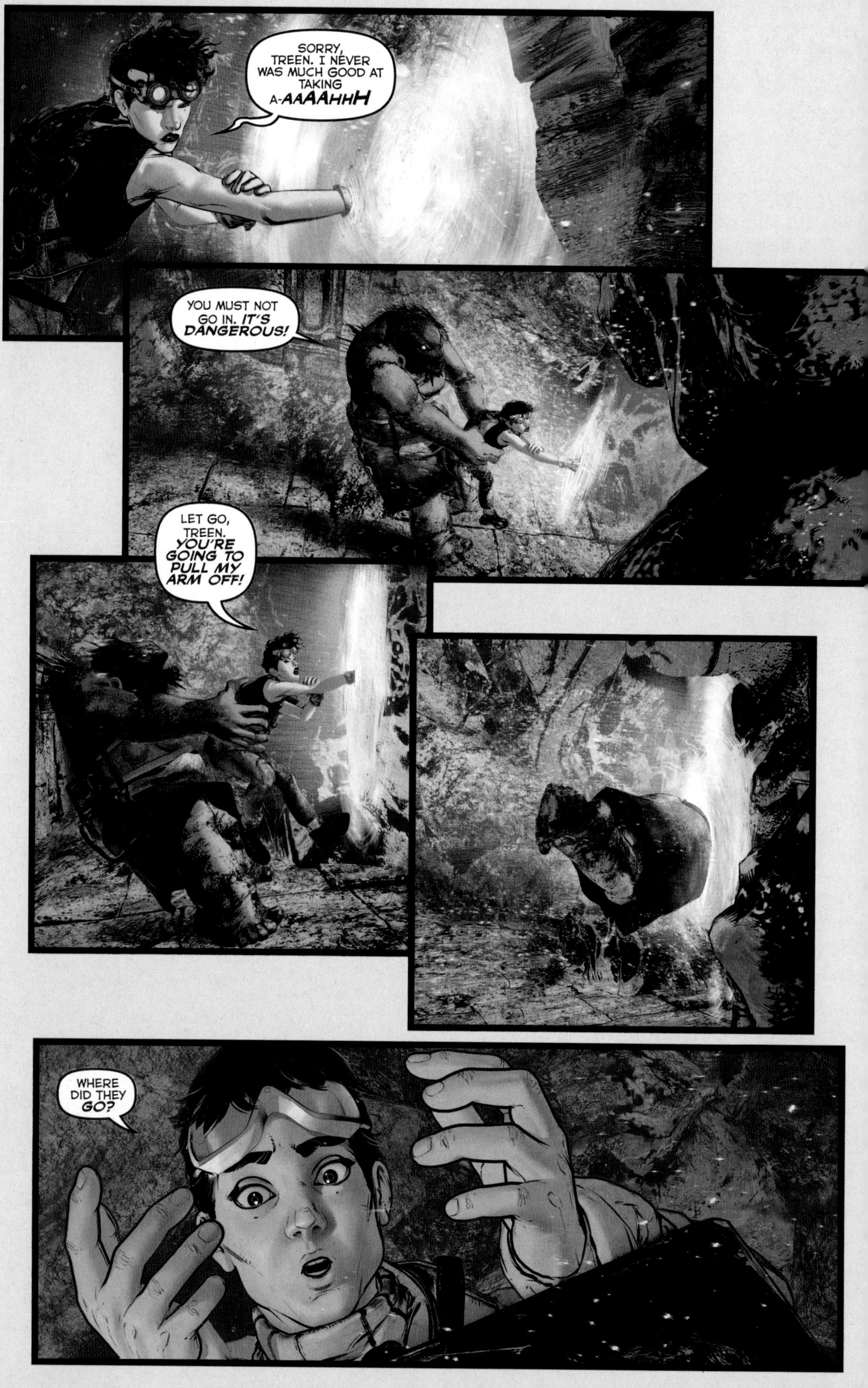
SORRY, TREEN. I NEVER WAS MUCH GOOD AT TAKING A-AAAAHHH
YOU MUST NOT GO IN. IT'S DANGEROUS!
LET GO, TREEN. YOU'RE GOING TO PULL MY ARM OFF!
WHERE DID THEY GO?

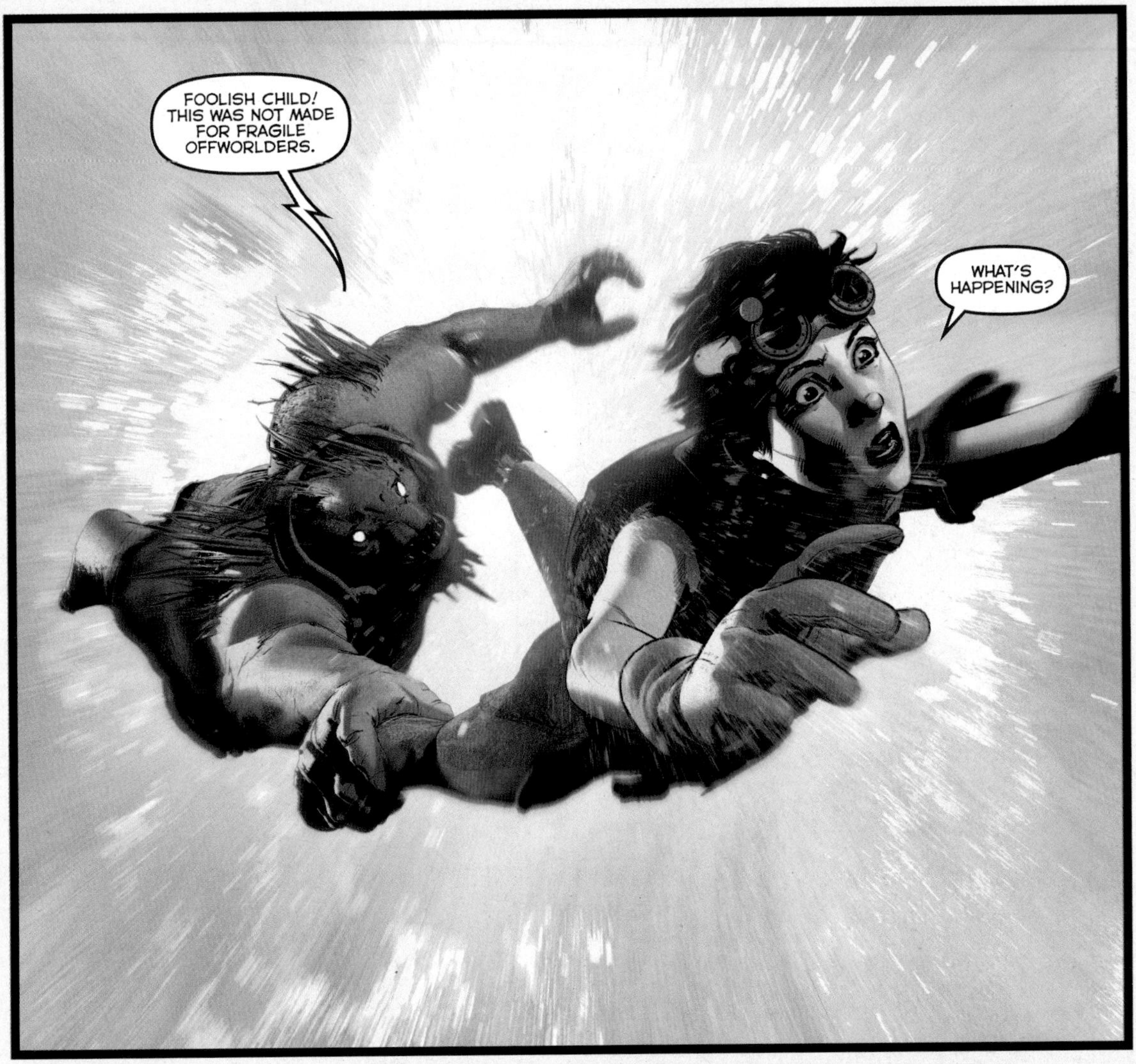
FOOLISH CHILD! THIS WAS NOT MADE FOR FRAGILE OFFWORLDERS.
WHAT'S HAPPENING?

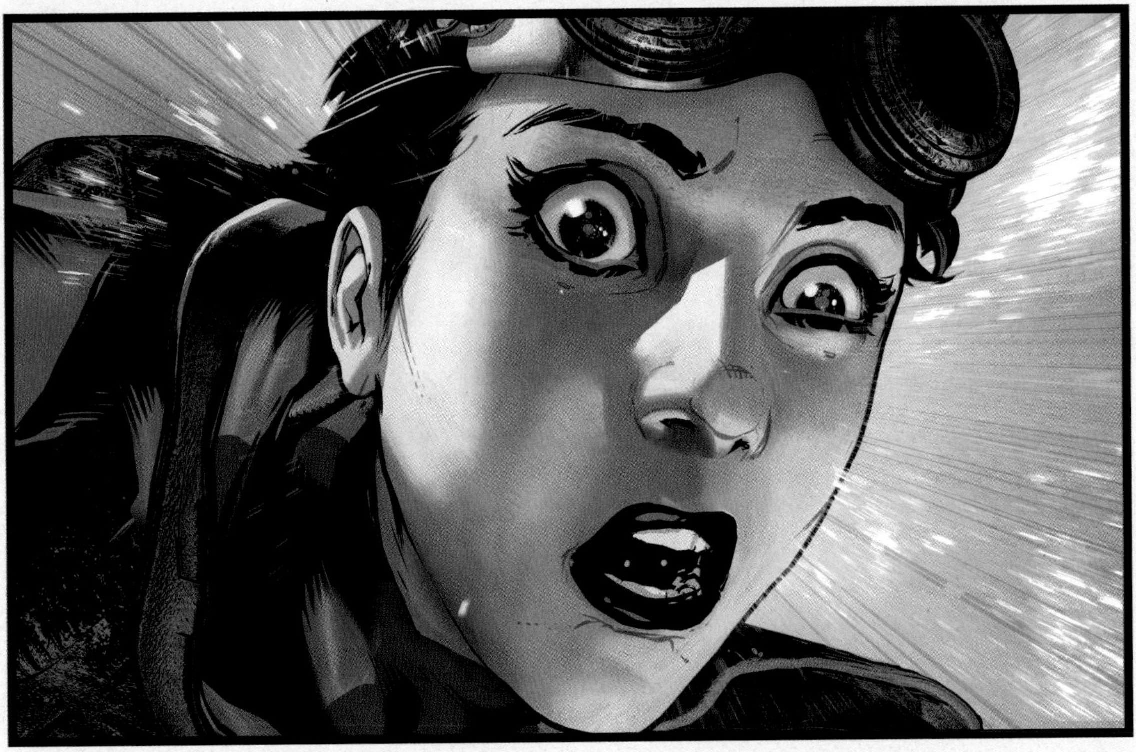

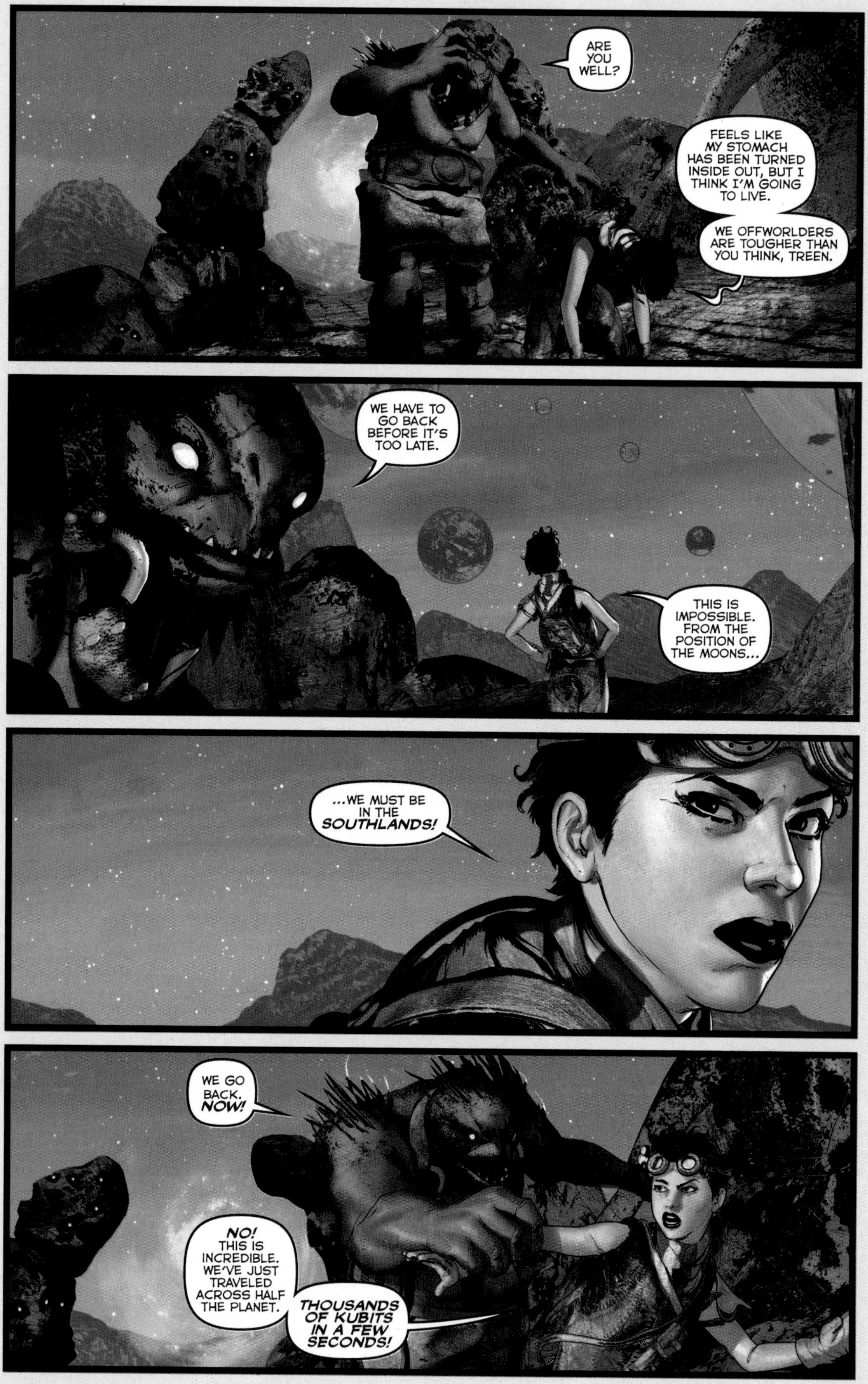
ARE YOU WELL?
FEELS LIKE MY STOMACH HAS BEEN TURNED INSIDE OUT, BUT I THINK I'M GOING TO LIVE.
WE OFFWORLDERS ARE TOUGHER THAN YOU THINK, TREEN.
WE HAVE TO GO BACK BEFORE IT'S TOO LATE.
THIS IS IMPOSSIBLE. FROM THE POSITION OF THE MOONS...
...WE MUST BE IN THE *SOUTHLANDS!*
WE GO BACK. *NOW!*
NO! THIS IS INCREDIBLE. WE'VE JUST TRAVELED ACROSS HALF THE PLANET.
THOUSANDS OF KUBITS IN A FEW SECONDS!

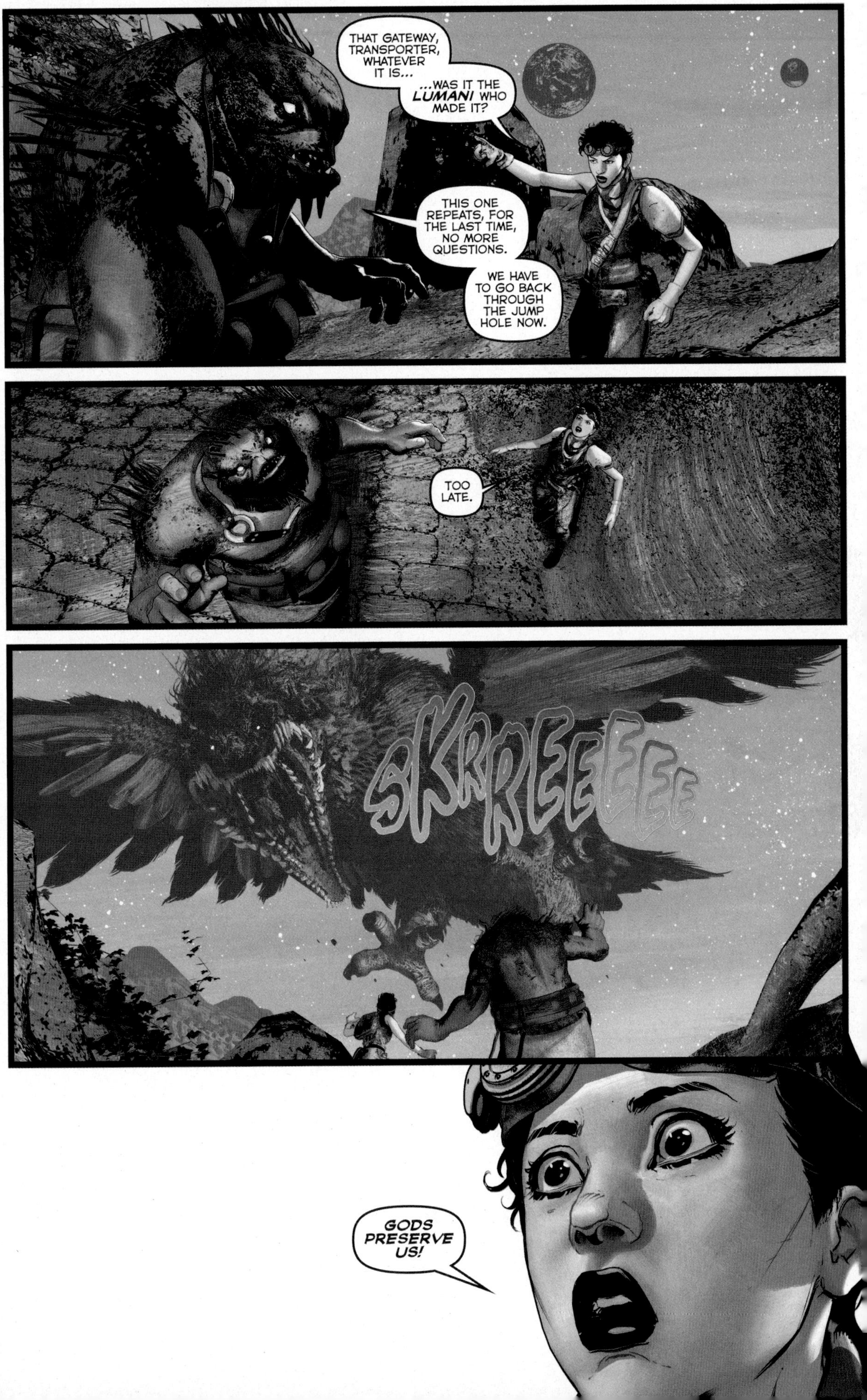

THAT GATEWAY, TRANSPORTER, WHATEVER IT IS...
...WAS IT THE *LUMANI* WHO MADE IT?
THIS ONE REPEATS, FOR THE LAST TIME, NO MORE QUESTIONS.
WE HAVE TO GO BACK THROUGH THE JUMP HOLE NOW.
TOO LATE.
SKRREEEEE
GODS PRESERVE US!

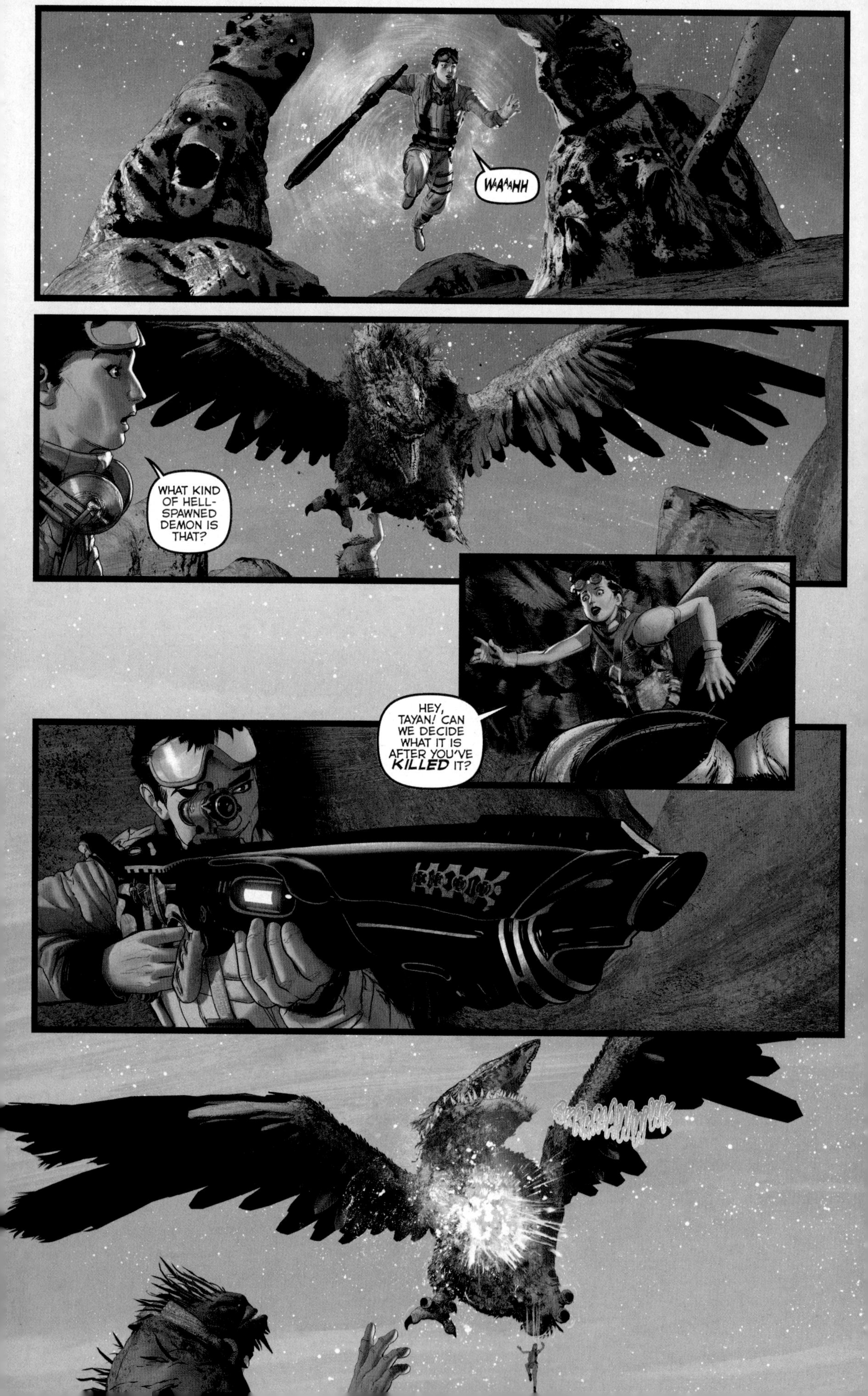
WAAAAHH
WHAT KIND OF HELL-SPAWNED DEMON IS THAT?
HEY, TAYAN! CAN WE DECIDE WHAT IT IS AFTER YOU'VE **KILLED** IT?

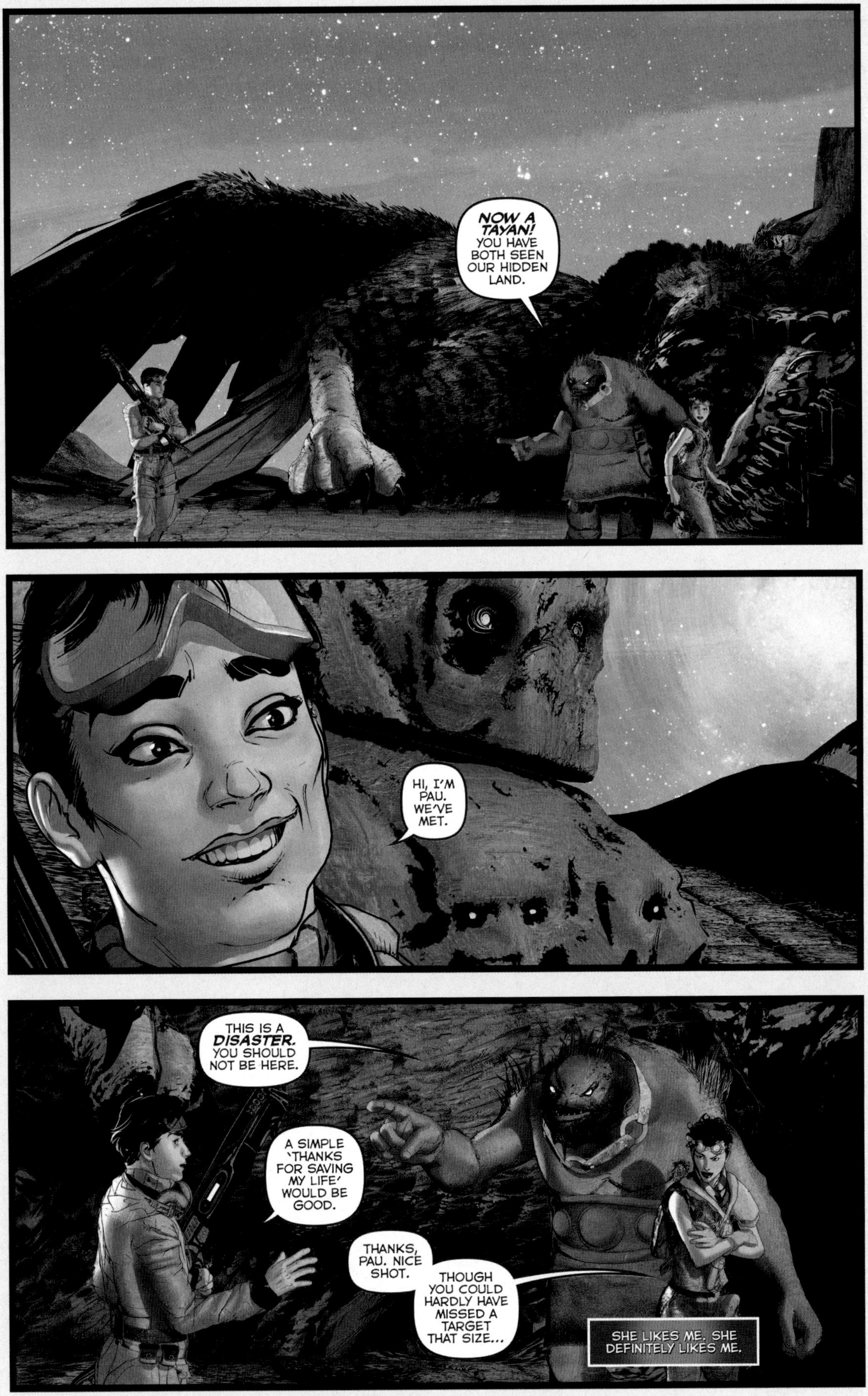
NOW A TAYAN! YOU HAVE BOTH SEEN OUR HIDDEN LAND.
HI, I'M PAU. WE'VE MET.
THIS IS A DISASTER. YOU SHOULD NOT BE HERE.
A SIMPLE 'THANKS FOR SAVING MY LIFE' WOULD BE GOOD.
THANKS, PAU. NICE SHOT.
THOUGH YOU COULD HARDLY HAVE MISSED A TARGET THAT SIZE...
SHE LIKES ME. SHE DEFINITELY LIKES ME.

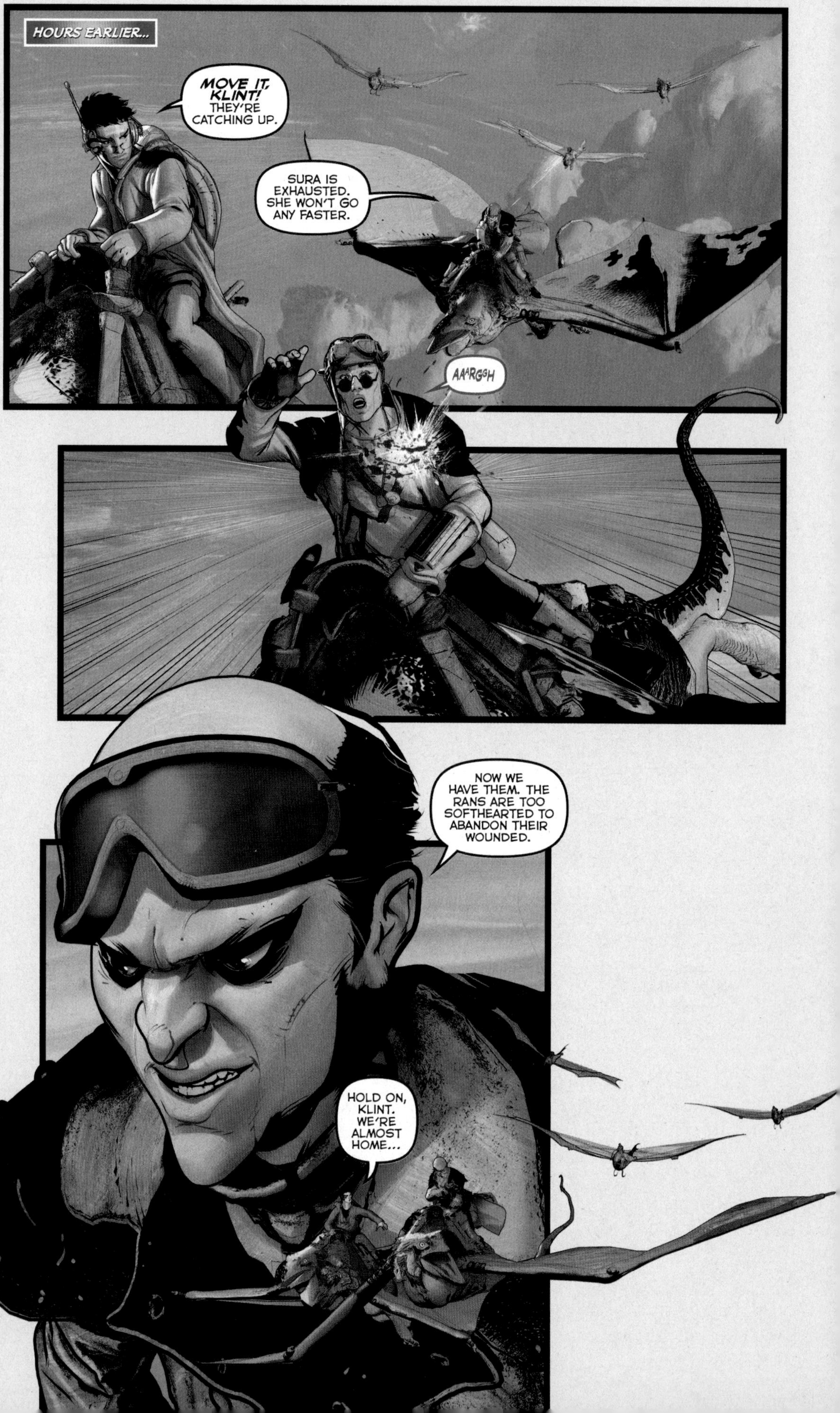
HOURS EARLIER...
MOVE IT, KLINT! THEY'RE CATCHING UP.
SURA IS EXHAUSTED. SHE WON'T GO ANY FASTER.
AAARGGH
NOW WE HAVE THEM. THE RANS ARE TOO SOFTHEARTED TO ABANDON THEIR WOUNDED.
HOLD ON, KLINT. WE'RE ALMOST HOME...

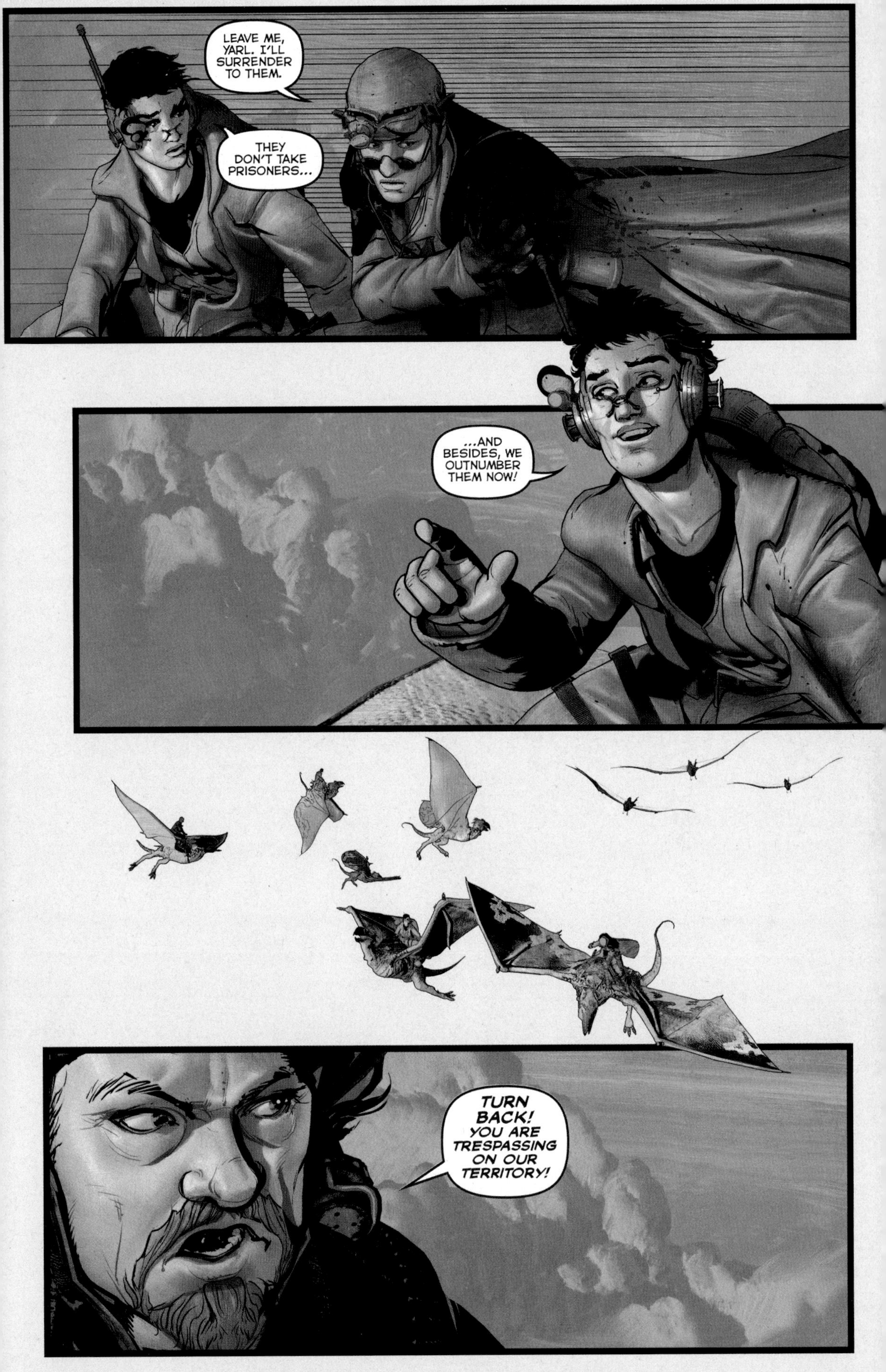
LEAVE ME, YARL. I'LL SURRENDER TO THEM.
THEY DON'T TAKE PRISONERS...
...AND BESIDES, WE OUTNUMBER THEM NOW!
TURN BACK! YOU ARE TRESPASSING ON OUR TERRITORY!

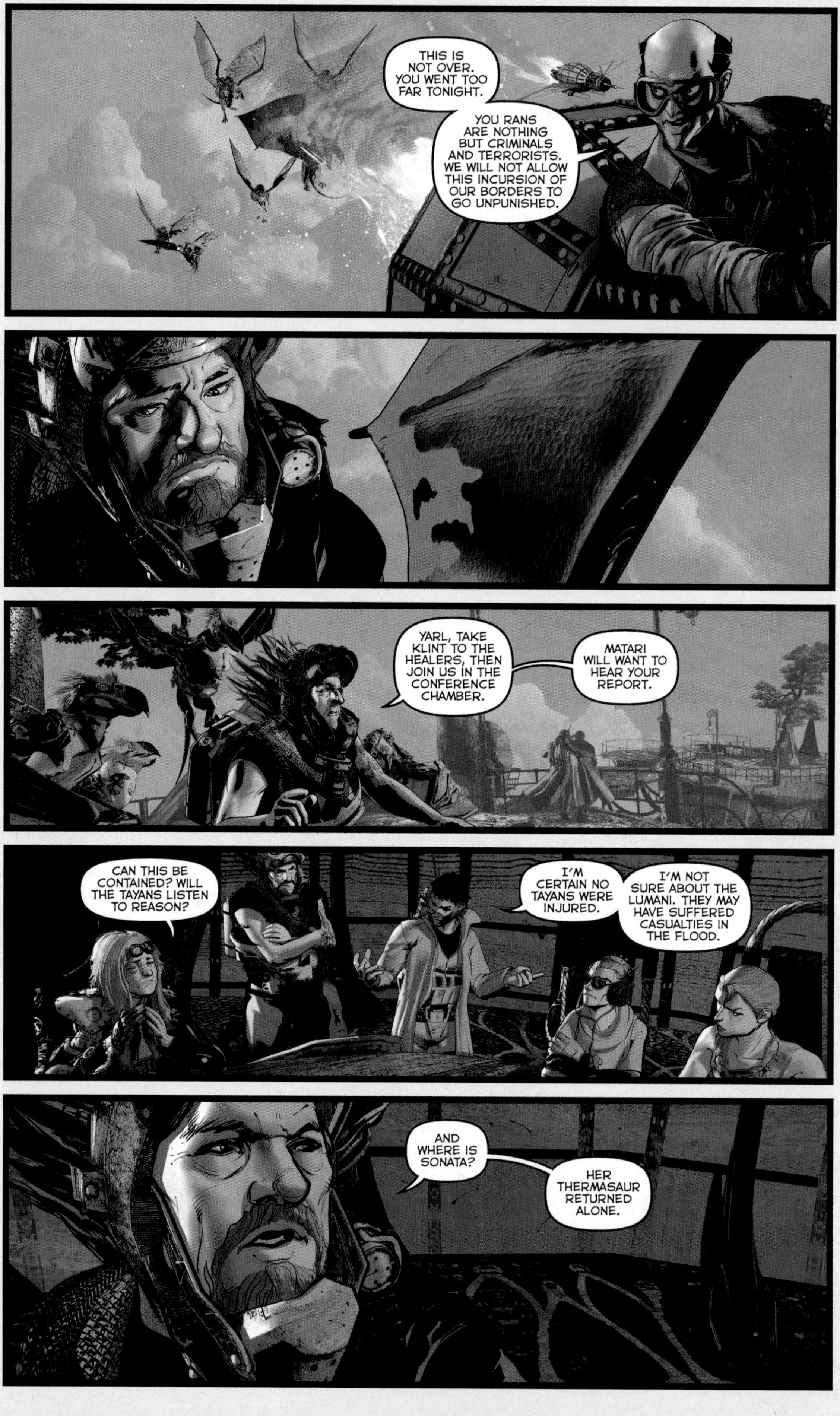
THIS IS NOT OVER. YOU WENT TOO FAR TONIGHT.
YOU RANS ARE NOTHING BUT CRIMINALS AND TERRORISTS. WE WILL NOT ALLOW THIS INCURSION OF OUR BORDERS TO GO UNPUNISHED.
YARL, TAKE KLINT TO THE HEALERS, THEN JOIN US IN THE CONFERENCE CHAMBER.
MATARI WILL WANT TO HEAR YOUR REPORT.
CAN THIS BE CONTAINED? WILL THE TAYANS LISTEN TO REASON?
I'M CERTAIN NO TAYANS WERE INJURED.
I'M NOT SURE ABOUT THE LUMANI. THEY MAY HAVE SUFFERED CASUALTIES IN THE FLOOD.
AND WHERE IS SONATA?
HER THERMASAUR RETURNED ALONE.

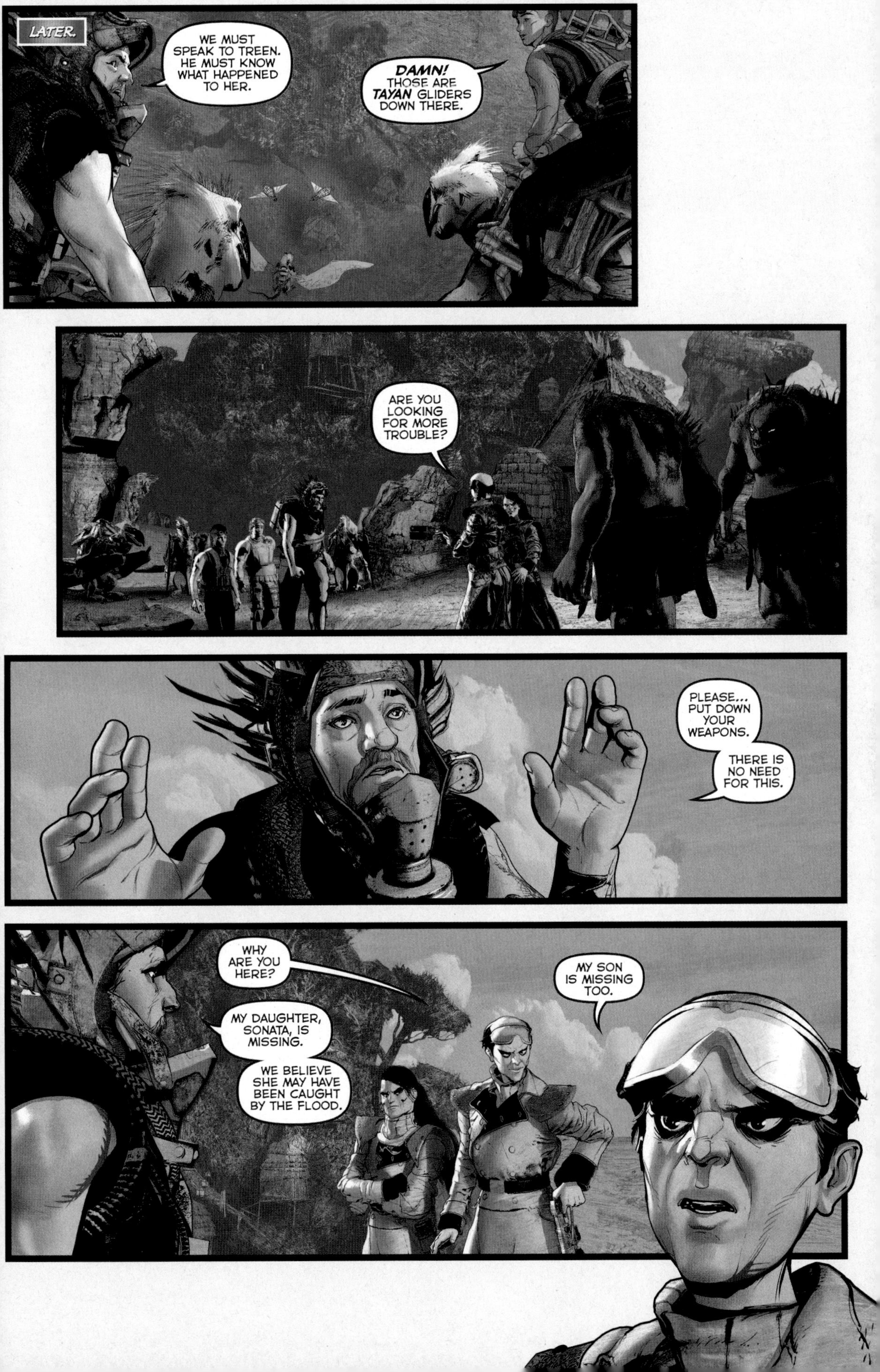
LATER.
WE MUST SPEAK TO TREEN. HE MUST KNOW WHAT HAPPENED TO HER.
DAMN! THOSE ARE TAYAN GLIDERS DOWN THERE.
ARE YOU LOOKING FOR MORE TROUBLE?
PLEASE... PUT DOWN YOUR WEAPONS.
THERE IS NO NEED FOR THIS.
WHY ARE YOU HERE?
MY DAUGHTER, SONATA, IS MISSING.
WE BELIEVE SHE MAY HAVE BEEN CAUGHT BY THE FLOOD.
MY SON IS MISSING TOO.

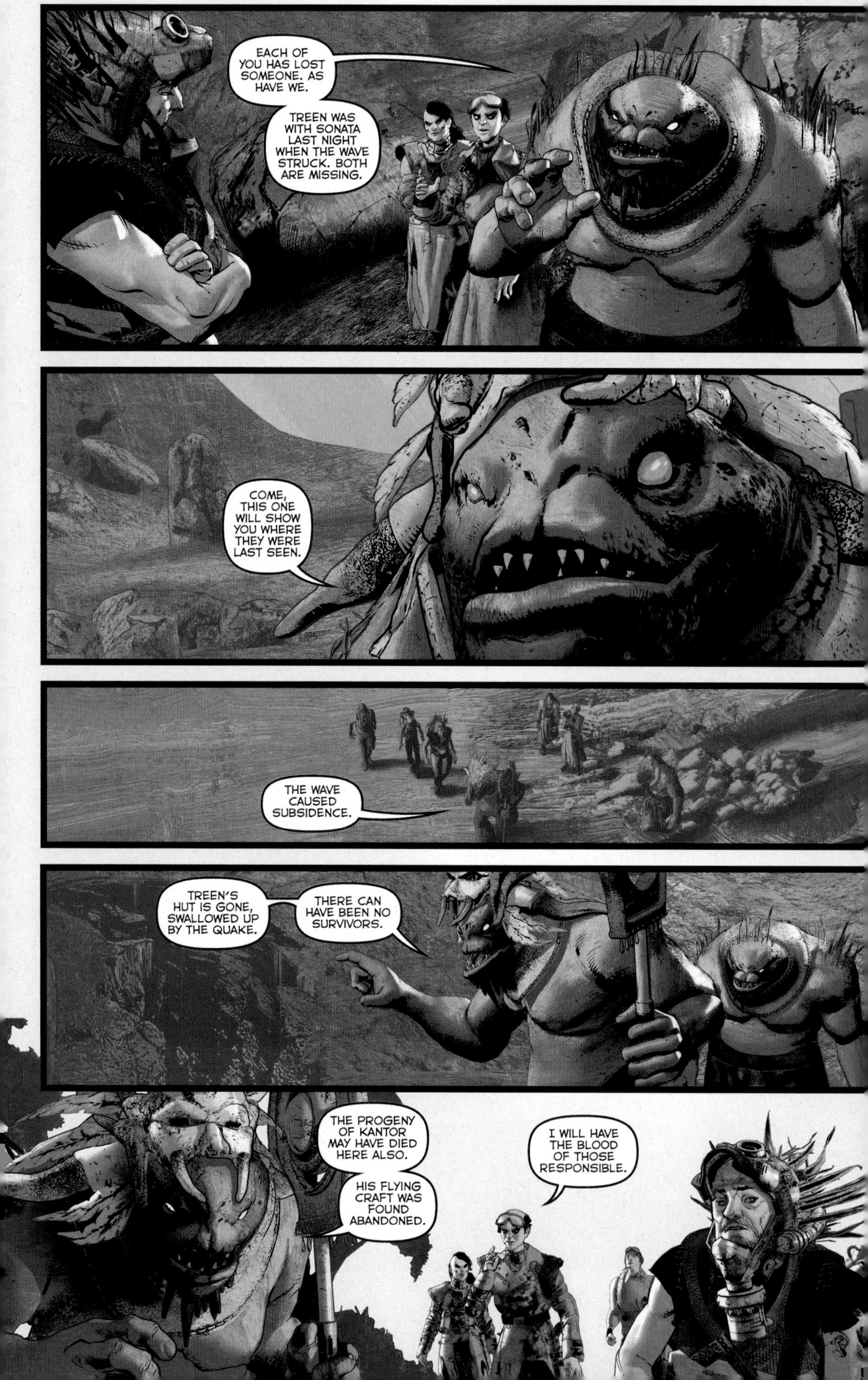
EACH OF YOU HAS LOST SOMEONE. AS HAVE WE.
TREEN WAS WITH SONATA LAST NIGHT WHEN THE WAVE STRUCK. BOTH ARE MISSING.
COME, THIS ONE WILL SHOW YOU WHERE THEY WERE LAST SEEN.
THE WAVE CAUSED SUBSIDENCE.
TREEN'S HUT IS GONE, SWALLOWED UP BY THE QUAKE.
THERE CAN HAVE BEEN NO SURVIVORS.
THE PROGENY OF KANTOR MAY HAVE DIED HERE ALSO.
HIS FLYING CRAFT WAS FOUND ABANDONED.
I WILL HAVE THE BLOOD OF THOSE RESPONSIBLE.

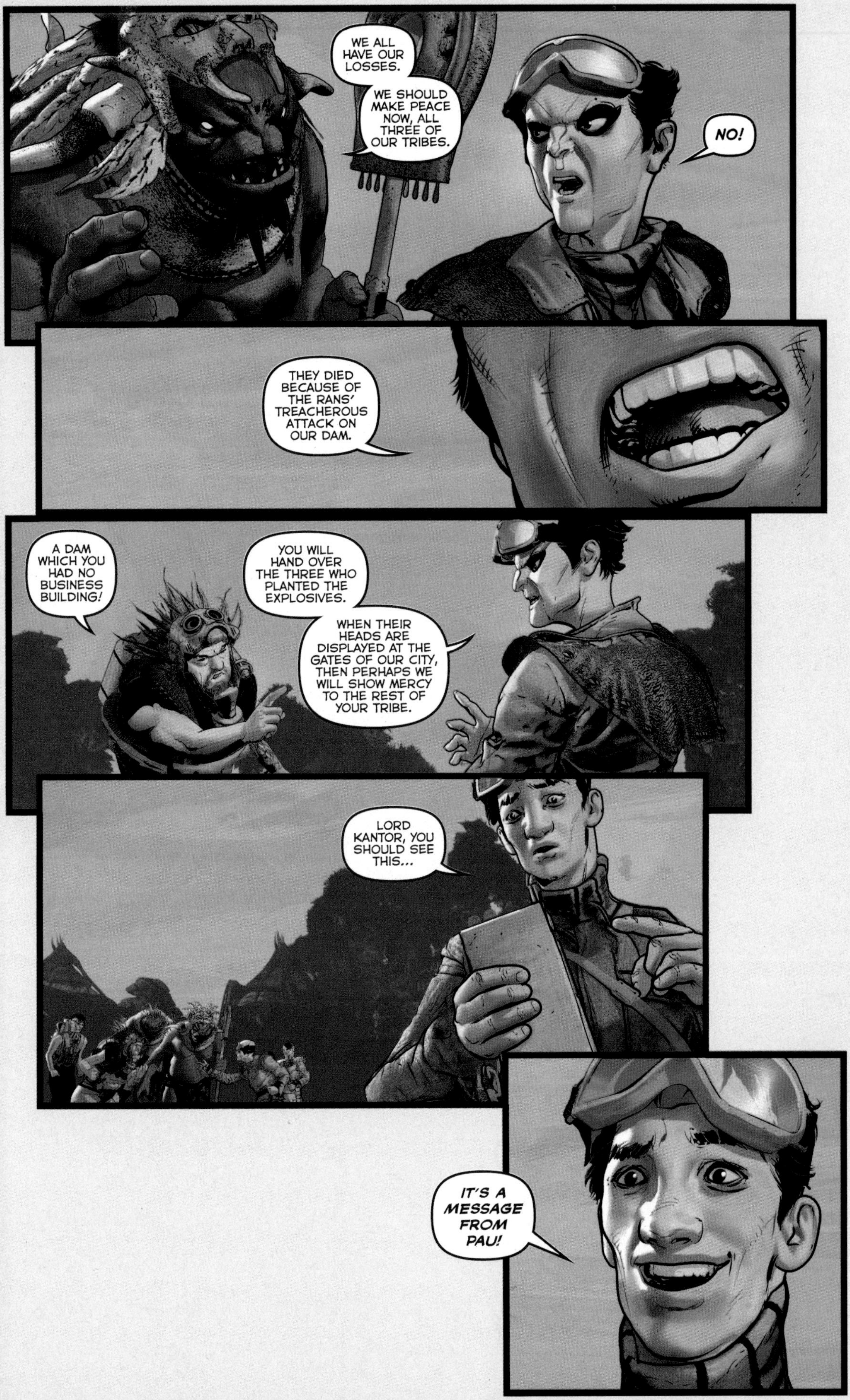

WE ALL HAVE OUR LOSSES.
WE SHOULD MAKE PEACE NOW, ALL THREE OF OUR TRIBES.
NO!
THEY DIED BECAUSE OF THE RANS' TREACHEROUS ATTACK ON OUR DAM.
A DAM WHICH YOU HAD NO BUSINESS BUILDING!
YOU WILL HAND OVER THE THREE WHO PLANTED THE EXPLOSIVES.
WHEN THEIR HEADS ARE DISPLAYED AT THE GATES OF OUR CITY, THEN PERHAPS WE WILL SHOW MERCY TO THE REST OF YOUR TRIBE.
LORD KANTOR, YOU SHOULD SEE THIS...
IT'S A MESSAGE FROM PAU!

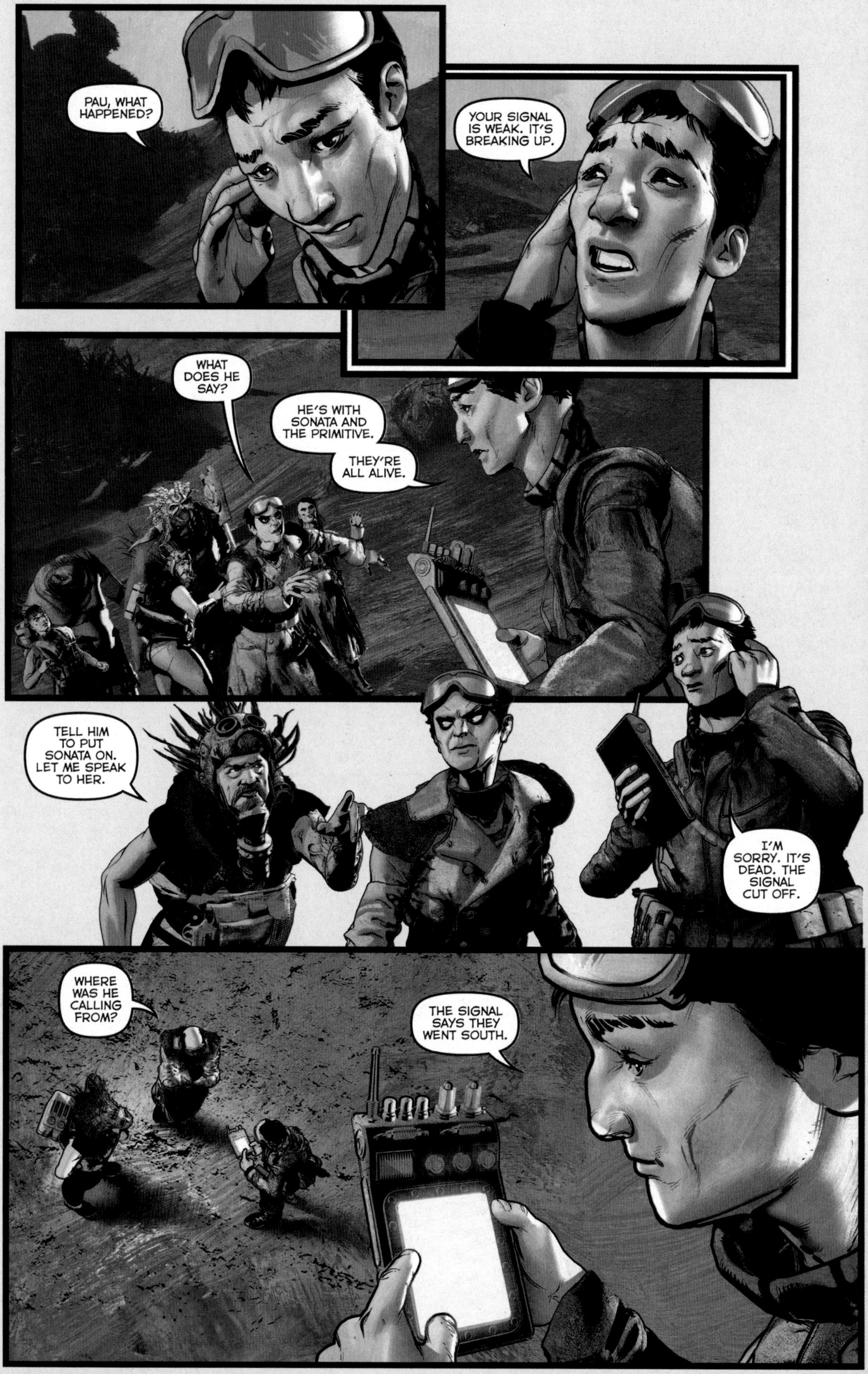
PAU, WHAT HAPPENED?
YOUR SIGNAL IS WEAK. IT'S BREAKING UP.
WHAT DOES HE SAY?
HE'S WITH SONATA AND THE PRIMITIVE.
THEY'RE ALL ALIVE.
TELL HIM TO PUT SONATA ON. LET ME SPEAK TO HER.
I'M SORRY. IT'S DEAD. THE SIGNAL CUT OFF.
WHERE WAS HE CALLING FROM?
THE SIGNAL SAYS THEY WENT SOUTH.

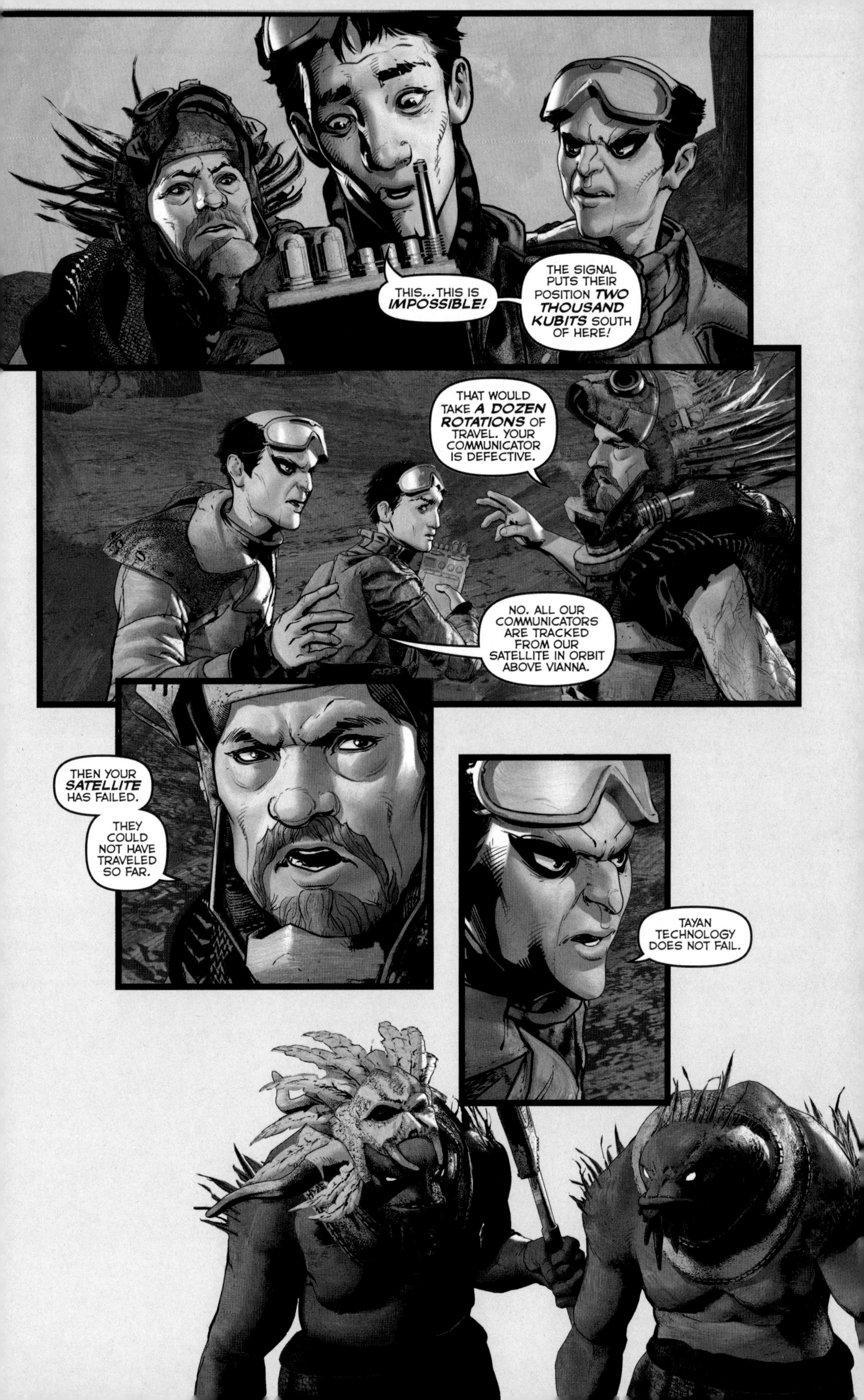
THIS...THIS IS IMPOSSIBLE!
THE SIGNAL PUTS THEIR POSITION TWO THOUSAND KUBITS SOUTH OF HERE!
THAT WOULD TAKE A DOZEN ROTATIONS OF TRAVEL. YOUR COMMUNICATOR IS DEFECTIVE.
NO. ALL OUR COMMUNICATORS ARE TRACKED FROM OUR SATELLITE IN ORBIT ABOVE VIANNA.
THEN YOUR SATELLITE HAS FAILED.
THEY COULD NOT HAVE TRAVELED SO FAR.
TAYAN TECHNOLOGY DOES NOT FAIL.

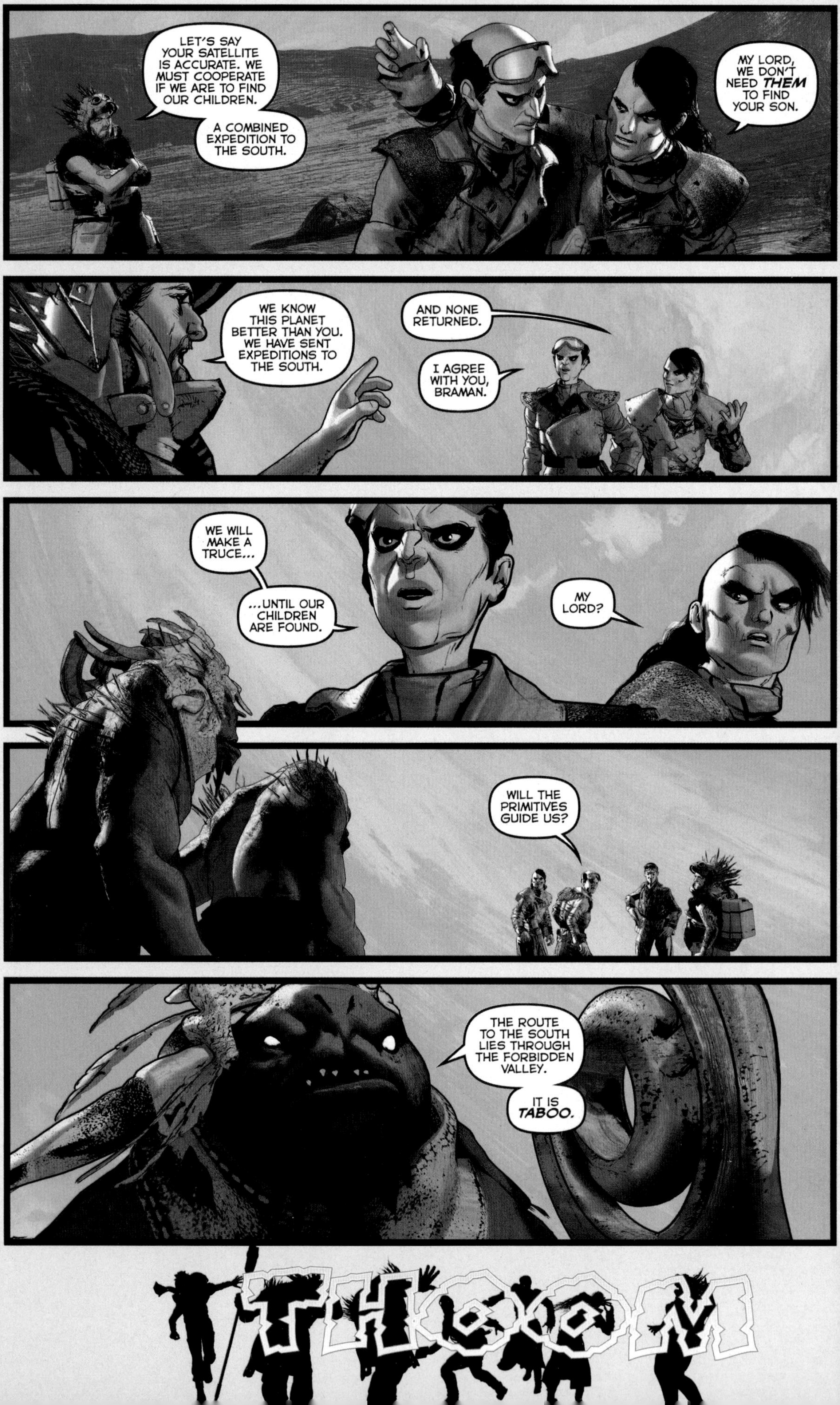
LET'S SAY YOUR SATELLITE IS ACCURATE. WE MUST COOPERATE IF WE ARE TO FIND OUR CHILDREN.
A COMBINED EXPEDITION TO THE SOUTH.
MY LORD, WE DON'T NEED *THEM* TO FIND YOUR SON.
WE KNOW THIS PLANET BETTER THAN YOU. WE HAVE SENT EXPEDITIONS TO THE SOUTH.
AND NONE RETURNED.
I AGREE WITH YOU, BRAMAN.
WE WILL MAKE A TRUCE...
...UNTIL OUR CHILDREN ARE FOUND.
MY LORD?
WILL THE PRIMITIVES GUIDE US?
THE ROUTE TO THE SOUTH LIES THROUGH THE FORBIDDEN VALLEY.
IT IS *TABOO.*

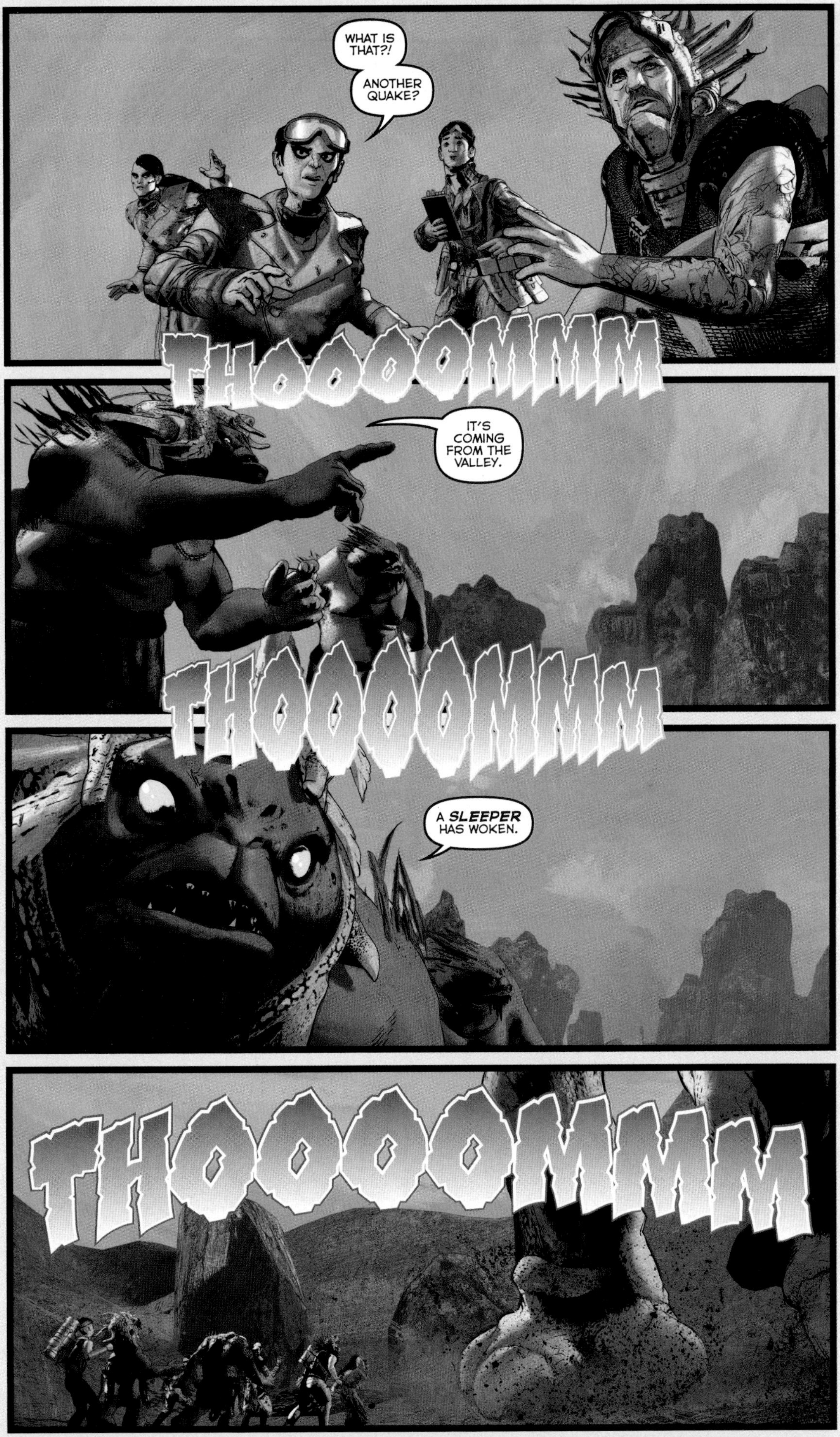
WHAT IS THAT?!
ANOTHER QUAKE?
THOOOOMMM
IT'S COMING FROM THE VALLEY.
THOOOOMMM
A *SLEEPER* HAS WOKEN.
THOOOOMMM

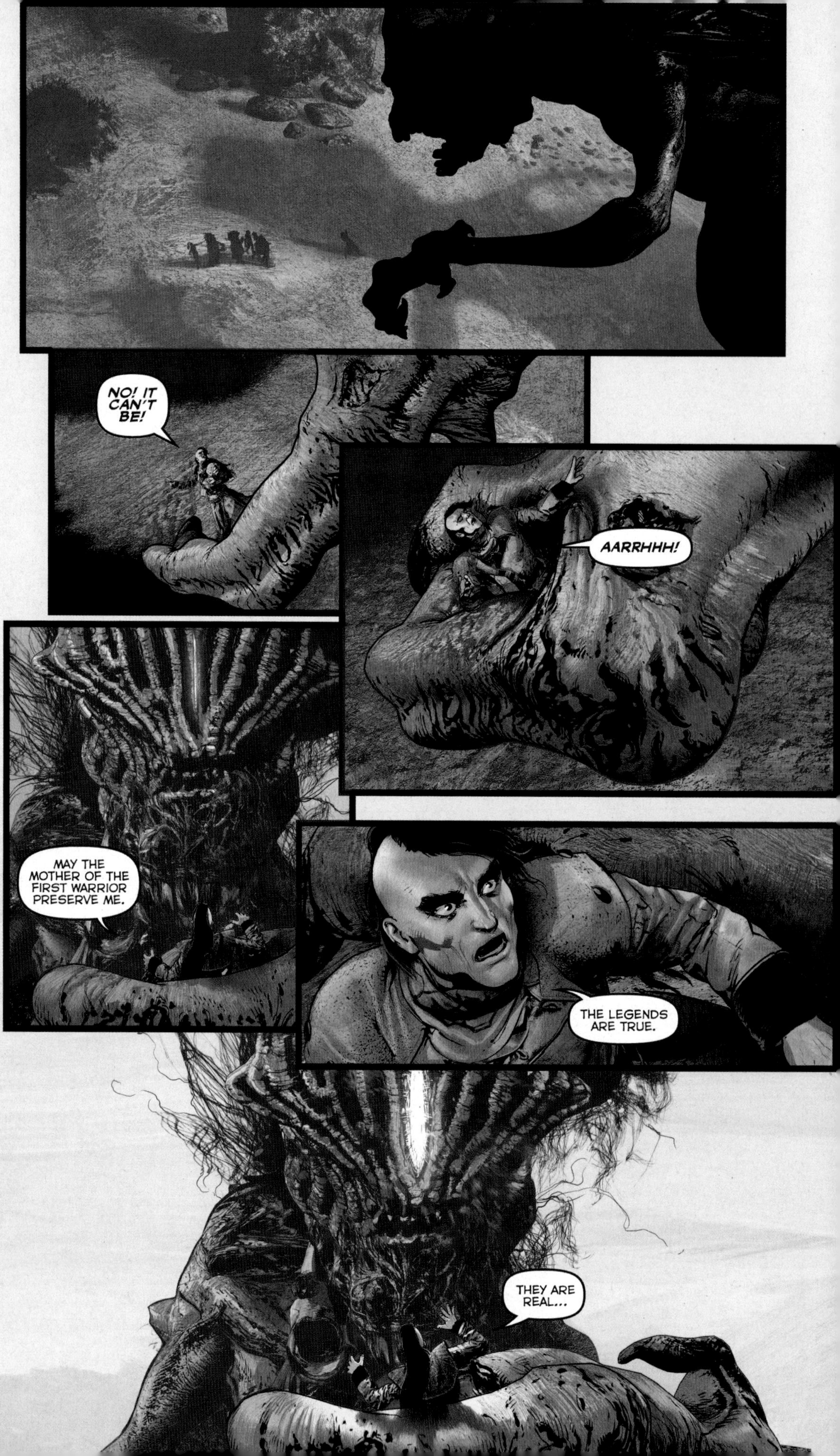
NO! IT CAN'T BE!
AARRHHH!
MAY THE MOTHER OF THE FIRST WARRIOR PRESERVE ME.
THE LEGENDS ARE TRUE.
THEY ARE REAL...

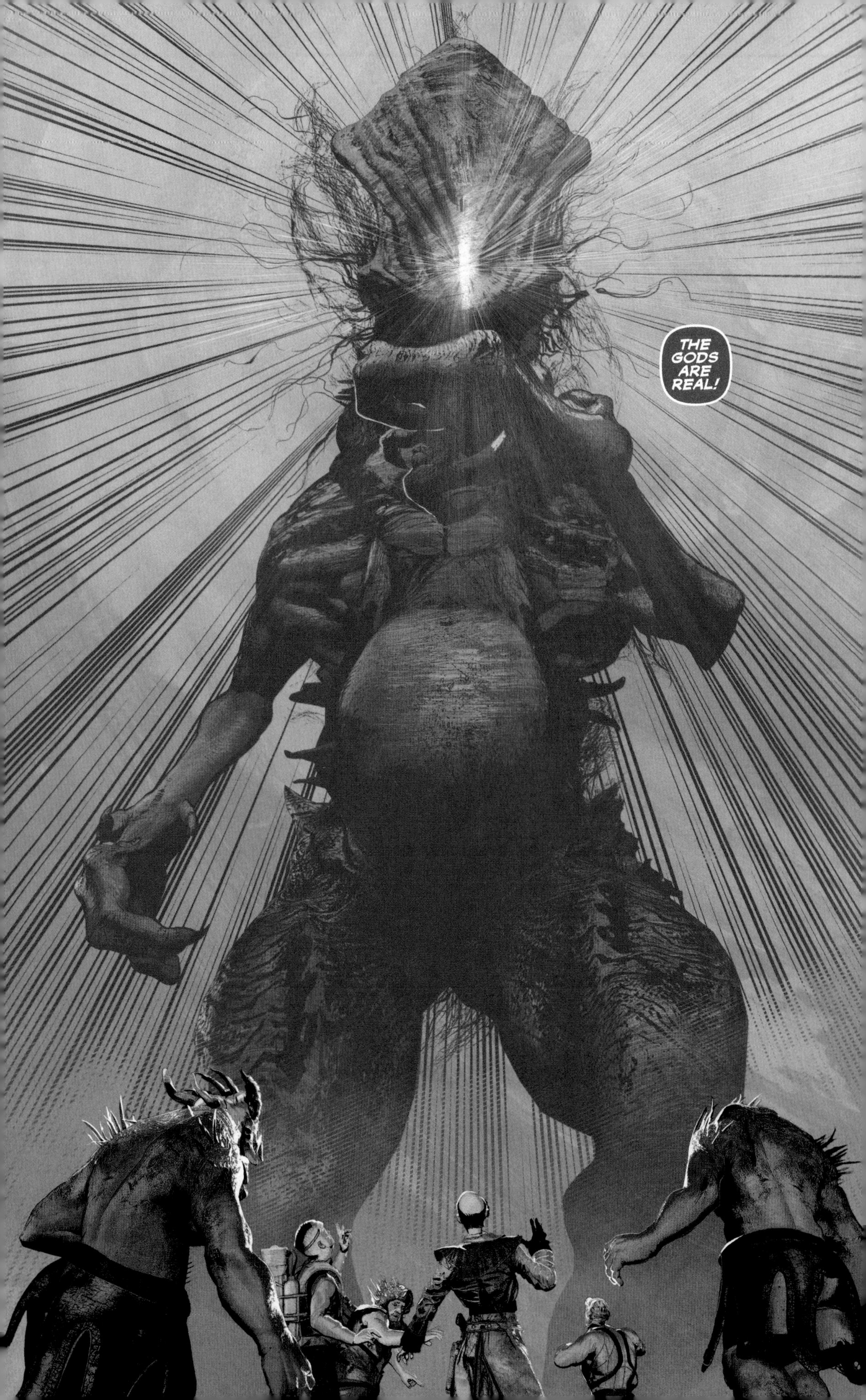
THE GODS ARE REAL!

Issue #1 Second Printing Cover

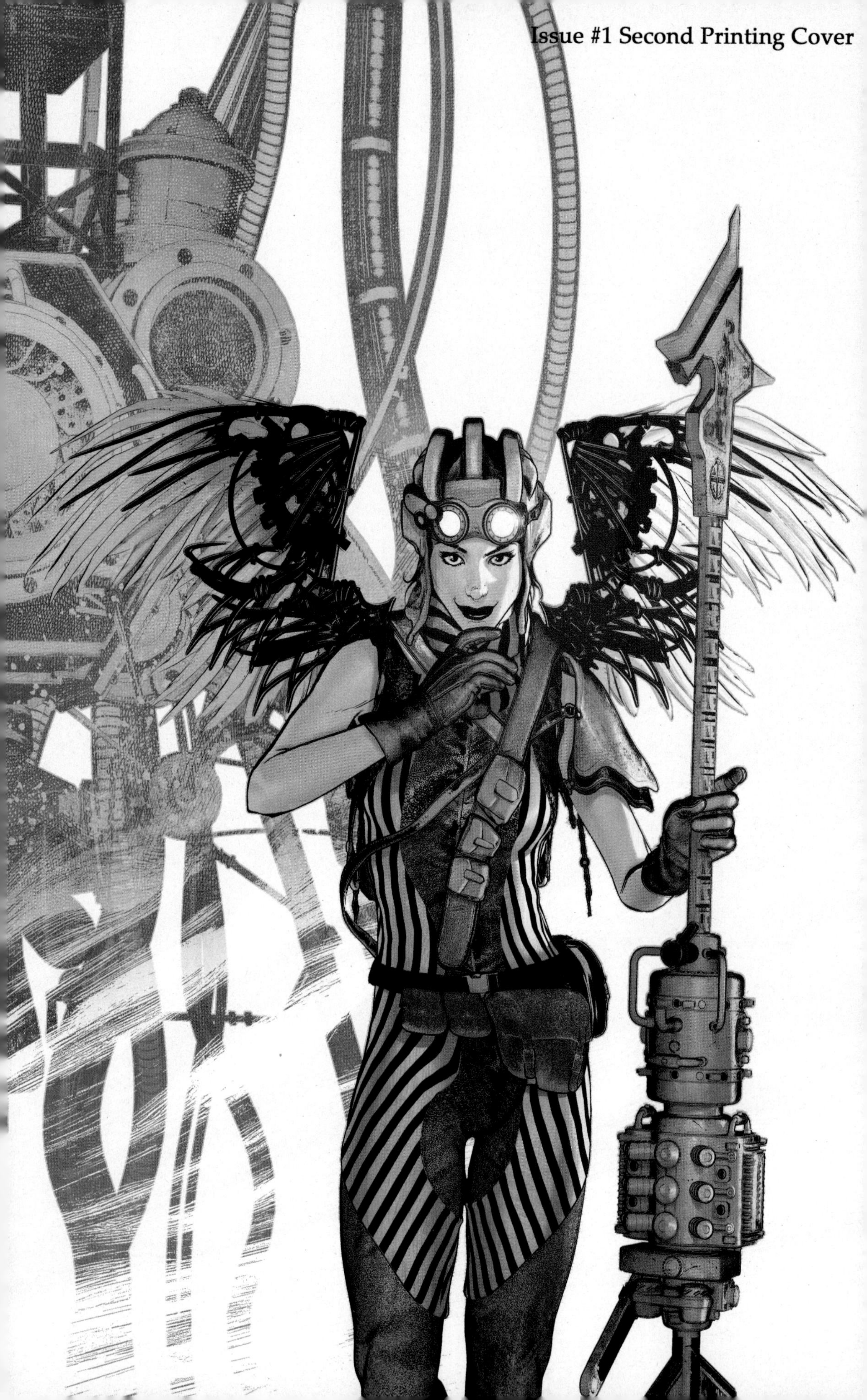

Issue #3 Cover A

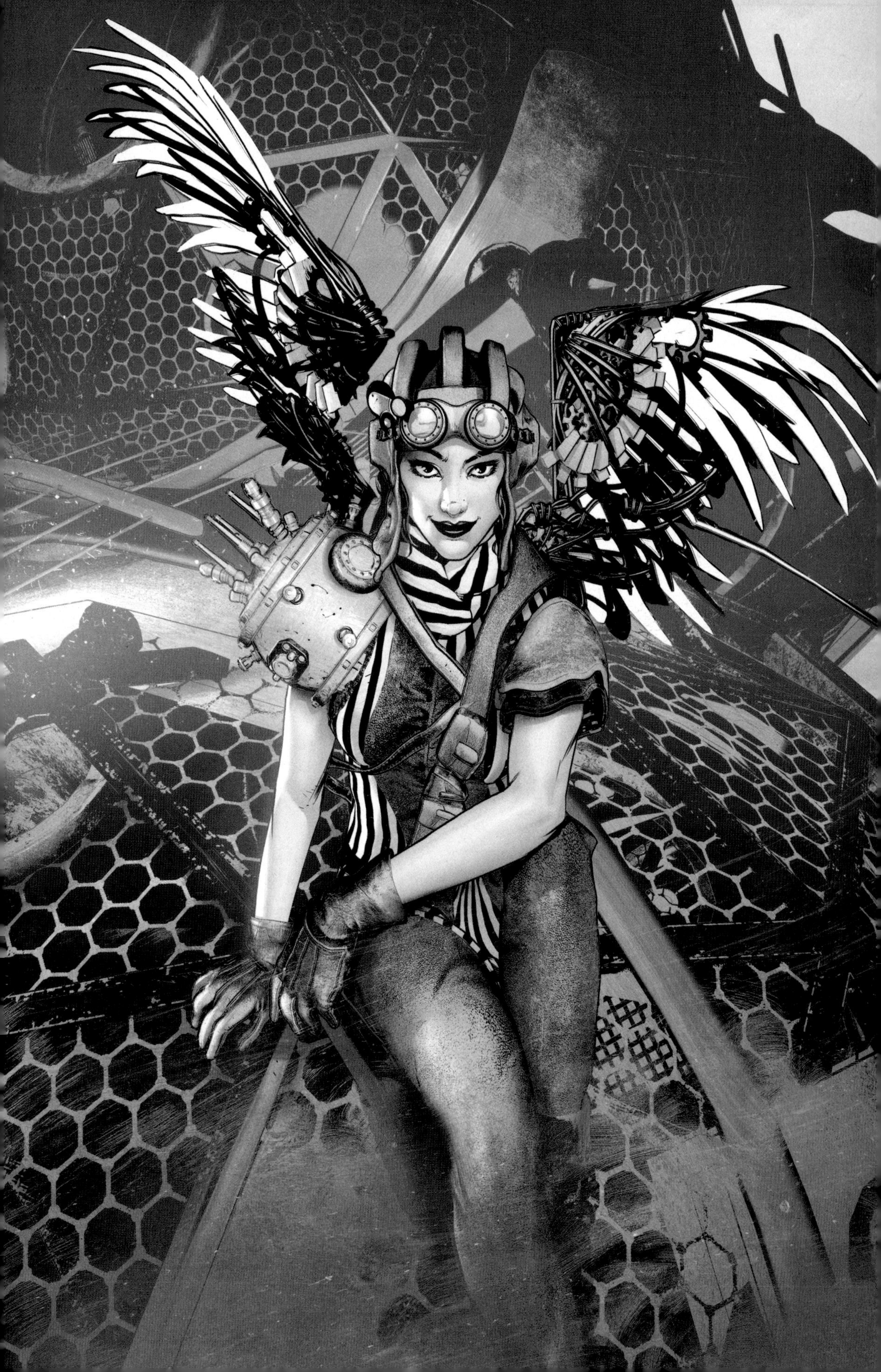

Issue #3 Cover B

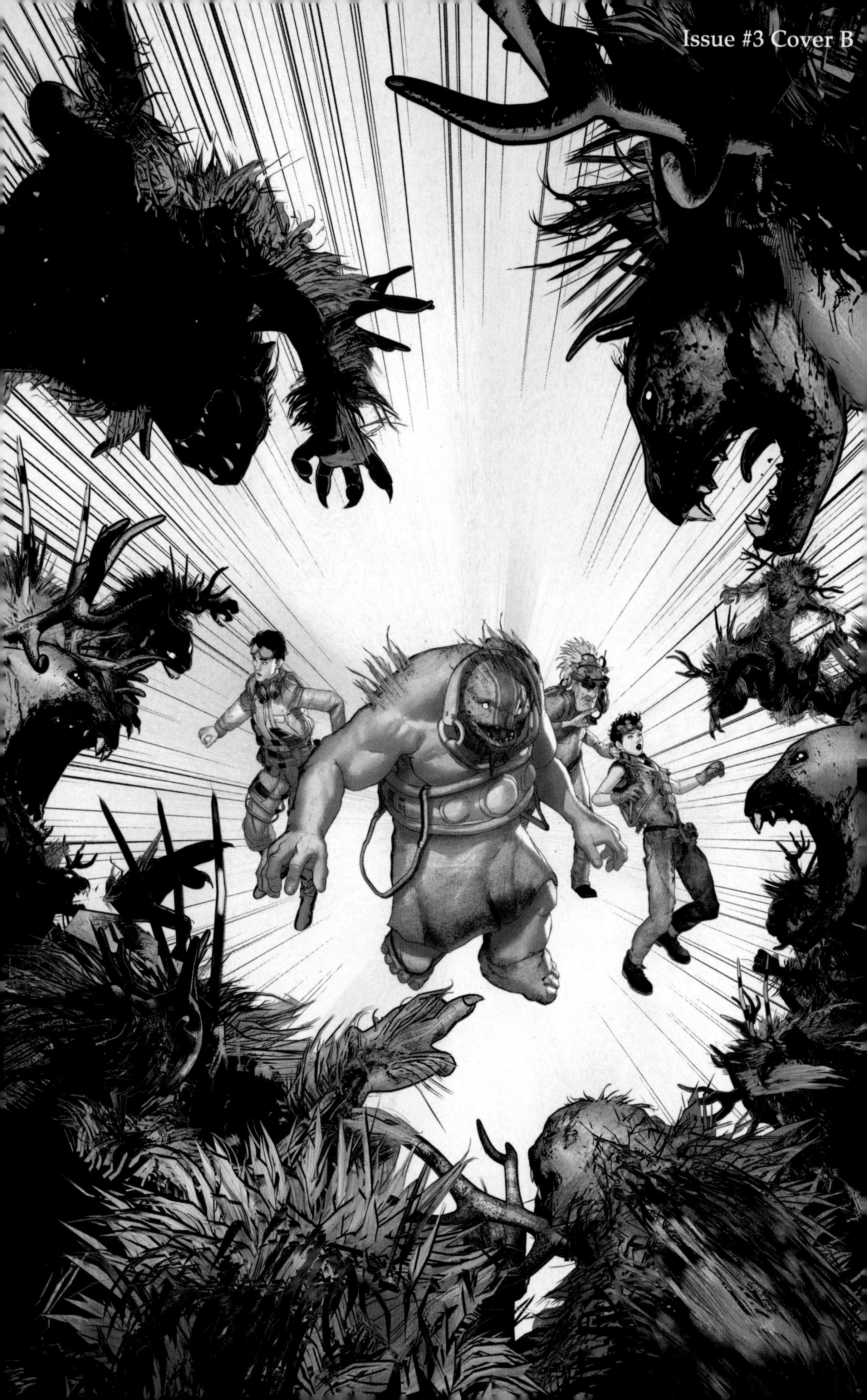

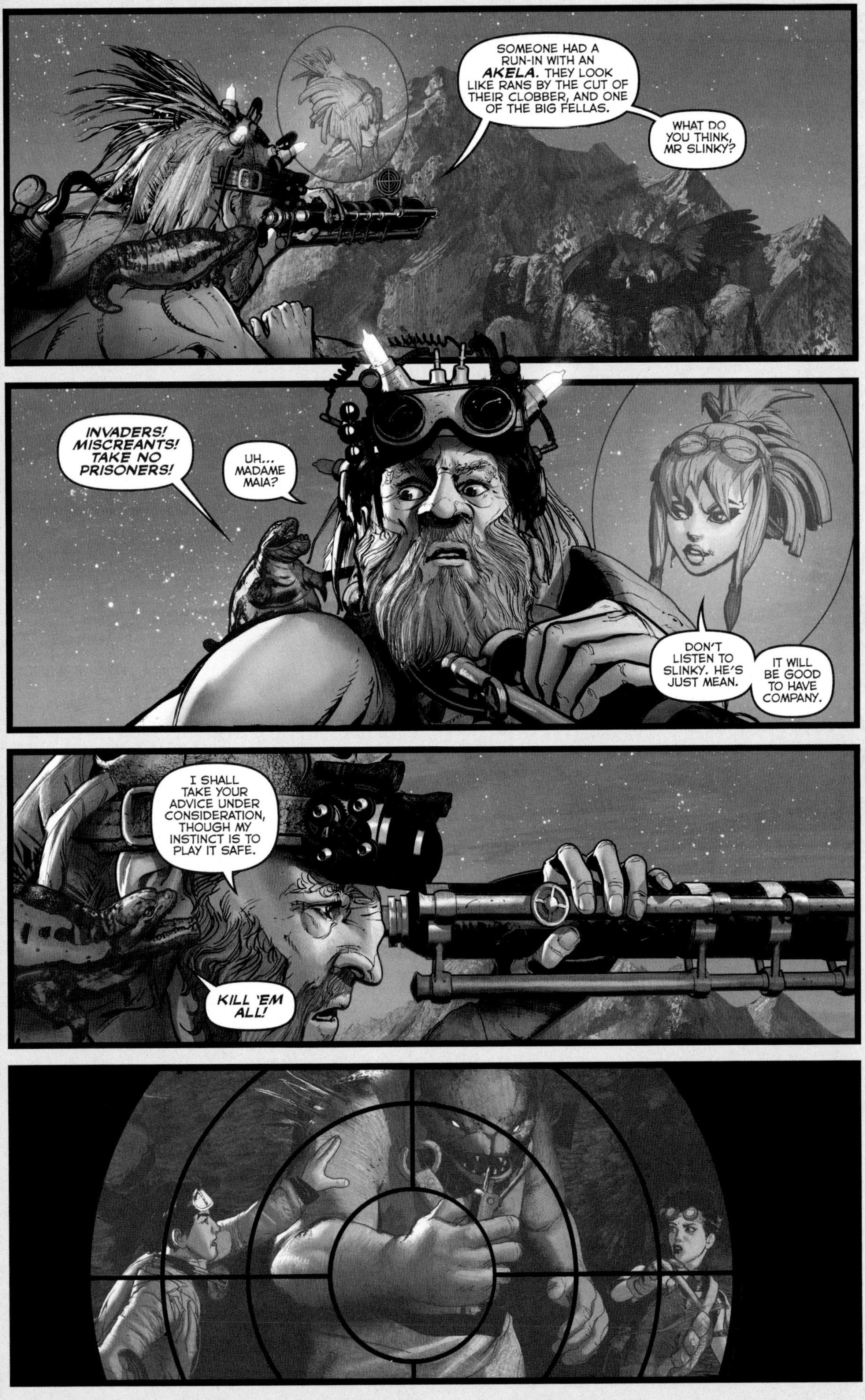
SOMEONE HAD A RUN-IN WITH AN AKELA. THEY LOOK LIKE RANS BY THE CUT OF THEIR CLOBBER, AND ONE OF THE BIG FELLAS.
WHAT DO YOU THINK, MR SLINKY?
INVADERS! MISCREANTS! TAKE NO PRISONERS!
UH... MADAME MAIA?
DON'T LISTEN TO SLINKY. HE'S JUST MEAN.
IT WILL BE GOOD TO HAVE COMPANY.
I SHALL TAKE YOUR ADVICE UNDER CONSIDERATION, THOUGH MY INSTINCT IS TO PLAY IT SAFE.
KILL 'EM ALL!

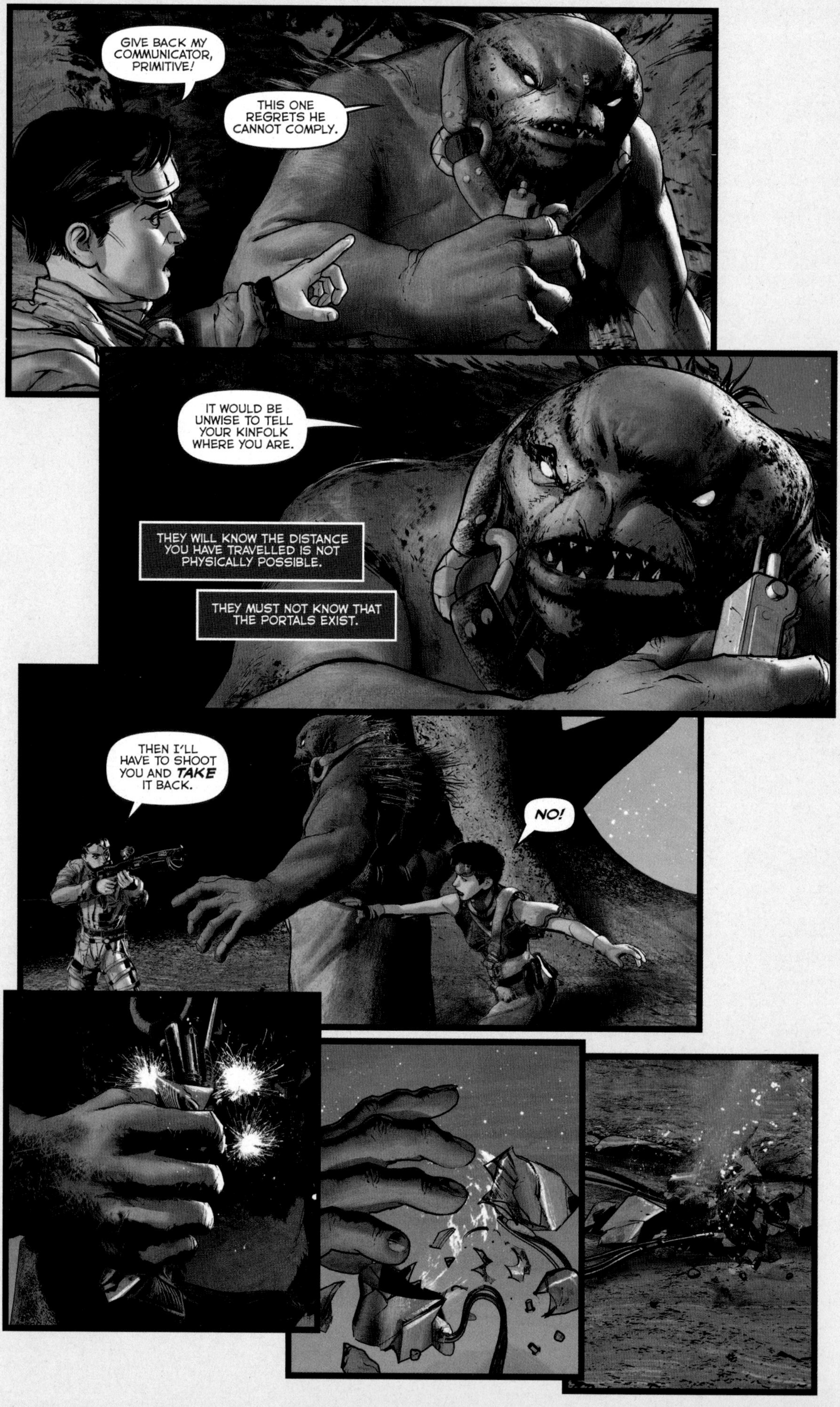
GIVE BACK MY COMMUNICATOR, PRIMITIVE!
THIS ONE REGRETS HE CANNOT COMPLY.
IT WOULD BE UNWISE TO TELL YOUR KINFOLK WHERE YOU ARE.
THEY WILL KNOW THE DISTANCE YOU HAVE TRAVELLED IS NOT PHYSICALLY POSSIBLE.
THEY MUST NOT KNOW THAT THE PORTALS EXIST.
THEN I'LL HAVE TO SHOOT YOU AND TAKE IT BACK.
NO!

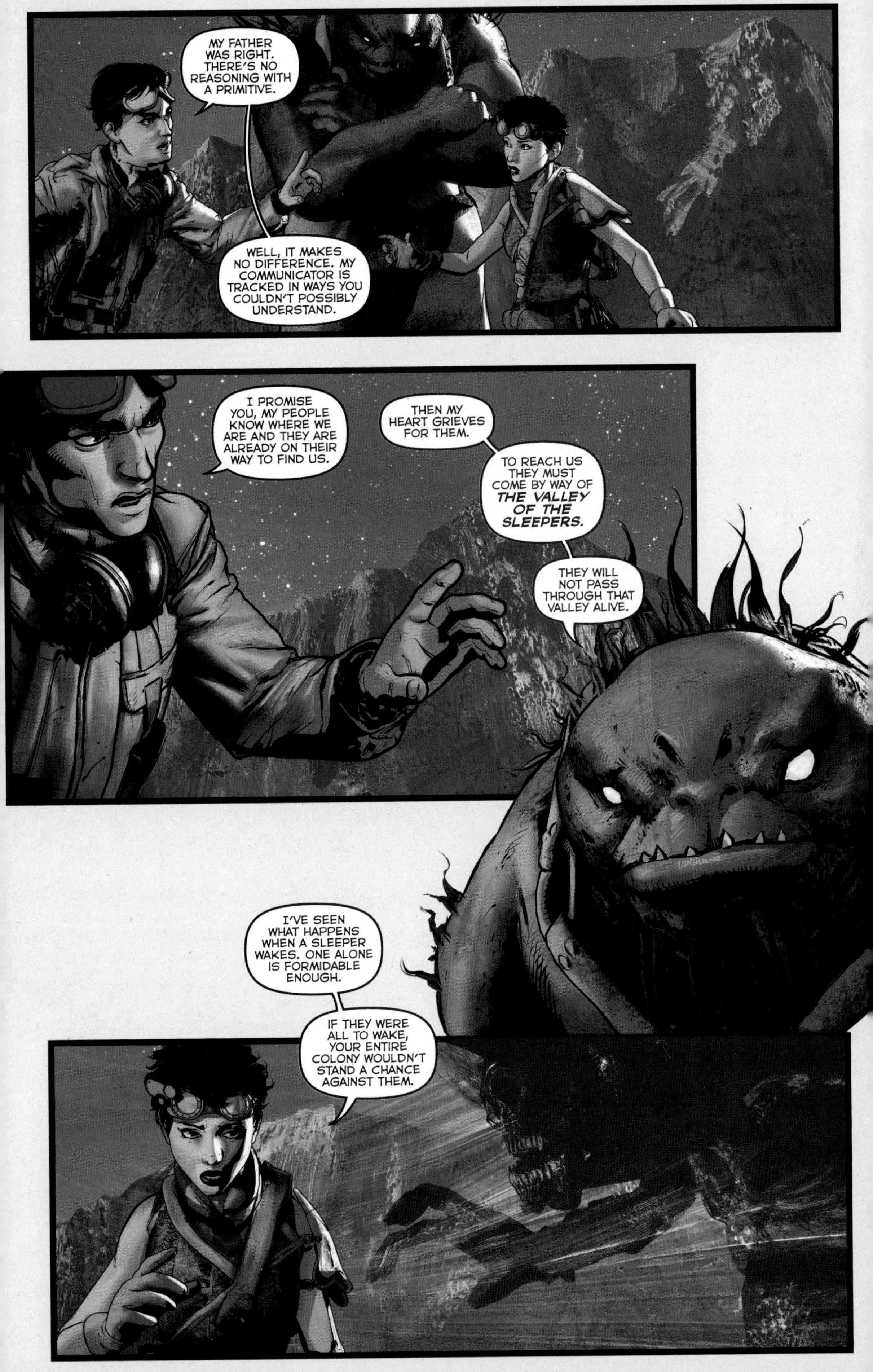
MY FATHER WAS RIGHT. THERE'S NO REASONING WITH A PRIMITIVE.
WELL, IT MAKES NO DIFFERENCE. MY COMMUNICATOR IS TRACKED IN WAYS YOU COULDN'T POSSIBLY UNDERSTAND.
I PROMISE YOU, MY PEOPLE KNOW WHERE WE ARE AND THEY ARE ALREADY ON THEIR WAY TO FIND US.
THEN MY HEART GRIEVES FOR THEM.
TO REACH US THEY MUST COME BY WAY OF *THE VALLEY OF THE SLEEPERS.*
THEY WILL NOT PASS THROUGH THAT VALLEY ALIVE.
I'VE SEEN WHAT HAPPENS WHEN A SLEEPER WAKES. ONE ALONE IS FORMIDABLE ENOUGH.
IF THEY WERE ALL TO WAKE, YOUR ENTIRE COLONY WOULDN'T STAND A CHANCE AGAINST THEM.

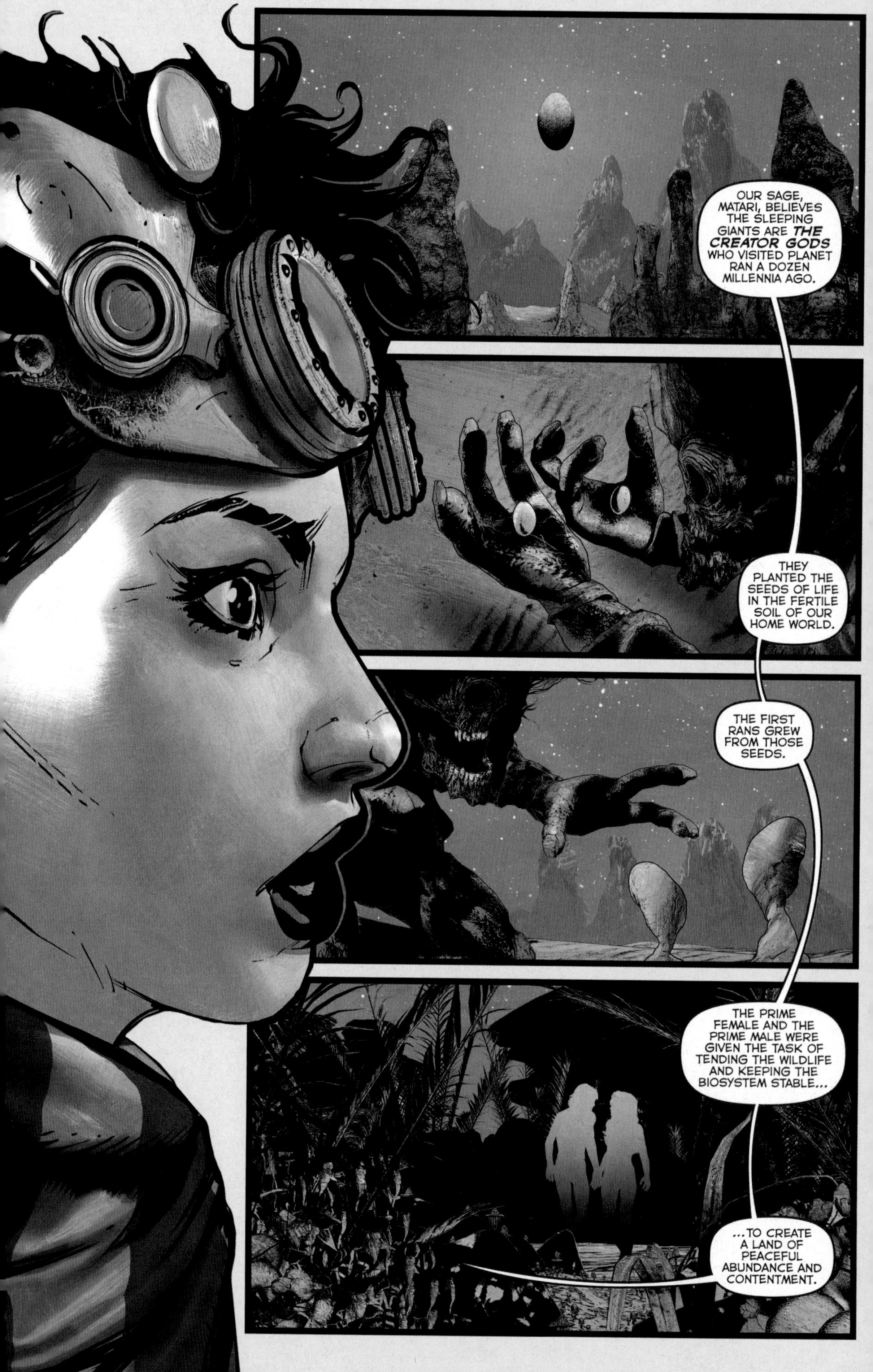
OUR SAGE, MATARI, BELIEVES THE SLEEPING GIANTS ARE ***THE CREATOR GODS*** WHO VISITED PLANET RAN A DOZEN MILLENNIA AGO.
THEY PLANTED THE SEEDS OF LIFE IN THE FERTILE SOIL OF OUR HOME WORLD.
THE FIRST RANS GREW FROM THOSE SEEDS.
THE PRIME FEMALE AND THE PRIME MALE WERE GIVEN THE TASK OF TENDING THE WILDLIFE AND KEEPING THE BIOSYSTEM STABLE...
...TO CREATE A LAND OF PEACEFUL ABUNDANCE AND CONTENTMENT.

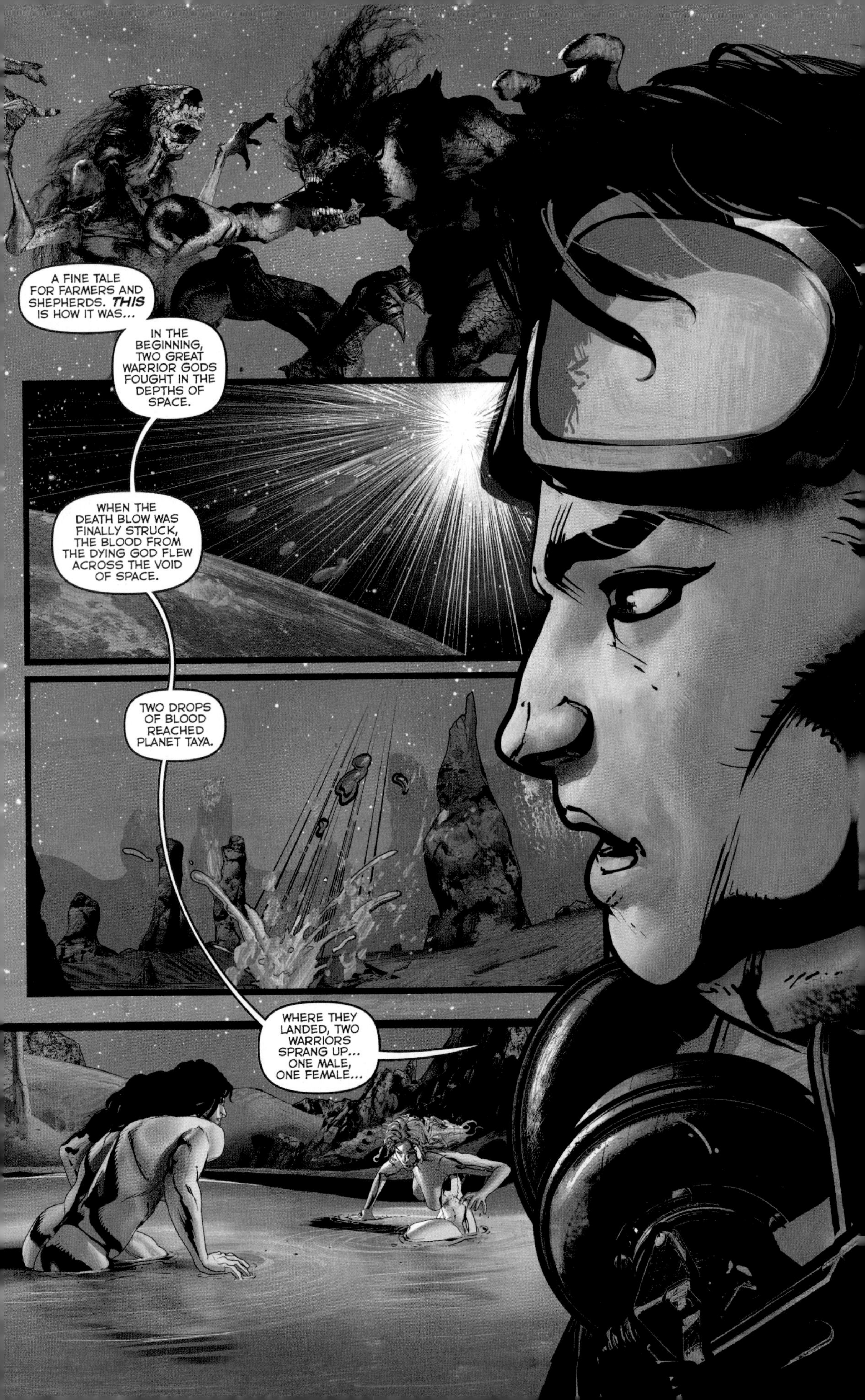
A FINE TALE FOR FARMERS AND SHEPHERDS. *THIS* IS HOW IT WAS...
IN THE BEGINNING, TWO GREAT WARRIOR GODS FOUGHT IN THE DEPTHS OF SPACE.
WHEN THE DEATH BLOW WAS FINALLY STRUCK, THE BLOOD FROM THE DYING GOD FLEW ACROSS THE VOID OF SPACE.
TWO DROPS OF BLOOD REACHED PLANET TAYA.
WHERE THEY LANDED, TWO WARRIORS SPRANG UP... ONE MALE, ONE FEMALE...

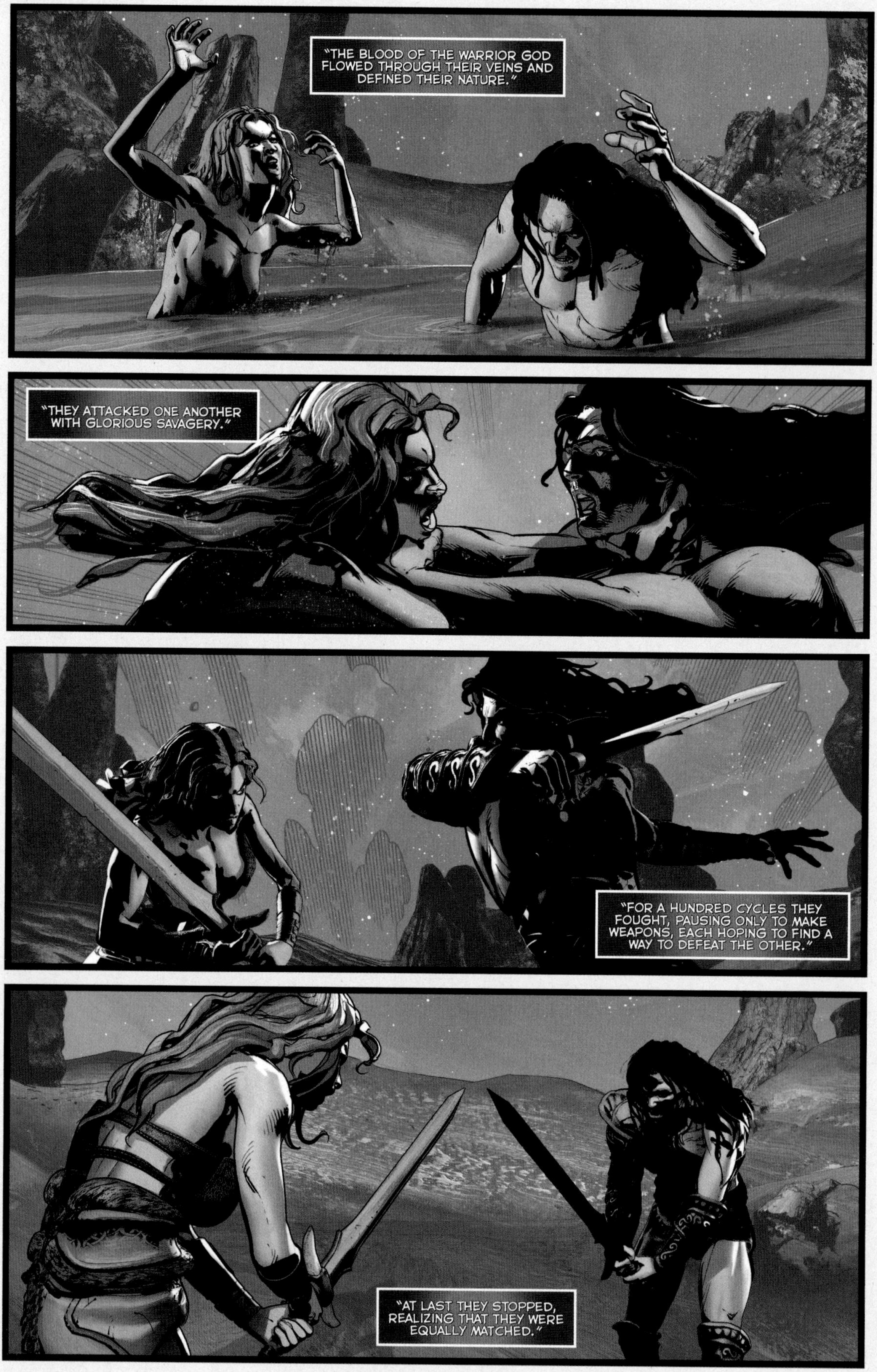
"THE BLOOD OF THE WARRIOR GOD FLOWED THROUGH THEIR VEINS AND DEFINED THEIR NATURE."
"THEY ATTACKED ONE ANOTHER WITH GLORIOUS SAVAGERY."
"FOR A HUNDRED CYCLES THEY FOUGHT, PAUSING ONLY TO MAKE WEAPONS, EACH HOPING TO FIND A WAY TO DEFEAT THE OTHER."
"AT LAST THEY STOPPED, REALIZING THAT THEY WERE EQUALLY MATCHED."

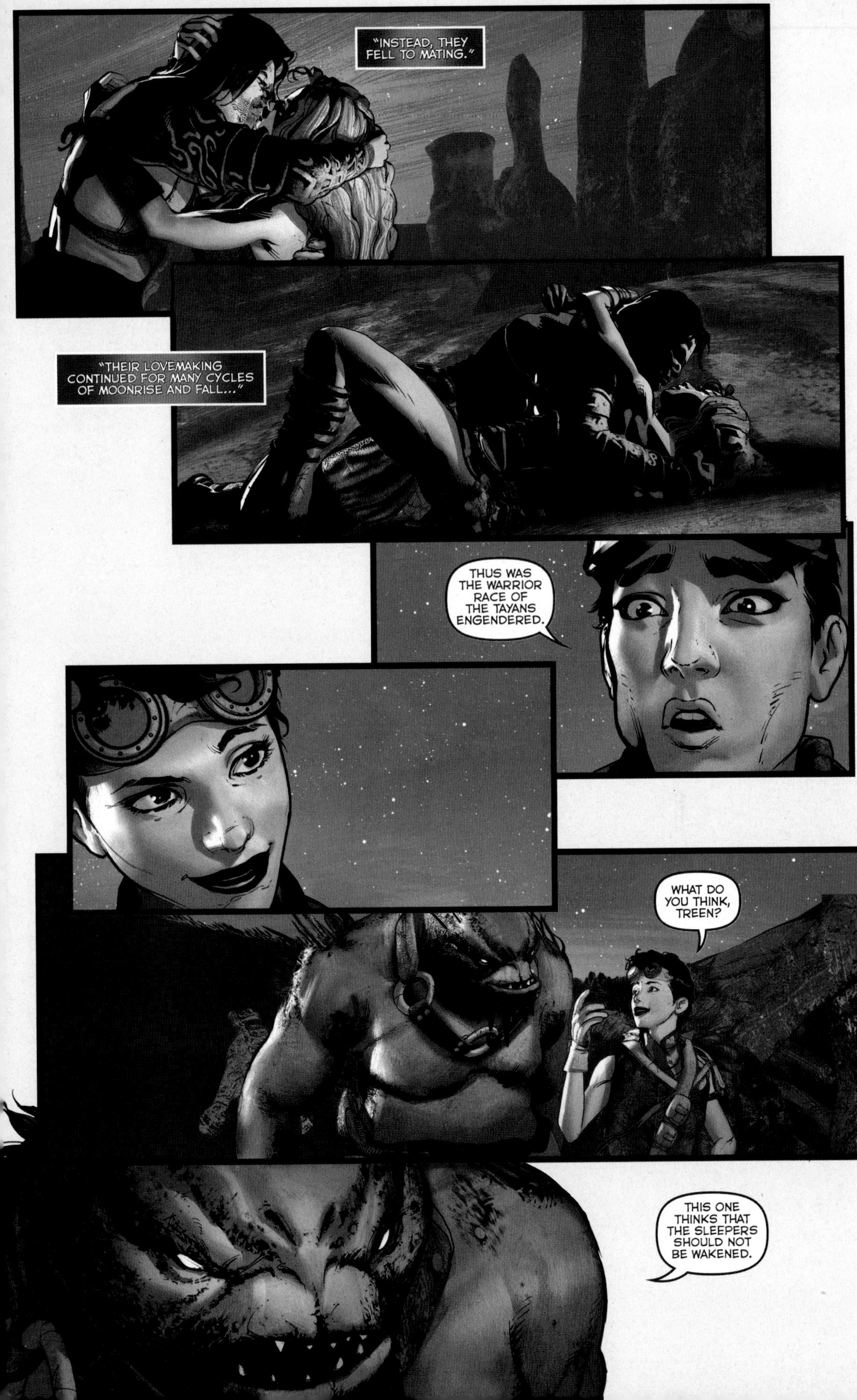
"INSTEAD, THEY FELL TO MATING."
"THEIR LOVEMAKING CONTINUED FOR MANY CYCLES OF MOONRISE AND FALL..."
THUS WAS THE WARRIOR RACE OF THE TAYANS ENGENDERED.
WHAT DO YOU THINK, TREEN?
THIS ONE THINKS THAT THE SLEEPERS SHOULD NOT BE WAKENED.

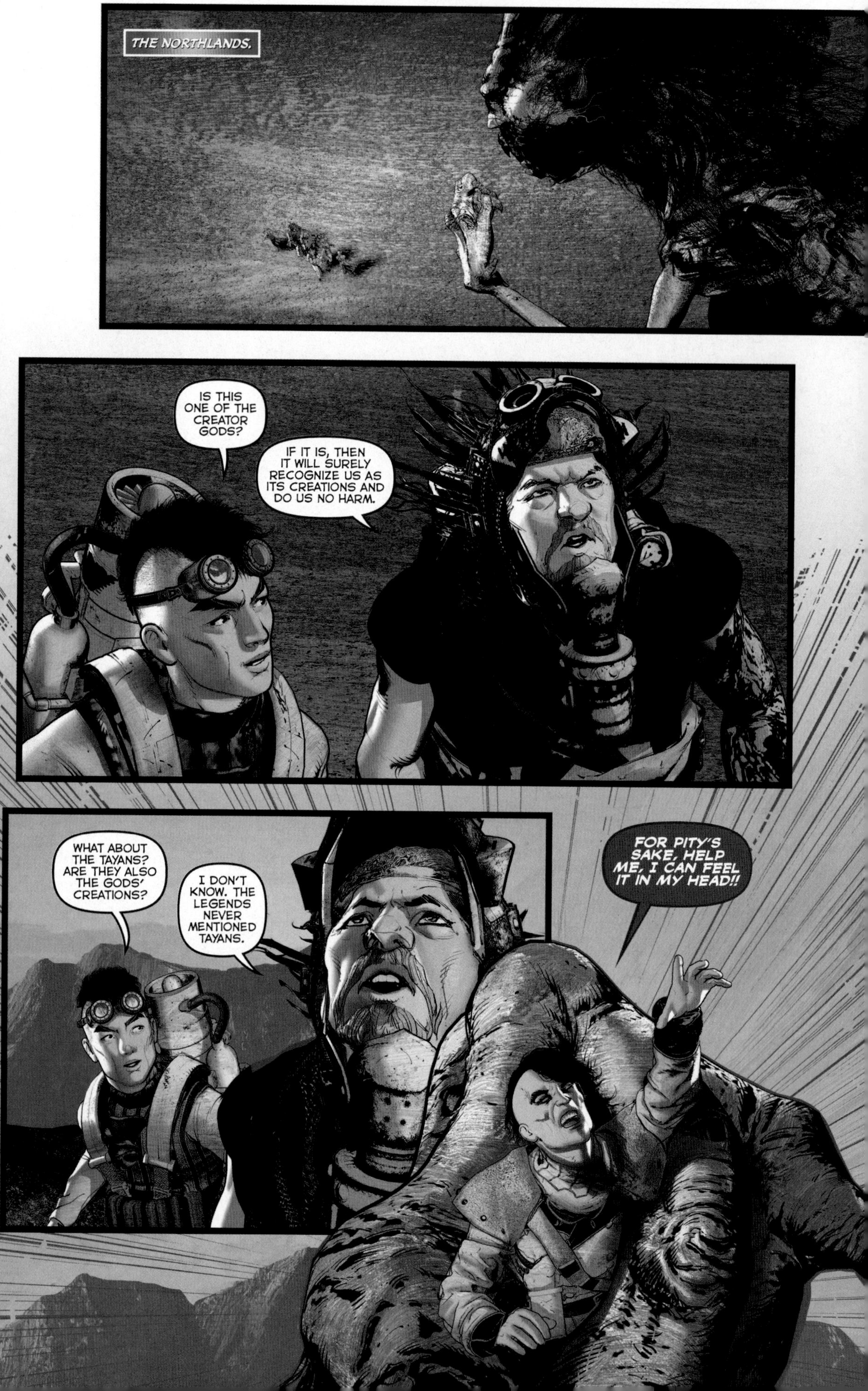
THE NORTHLANDS.
IS THIS ONE OF THE CREATOR GODS?
IF IT IS, THEN IT WILL SURELY RECOGNIZE US AS ITS CREATIONS AND DO US NO HARM.
WHAT ABOUT THE TAYANS? ARE THEY ALSO THE GODS' CREATIONS?
I DON'T KNOW. THE LEGENDS NEVER MENTIONED TAYANS.
FOR PITY'S SAKE, HELP ME, I CAN FEEL IT IN MY HEAD!!

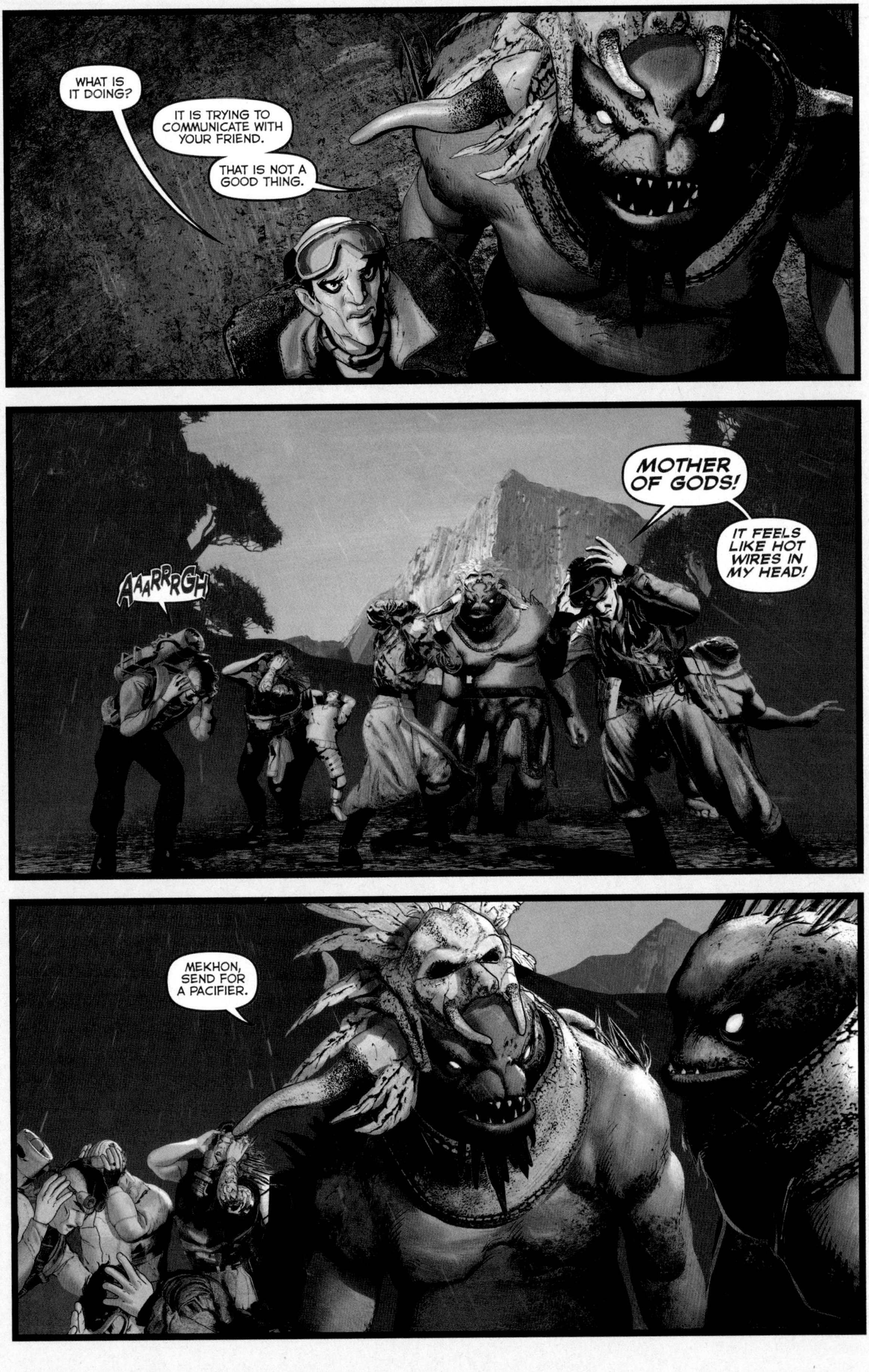
WHAT IS IT DOING?
IT IS TRYING TO COMMUNICATE WITH YOUR FRIEND.
THAT IS NOT A GOOD THING.
MOTHER OF GODS!
IT FEELS LIKE HOT WIRES IN MY HEAD!
AAARRRGH
MEKHON, SEND FOR A PACIFIER.

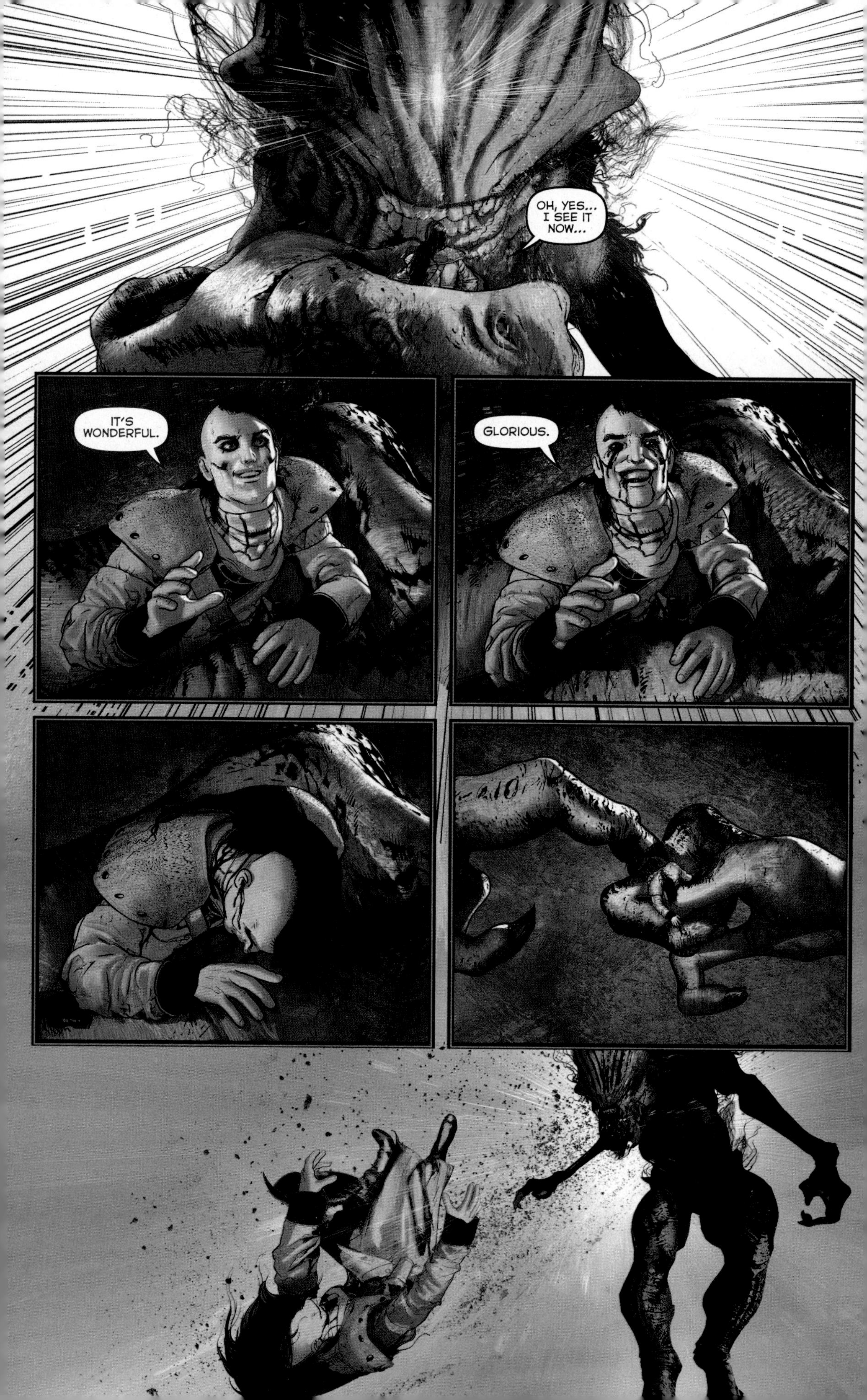
OH, YES... I SEE IT NOW...
IT'S WONDERFUL.
GLORIOUS.

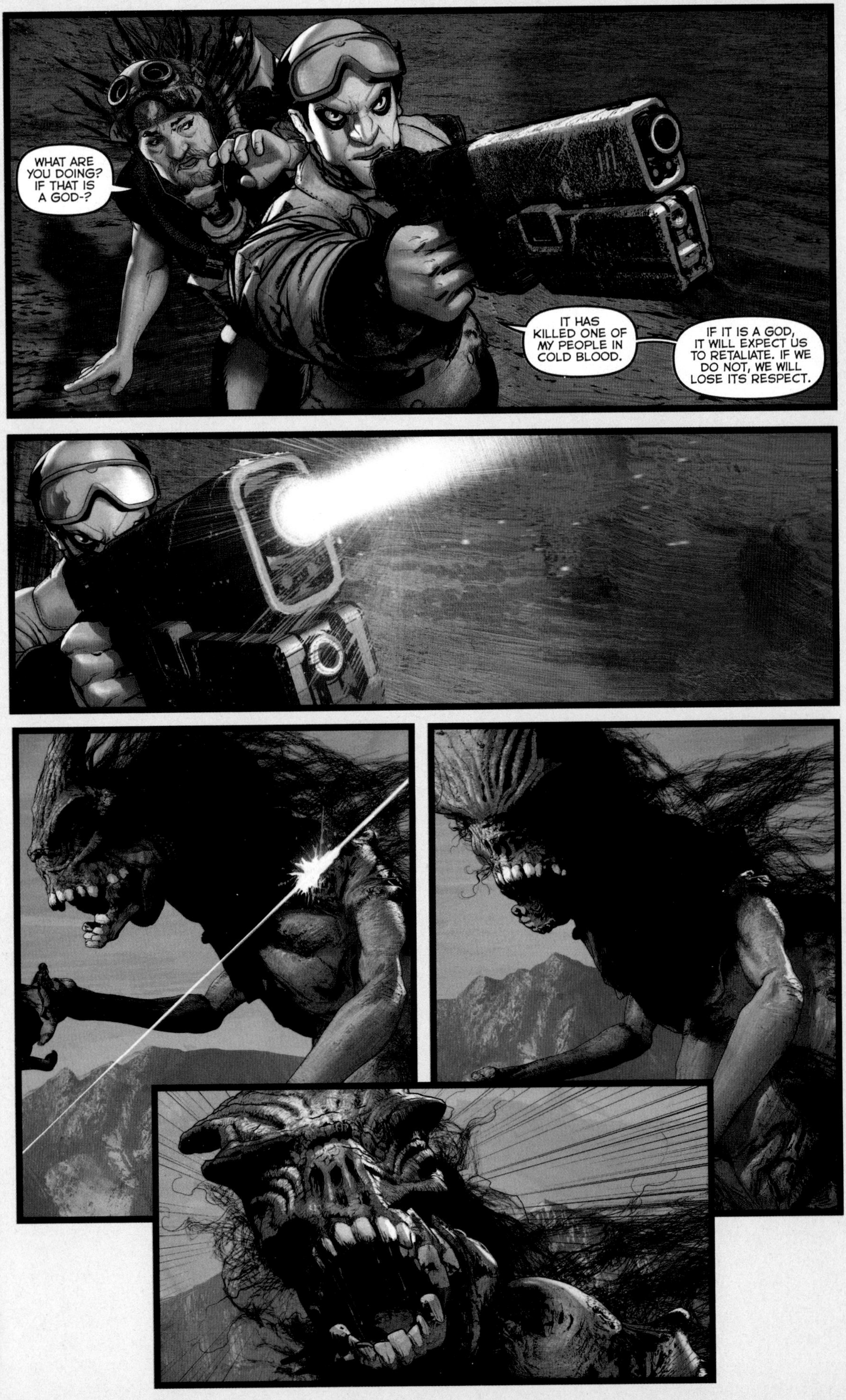
WHAT ARE YOU DOING? IF THAT IS A GOD-?
IT HAS KILLED ONE OF MY PEOPLE IN COLD BLOOD.
IF IT IS A GOD, IT WILL EXPECT US TO RETALIATE. IF WE DO NOT, WE WILL LOSE ITS RESPECT.

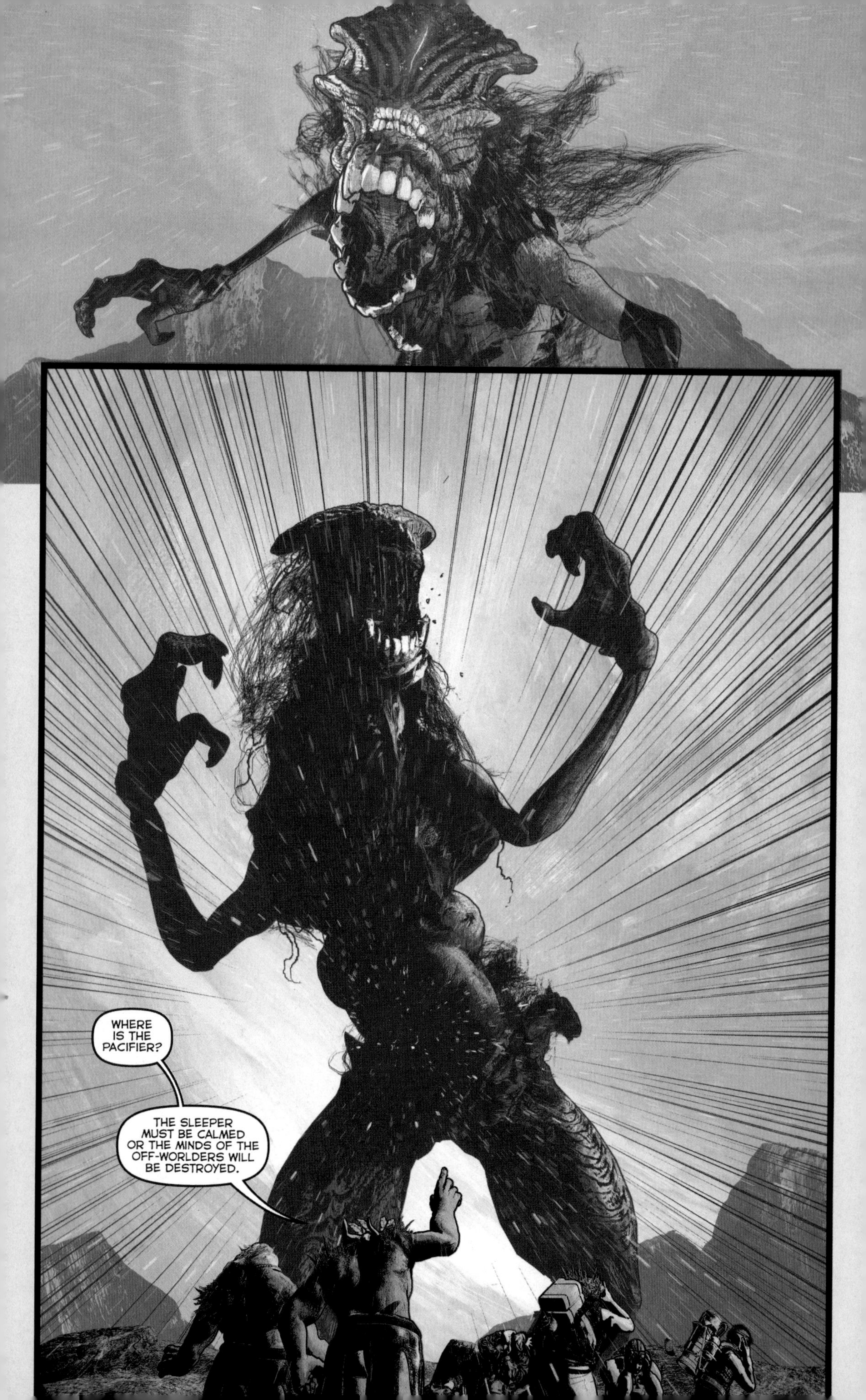
WHERE IS THE PACIFIER?
THE SLEEPER MUST BE CALMED OR THE MINDS OF THE OFF-WORLDERS WILL BE DESTROYED.

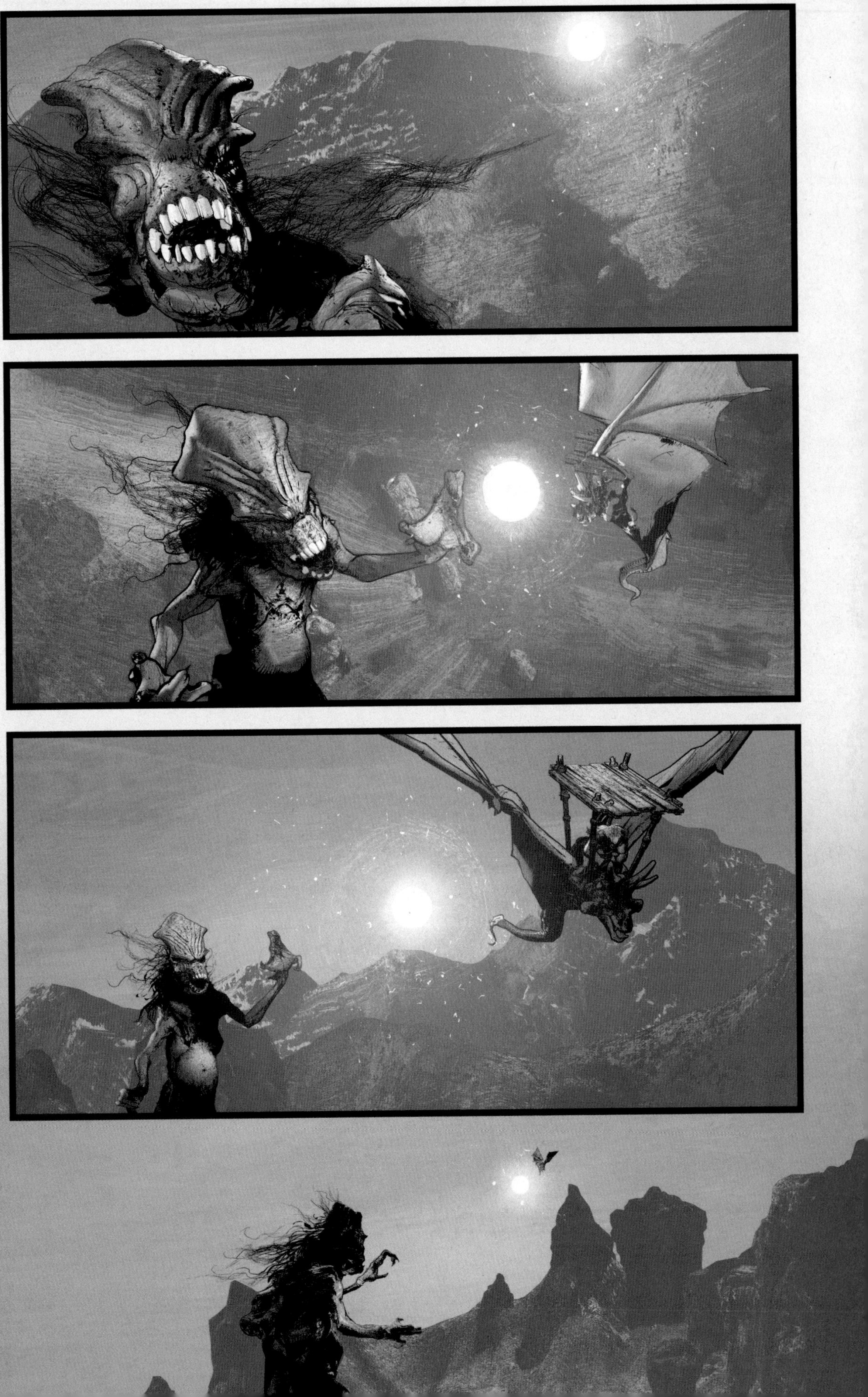

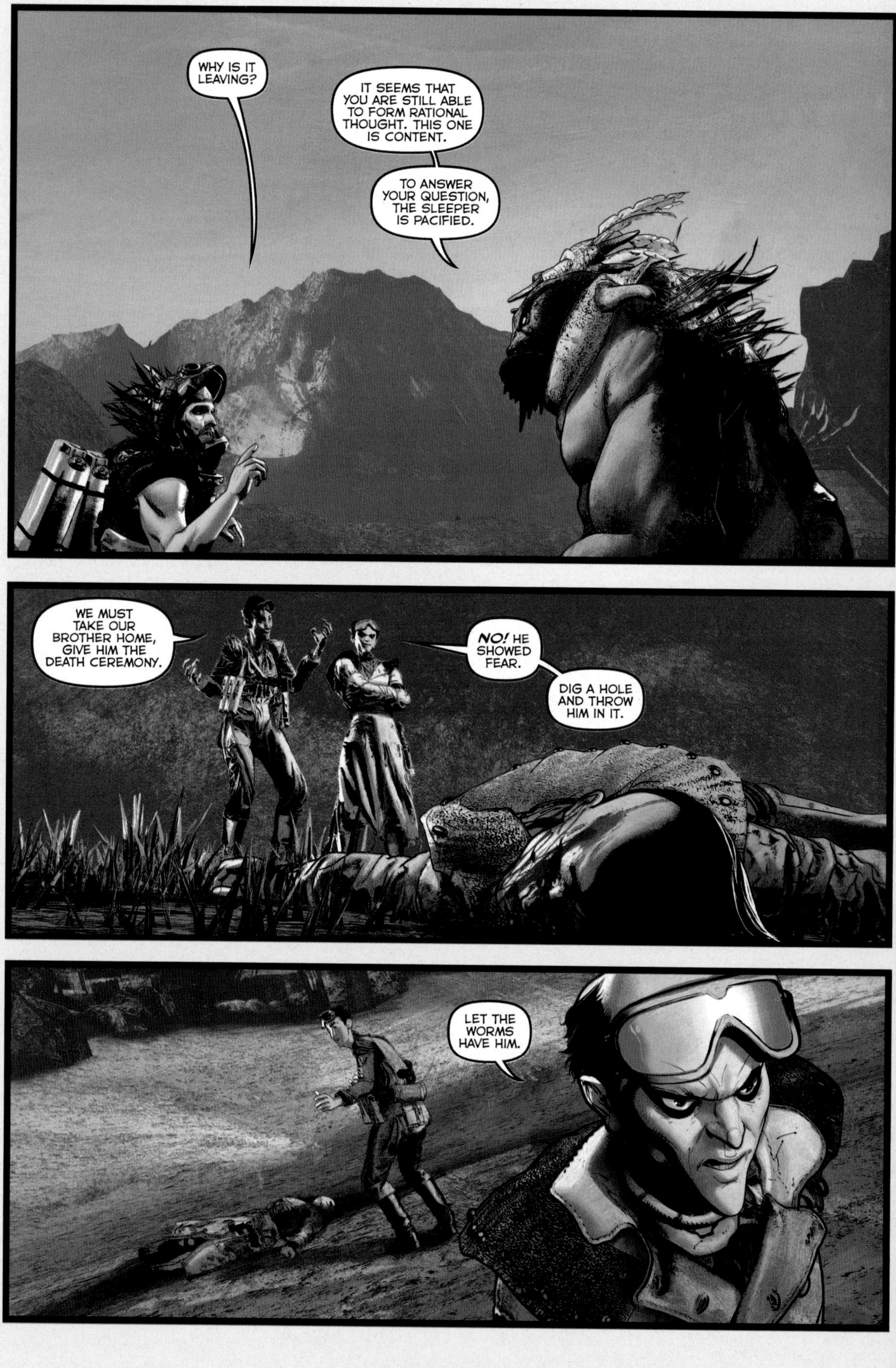
WHY IS IT LEAVING?
IT SEEMS THAT YOU ARE STILL ABLE TO FORM RATIONAL THOUGHT. THIS ONE IS CONTENT.
TO ANSWER YOUR QUESTION, THE SLEEPER IS PACIFIED.
WE MUST TAKE OUR BROTHER HOME, GIVE HIM THE DEATH CEREMONY.
NO! HE SHOWED FEAR.
DIG A HOLE AND THROW HIM IN IT.
LET THE WORMS HAVE HIM.

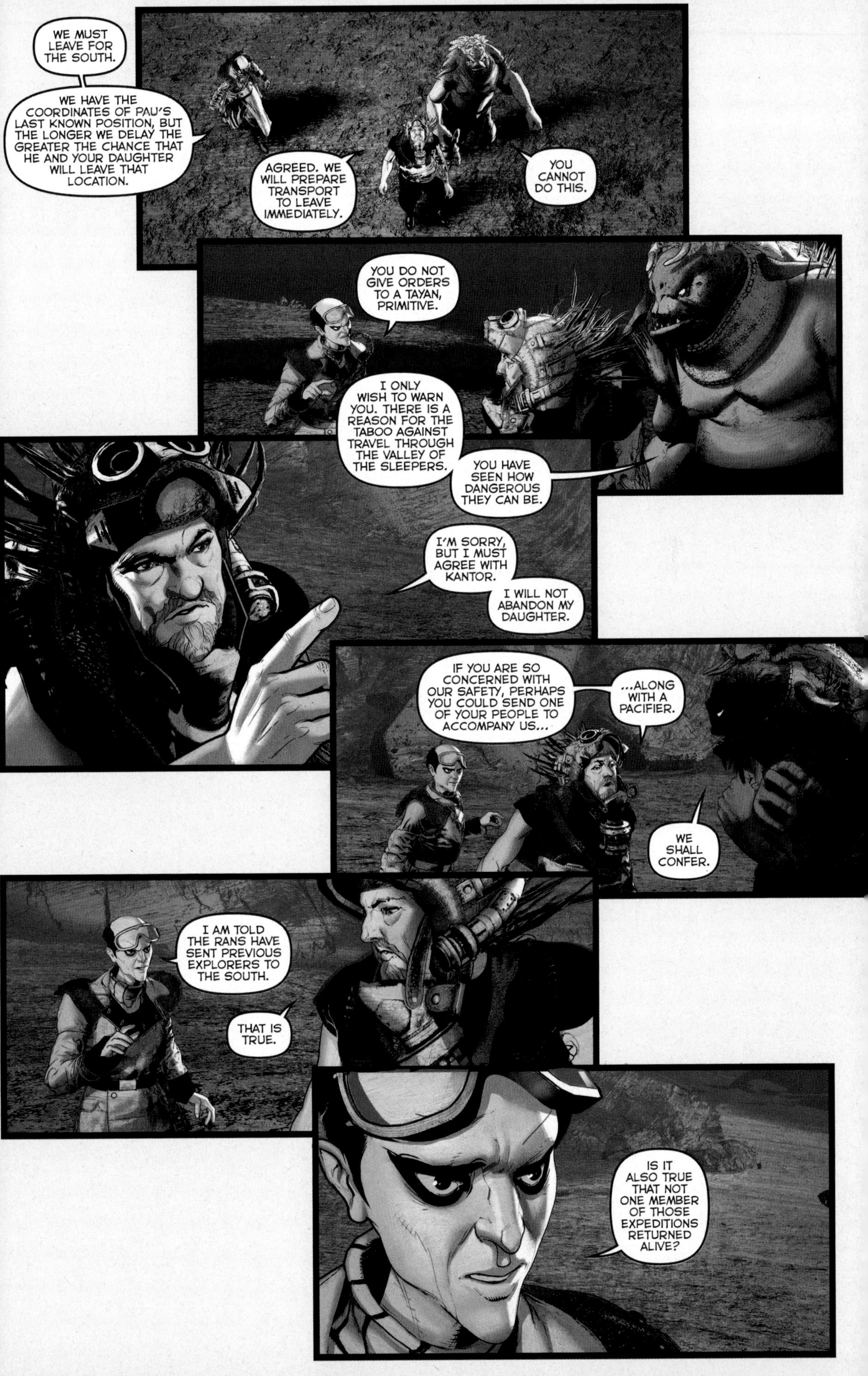
WE MUST LEAVE FOR THE SOUTH.
WE HAVE THE COORDINATES OF PAU'S LAST KNOWN POSITION, BUT THE LONGER WE DELAY THE GREATER THE CHANCE THAT HE AND YOUR DAUGHTER WILL LEAVE THAT LOCATION.
AGREED. WE WILL PREPARE TRANSPORT TO LEAVE IMMEDIATELY.
YOU CANNOT DO THIS.
YOU DO NOT GIVE ORDERS TO A TAYAN, PRIMITIVE.
I ONLY WISH TO WARN YOU. THERE IS A REASON FOR THE TABOO AGAINST TRAVEL THROUGH THE VALLEY OF THE SLEEPERS.
YOU HAVE SEEN HOW DANGEROUS THEY CAN BE.
I'M SORRY, BUT I MUST AGREE WITH KANTOR.
I WILL NOT ABANDON MY DAUGHTER.
IF YOU ARE SO CONCERNED WITH OUR SAFETY, PERHAPS YOU COULD SEND ONE OF YOUR PEOPLE TO ACCOMPANY US...
...ALONG WITH A PACIFIER.
WE SHALL CONFER.
I AM TOLD THE RANS HAVE SENT PREVIOUS EXPLORERS TO THE SOUTH.
THAT IS TRUE.
IS IT ALSO TRUE THAT NOT ONE MEMBER OF THOSE EXPEDITIONS RETURNED ALIVE?

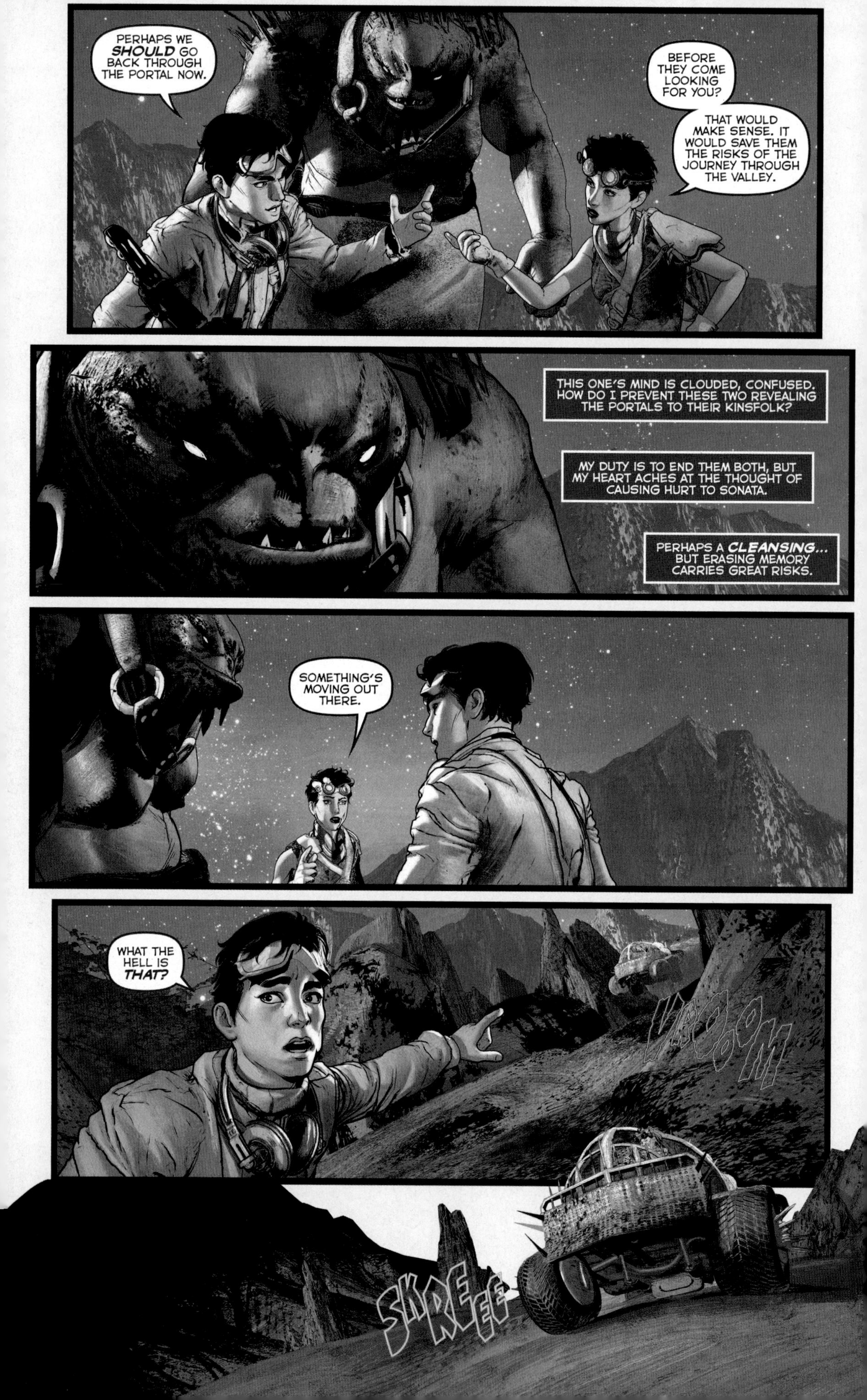
PERHAPS WE SHOULD GO BACK THROUGH THE PORTAL NOW.
BEFORE THEY COME LOOKING FOR YOU?
THAT WOULD MAKE SENSE. IT WOULD SAVE THEM THE RISKS OF THE JOURNEY THROUGH THE VALLEY.
THIS ONE'S MIND IS CLOUDED, CONFUSED. HOW DO I PREVENT THESE TWO REVEALING THE PORTALS TO THEIR KINSFOLK?
MY DUTY IS TO END THEM BOTH, BUT MY HEART ACHES AT THE THOUGHT OF CAUSING HURT TO SONATA.
PERHAPS A CLEANSING... BUT ERASING MEMORY CARRIES GREAT RISKS.
SOMETHING'S MOVING OUT THERE.
WHAT THE HELL IS THAT?
VROOOM
SKREEE

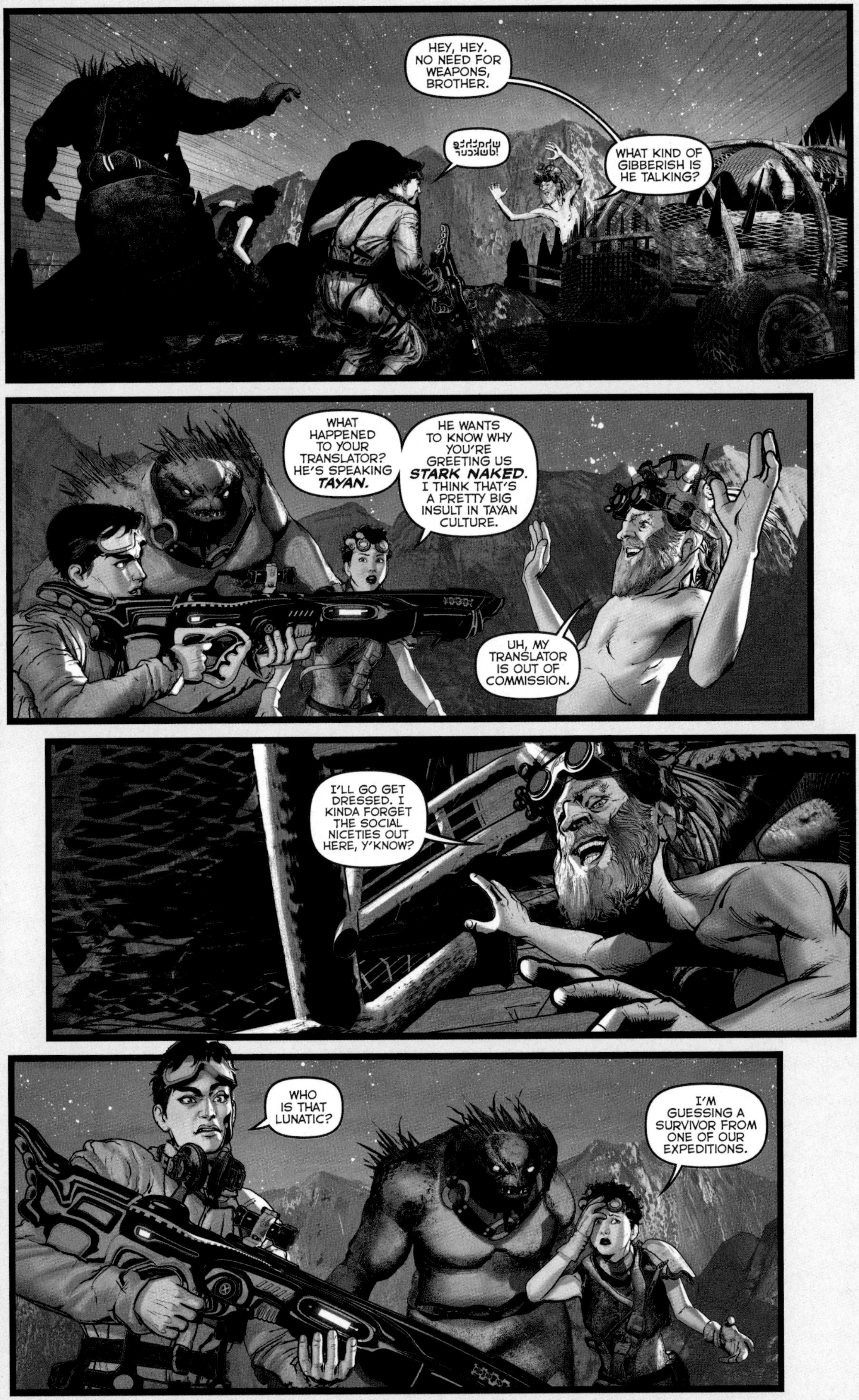
HEY, HEY. NO NEED FOR WEAPONS, BROTHER.
WHAT KIND OF GIBBERISH IS HE TALKING?
WHAT HAPPENED TO YOUR TRANSLATOR? HE'S SPEAKING *TAYAN.*
HE WANTS TO KNOW WHY YOU'RE GREETING US **STARK NAKED**. I THINK THAT'S A PRETTY BIG INSULT IN TAYAN CULTURE.
UH, MY TRANSLATOR IS OUT OF COMMISSION.
I'LL GO GET DRESSED. I KINDA FORGET THE SOCIAL NICETIES OUT HERE, Y'KNOW?
WHO IS THAT LUNATIC?
I'M GUESSING A SURVIVOR FROM ONE OF OUR EXPEDITIONS.

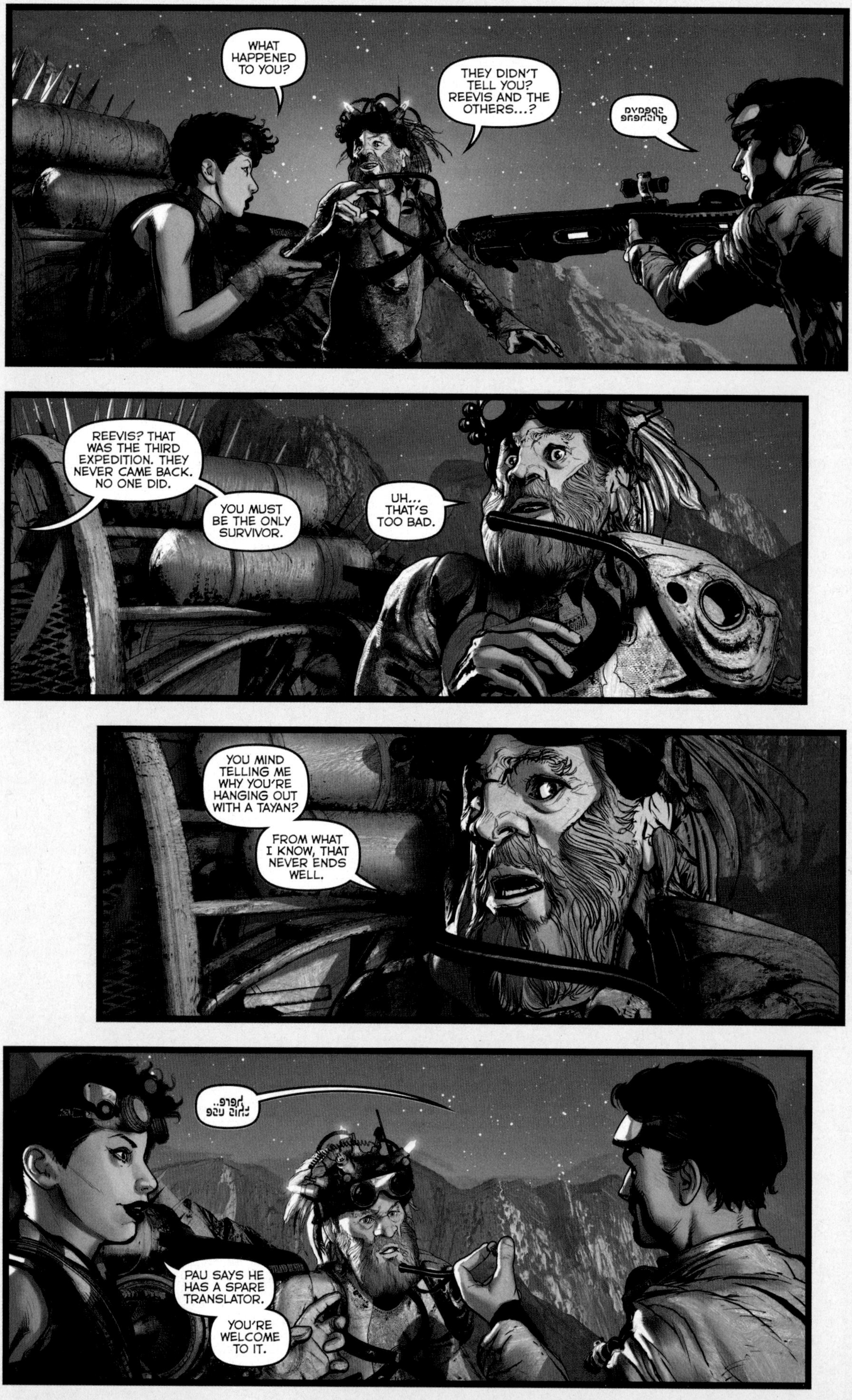
WHAT HAPPENED TO YOU?
THEY DIDN'T TELL YOU? REEVIS AND THE OTHERS...?
REEVIS? THAT WAS THE THIRD EXPEDITION. THEY NEVER CAME BACK. NO ONE DID.
YOU MUST BE THE ONLY SURVIVOR.
UH... THAT'S TOO BAD.
YOU MIND TELLING ME WHY YOU'RE HANGING OUT WITH A TAYAN?
FROM WHAT I KNOW, THAT NEVER ENDS WELL.
PAU SAYS HE HAS A SPARE TRANSLATOR.
YOU'RE WELCOME TO IT.

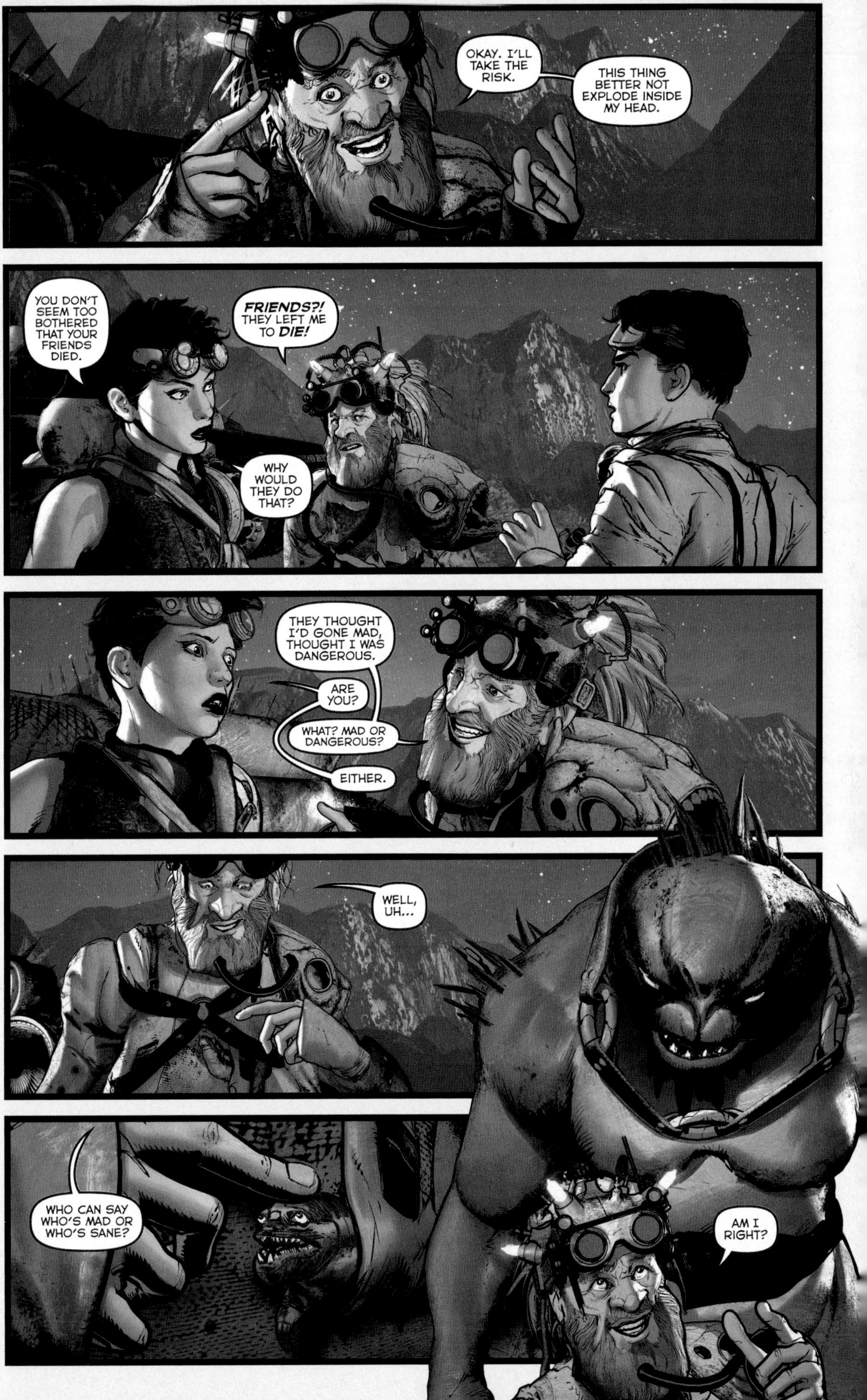

OKAY. I'LL TAKE THE RISK.
THIS THING BETTER NOT EXPLODE INSIDE MY HEAD.
YOU DON'T SEEM TOO BOTHERED THAT YOUR FRIENDS DIED.
FRIENDS?! THEY LEFT ME TO **DIE!**
WHY WOULD THEY DO THAT?
THEY THOUGHT I'D GONE MAD, THOUGHT I WAS DANGEROUS.
ARE YOU?
WHAT? MAD OR DANGEROUS?
EITHER.
WELL, UH...
WHO CAN SAY WHO'S MAD OR WHO'S SANE?
AM I RIGHT?

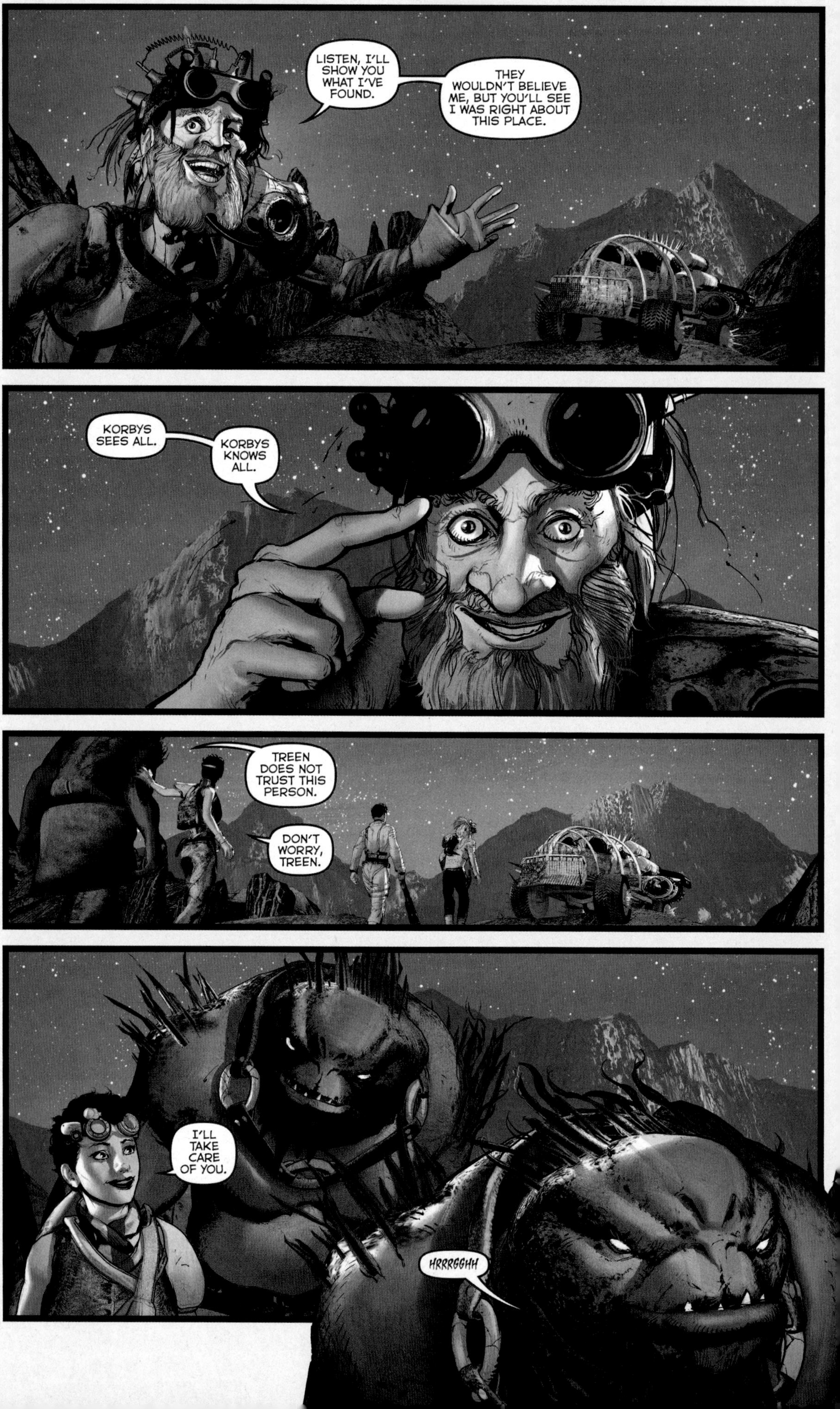
LISTEN, I'LL SHOW YOU WHAT I'VE FOUND.
THEY WOULDN'T BELIEVE ME, BUT YOU'LL SEE I WAS RIGHT ABOUT THIS PLACE.
KORBYS SEES ALL.
KORBYS KNOWS ALL.
TREEN DOES NOT TRUST THIS PERSON.
DON'T WORRY, TREEN.
I'LL TAKE CARE OF YOU.
HRRRGGHH

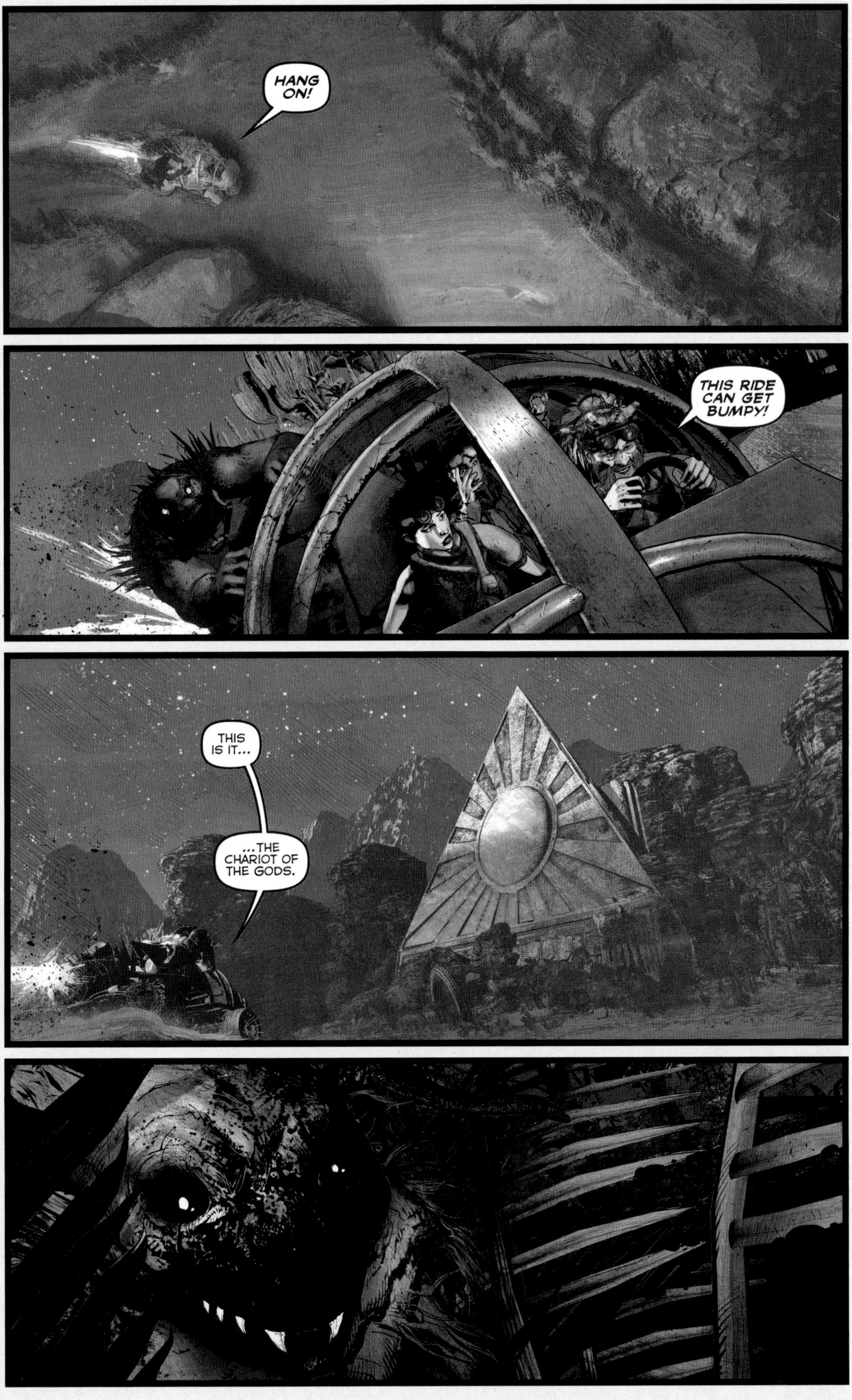
HANG ON!
THIS RIDE CAN GET BUMPY!
THIS IS IT...
...THE CHARIOT OF THE GODS.

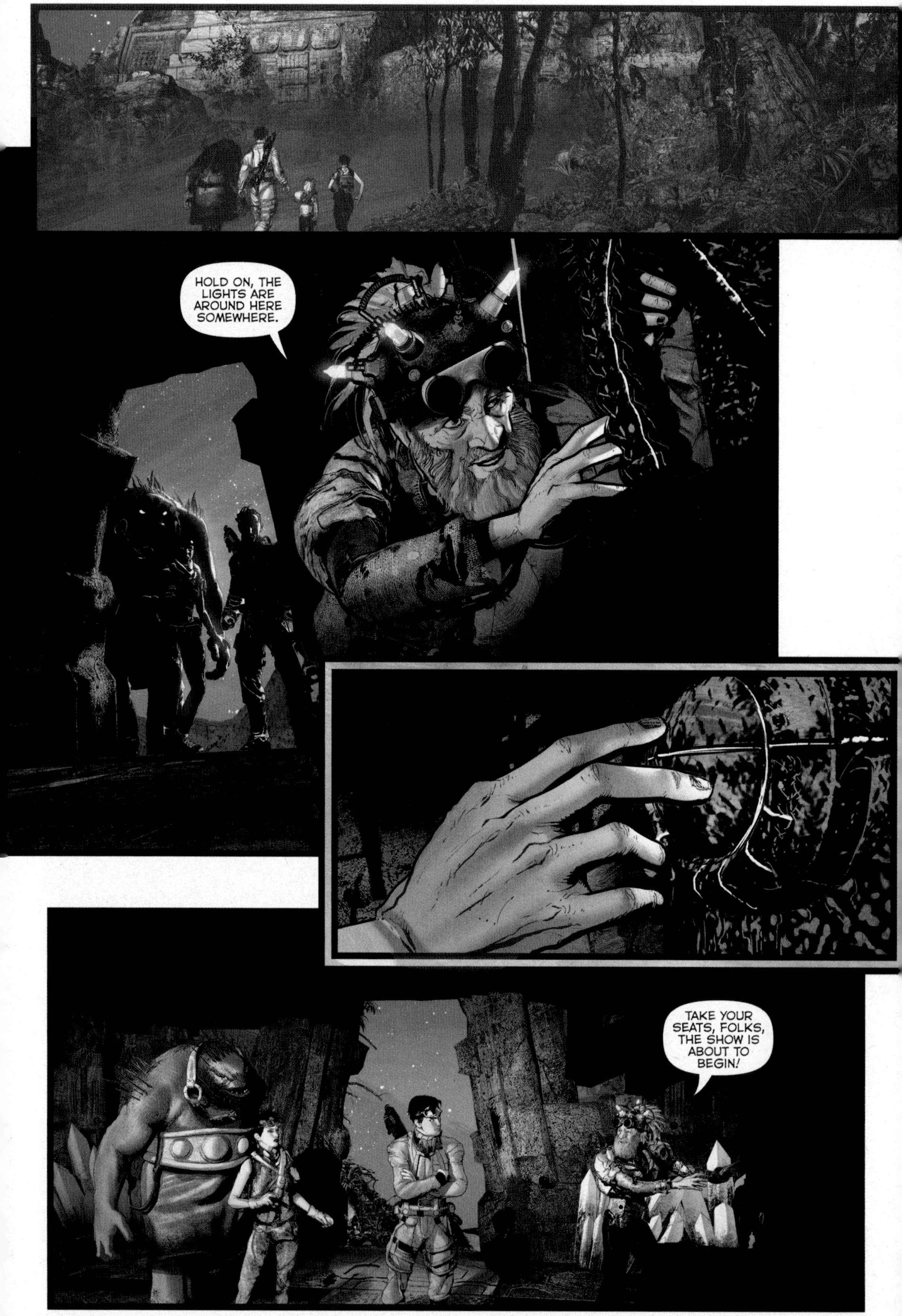
HOLD ON, THE LIGHTS ARE AROUND HERE SOMEWHERE.
TAKE YOUR SEATS, FOLKS, THE SHOW IS ABOUT TO BEGIN!

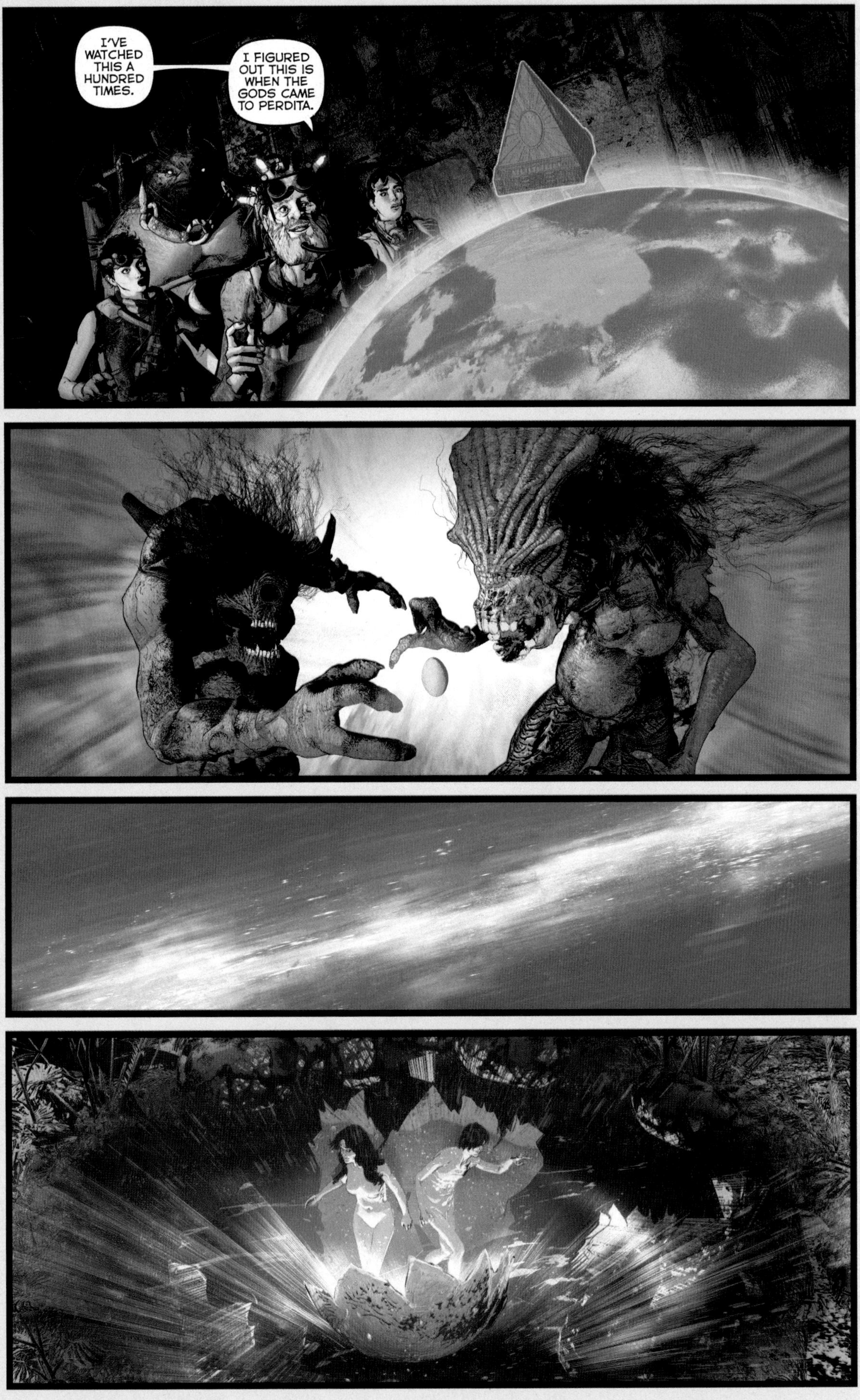
I'VE WATCHED THIS A HUNDRED TIMES.
I FIGURED OUT THIS IS WHEN THE GODS CAME TO PERDITA.

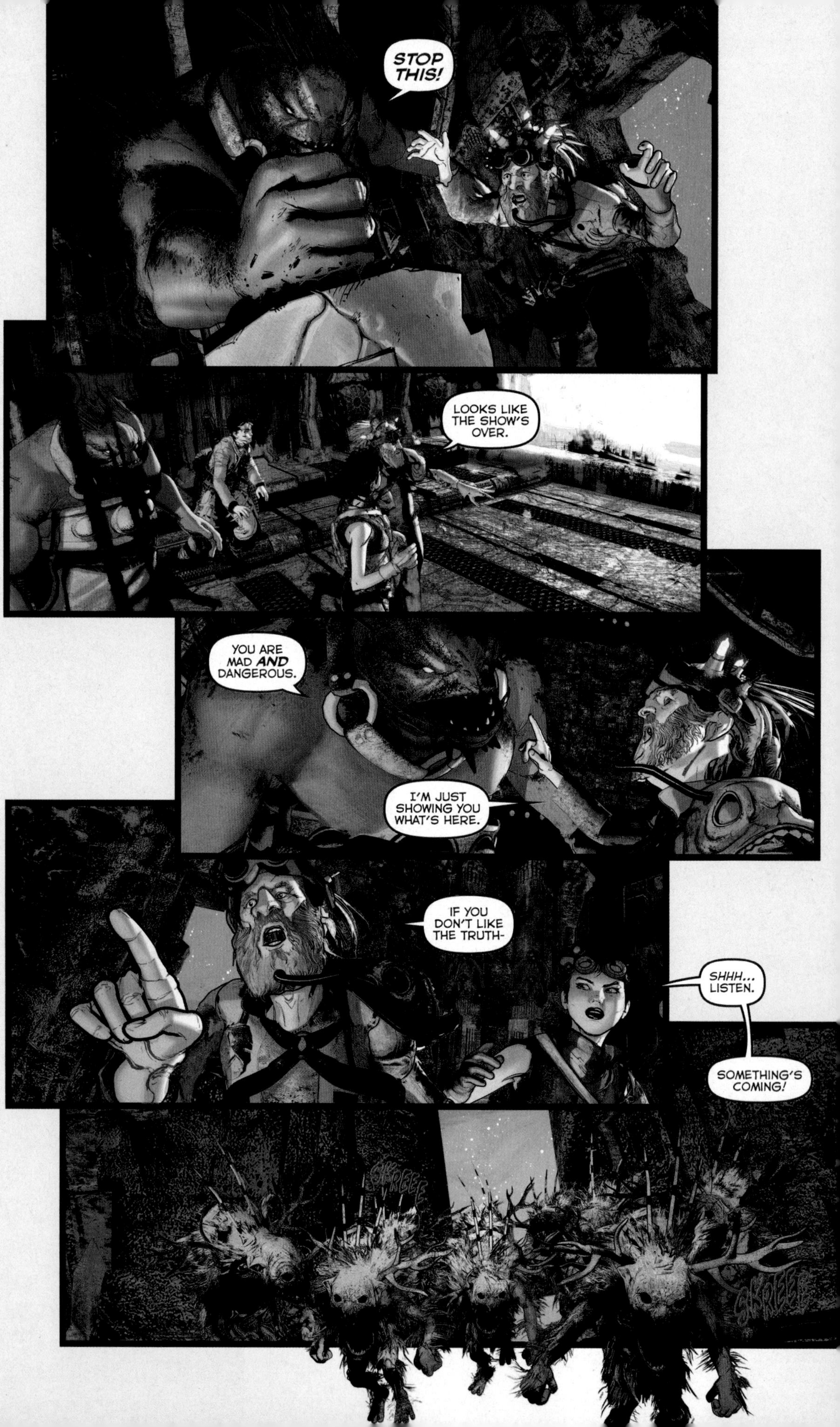
STOP THIS!
LOOKS LIKE THE SHOW'S OVER.
YOU ARE MAD *AND* DANGEROUS.
I'M JUST SHOWING YOU WHAT'S HERE.
IF YOU DON'T LIKE THE TRUTH-
SHHH... LISTEN.
SOMETHING'S COMING!

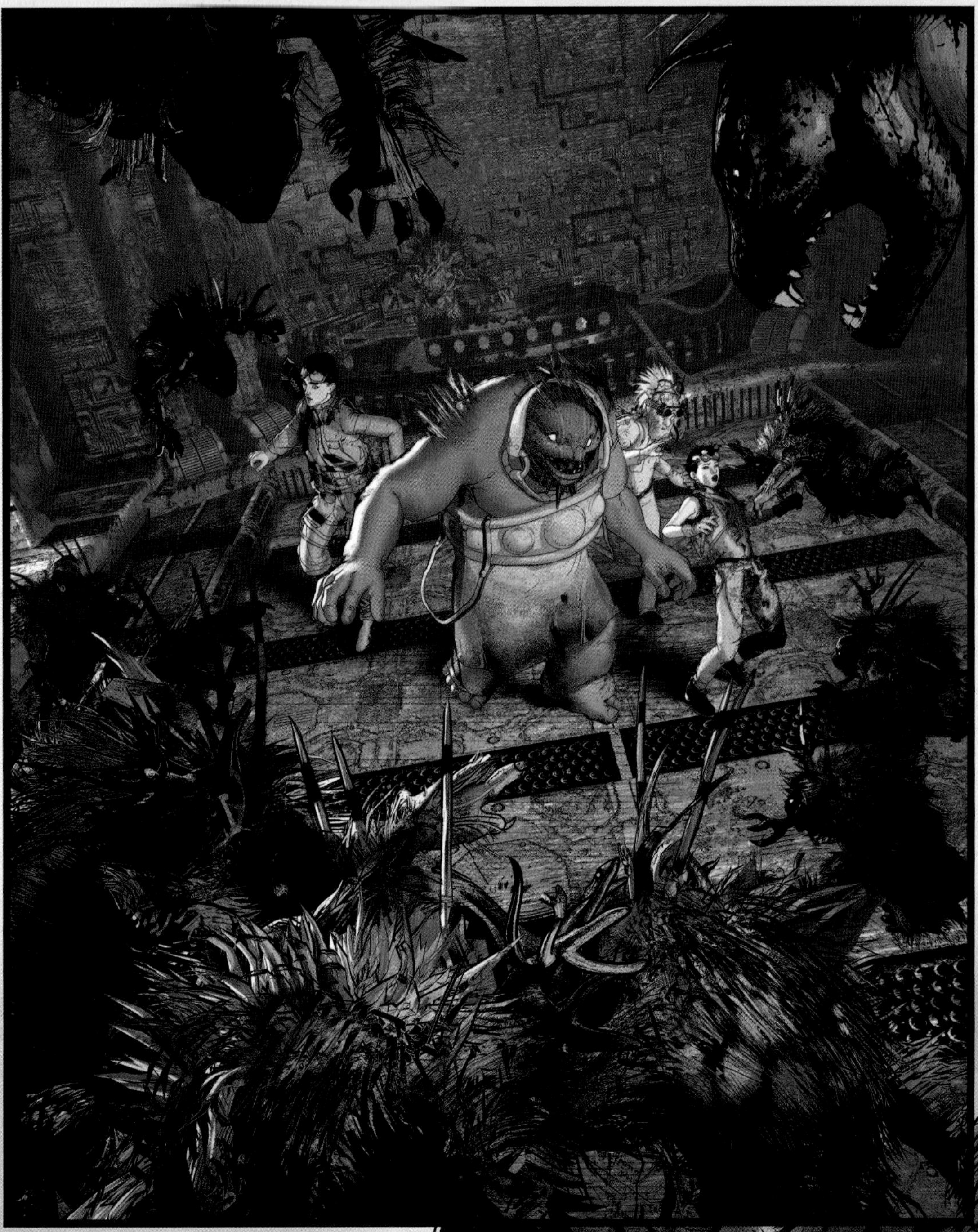

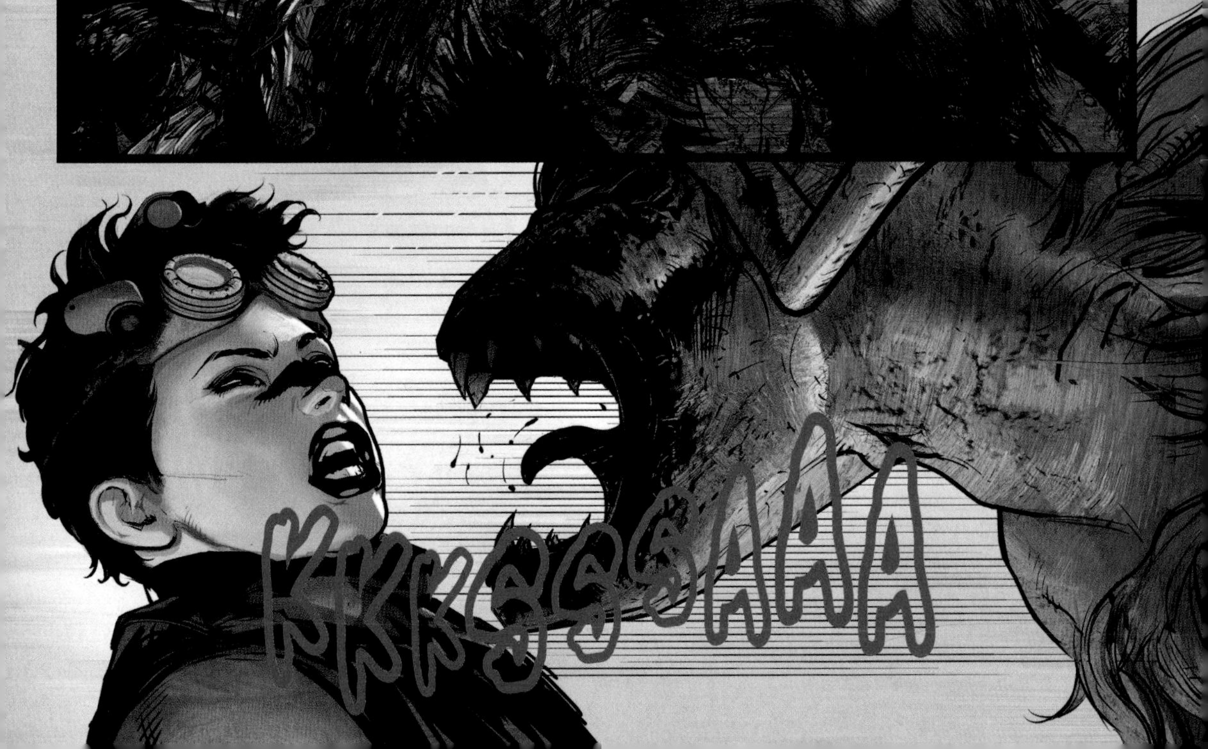
KKKSSSHAA

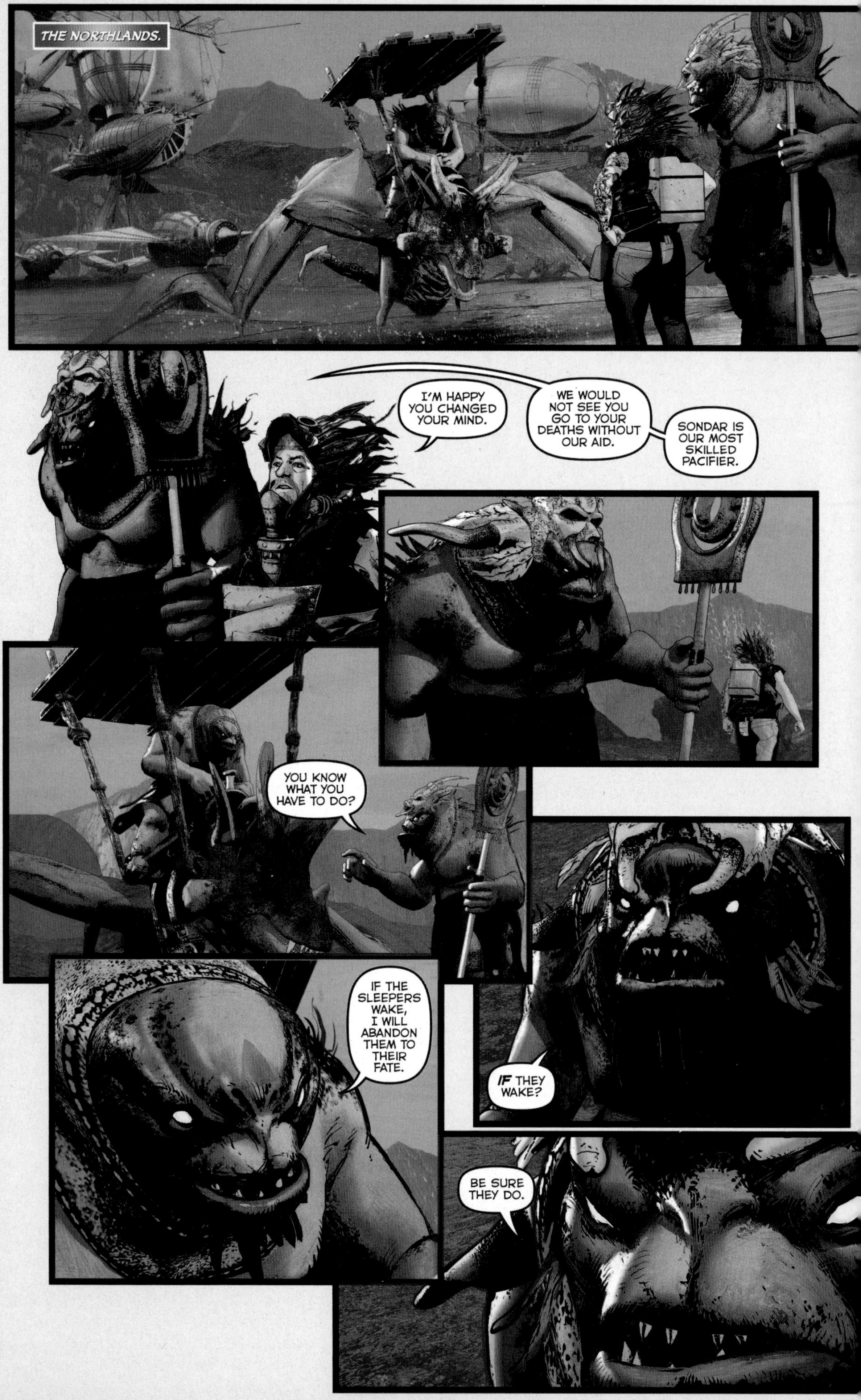
THE NORTHLANDS.
I'M HAPPY YOU CHANGED YOUR MIND.
WE WOULD NOT SEE YOU GO TO YOUR DEATHS WITHOUT OUR AID.
SONDAR IS OUR MOST SKILLED PACIFIER.
YOU KNOW WHAT YOU HAVE TO DO?
IF THE SLEEPERS WAKE, I WILL ABANDON THEM TO THEIR FATE.
IF THEY WAKE?
BE SURE THEY DO.

Issue #4 Cover A

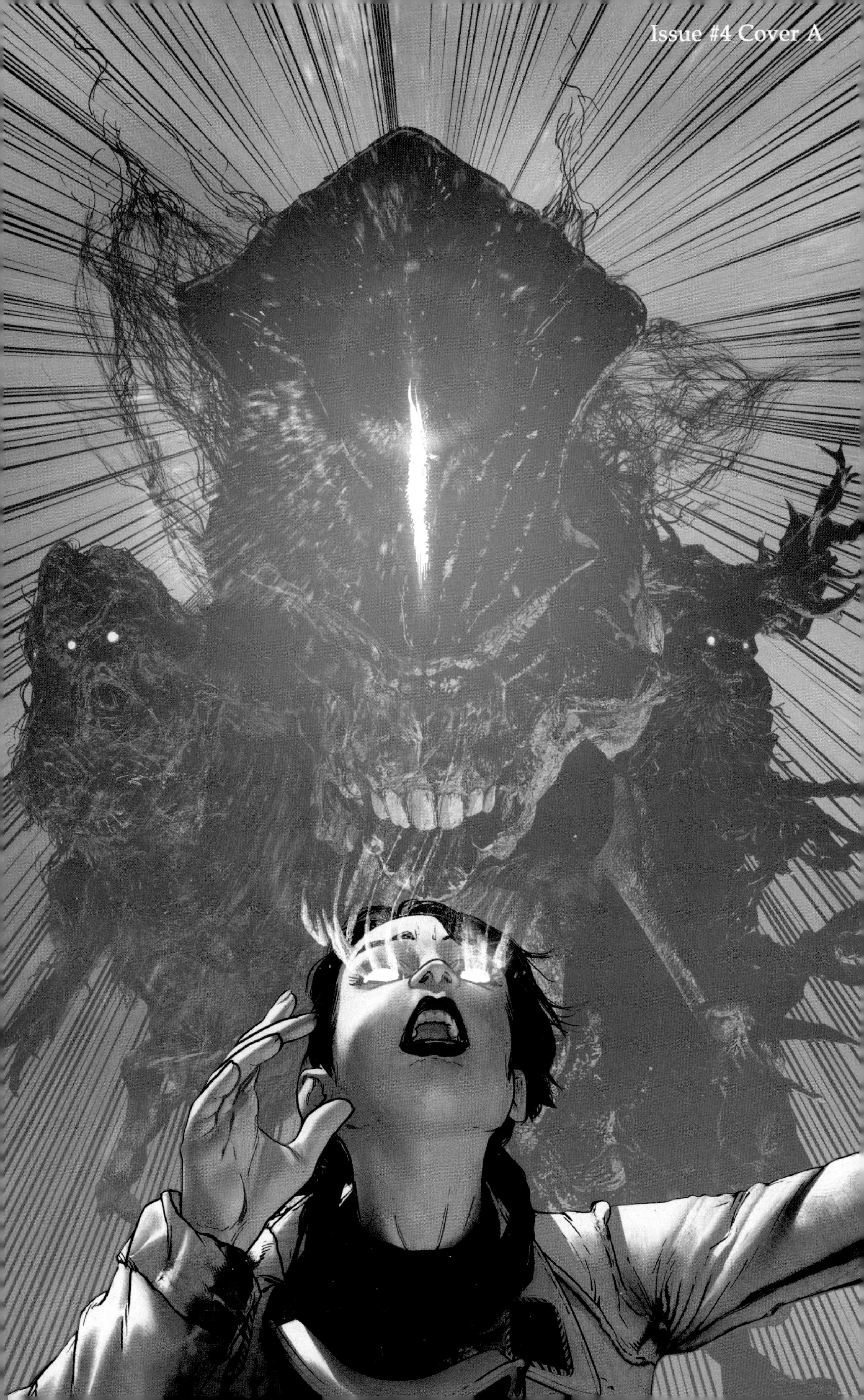

Issue #4 Cover B

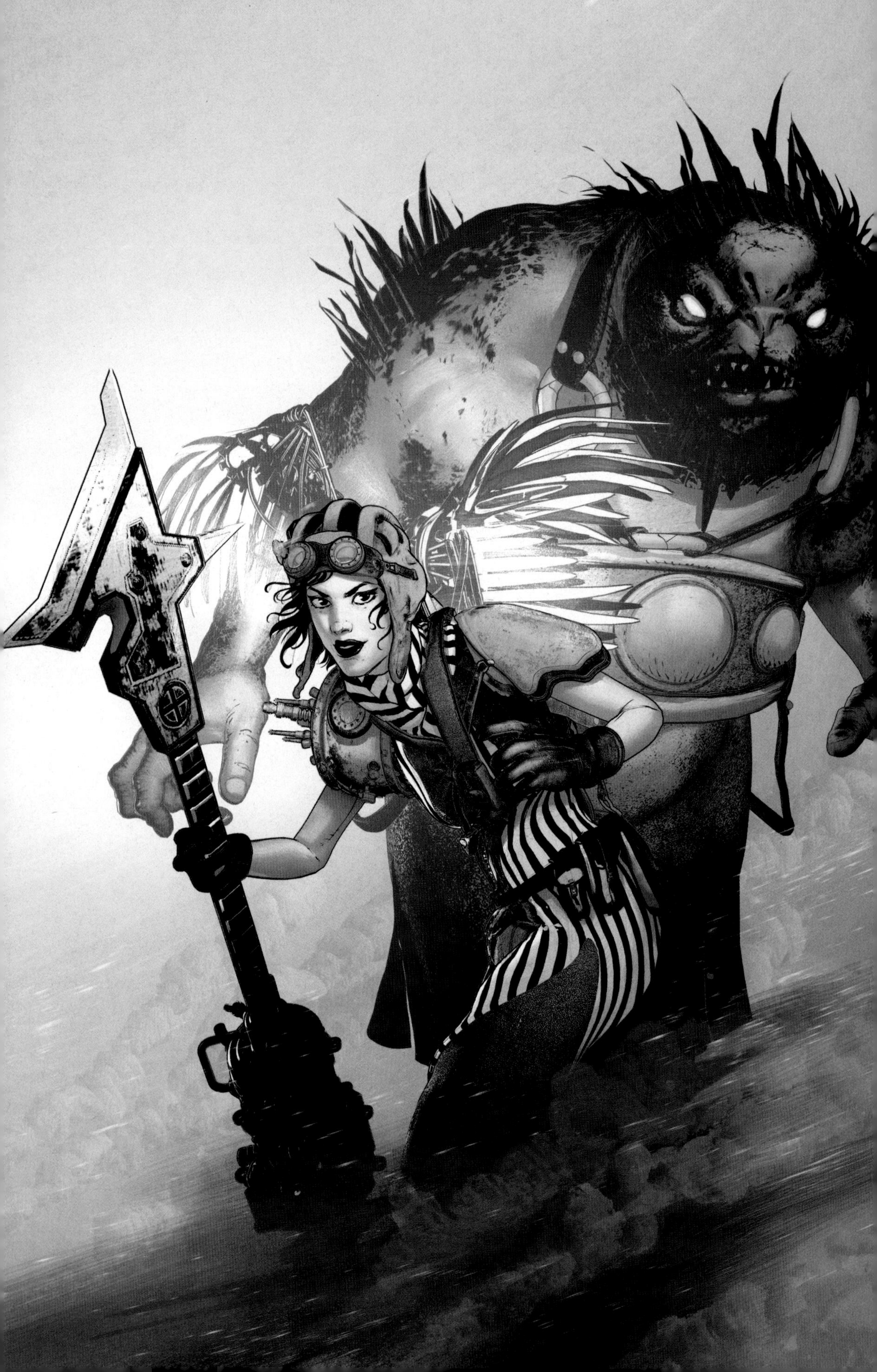

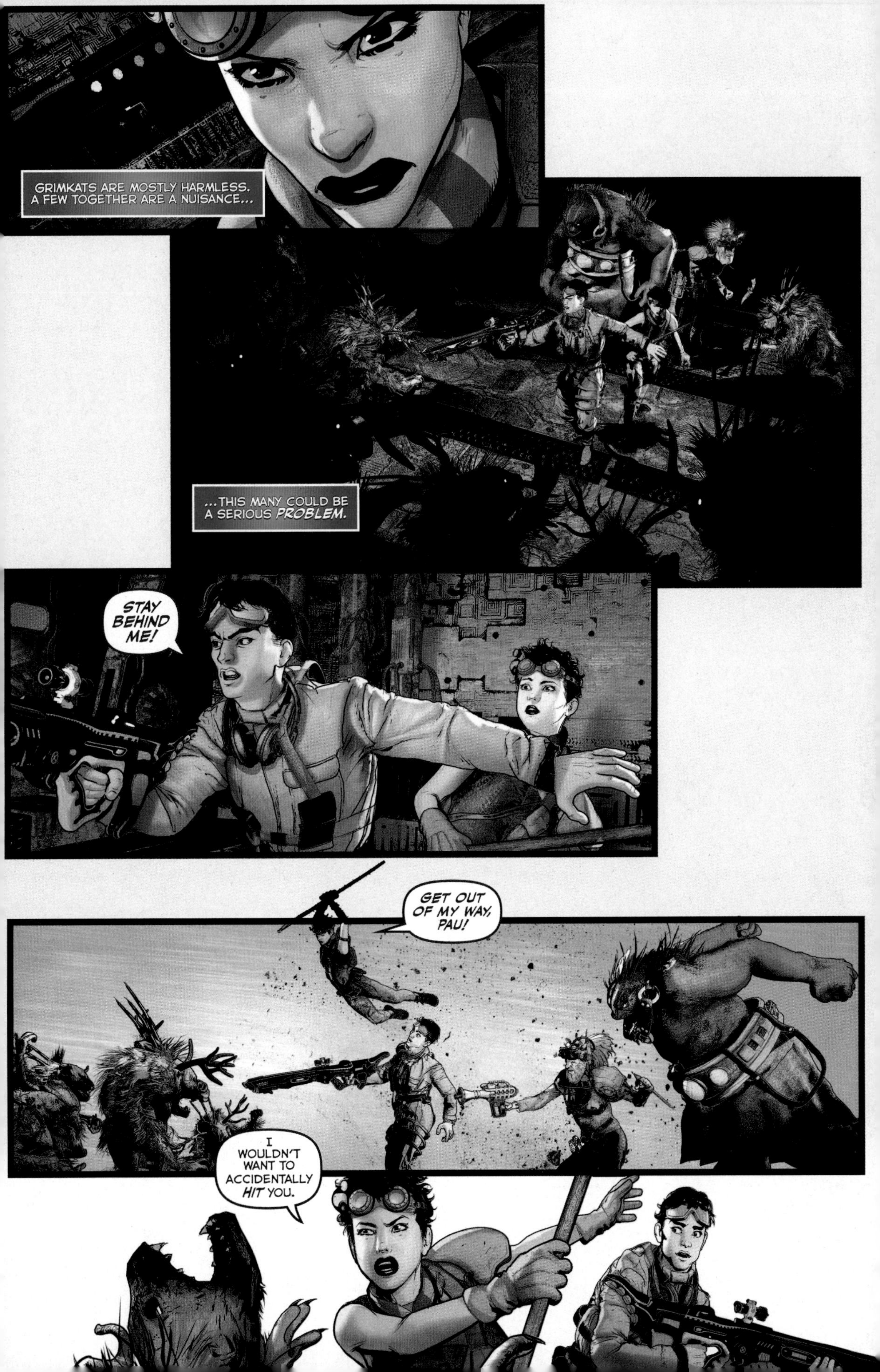
GRIMKATS ARE MOSTLY HARMLESS. A FEW TOGETHER ARE A NUISANCE...
...THIS MANY COULD BE A SERIOUS PROBLEM.
STAY BEHIND ME!
GET OUT OF MY WAY, PAU!
I WOULDN'T WANT TO ACCIDENTALLY HIT YOU.

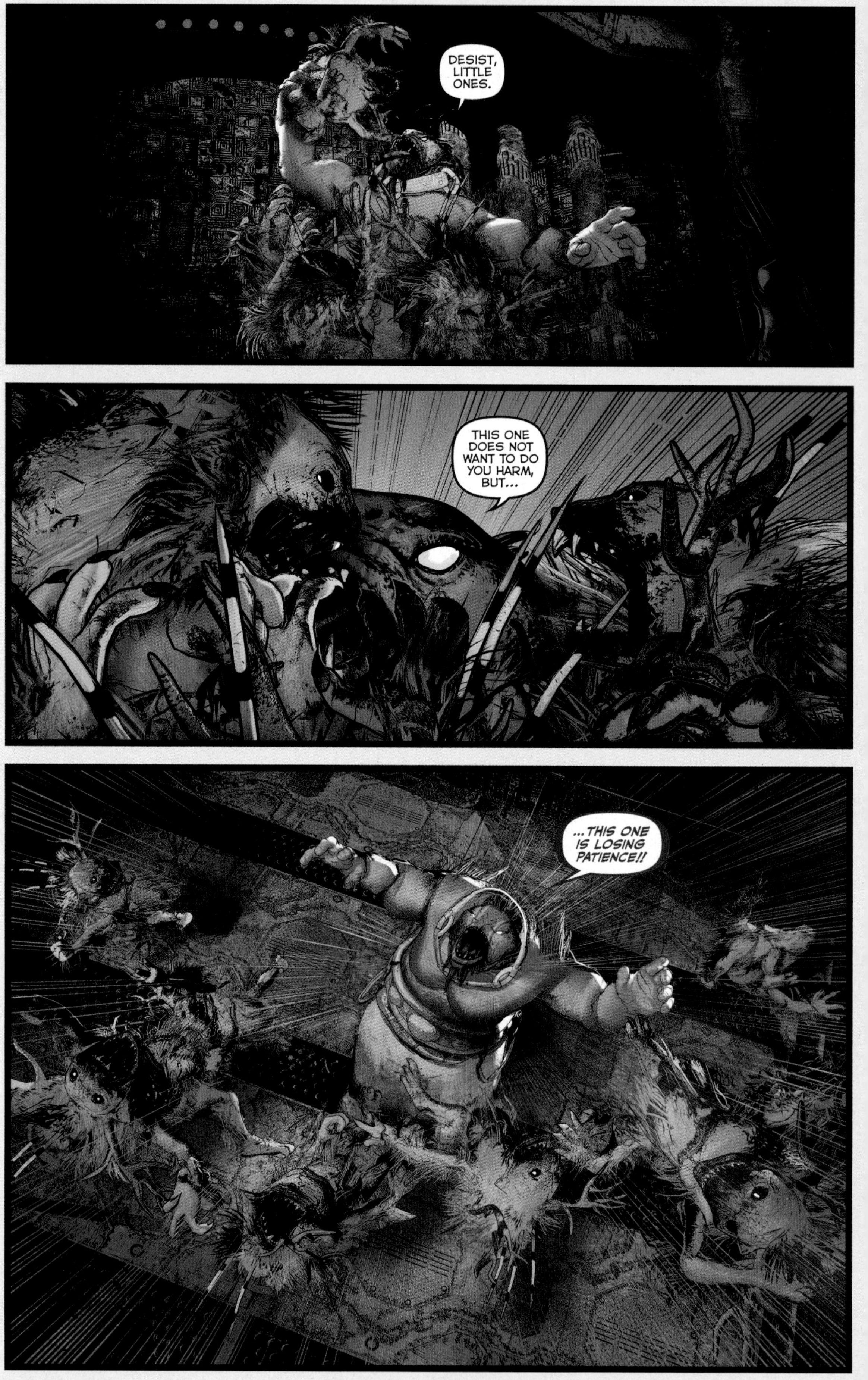
DESIST, LITTLE ONES.
THIS ONE DOES NOT WANT TO DO YOU HARM, BUT...
...THIS ONE IS LOSING PATIENCE!!

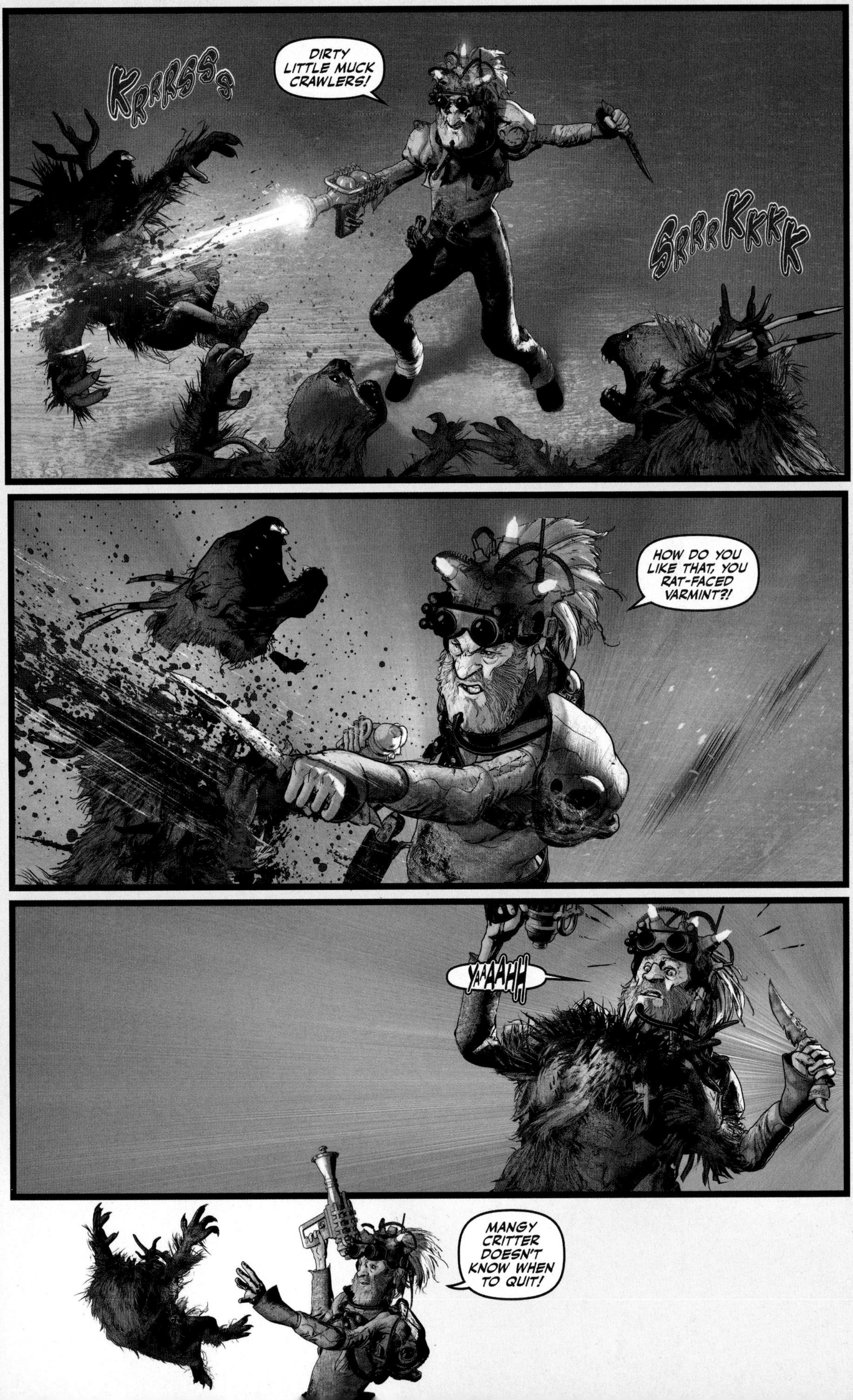
KRRRSSS
DIRTY LITTLE MUCK CRAWLERS!
SRRRKKKK
HOW DO YOU LIKE THAT, YOU RAT-FACED VARMINT?!
YAAAAHH
MANGY CRITTER DOESN'T KNOW WHEN TO QUIT!

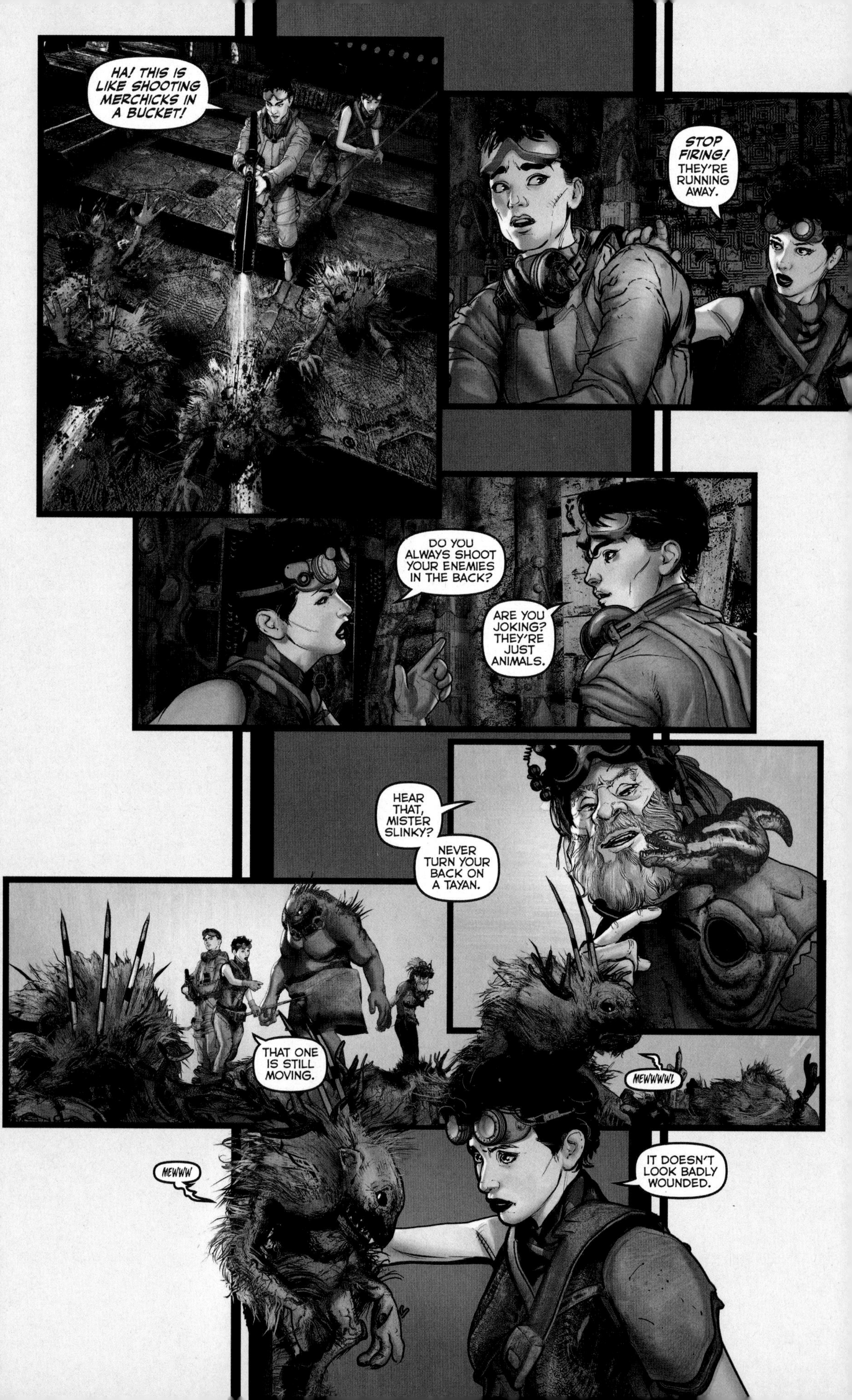
HA! THIS IS LIKE SHOOTING MERCHICKS IN A BUCKET!
STOP FIRING! THEY'RE RUNNING AWAY.
DO YOU ALWAYS SHOOT YOUR ENEMIES IN THE BACK?
ARE YOU JOKING? THEY'RE JUST ANIMALS.
HEAR THAT, MISTER SLINKY?
NEVER TURN YOUR BACK ON A TAYAN.
THAT ONE IS STILL MOVING.
MEWWWWL
MEWWW
IT DOESN'T LOOK BADLY WOUNDED.

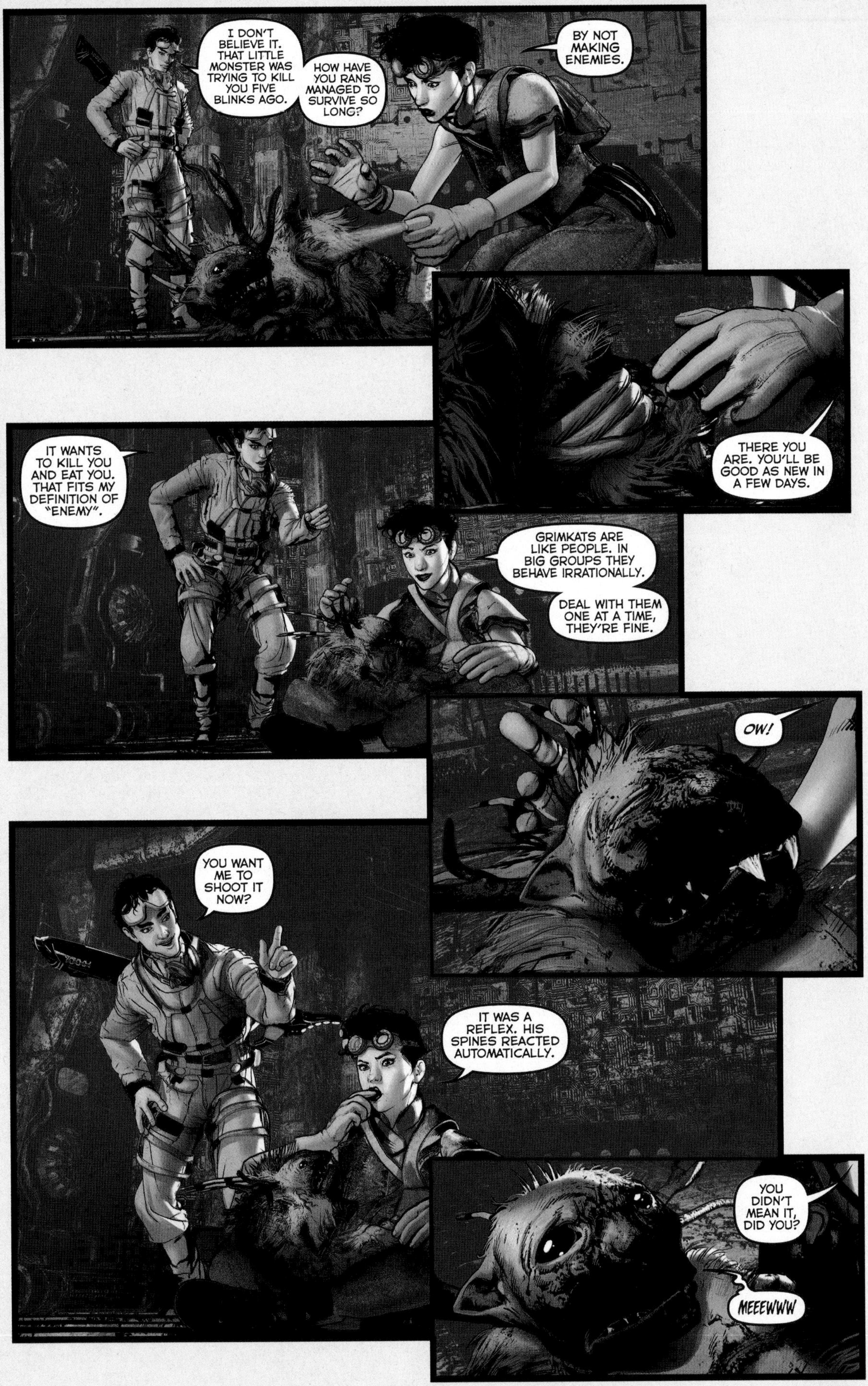
I DON'T BELIEVE IT. THAT LITTLE MONSTER WAS TRYING TO KILL YOU FIVE BLINKS AGO.
HOW HAVE YOU RANS MANAGED TO SURVIVE SO LONG?
BY NOT MAKING ENEMIES.
THERE YOU ARE. YOU'LL BE GOOD AS NEW IN A FEW DAYS.
IT WANTS TO KILL YOU AND EAT YOU. THAT FITS MY DEFINITION OF "ENEMY".
GRIMKATS ARE LIKE PEOPLE. IN BIG GROUPS THEY BEHAVE IRRATIONALLY.
DEAL WITH THEM ONE AT A TIME, THEY'RE FINE.
OW!
YOU WANT ME TO SHOOT IT NOW?
IT WAS A REFLEX. HIS SPINES REACTED AUTOMATICALLY.
YOU DIDN'T MEAN IT, DID YOU?
MEEEWWW

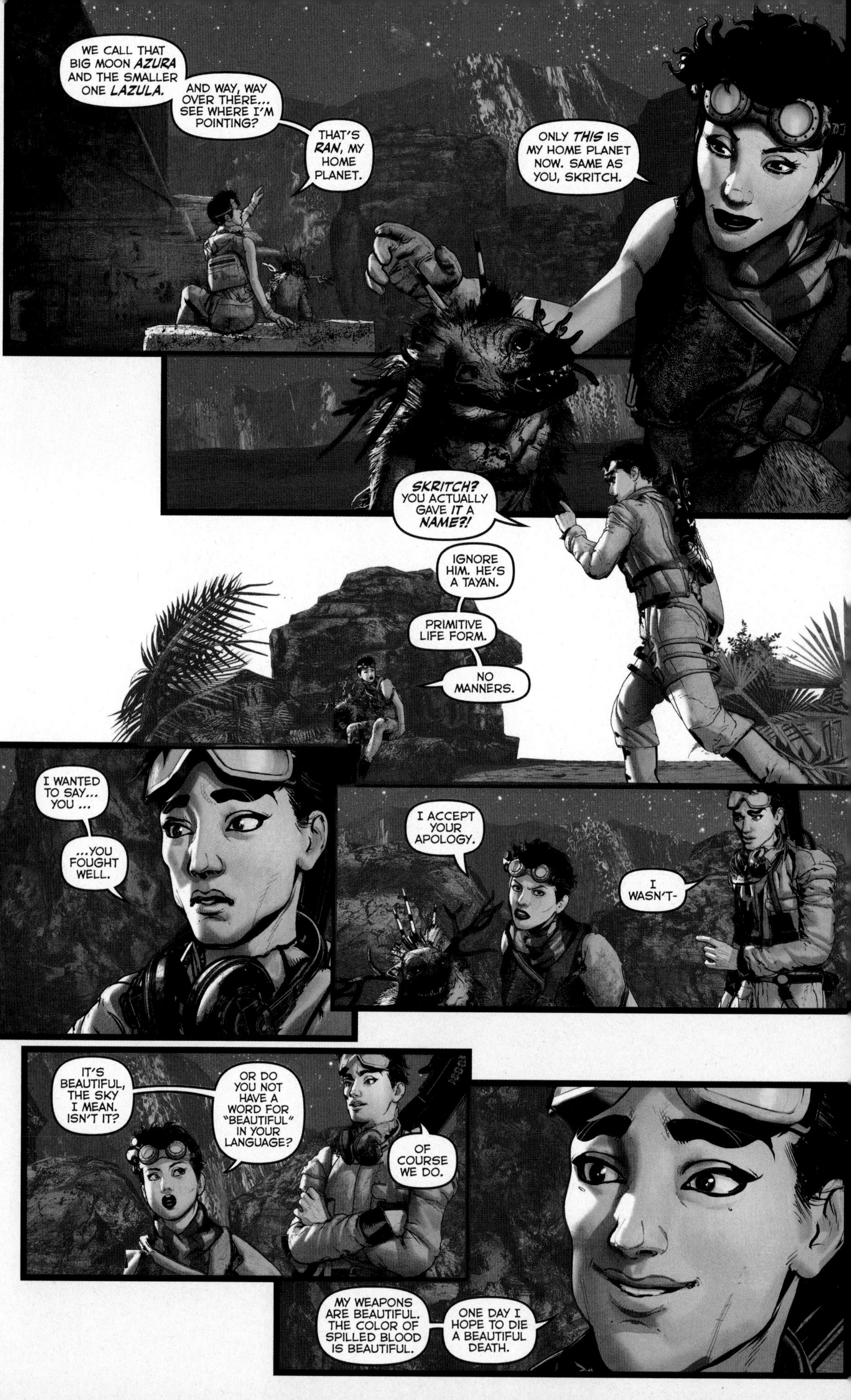
WE CALL THAT BIG MOON AZURA AND THE SMALLER ONE LAZULA.
AND WAY, WAY OVER THERE... SEE WHERE I'M POINTING?
THAT'S RAN, MY HOME PLANET.
ONLY THIS IS MY HOME PLANET NOW. SAME AS YOU, SKRITCH.
SKRITCH? YOU ACTUALLY GAVE IT A NAME?!
IGNORE HIM. HE'S A TAYAN.
PRIMITIVE LIFE FORM.
NO MANNERS.
I WANTED TO SAY... YOU ...
...YOU FOUGHT WELL.
I ACCEPT YOUR APOLOGY.
I WASN'T-
IT'S BEAUTIFUL, THE SKY I MEAN. ISN'T IT?
OR DO YOU NOT HAVE A WORD FOR "BEAUTIFUL" IN YOUR LANGUAGE?
OF COURSE WE DO.
MY WEAPONS ARE BEAUTIFUL. THE COLOR OF SPILLED BLOOD IS BEAUTIFUL.
ONE DAY I HOPE TO DIE A BEAUTIFUL DEATH.

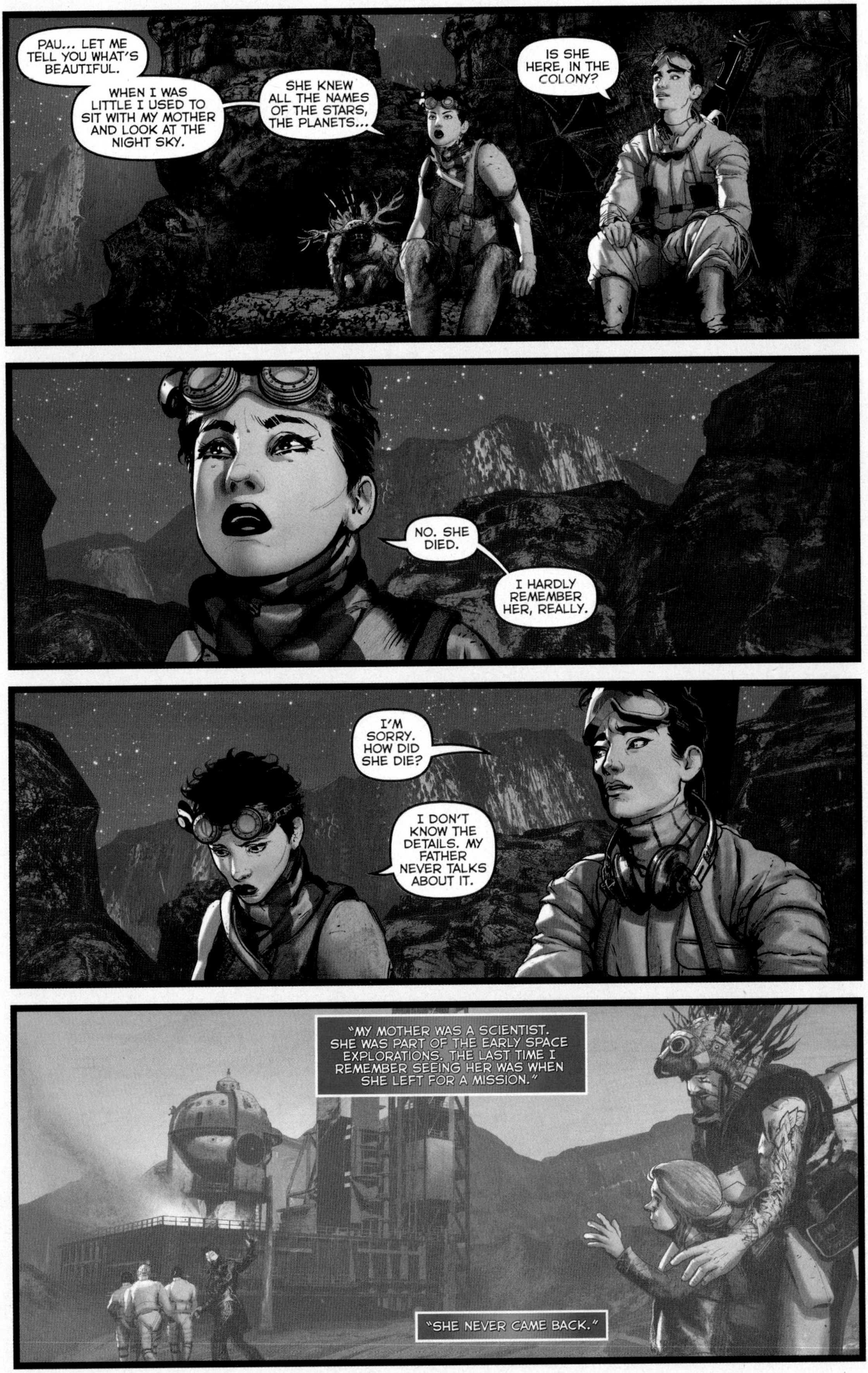
PAU... LET ME TELL YOU WHAT'S BEAUTIFUL.
WHEN I WAS LITTLE I USED TO SIT WITH MY MOTHER AND LOOK AT THE NIGHT SKY.
SHE KNEW ALL THE NAMES OF THE STARS, THE PLANETS...
IS SHE HERE, IN THE COLONY?
NO. SHE DIED.
I HARDLY REMEMBER HER, REALLY.
I'M SORRY. HOW DID SHE DIE?
I DON'T KNOW THE DETAILS. MY FATHER NEVER TALKS ABOUT IT.
"MY MOTHER WAS A SCIENTIST. SHE WAS PART OF THE EARLY SPACE EXPLORATIONS. THE LAST TIME I REMEMBER SEEING HER WAS WHEN SHE LEFT FOR A MISSION."
"SHE NEVER CAME BACK."

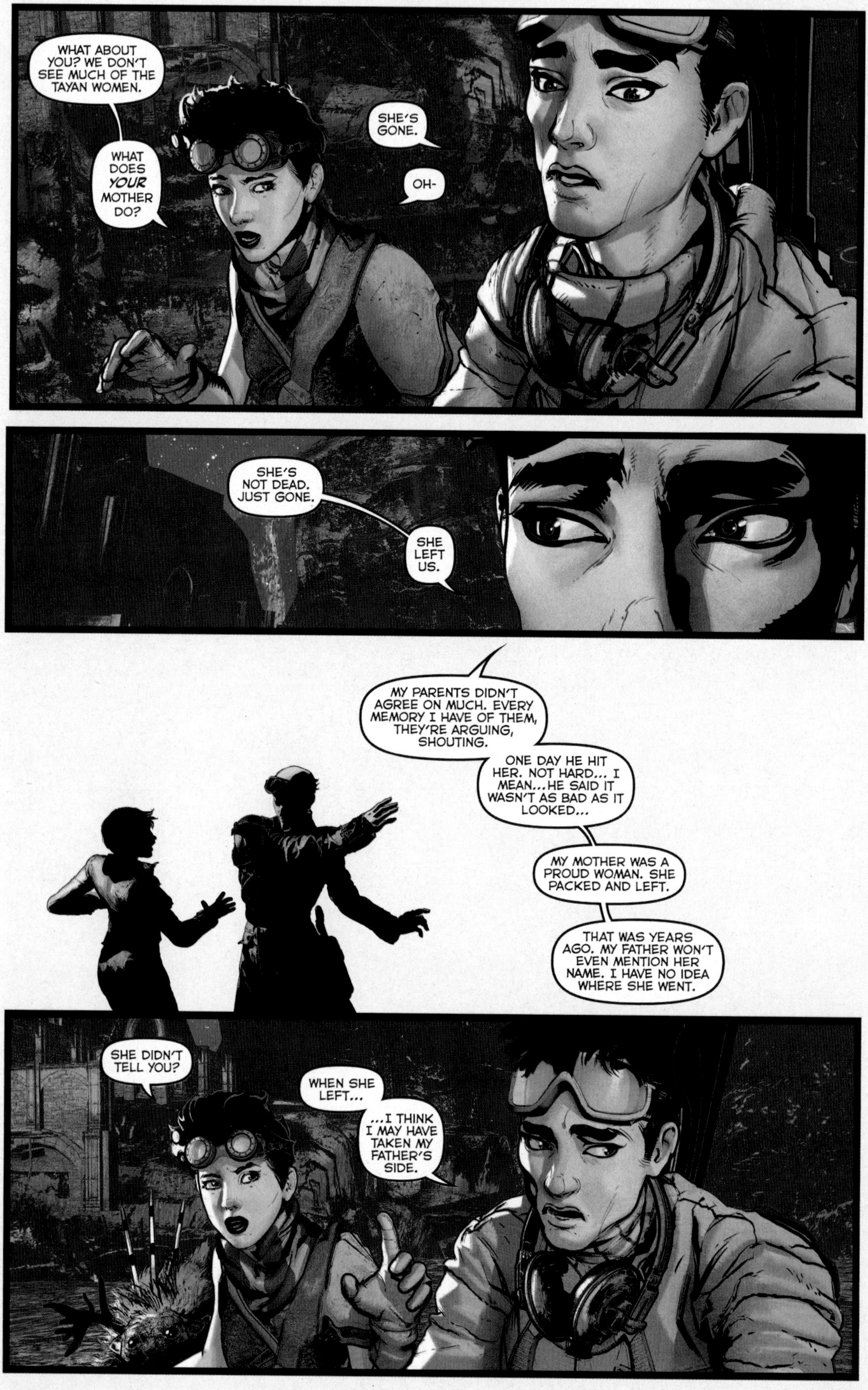
WHAT ABOUT YOU? WE DON'T SEE MUCH OF THE TAYAN WOMEN.
WHAT DOES *YOUR* MOTHER DO?
SHE'S GONE.
OH-
SHE'S NOT DEAD. JUST GONE.
SHE LEFT US.
MY PARENTS DIDN'T AGREE ON MUCH. EVERY MEMORY I HAVE OF THEM, THEY'RE ARGUING, SHOUTING.
ONE DAY HE HIT HER. NOT HARD... I MEAN...HE SAID IT WASN'T AS BAD AS IT LOOKED...
MY MOTHER WAS A PROUD WOMAN. SHE PACKED AND LEFT.
THAT WAS YEARS AGO. MY FATHER WON'T EVEN MENTION HER NAME. I HAVE NO IDEA WHERE SHE WENT.
SHE DIDN'T TELL YOU?
WHEN SHE LEFT...
...I THINK I MAY HAVE TAKEN MY FATHER'S SIDE.

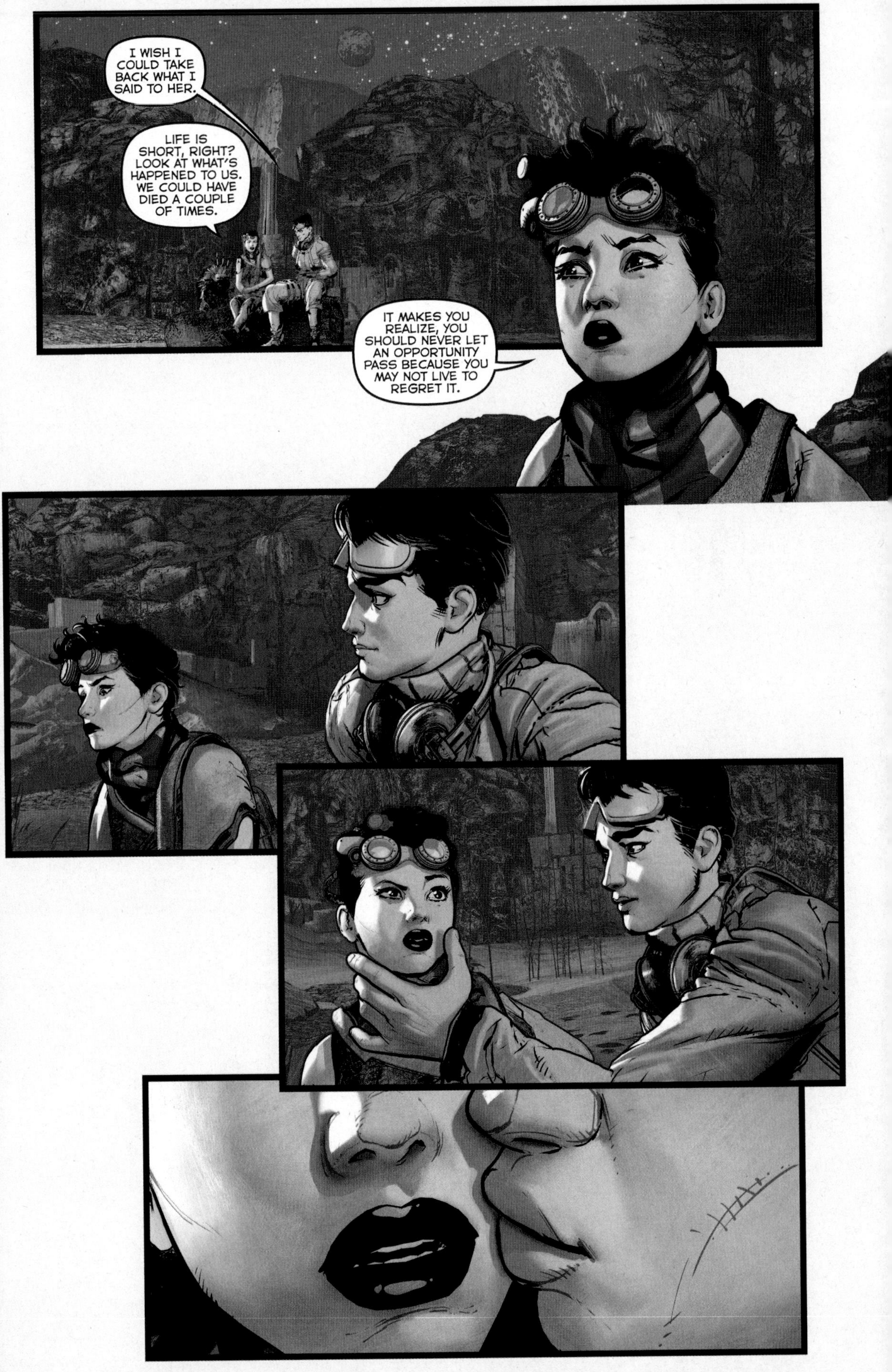
I WISH I COULD TAKE BACK WHAT I SAID TO HER.
LIFE IS SHORT, RIGHT? LOOK AT WHAT'S HAPPENED TO US. WE COULD HAVE DIED A COUPLE OF TIMES.
IT MAKES YOU REALIZE, YOU SHOULD NEVER LET AN OPPORTUNITY PASS BECAUSE YOU MAY NOT LIVE TO REGRET IT.

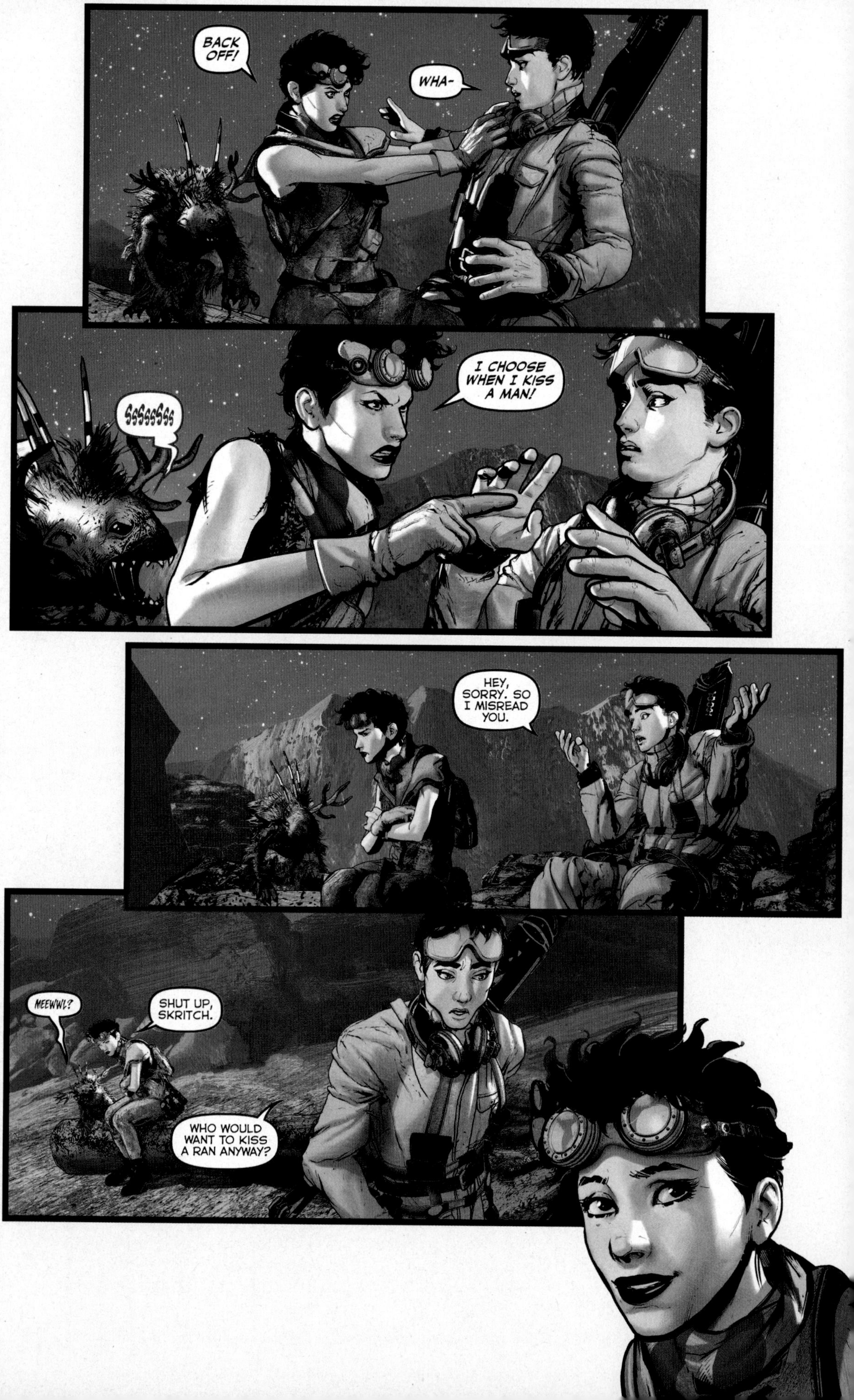
BACK OFF!
WHA-
I CHOOSE WHEN I KISS A MAN!
SSSSSSSS
HEY, SORRY. SO I MISREAD YOU.
MEEWWL?
SHUT UP, SKRITCH.
WHO WOULD WANT TO KISS A RAN ANYWAY?

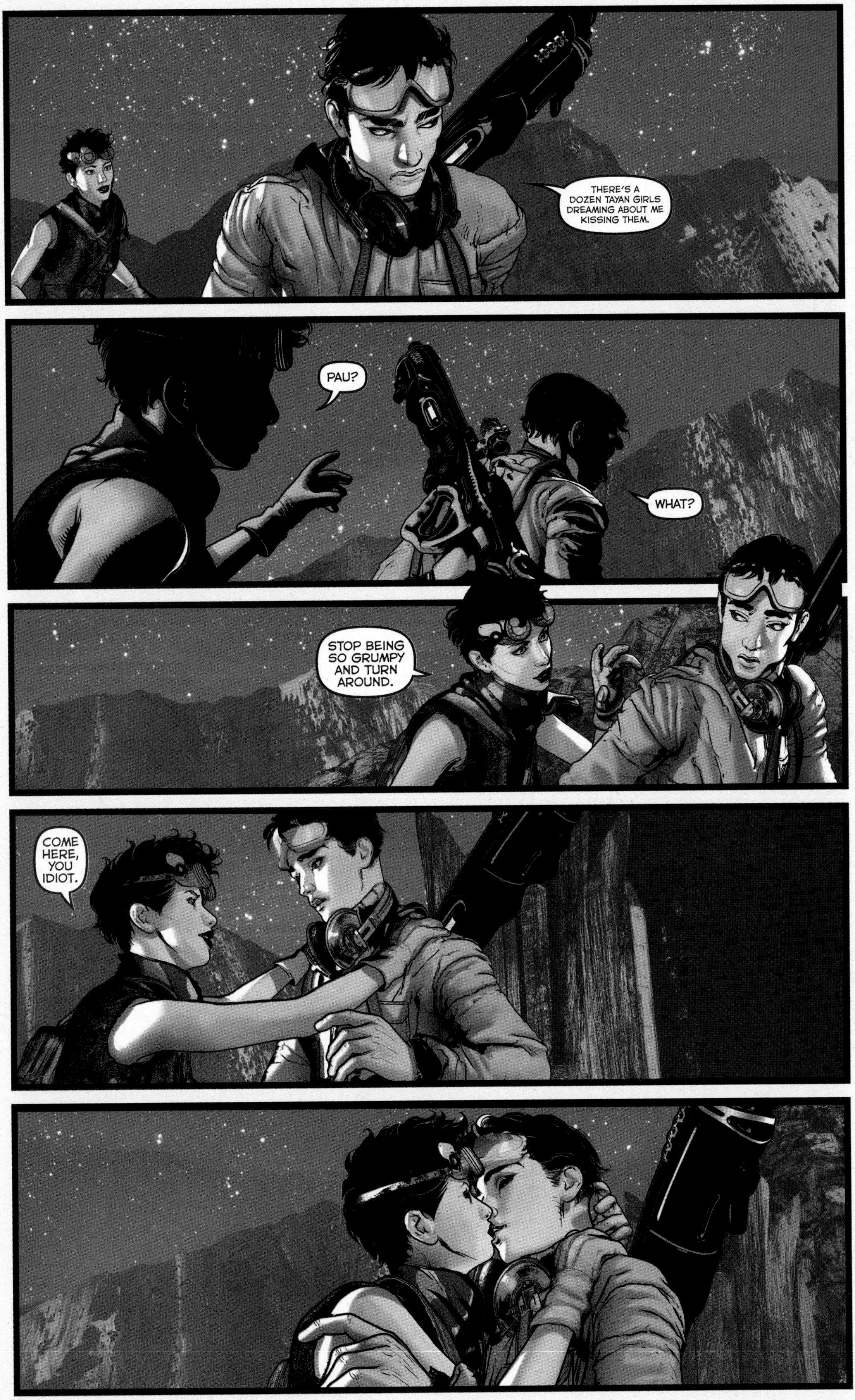
THERE'S A DOZEN TAYAN GIRLS DREAMING ABOUT ME KISSING THEM.
PAU?
WHAT?
STOP BEING SO GRUMPY AND TURN AROUND.
COME HERE, YOU IDIOT.

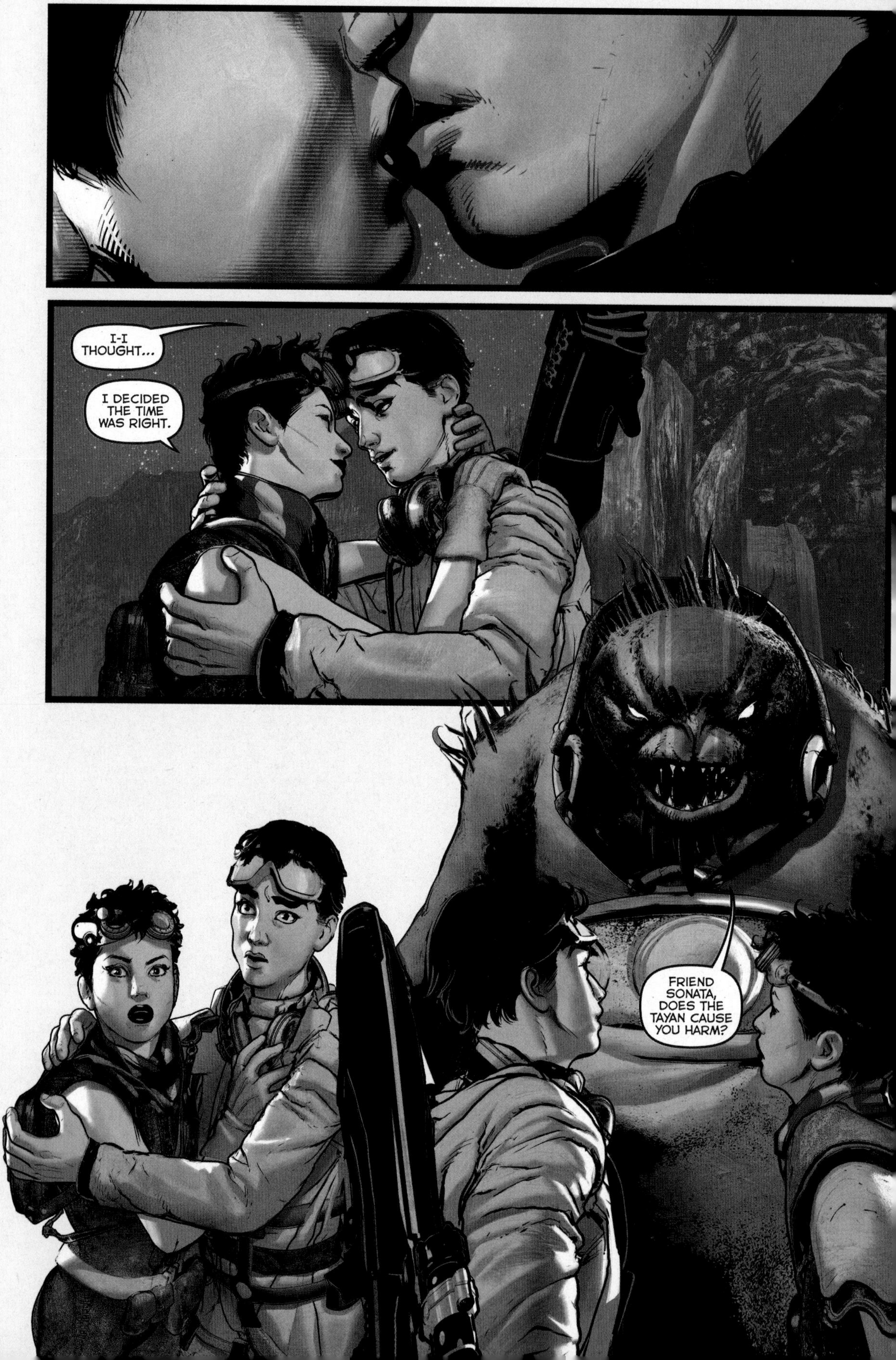
I-I THOUGHT...
I DECIDED THE TIME WAS RIGHT.
FRIEND SONATA, DOES THE TAYAN CAUSE YOU HARM?

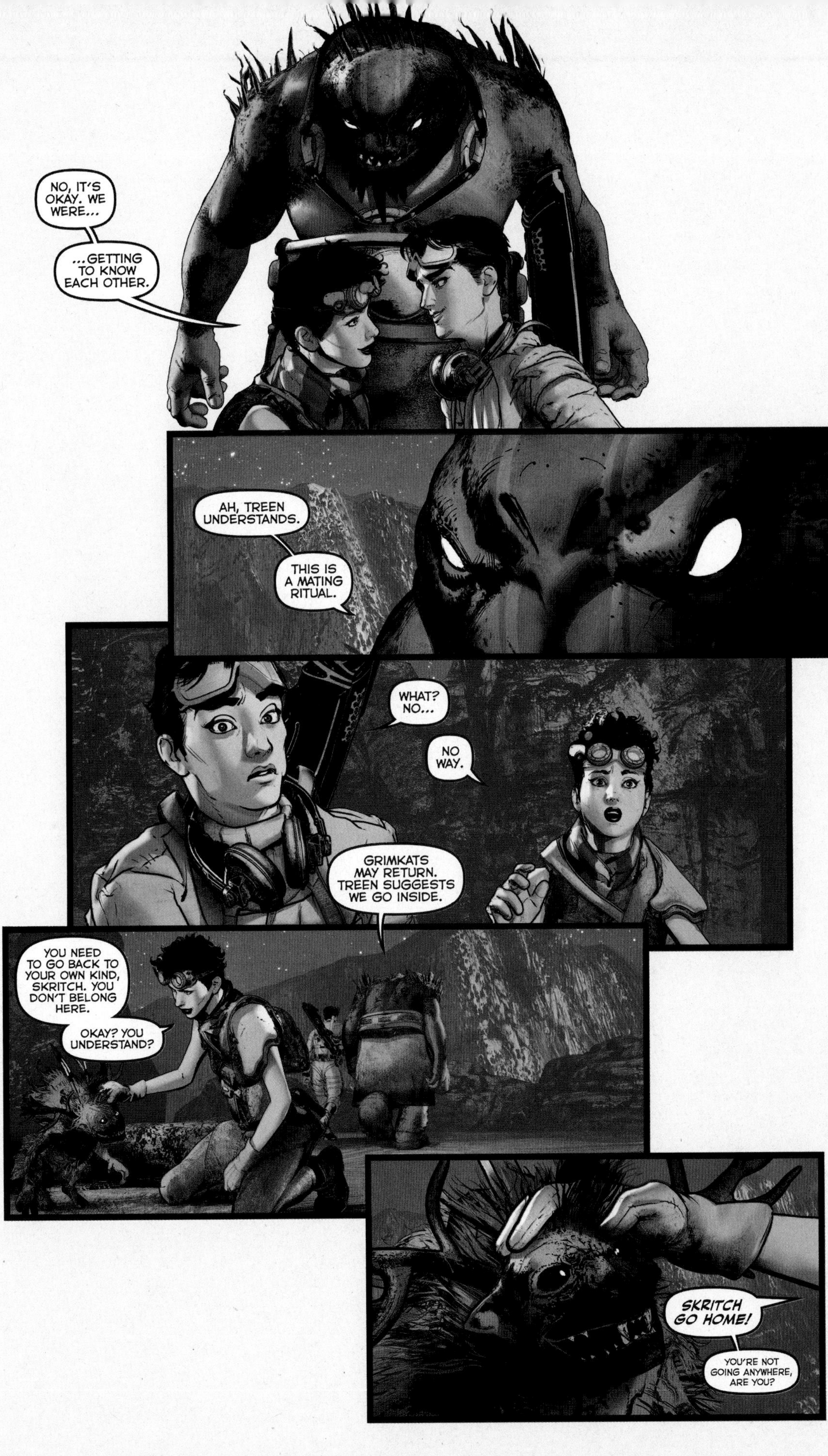
NO, IT'S OKAY. WE WERE...
...GETTING TO KNOW EACH OTHER.
AH, TREEN UNDERSTANDS.
THIS IS A MATING RITUAL.
WHAT? NO...
NO WAY.
GRIMKATS MAY RETURN. TREEN SUGGESTS WE GO INSIDE.
YOU NEED TO GO BACK TO YOUR OWN KIND, SKRITCH. YOU DON'T BELONG HERE.
OKAY? YOU UNDERSTAND?
SKRITCH GO HOME!
YOU'RE NOT GOING ANYWHERE, ARE YOU?

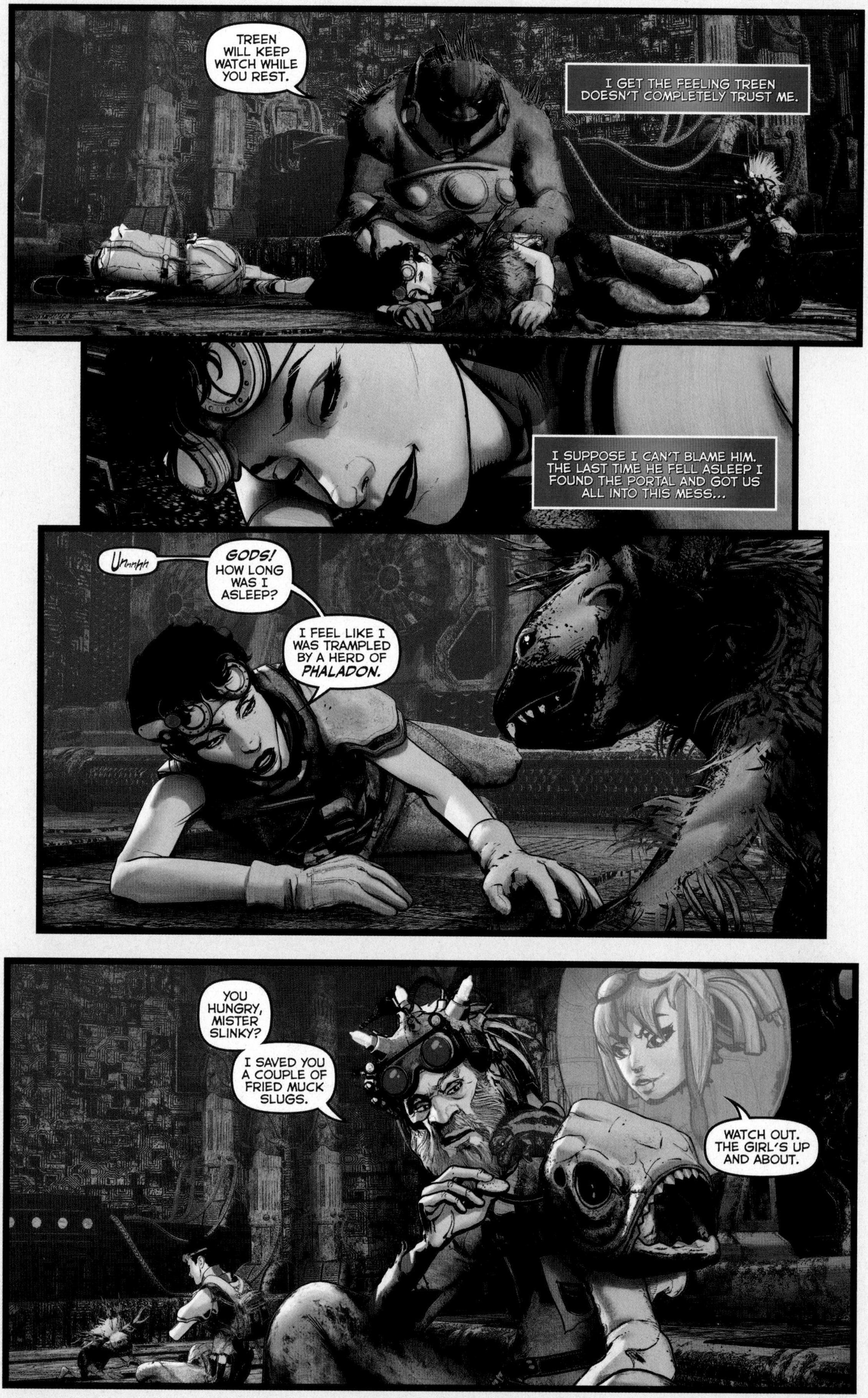
TREEN WILL KEEP WATCH WHILE YOU REST.
I GET THE FEELING TREEN DOESN'T COMPLETELY TRUST ME.
I SUPPOSE I CAN'T BLAME HIM. THE LAST TIME HE FELL ASLEEP I FOUND THE PORTAL AND GOT US ALL INTO THIS MESS...
Unnnhh
GODS! HOW LONG WAS I ASLEEP?
I FEEL LIKE I WAS TRAMPLED BY A HERD OF PHALADON.
YOU HUNGRY, MISTER SLINKY?
I SAVED YOU A COUPLE OF FRIED MUCK SLUGS.
WATCH OUT. THE GIRL'S UP AND ABOUT.

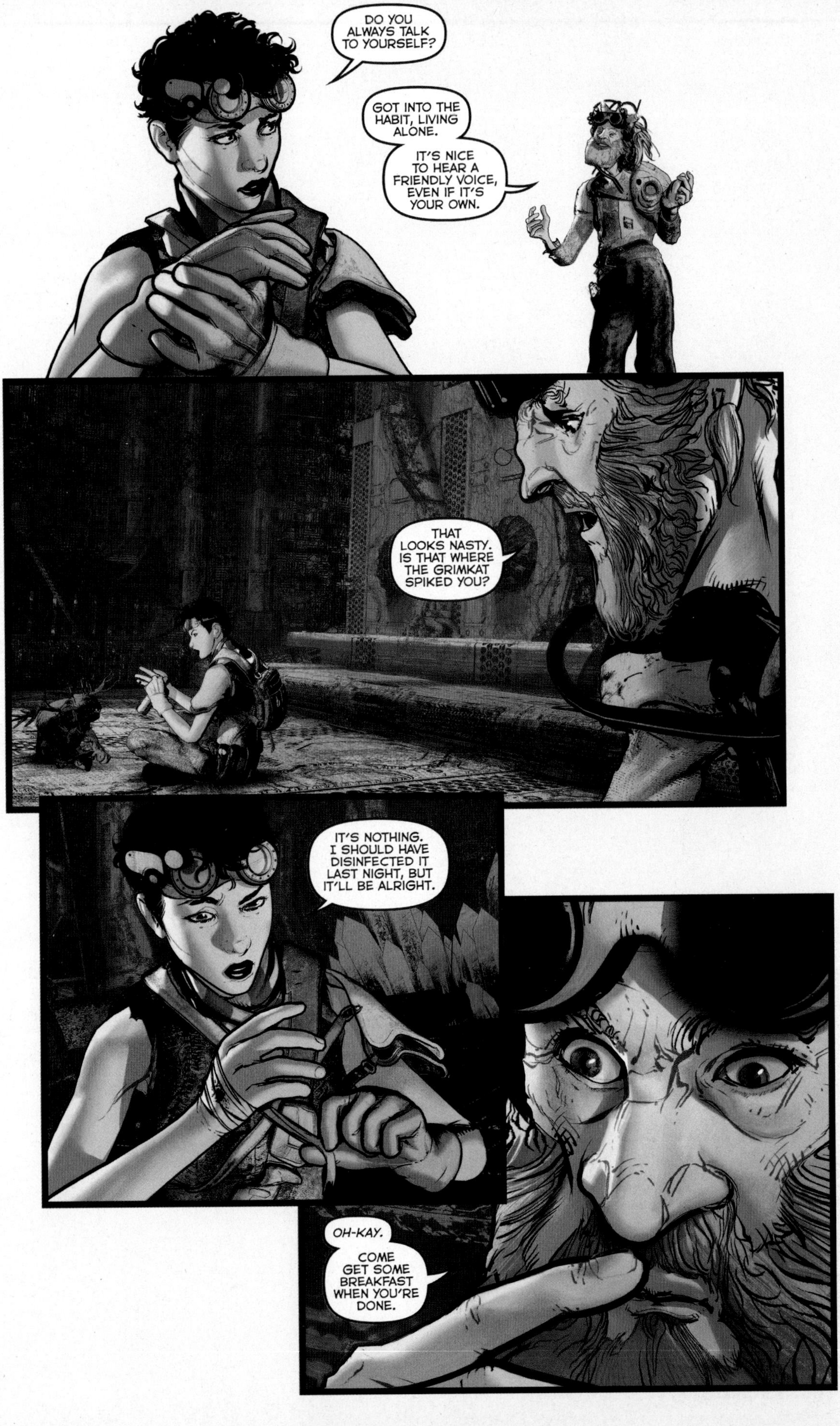
DO YOU ALWAYS TALK TO YOURSELF?
GOT INTO THE HABIT, LIVING ALONE.
IT'S NICE TO HEAR A FRIENDLY VOICE, EVEN IF IT'S YOUR OWN.
THAT LOOKS NASTY. IS THAT WHERE THE GRIMKAT SPIKED YOU?
IT'S NOTHING. I SHOULD HAVE DISINFECTED IT LAST NIGHT, BUT IT'LL BE ALRIGHT.
OH-KAY.
COME GET SOME BREAKFAST WHEN YOU'RE DONE.

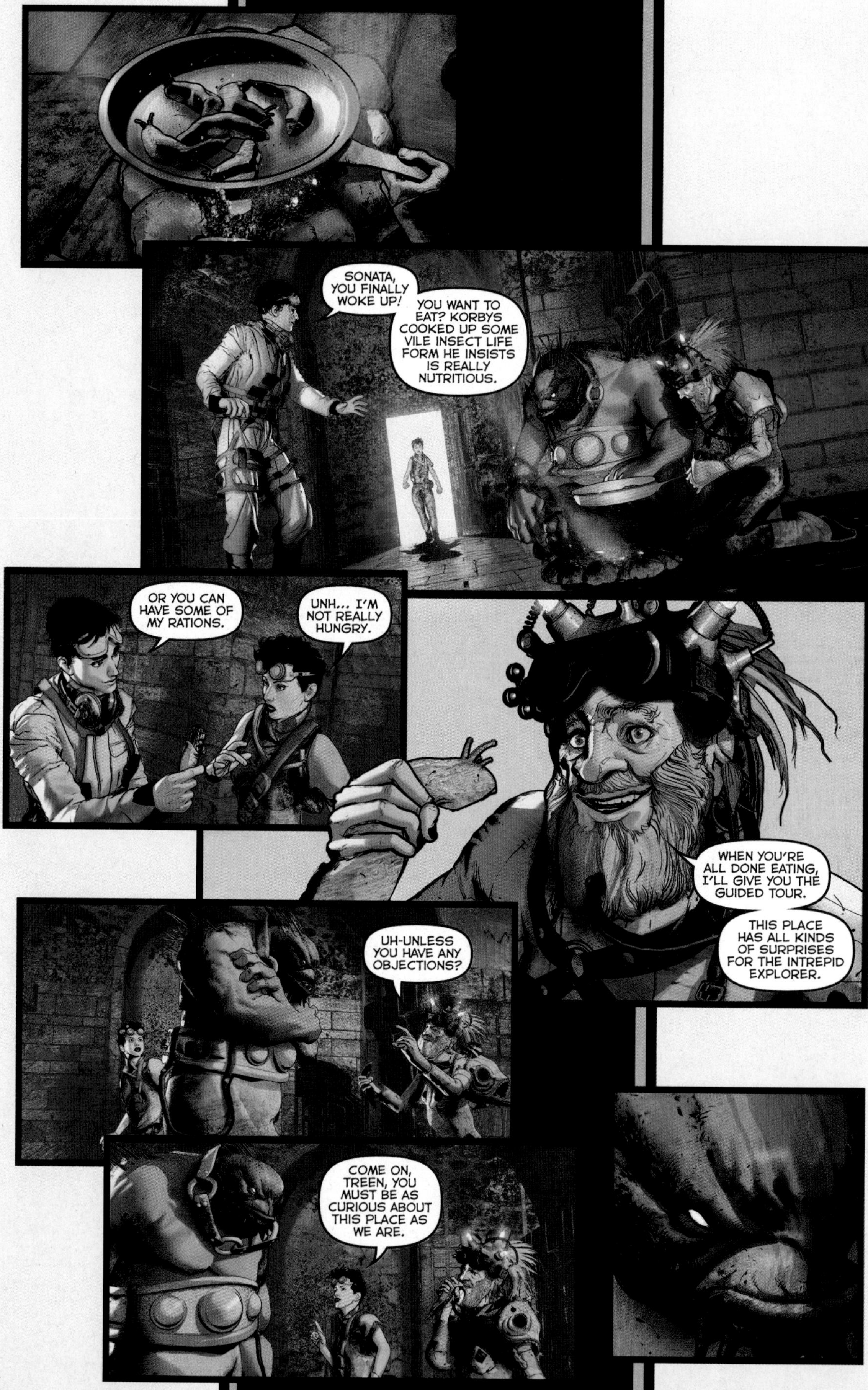
SONATA, YOU FINALLY WOKE UP!
YOU WANT TO EAT? KORBYS COOKED UP SOME VILE INSECT LIFE FORM HE INSISTS IS REALLY NUTRITIOUS.
OR YOU CAN HAVE SOME OF MY RATIONS.
UNH... I'M NOT REALLY HUNGRY.
WHEN YOU'RE ALL DONE EATING, I'LL GIVE YOU THE GUIDED TOUR.
THIS PLACE HAS ALL KINDS OF SURPRISES FOR THE INTREPID EXPLORER.
UH-UNLESS YOU HAVE ANY OBJECTIONS?
COME ON, TREEN, YOU MUST BE AS CURIOUS ABOUT THIS PLACE AS WE ARE.

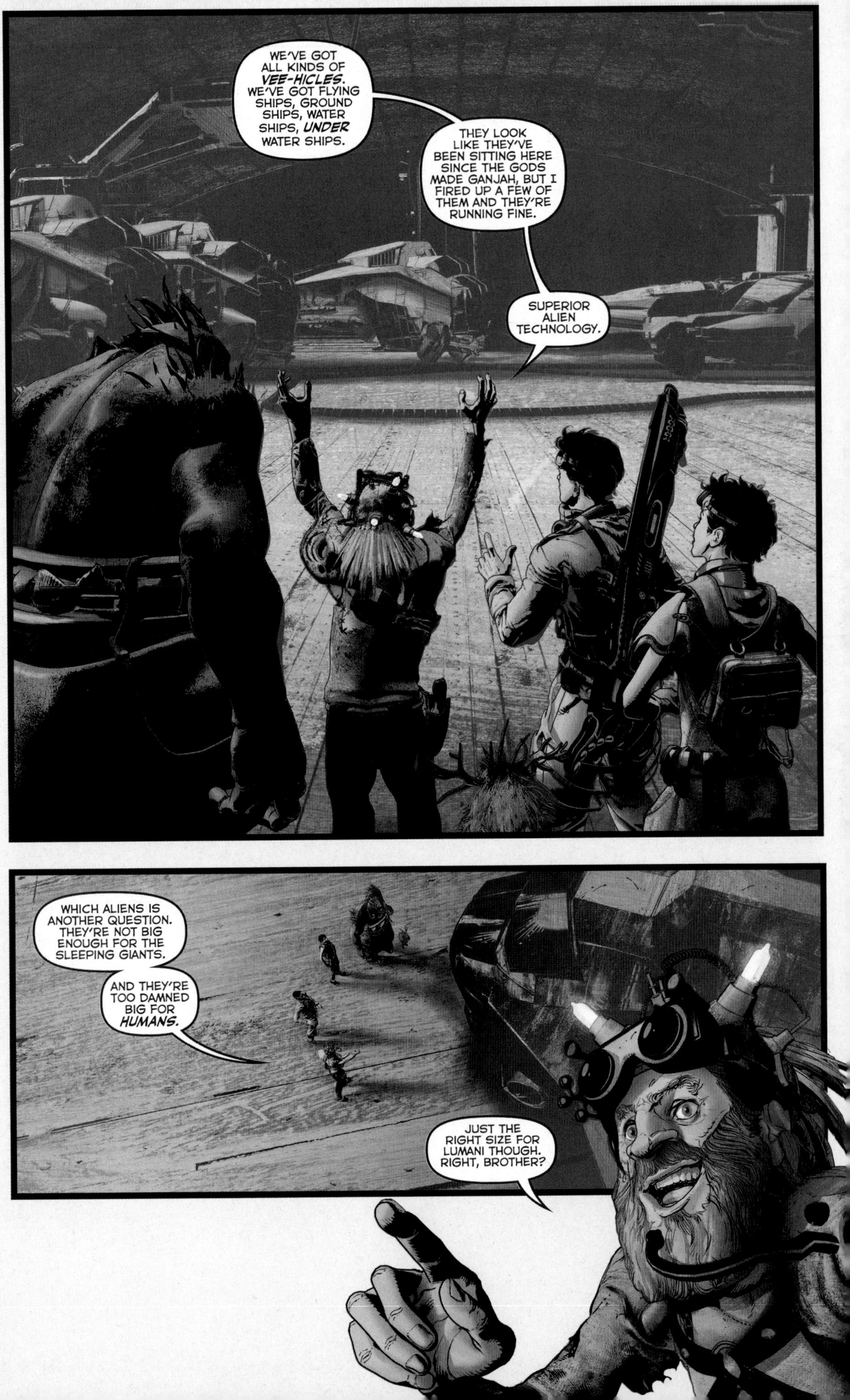

WE'VE GOT ALL KINDS OF *VEE-HICLES*. WE'VE GOT FLYING SHIPS, GROUND SHIPS, WATER SHIPS, *UNDER* WATER SHIPS.
THEY LOOK LIKE THEY'VE BEEN SITTING HERE SINCE THE GODS MADE GANJAH, BUT I FIRED UP A FEW OF THEM AND THEY'RE RUNNING FINE.
SUPERIOR ALIEN TECHNOLOGY.
WHICH ALIENS IS ANOTHER QUESTION. THEY'RE NOT BIG ENOUGH FOR THE SLEEPING GIANTS.
AND THEY'RE TOO DAMNED BIG FOR *HUMANS.*
JUST THE RIGHT SIZE FOR LUMANI THOUGH. RIGHT, BROTHER?

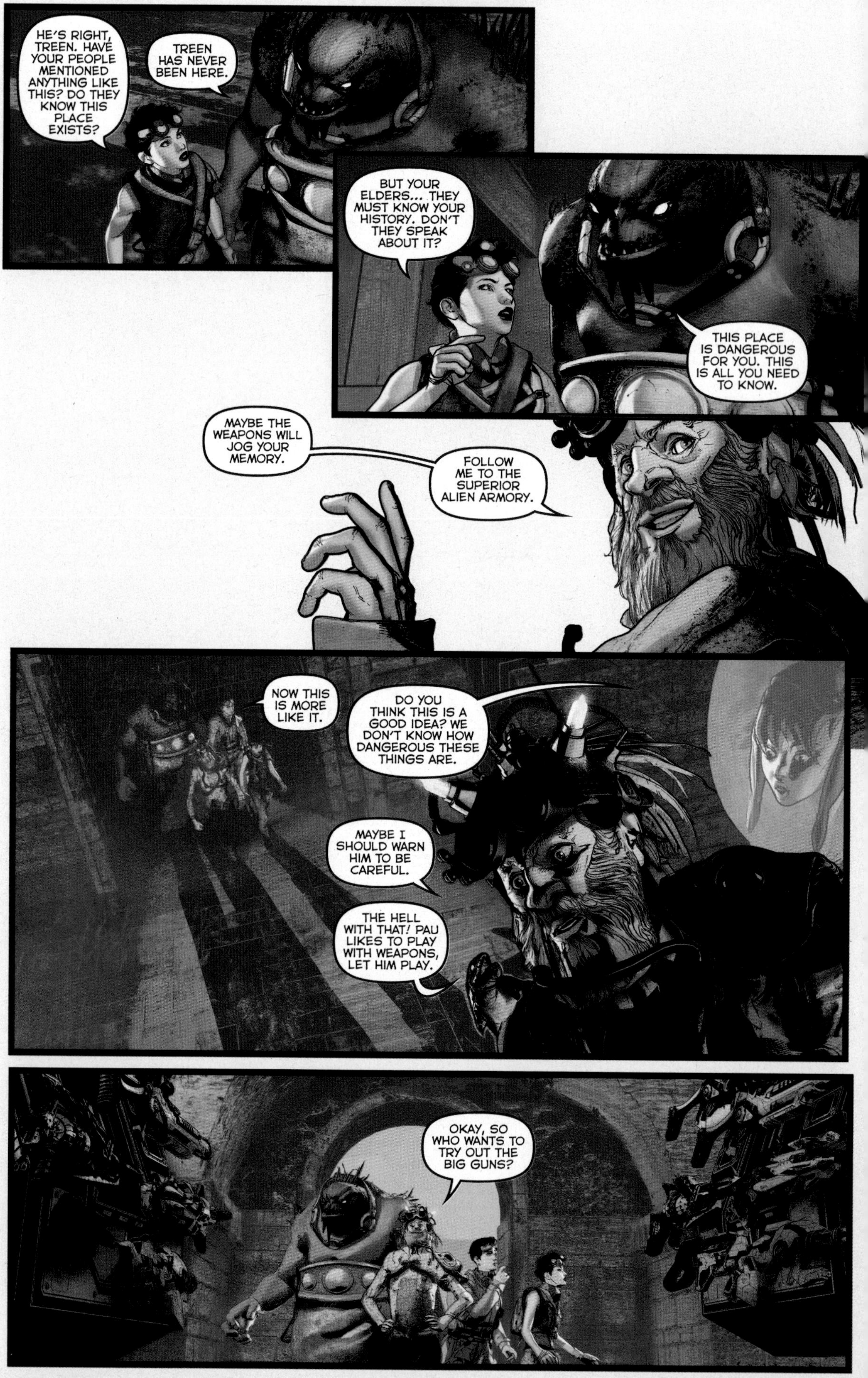
HE'S RIGHT, TREEN. HAVE YOUR PEOPLE MENTIONED ANYTHING LIKE THIS? DO THEY KNOW THIS PLACE EXISTS?
TREEN HAS NEVER BEEN HERE.
BUT YOUR ELDERS... THEY MUST KNOW YOUR HISTORY. DON'T THEY SPEAK ABOUT IT?
THIS PLACE IS DANGEROUS FOR YOU. THIS IS ALL YOU NEED TO KNOW.
MAYBE THE WEAPONS WILL JOG YOUR MEMORY.
FOLLOW ME TO THE SUPERIOR ALIEN ARMORY.
NOW THIS IS MORE LIKE IT.
DO YOU THINK THIS IS A GOOD IDEA? WE DON'T KNOW HOW DANGEROUS THESE THINGS ARE.
MAYBE I SHOULD WARN HIM TO BE CAREFUL.
THE HELL WITH THAT! PAU LIKES TO PLAY WITH WEAPONS, LET HIM PLAY.
OKAY, SO WHO WANTS TO TRY OUT THE BIG GUNS?

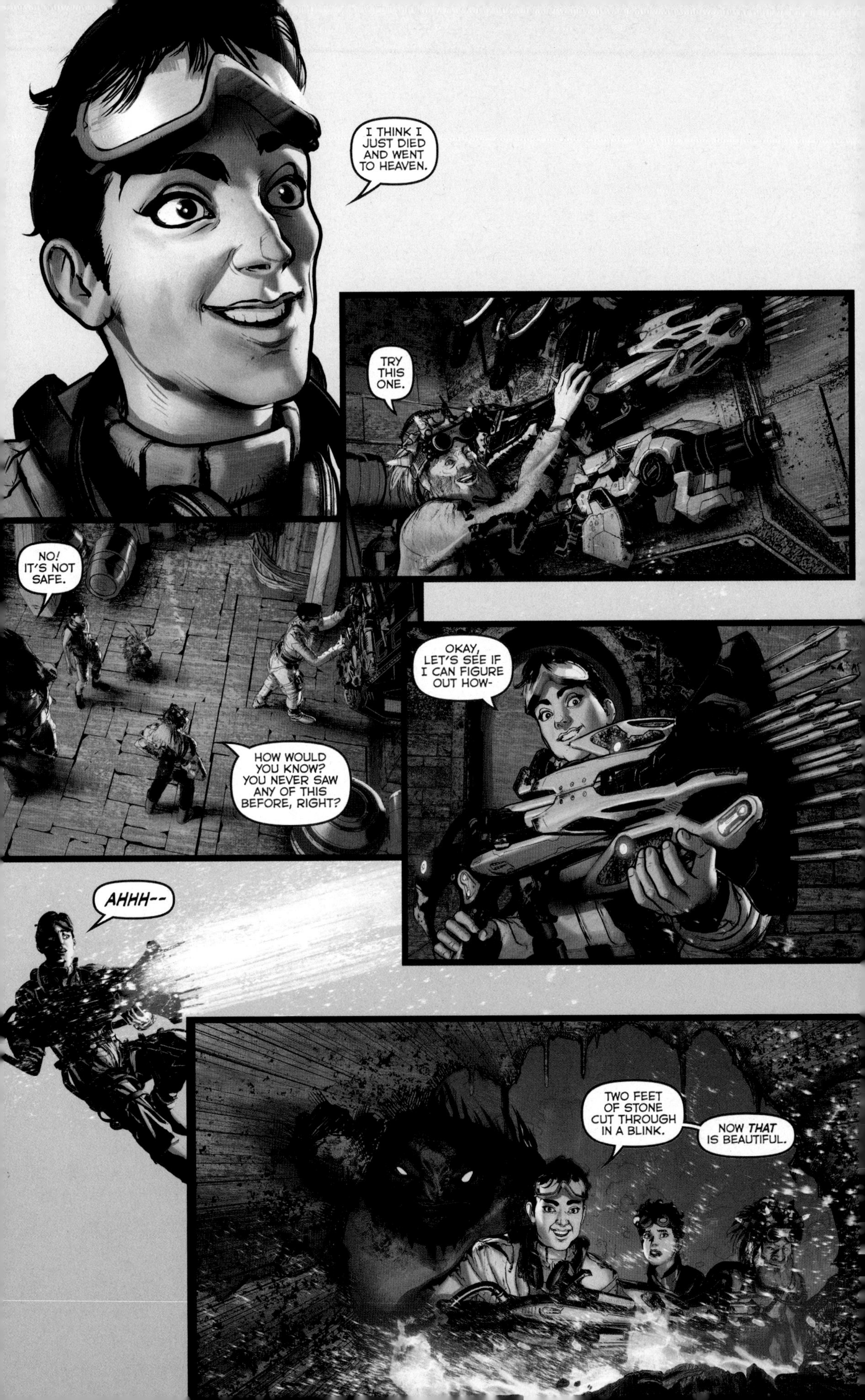
I THINK I JUST DIED AND WENT TO HEAVEN.
TRY THIS ONE.
NO! IT'S NOT SAFE.
HOW WOULD YOU KNOW? YOU NEVER SAW ANY OF THIS BEFORE, RIGHT?
OKAY, LET'S SEE IF I CAN FIGURE OUT HOW-
AHHH--
TWO FEET OF STONE CUT THROUGH IN A BLINK.
NOW THAT IS BEAUTIFUL.

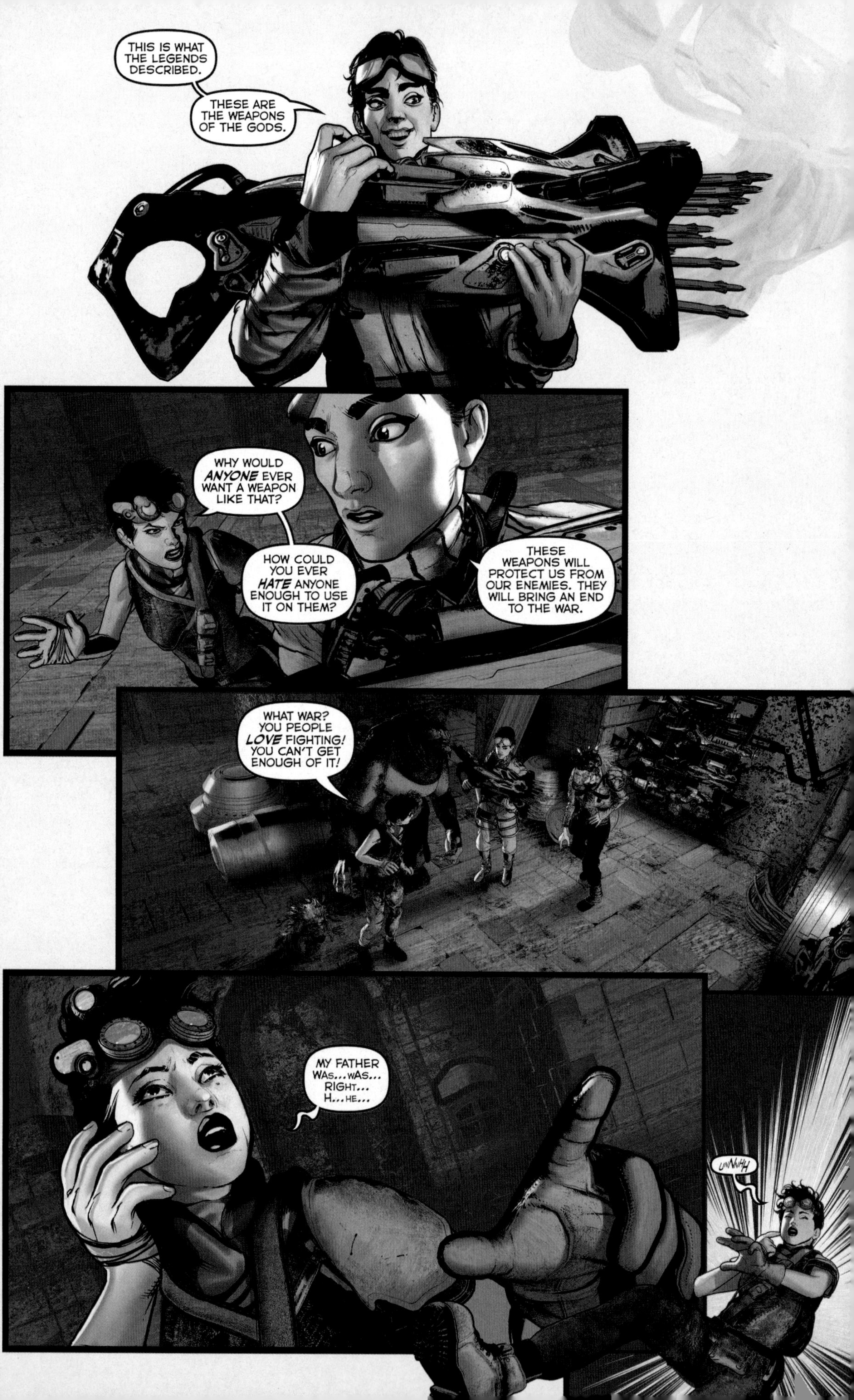
THIS IS WHAT THE LEGENDS DESCRIBED.
THESE ARE THE WEAPONS OF THE GODS.
WHY WOULD ANYONE EVER WANT A WEAPON LIKE THAT?
HOW COULD YOU EVER HATE ANYONE ENOUGH TO USE IT ON THEM?
THESE WEAPONS WILL PROTECT US FROM OUR ENEMIES. THEY WILL BRING AN END TO THE WAR.
WHAT WAR? YOU PEOPLE LOVE FIGHTING! YOU CAN'T GET ENOUGH OF IT!
MY FATHER WAS...WAS... RIGHT... H...HE...
UNNNHH

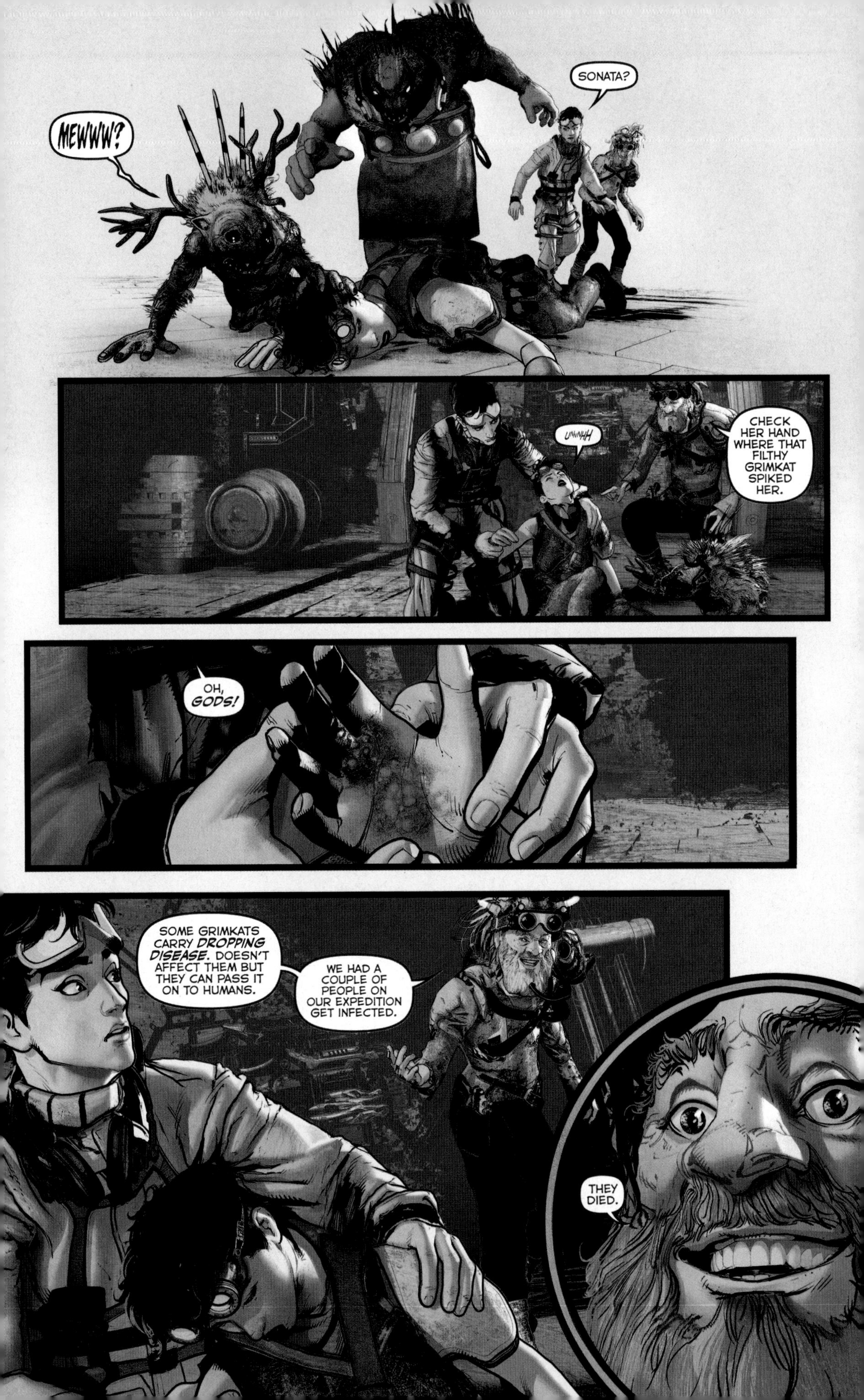
MEWWW?
SONATA?
UNNNHH
CHECK HER HAND WHERE THAT FILTHY GRIMKAT SPIKED HER.
OH, GODS!
SOME GRIMKATS CARRY DROPPING DISEASE. DOESN'T AFFECT THEM BUT THEY CAN PASS IT ON TO HUMANS.
WE HAD A COUPLE OF PEOPLE ON OUR EXPEDITION GET INFECTED.
THEY DIED.

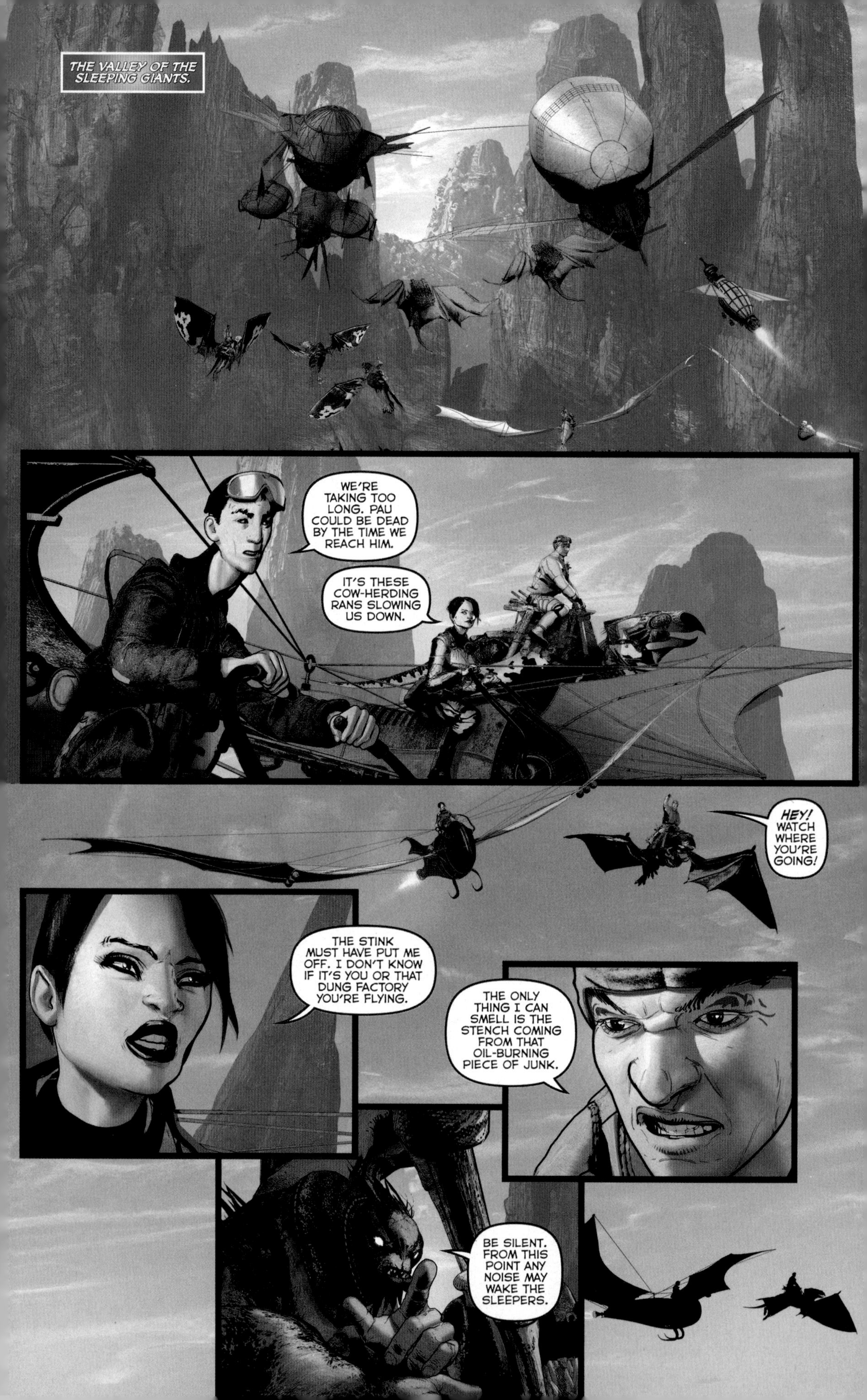
THE VALLEY OF THE SLEEPING GIANTS.
WE'RE TAKING TOO LONG. PAU COULD BE DEAD BY THE TIME WE REACH HIM.
IT'S THESE COW-HERDING RANS SLOWING US DOWN.
HEY! WATCH WHERE YOU'RE GOING!
THE STINK MUST HAVE PUT ME OFF. I DON'T KNOW IF IT'S YOU OR THAT DUNG FACTORY YOU'RE FLYING.
THE ONLY THING I CAN SMELL IS THE STENCH COMING FROM THAT OIL-BURNING PIECE OF JUNK.
BE SILENT. FROM THIS POINT ANY NOISE MAY WAKE THE SLEEPERS.

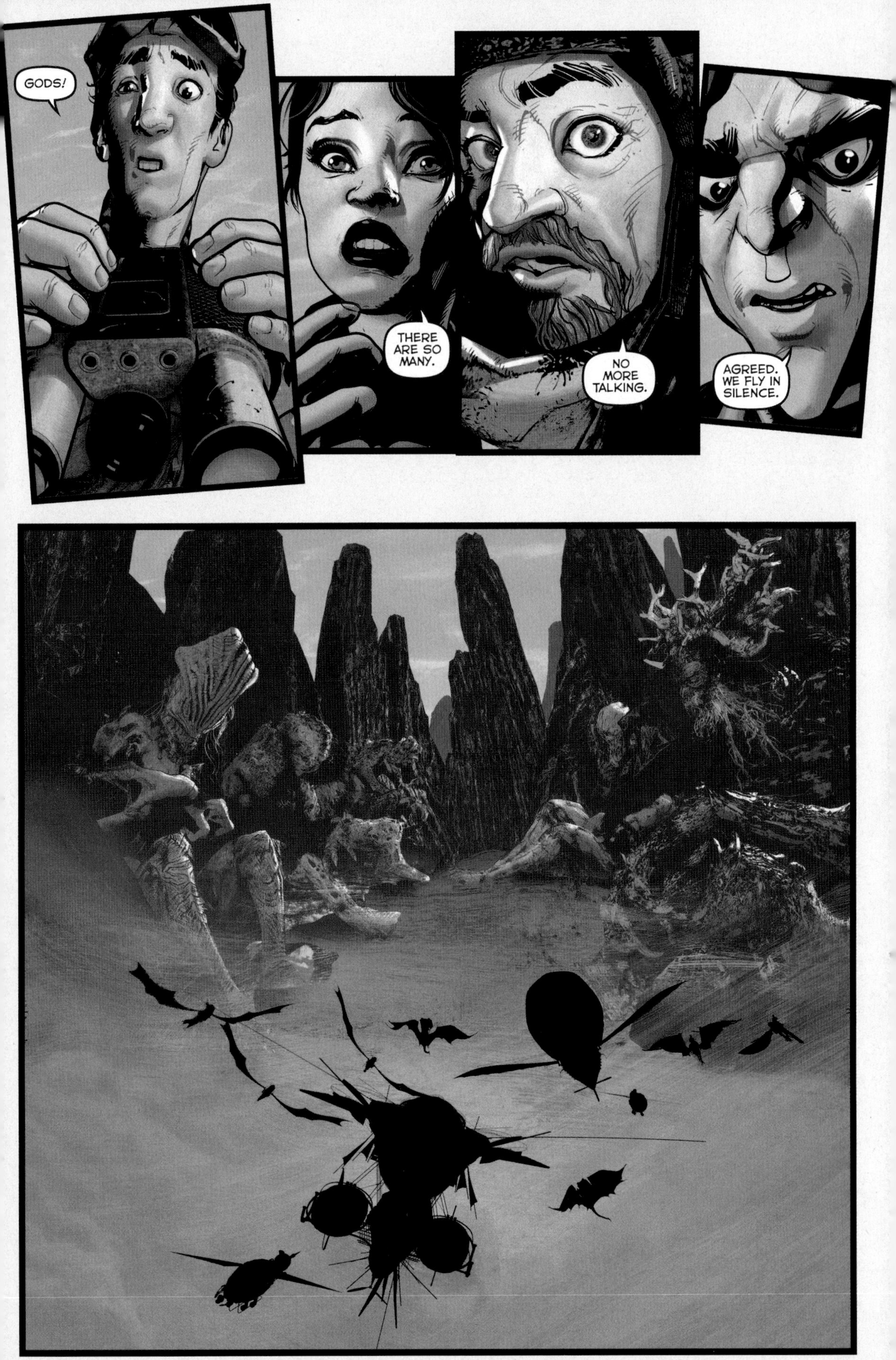
GODS!
THERE ARE SO MANY.
NO MORE TALKING.
AGREED. WE FLY IN SILENCE.

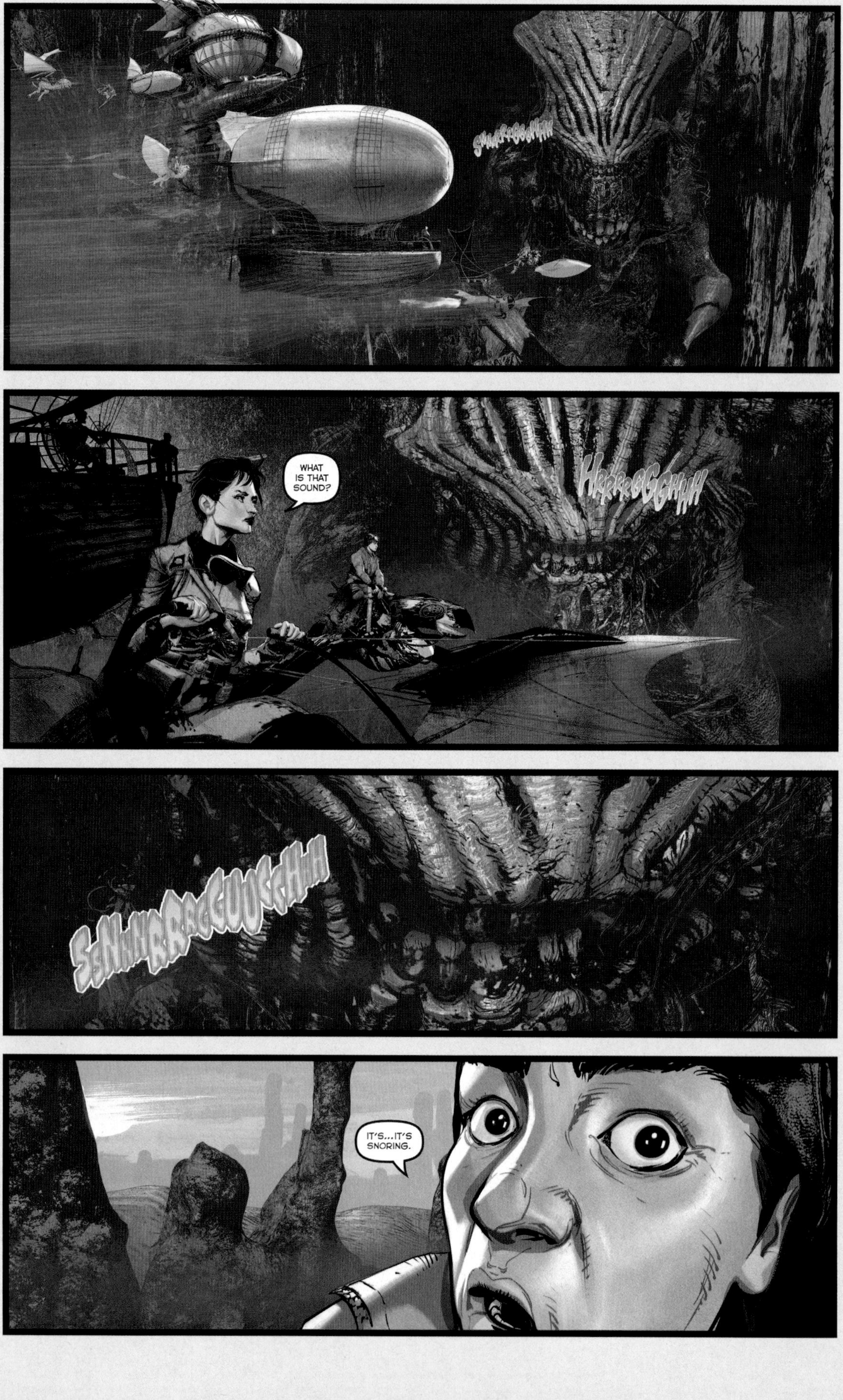
WHAT IS THAT SOUND?
IT'S...IT'S SNORING.

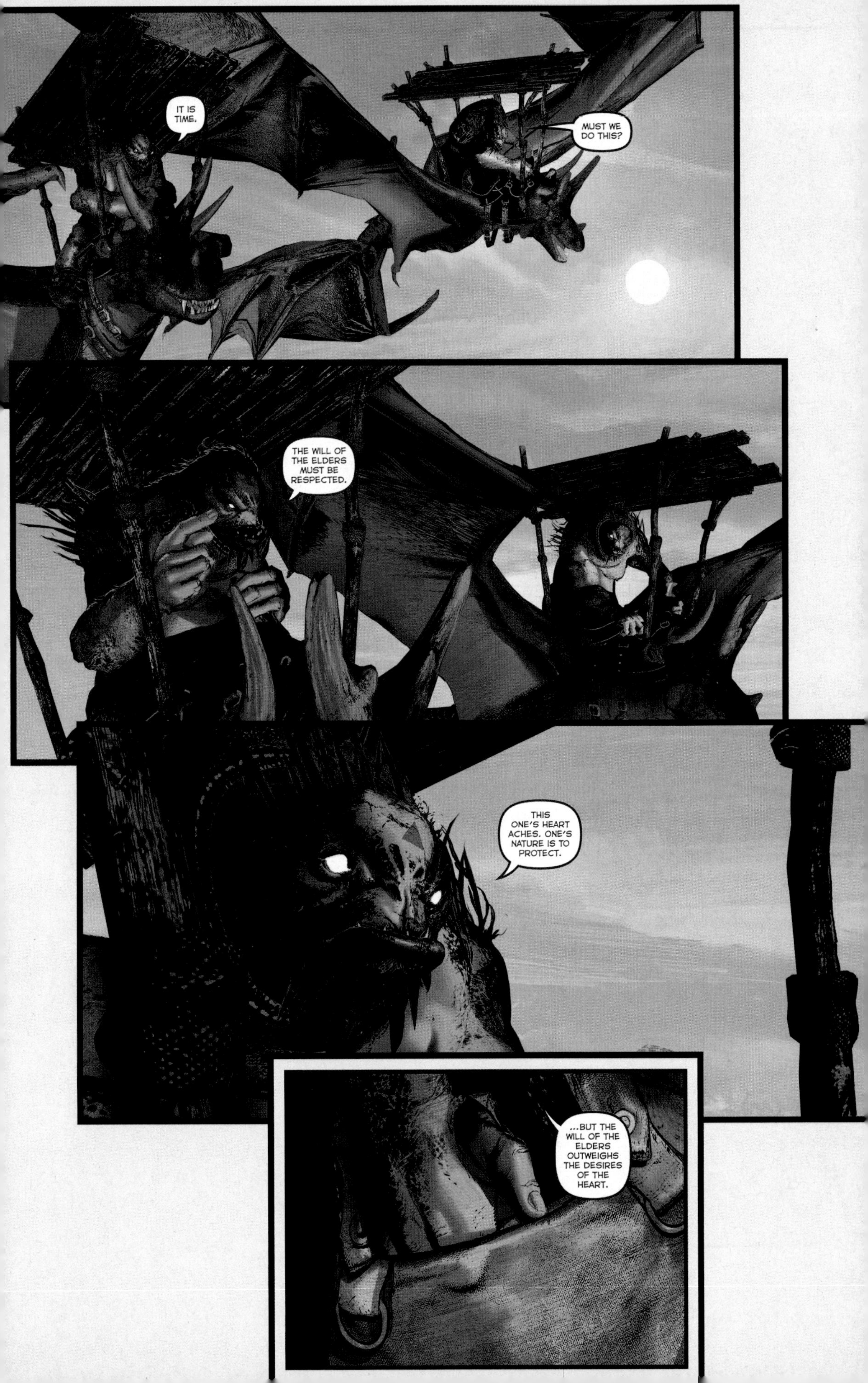
IT IS TIME.
MUST WE DO THIS?
THE WILL OF THE ELDERS MUST BE RESPECTED.
THIS ONE'S HEART ACHES. ONE'S NATURE IS TO PROTECT.
...BUT THE WILL OF THE ELDERS OUTWEIGHS THE DESIRES OF THE HEART.

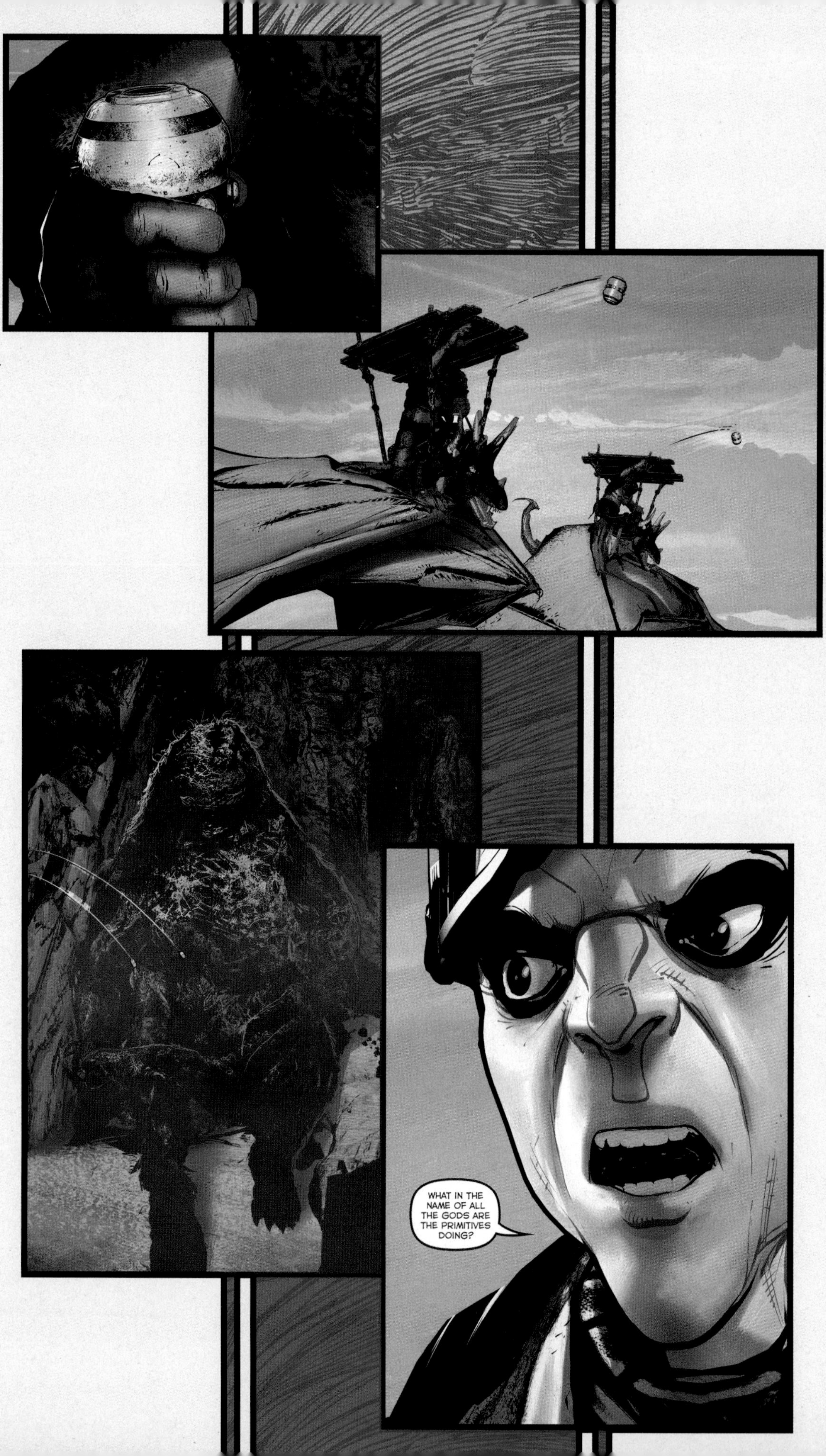
WHAT IN THE NAME OF ALL THE GODS ARE THE PRIMITIVES DOING?

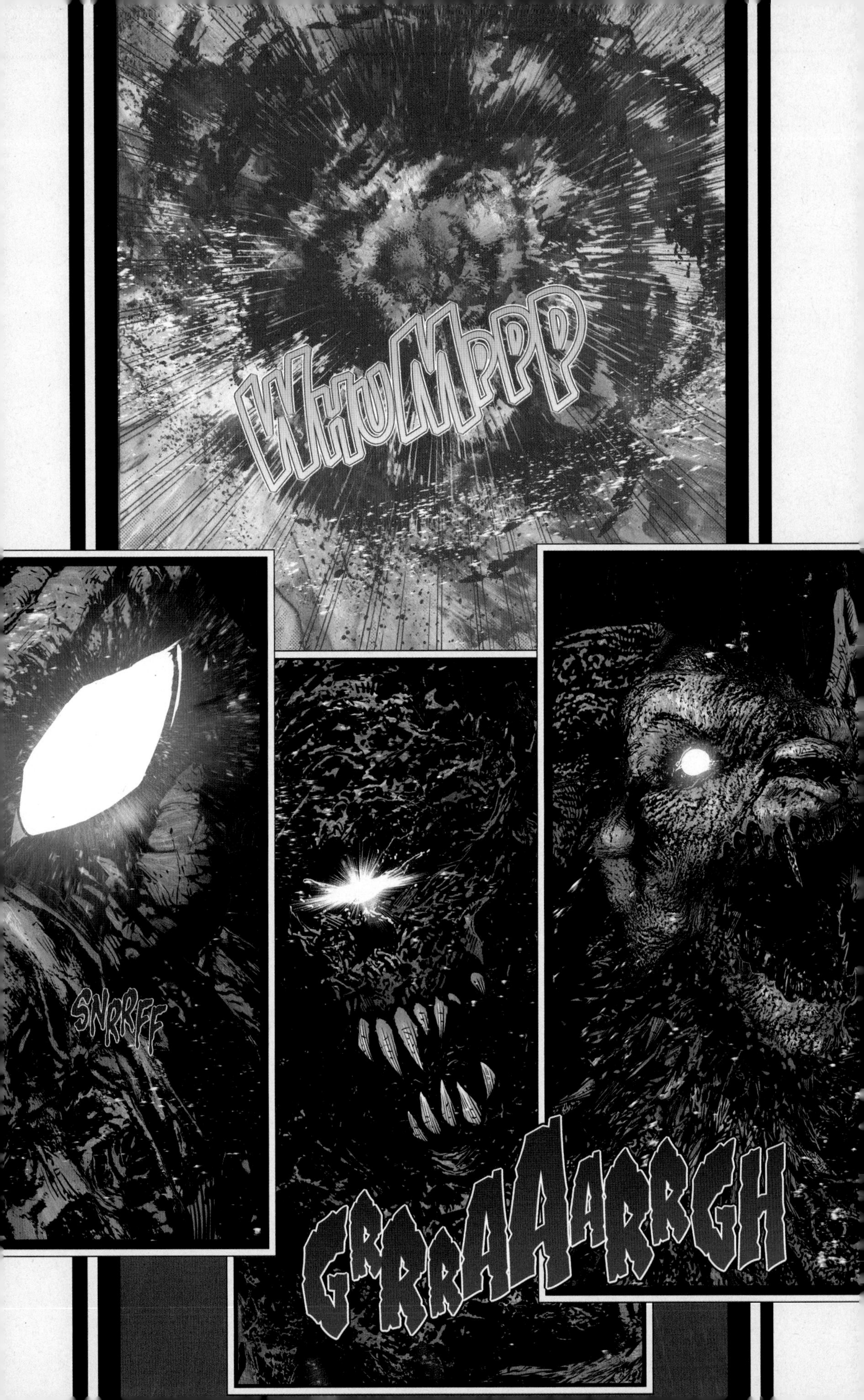
WHOMPPP
SNRFF
GRRRAAARRGH

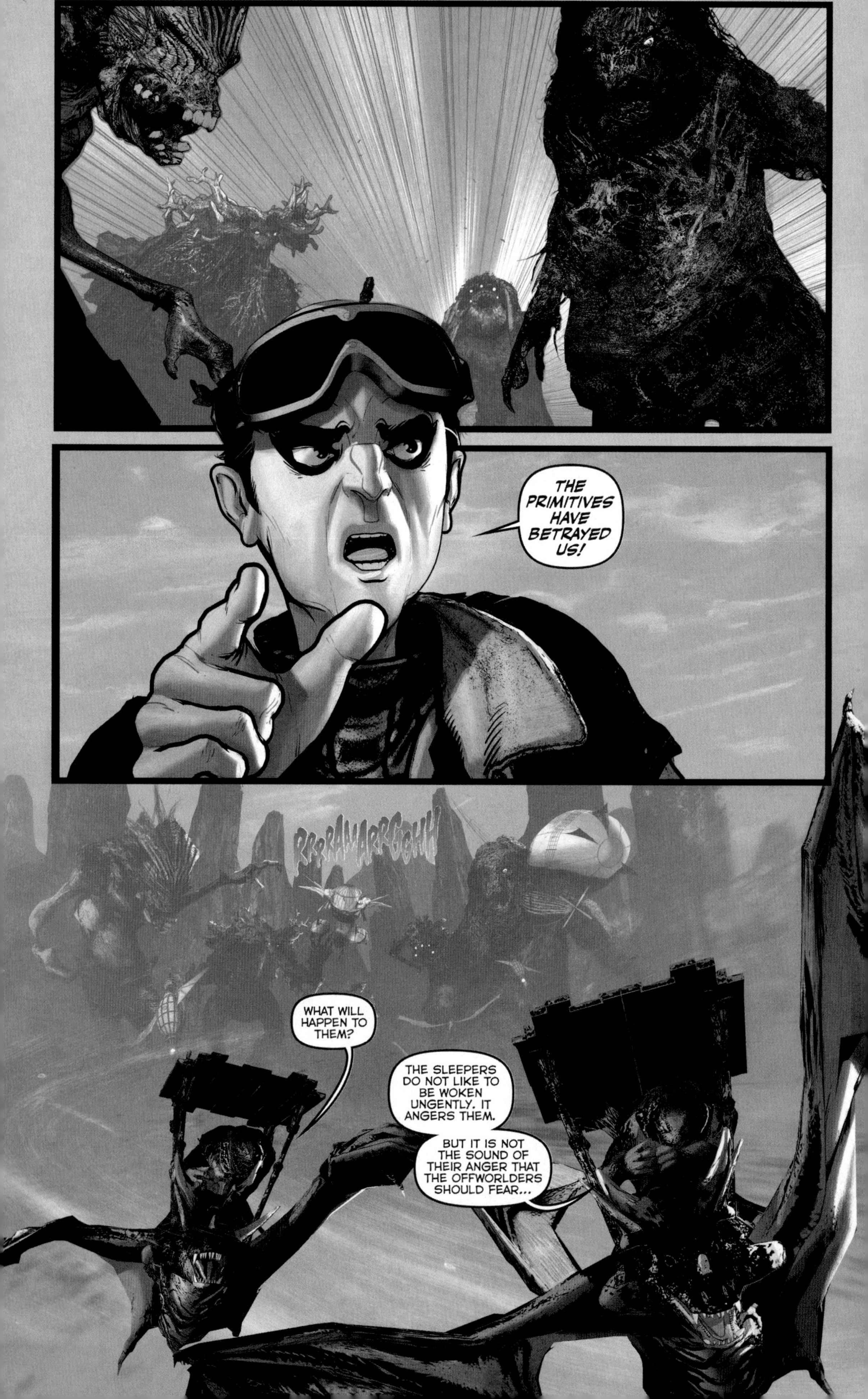
THE PRIMITIVES HAVE BETRAYED US!
RRRRAMARRGGHH
WHAT WILL HAPPEN TO THEM?
THE SLEEPERS DO NOT LIKE TO BE WOKEN UNGENTLY. IT ANGERS THEM.
BUT IT IS NOT THE SOUND OF THEIR ANGER THAT THE OFFWORLDERS SHOULD FEAR...

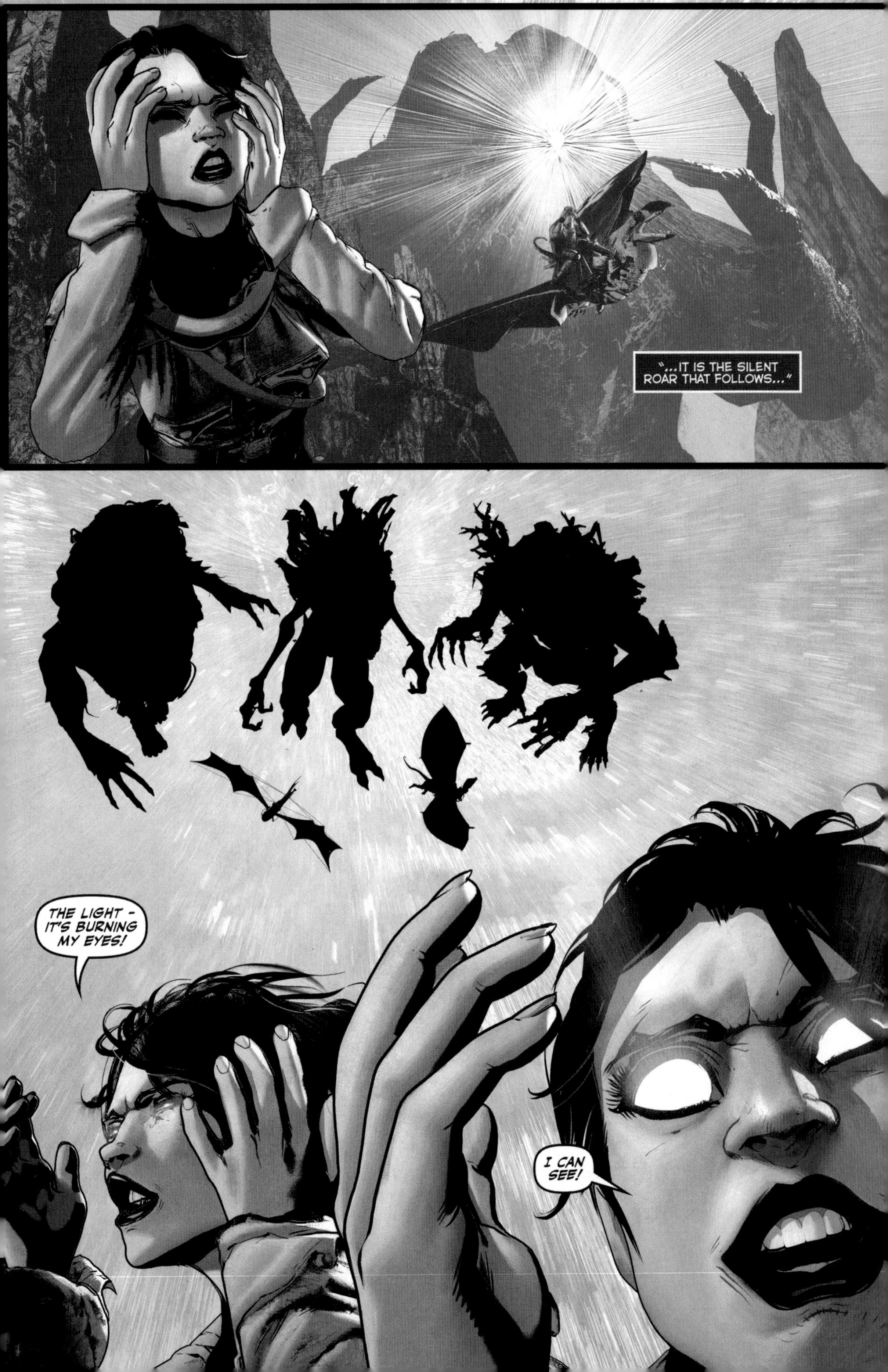
"...IT IS THE SILENT ROAR THAT FOLLOWS..."
THE LIGHT - IT'S BURNING MY EYES!
I CAN SEE!

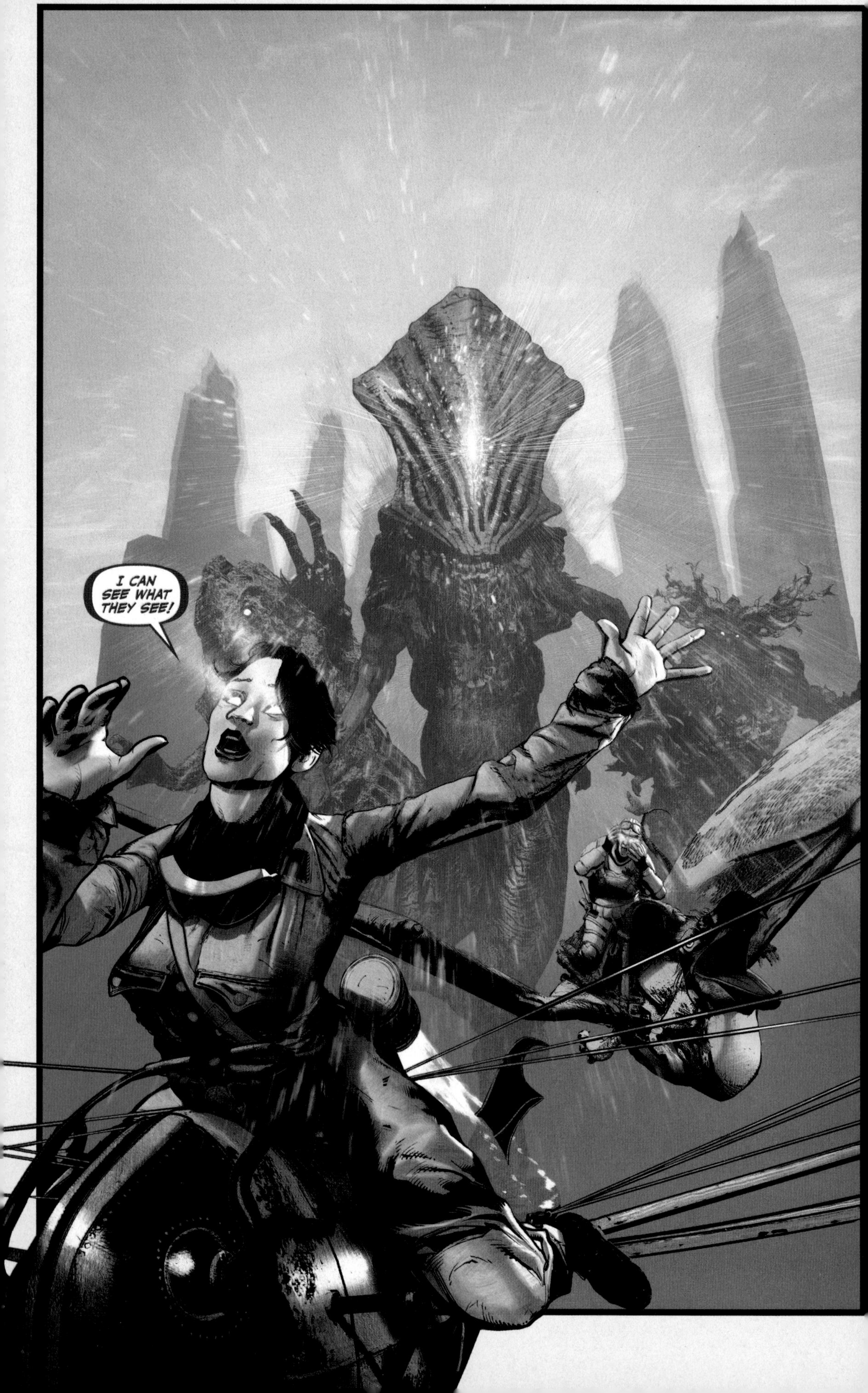
I CAN SEE WHAT THEY SEE!

Issue #5 Cover A

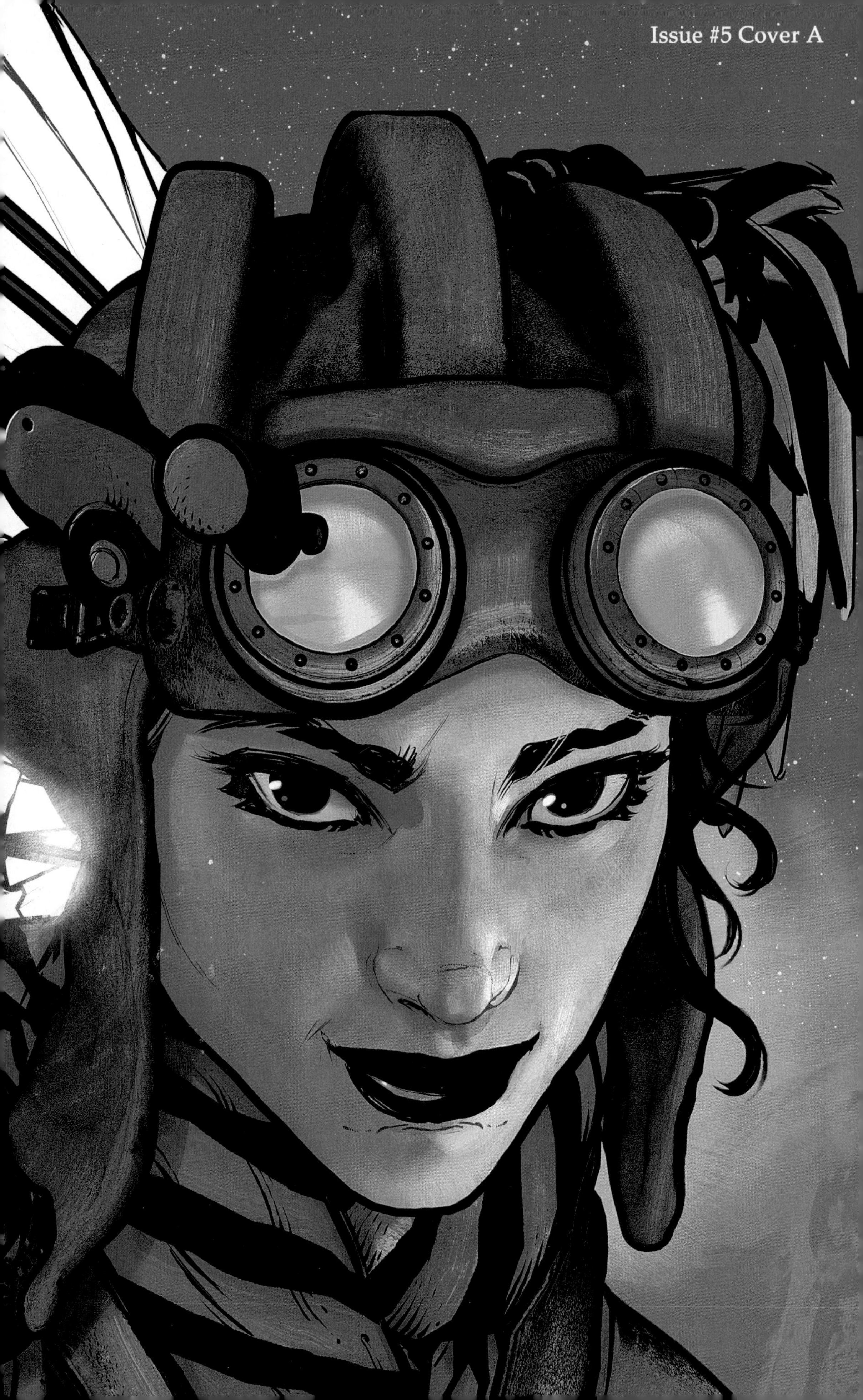

Issue #5 Cover B

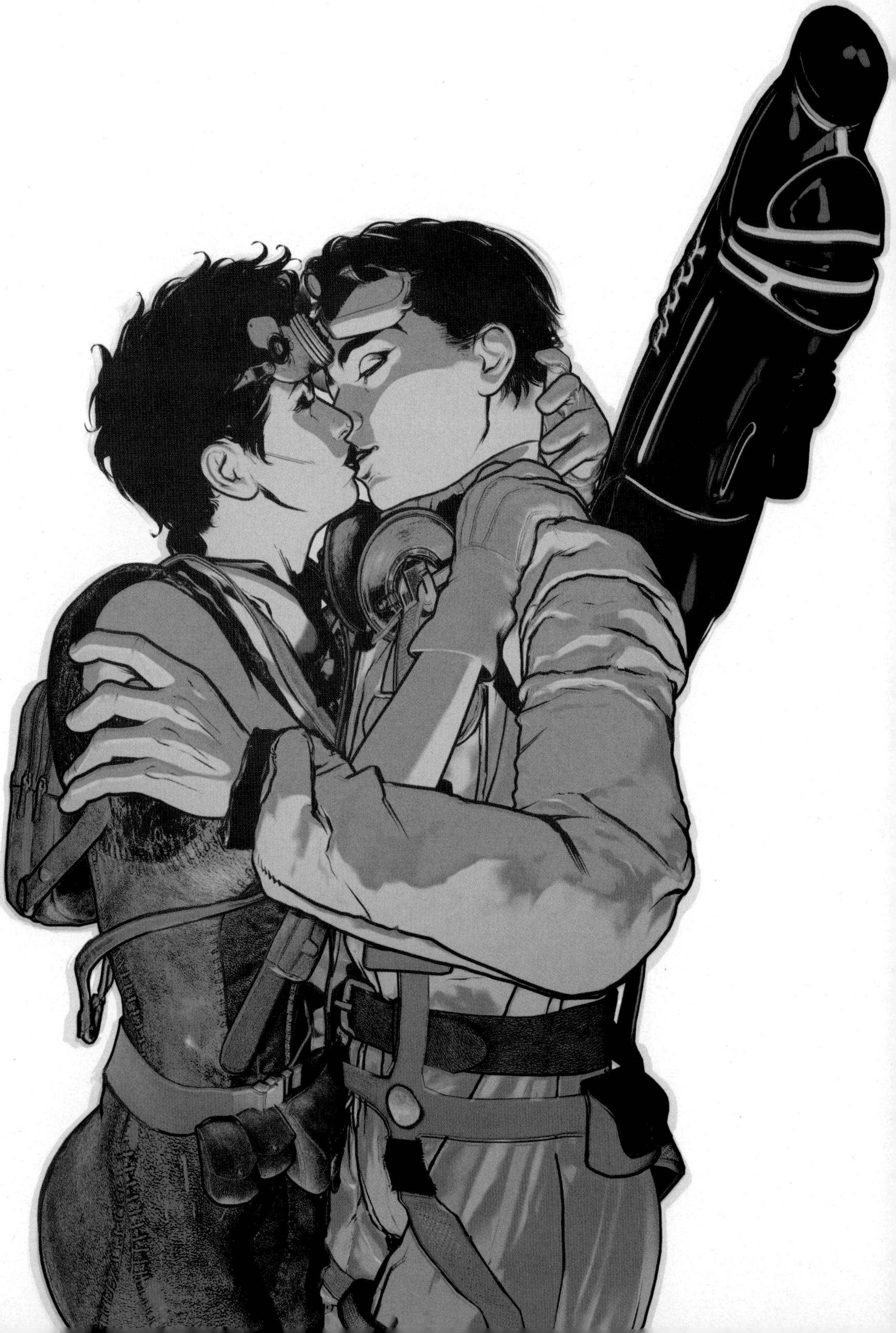

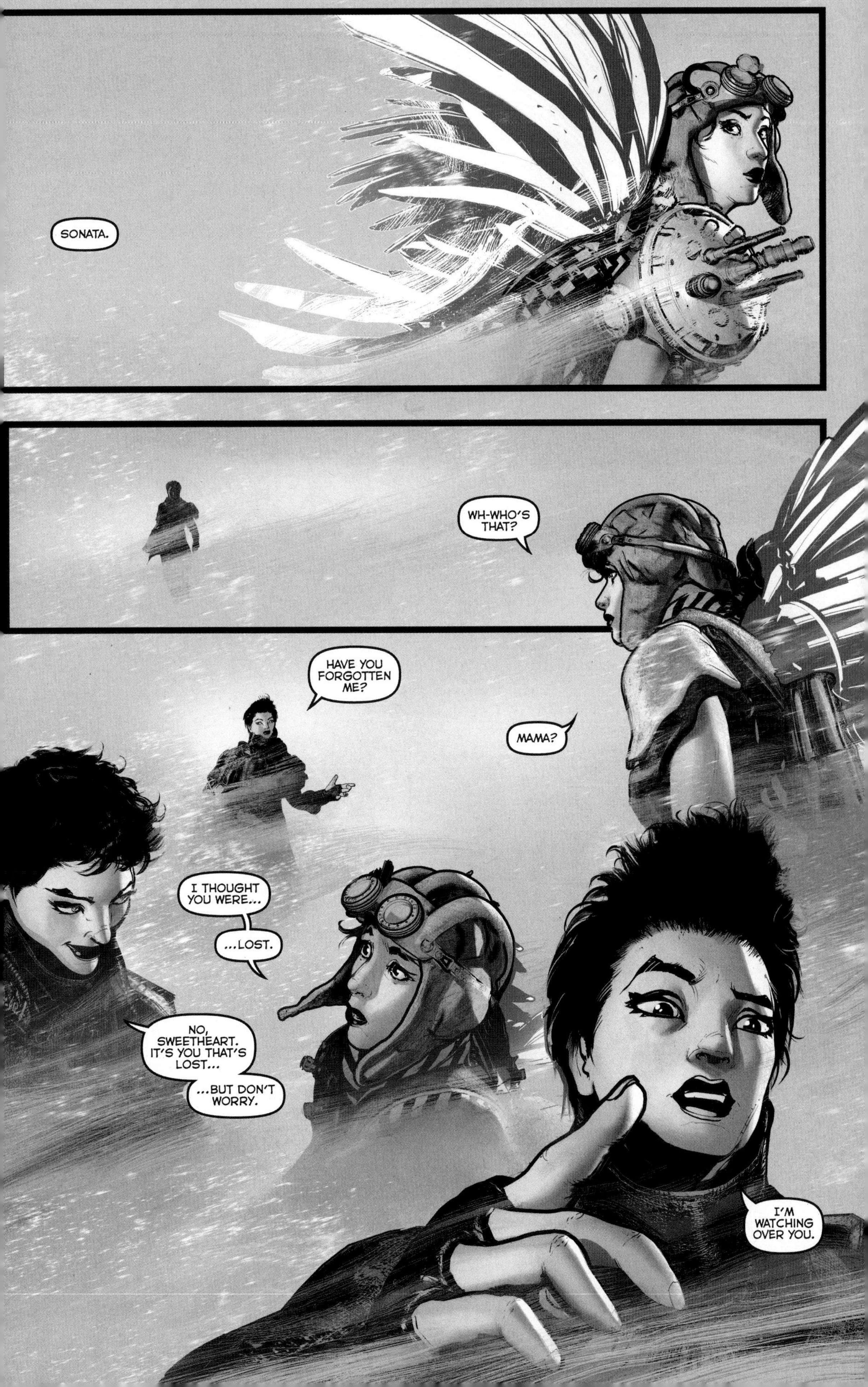
SONATA.
WH-WHO'S THAT?
HAVE YOU FORGOTTEN ME?
MAMA?
I THOUGHT YOU WERE...
...LOST.
NO, SWEETHEART. IT'S YOU THAT'S LOST...
...BUT DON'T WORRY.
I'M WATCHING OVER YOU.

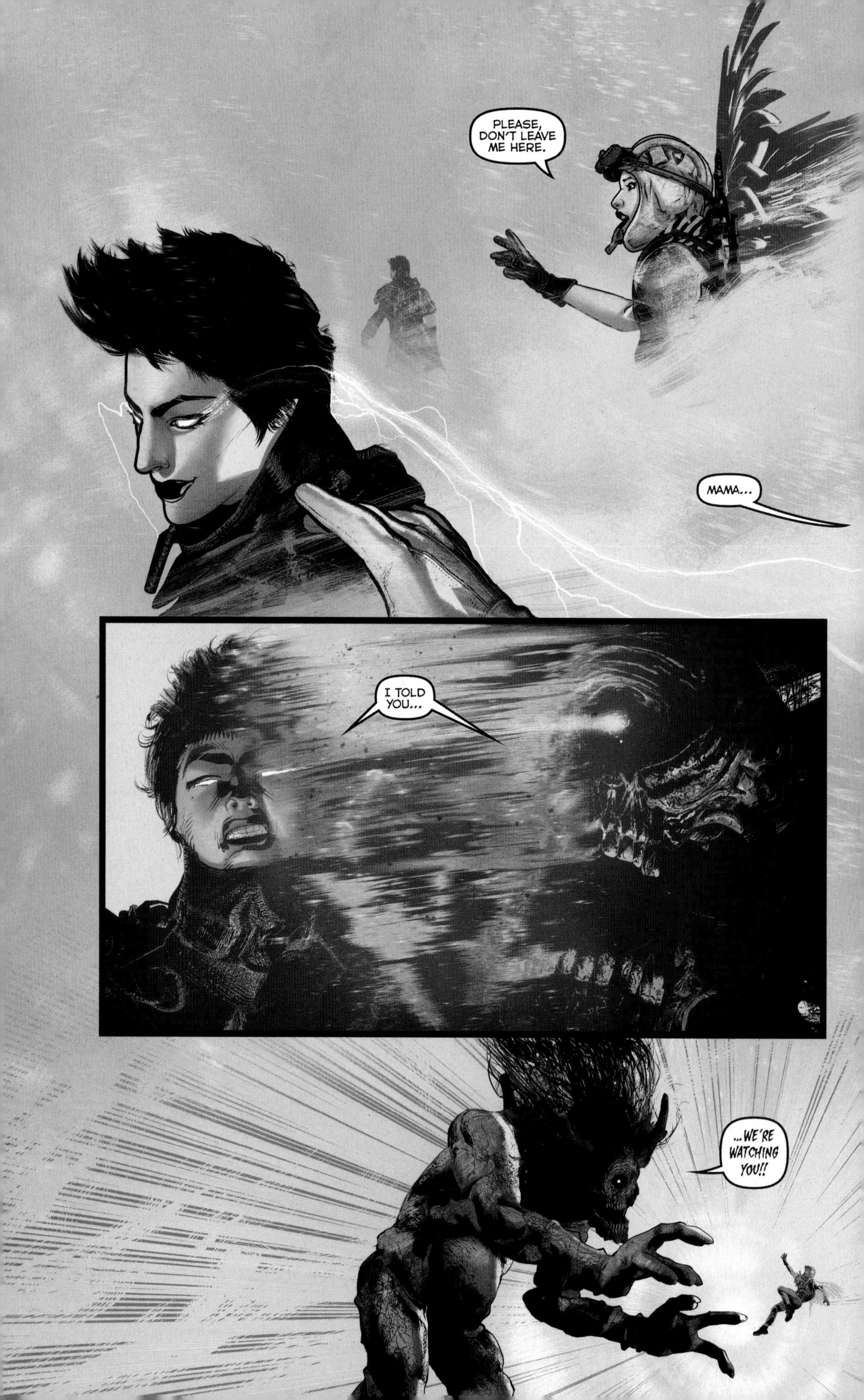
PLEASE, DON'T LEAVE ME HERE.
MAMA...
I TOLD YOU...
...WE'RE WATCHING YOU!!

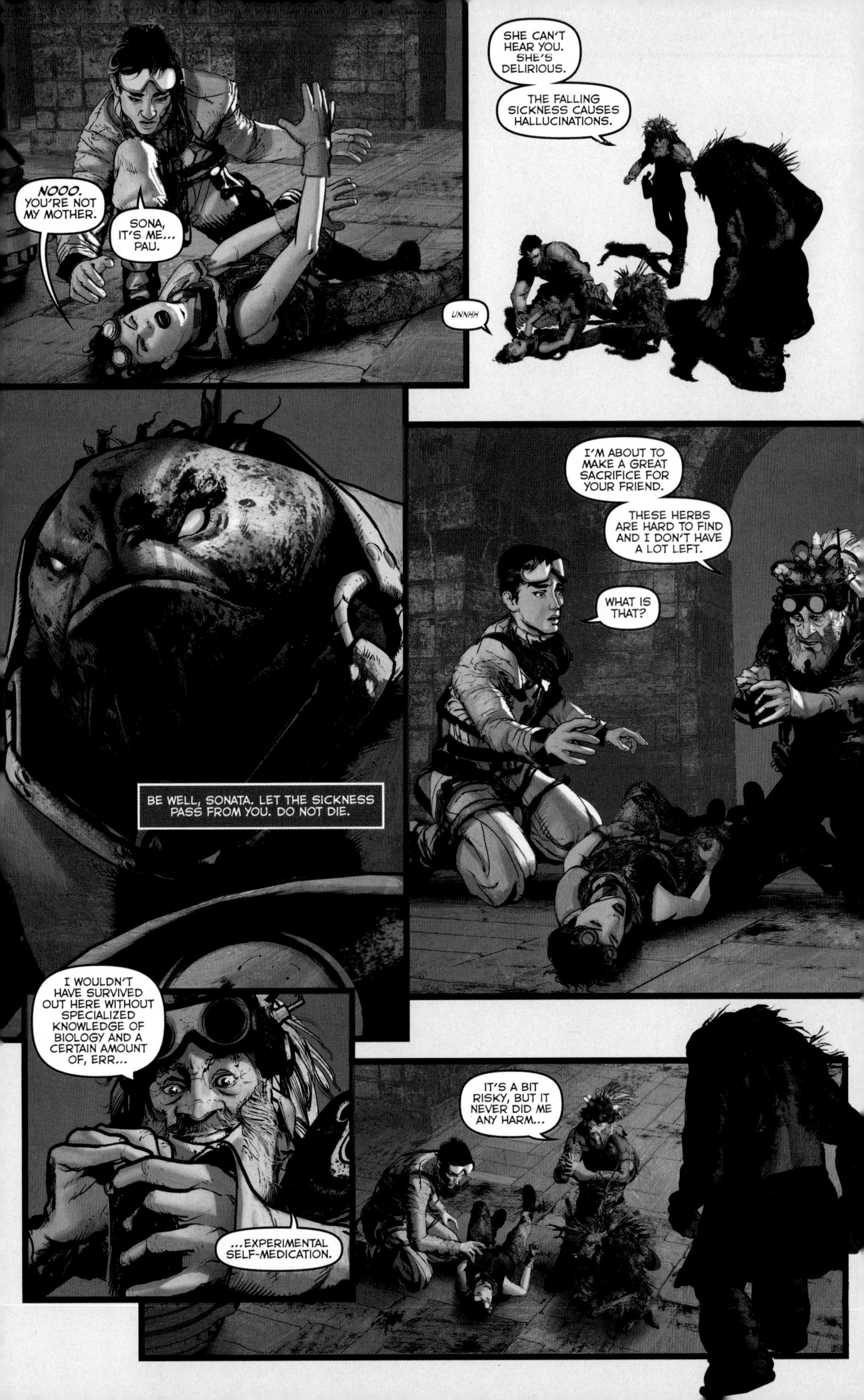
NOOO. YOU'RE NOT MY MOTHER.
SONA, IT'S ME... PAU.
SHE CAN'T HEAR YOU. SHE'S DELIRIOUS.
THE FALLING SICKNESS CAUSES HALLUCINATIONS.
UNNHH
BE WELL, SONATA. LET THE SICKNESS PASS FROM YOU. DO NOT DIE.
I'M ABOUT TO MAKE A GREAT SACRIFICE FOR YOUR FRIEND.
THESE HERBS ARE HARD TO FIND AND I DON'T HAVE A LOT LEFT.
WHAT IS THAT?
I WOULDN'T HAVE SURVIVED OUT HERE WITHOUT SPECIALIZED KNOWLEDGE OF BIOLOGY AND A CERTAIN AMOUNT OF, ERR...
...EXPERIMENTAL SELF-MEDICATION.
IT'S A BIT RISKY, BUT IT NEVER DID ME ANY HARM...

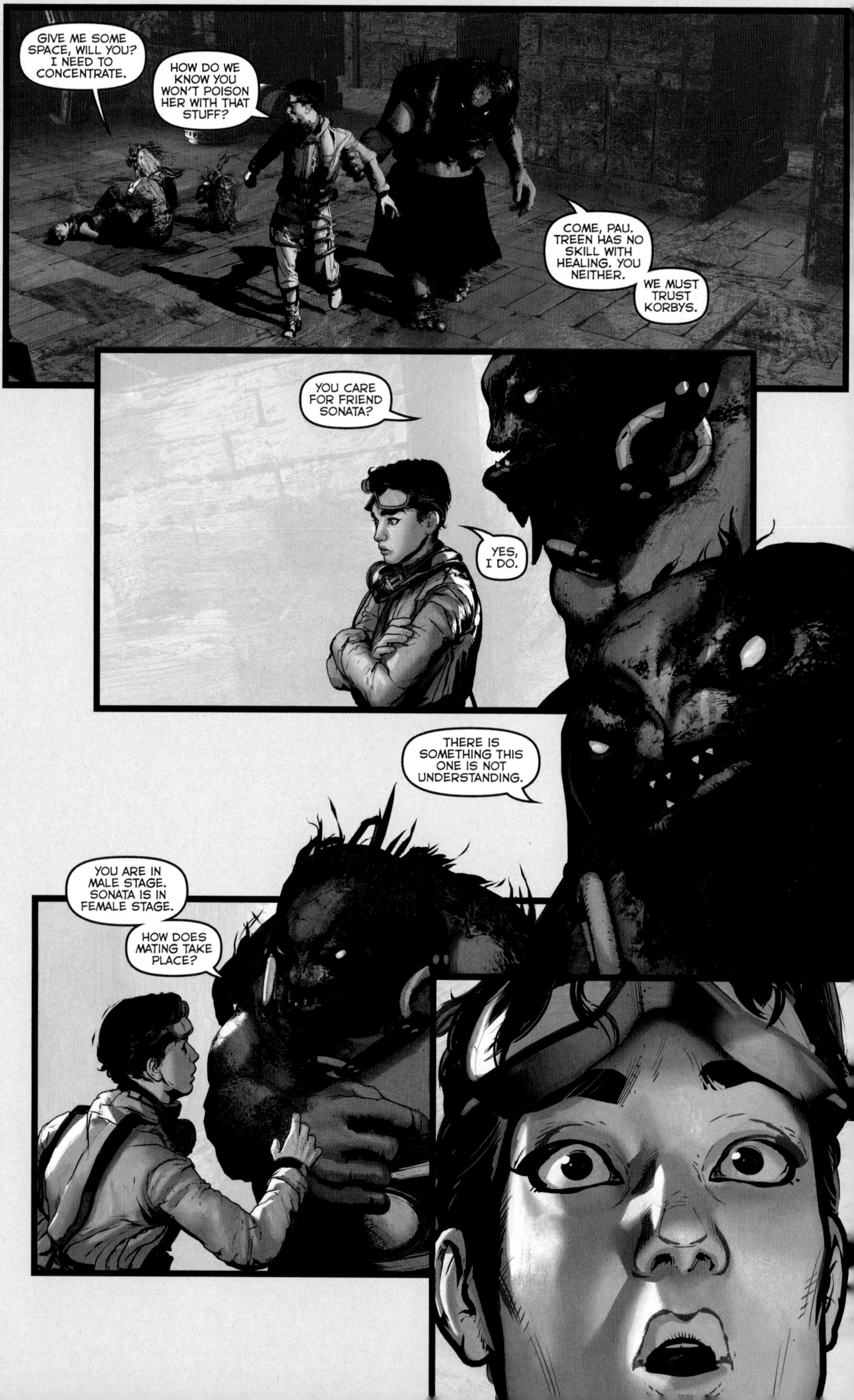
GIVE ME SOME SPACE, WILL YOU? I NEED TO CONCENTRATE.
HOW DO WE KNOW YOU WON'T POISON HER WITH THAT STUFF?
COME, PAU. TREEN HAS NO SKILL WITH HEALING. YOU NEITHER.
WE MUST TRUST KORBYS.
YOU CARE FOR FRIEND SONATA?
YES, I DO.
THERE IS SOMETHING THIS ONE IS NOT UNDERSTANDING.
YOU ARE IN MALE STAGE. SONATA IS IN FEMALE STAGE.
HOW DOES MATING TAKE PLACE?

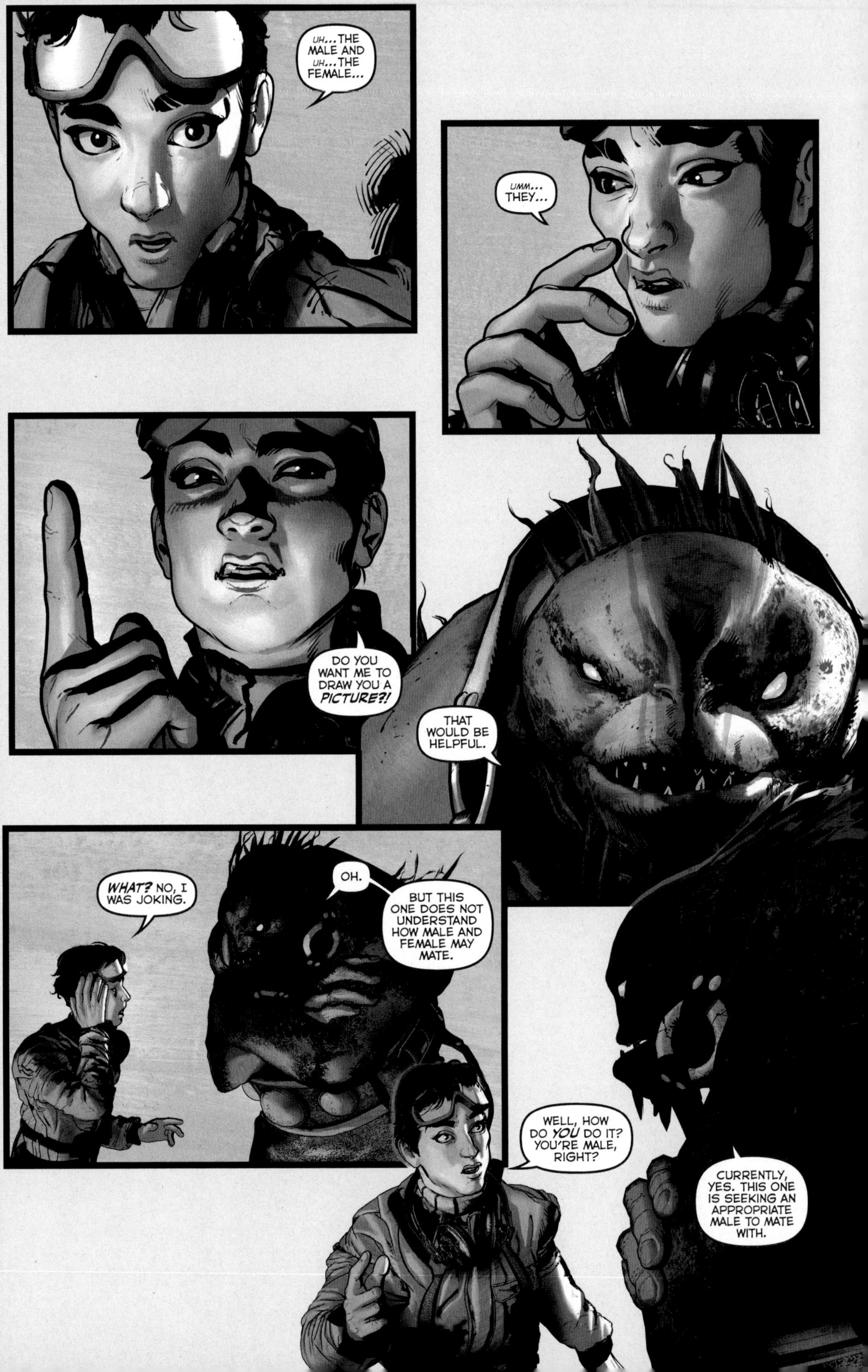
UH... THE MALE AND UH... THE FEMALE...
UMM... THEY...
DO YOU WANT ME TO DRAW YOU A PICTURE?!
THAT WOULD BE HELPFUL.
WHAT? NO, I WAS JOKING.
OH.
BUT THIS ONE DOES NOT UNDERSTAND HOW MALE AND FEMALE MAY MATE.
WELL, HOW DO YOU DO IT? YOU'RE MALE, RIGHT?
CURRENTLY, YES. THIS ONE IS SEEKING AN APPROPRIATE MALE TO MATE WITH.

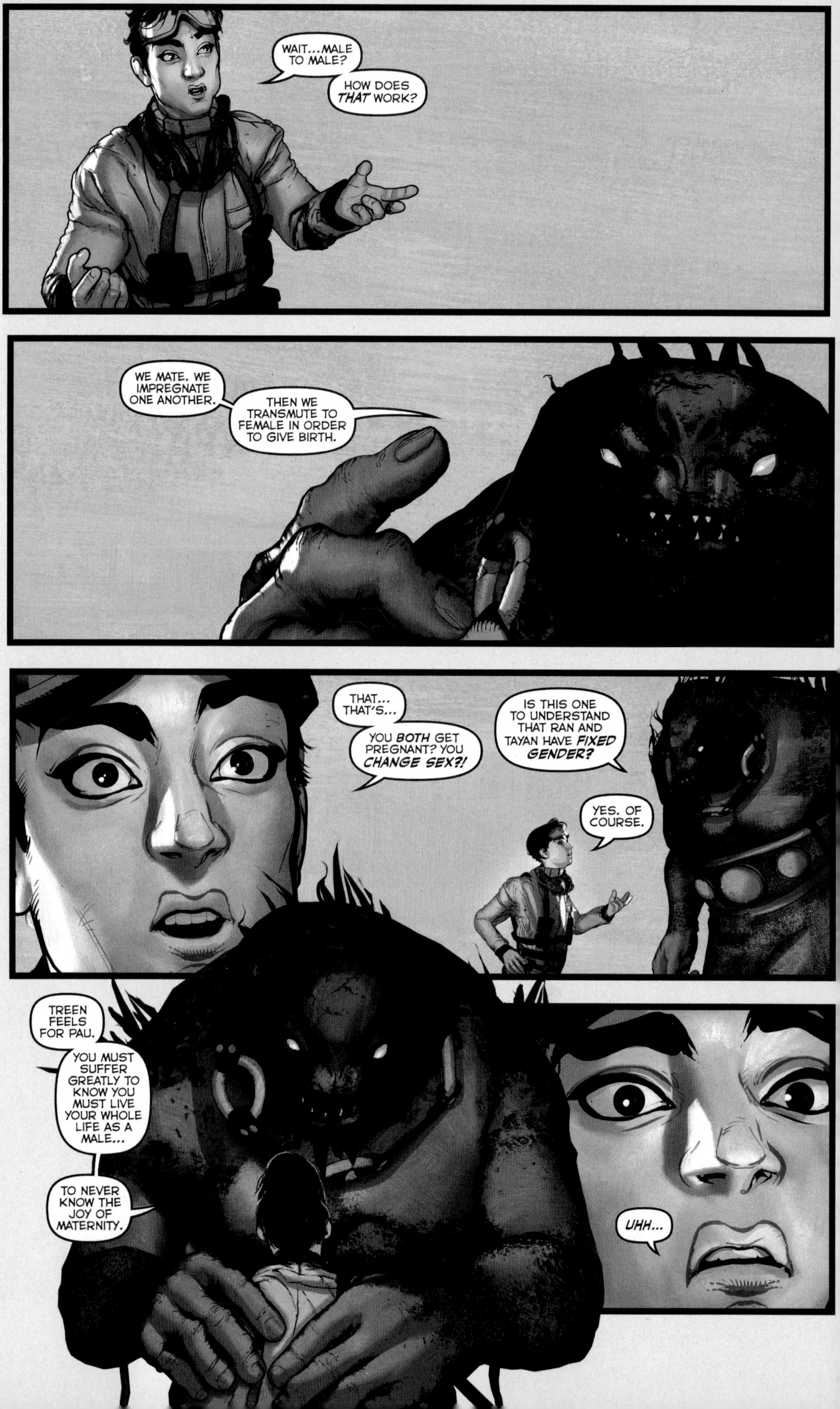
WAIT... MALE TO MALE?
HOW DOES *THAT* WORK?
WE MATE. WE IMPREGNATE ONE ANOTHER.
THEN WE TRANSMUTE TO FEMALE IN ORDER TO GIVE BIRTH.
THAT... THAT'S...
YOU *BOTH* GET PREGNANT? YOU *CHANGE SEX?!*
IS THIS ONE TO UNDERSTAND THAT RAN AND TAYAN HAVE *FIXED GENDER?*
YES. OF COURSE.
TREEN FEELS FOR PAU.
YOU MUST SUFFER GREATLY TO KNOW YOU MUST LIVE YOUR WHOLE LIFE AS A MALE...
TO NEVER KNOW THE JOY OF MATERNITY.
UHH...

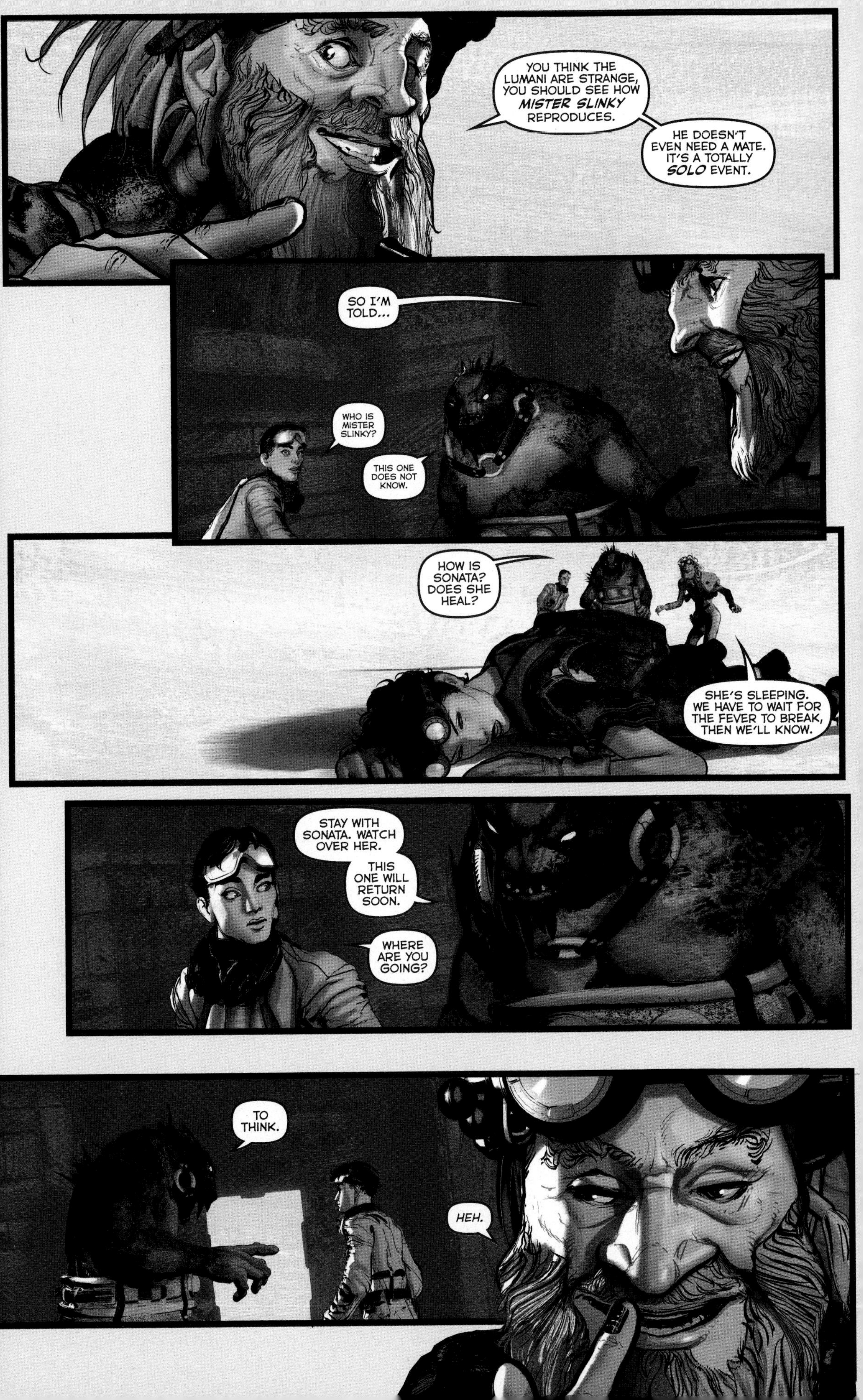
YOU THINK THE LUMANI ARE STRANGE, YOU SHOULD SEE HOW *MISTER SLINKY* REPRODUCES.
HE DOESN'T EVEN NEED A MATE. IT'S A TOTALLY *SOLO* EVENT.
SO I'M TOLD...
WHO IS MISTER SLINKY?
THIS ONE DOES NOT KNOW.
HOW IS SONATA? DOES SHE HEAL?
SHE'S SLEEPING. WE HAVE TO WAIT FOR THE FEVER TO BREAK, THEN WE'LL KNOW.
STAY WITH SONATA. WATCH OVER HER.
THIS ONE WILL RETURN SOON.
WHERE ARE YOU GOING?
TO THINK.
HEH.

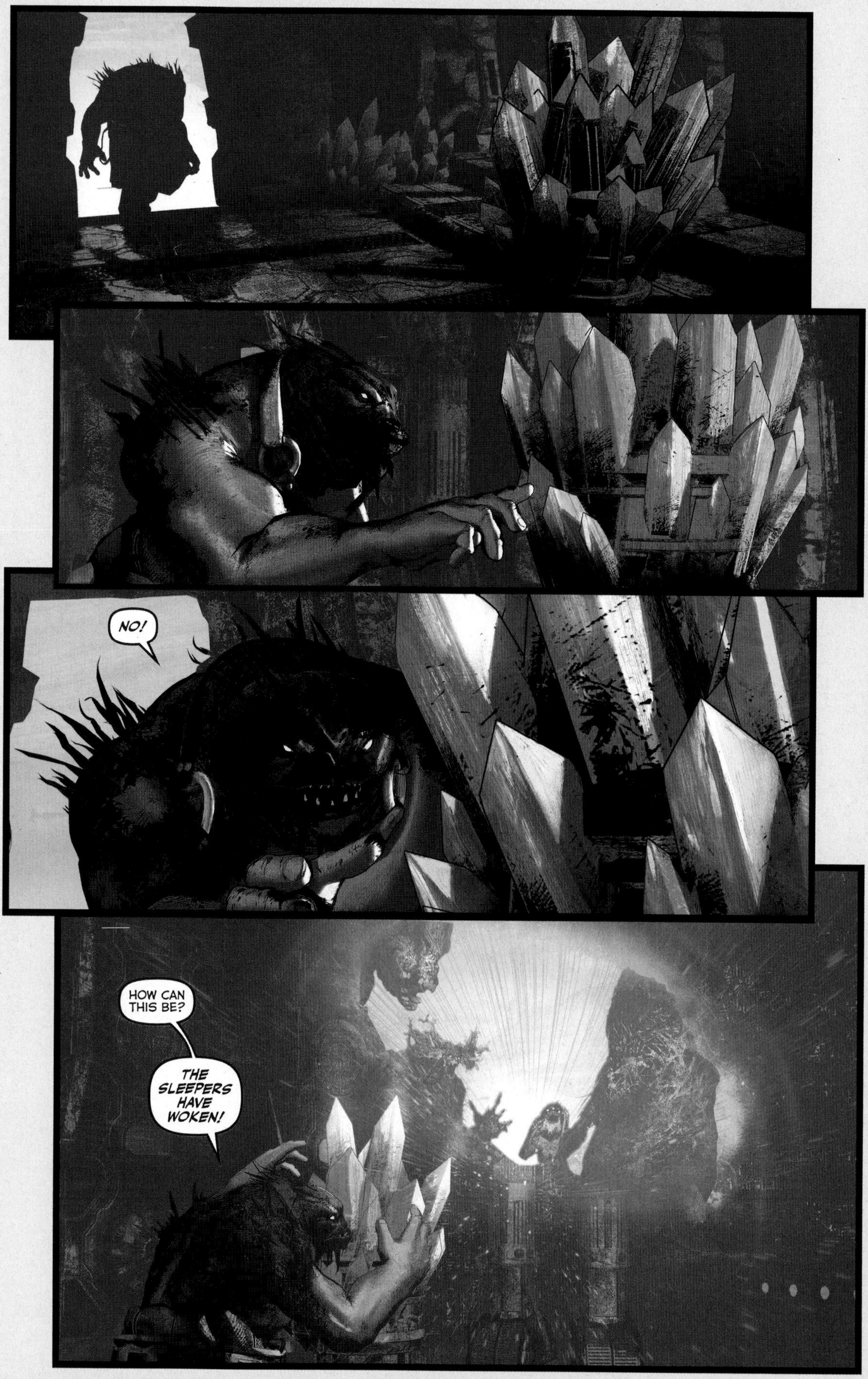
NO!
HOW CAN THIS BE?
THE SLEEPERS HAVE WOKEN!

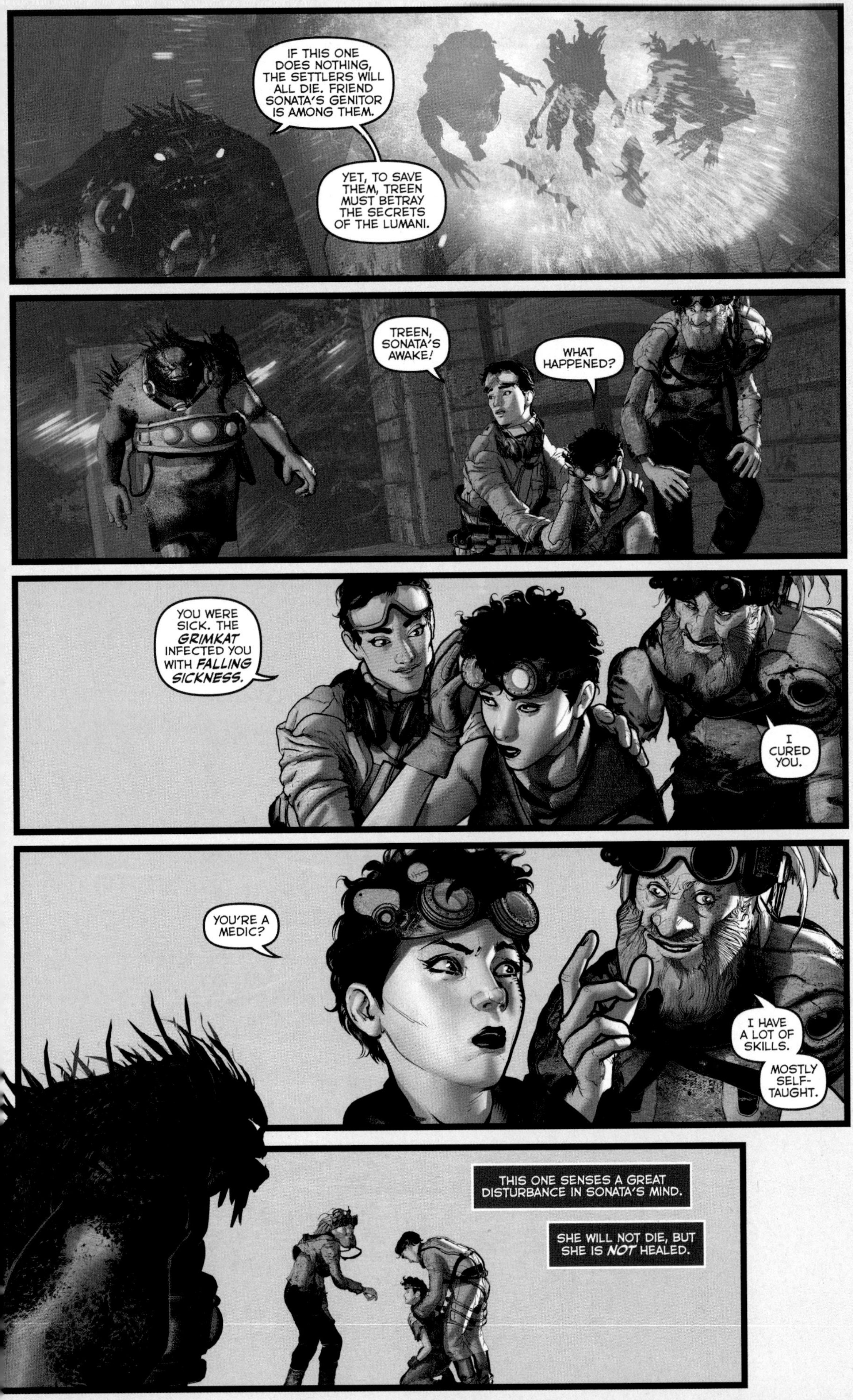
IF THIS ONE DOES NOTHING, THE SETTLERS WILL ALL DIE. FRIEND SONATA'S GENITOR IS AMONG THEM.
YET, TO SAVE THEM, TREEN MUST BETRAY THE SECRETS OF THE LUMANI.
TREEN, SONATA'S AWAKE!
WHAT HAPPENED?
YOU WERE SICK. THE *GRIMKAT* INFECTED YOU WITH *FALLING SICKNESS*.
I CURED YOU.
YOU'RE A MEDIC?
I HAVE A LOT OF SKILLS.
MOSTLY SELF-TAUGHT.
THIS ONE SENSES A GREAT DISTURBANCE IN SONATA'S MIND.
SHE WILL NOT DIE, BUT SHE IS *NOT* HEALED.

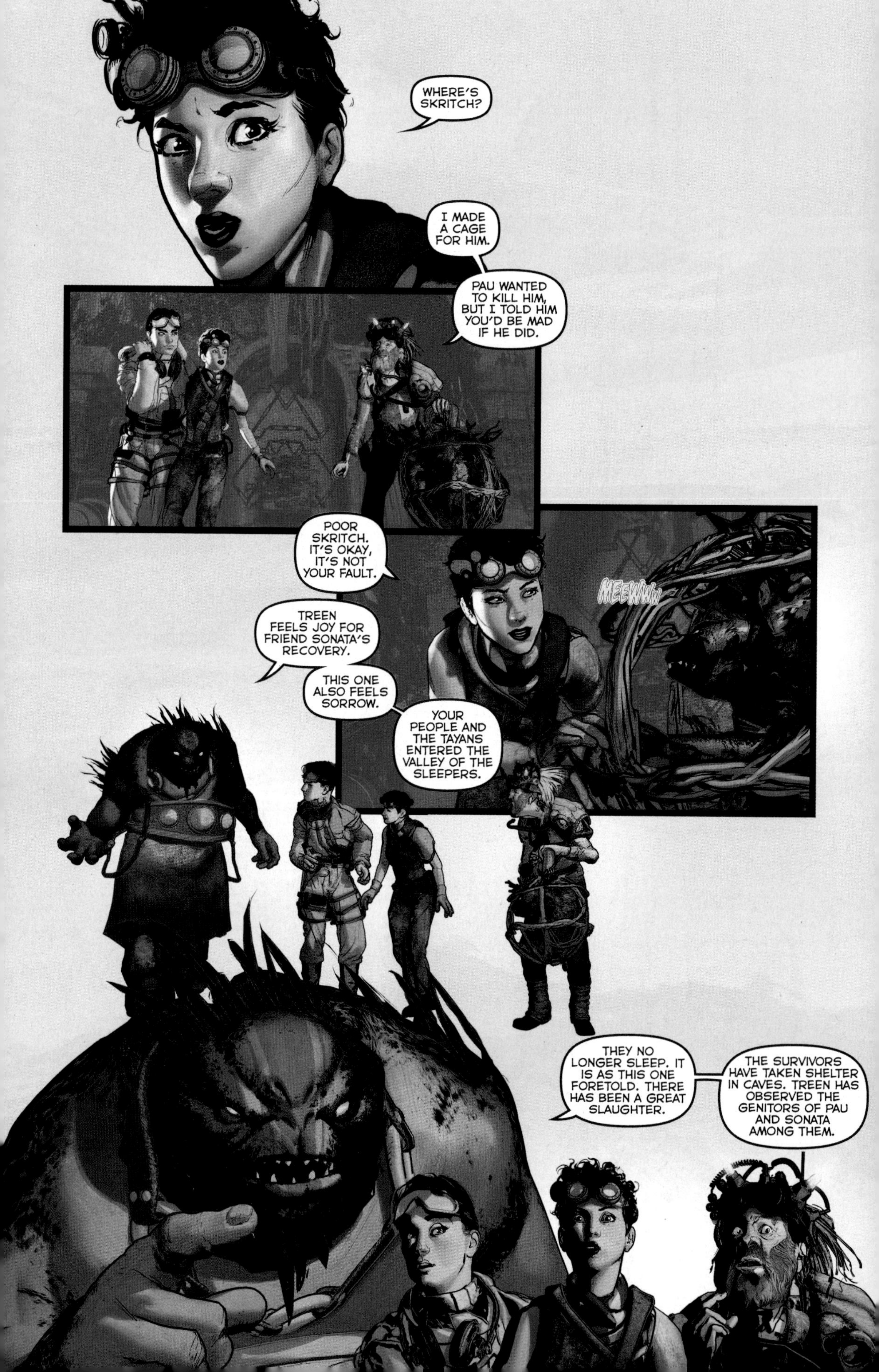
WHERE'S SKRITCH?
I MADE A CAGE FOR HIM.
PAU WANTED TO KILL HIM, BUT I TOLD HIM YOU'D BE MAD IF HE DID.
POOR SKRITCH. IT'S OKAY, IT'S NOT YOUR FAULT.
MEEWWW
TREEN FEELS JOY FOR FRIEND SONATA'S RECOVERY.
THIS ONE ALSO FEELS SORROW.
YOUR PEOPLE AND THE TAYANS ENTERED THE VALLEY OF THE SLEEPERS.
THEY NO LONGER SLEEP. IT IS AS THIS ONE FORETOLD. THERE HAS BEEN A GREAT SLAUGHTER.
THE SURVIVORS HAVE TAKEN SHELTER IN CAVES. TREEN HAS OBSERVED THE GENITORS OF PAU AND SONATA AMONG THEM.

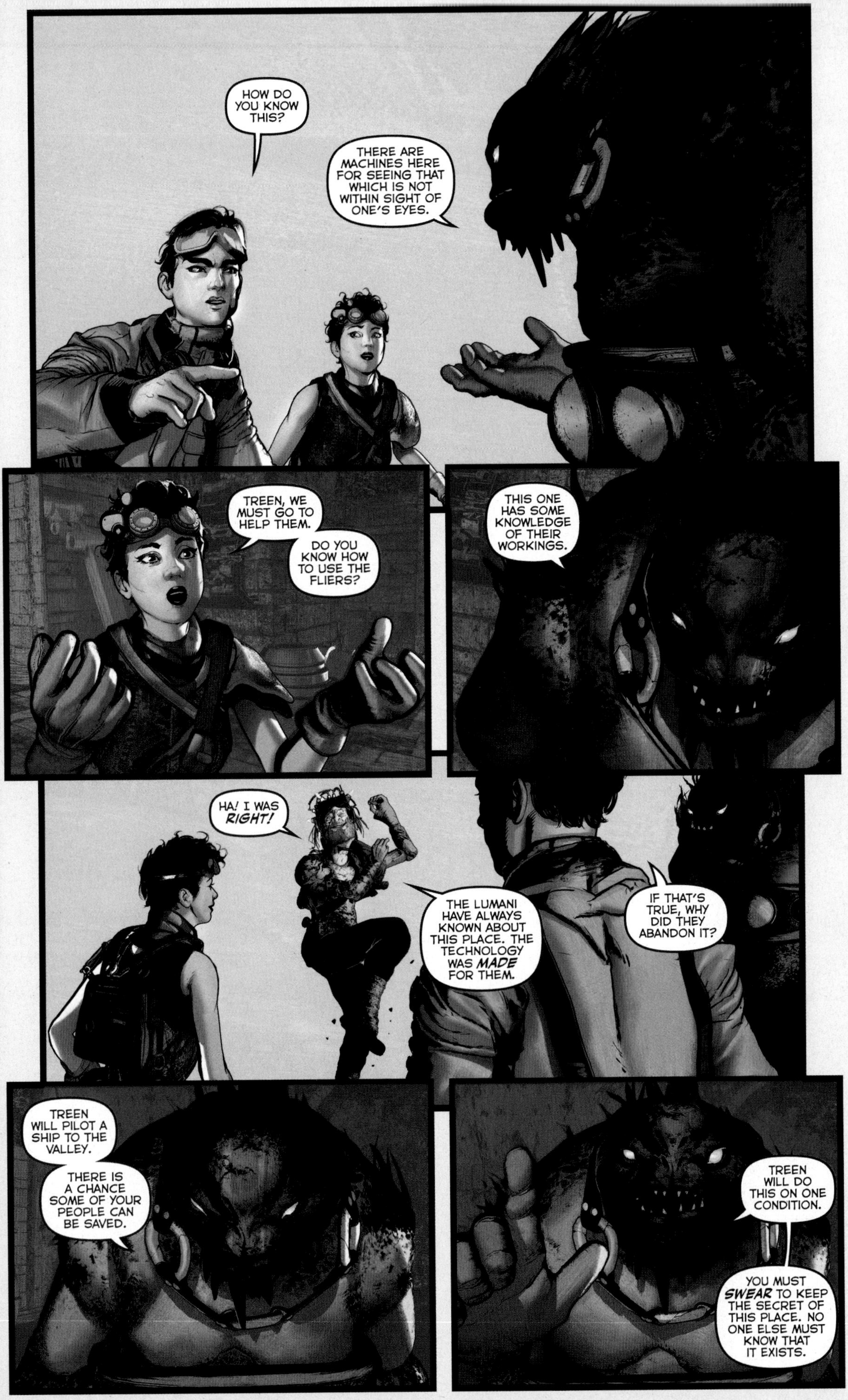
HOW DO YOU KNOW THIS?
THERE ARE MACHINES HERE FOR SEEING THAT WHICH IS NOT WITHIN SIGHT OF ONE'S EYES.
TREEN, WE MUST GO TO HELP THEM.
DO YOU KNOW HOW TO USE THE FLIERS?
THIS ONE HAS SOME KNOWLEDGE OF THEIR WORKINGS.
HA! I WAS RIGHT!
THE LUMANI HAVE ALWAYS KNOWN ABOUT THIS PLACE. THE TECHNOLOGY WAS MADE FOR THEM.
IF THAT'S TRUE, WHY DID THEY ABANDON IT?
TREEN WILL PILOT A SHIP TO THE VALLEY.
THERE IS A CHANCE SOME OF YOUR PEOPLE CAN BE SAVED.
TREEN WILL DO THIS ON ONE CONDITION.
YOU MUST SWEAR TO KEEP THE SECRET OF THIS PLACE. NO ONE ELSE MUST KNOW THAT IT EXISTS.

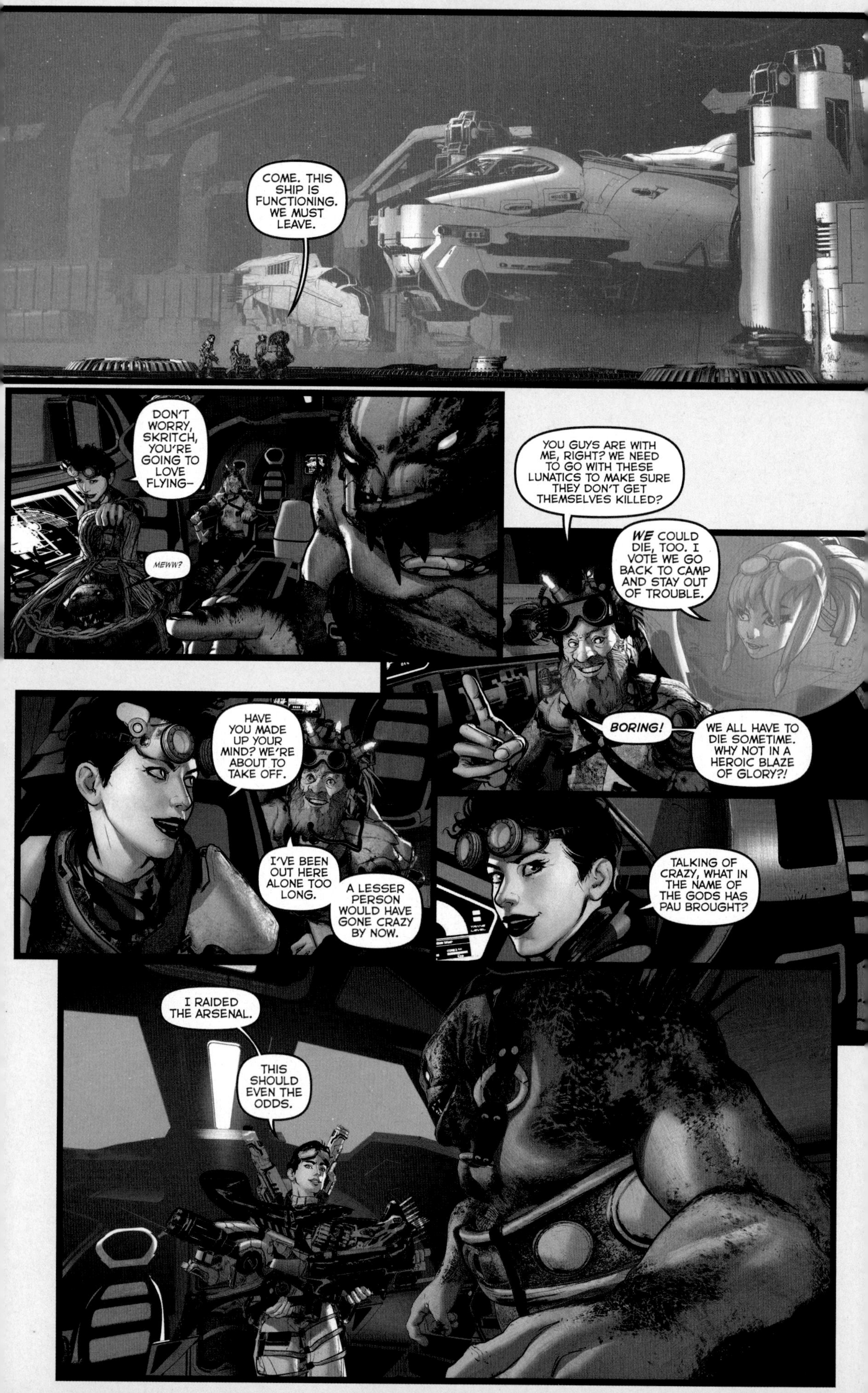
COME. THIS SHIP IS FUNCTIONING. WE MUST LEAVE.
DON'T WORRY, SKRITCH, YOU'RE GOING TO LOVE FLYING–
MEWW?
YOU GUYS ARE WITH ME, RIGHT? WE NEED TO GO WITH THESE LUNATICS TO MAKE SURE THEY DON'T GET THEMSELVES KILLED?
WE COULD DIE, TOO. I VOTE WE GO BACK TO CAMP AND STAY OUT OF TROUBLE.
BORING!
WE ALL HAVE TO DIE SOMETIME. WHY NOT IN A HEROIC BLAZE OF GLORY?!
HAVE YOU MADE UP YOUR MIND? WE'RE ABOUT TO TAKE OFF.
I'VE BEEN OUT HERE ALONE TOO LONG.
A LESSER PERSON WOULD HAVE GONE CRAZY BY NOW.
TALKING OF CRAZY, WHAT IN THE NAME OF THE GODS HAS PAU BROUGHT?
I RAIDED THE ARSENAL.
THIS SHOULD EVEN THE ODDS.

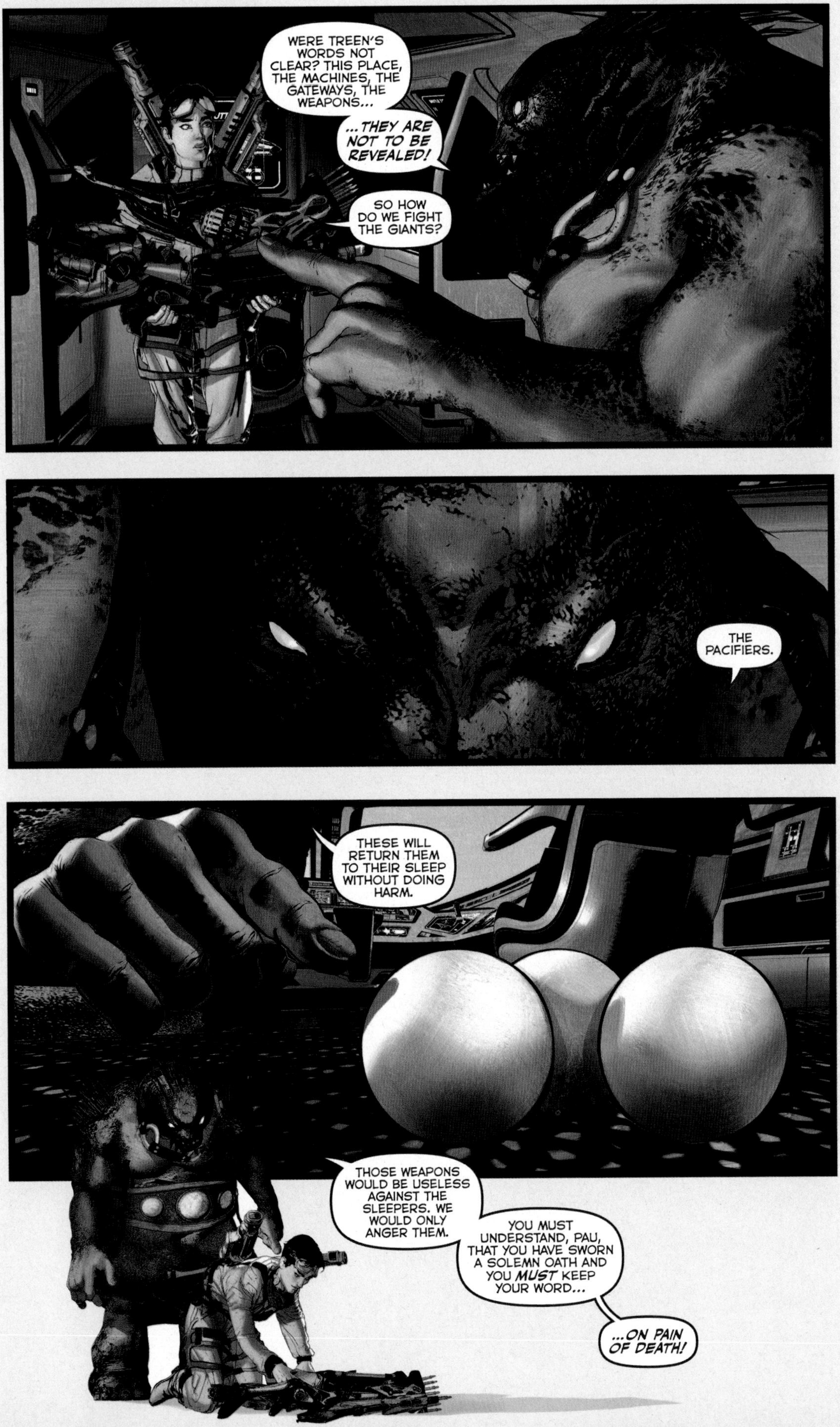
WERE TREEN'S WORDS NOT CLEAR? THIS PLACE, THE MACHINES, THE GATEWAYS, THE WEAPONS...
...THEY ARE NOT TO BE REVEALED!
SO HOW DO WE FIGHT THE GIANTS?
THE PACIFIERS.
THESE WILL RETURN THEM TO THEIR SLEEP WITHOUT DOING HARM.
THOSE WEAPONS WOULD BE USELESS AGAINST THE SLEEPERS. WE WOULD ONLY ANGER THEM.
YOU MUST UNDERSTAND, PAU, THAT YOU HAVE SWORN A SOLEMN OATH AND YOU MUST KEEP YOUR WORD...
...ON PAIN OF DEATH!

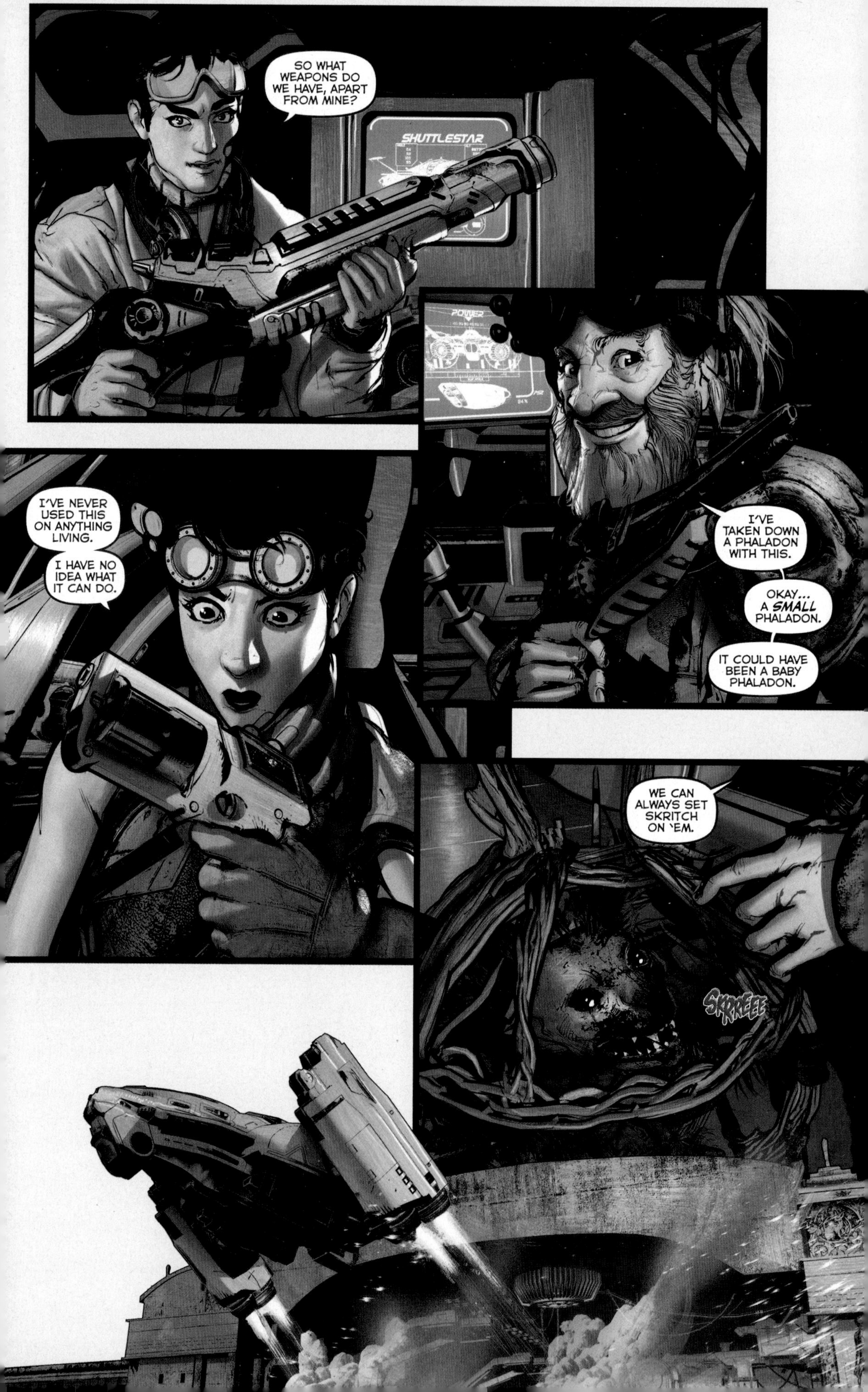
SO WHAT WEAPONS DO WE HAVE, APART FROM MINE?
SHUTTLESTAR
POWER
I'VE TAKEN DOWN A PHALADON WITH THIS.
OKAY... A *SMALL* PHALADON.
IT COULD HAVE BEEN A BABY PHALADON.
I'VE NEVER USED THIS ON ANYTHING LIVING.
I HAVE NO IDEA WHAT IT CAN DO.
WE CAN ALWAYS SET SKRITCH ON 'EM.
SKREEEE

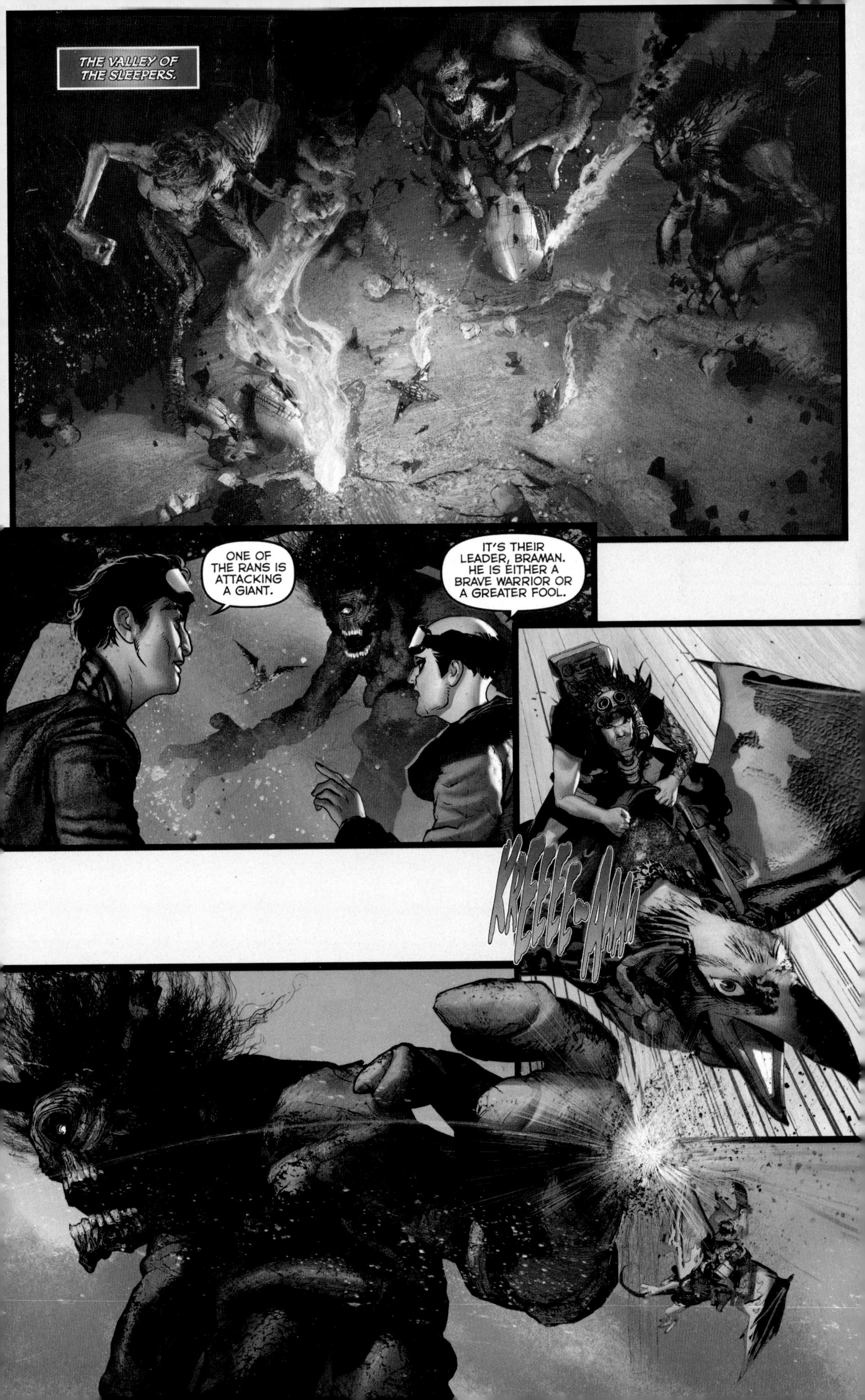
THE VALLEY OF THE SLEEPERS.
ONE OF THE RANS IS ATTACKING A GIANT.
IT'S THEIR LEADER, BRAMAN. HE IS EITHER A BRAVE WARRIOR OR A GREATER FOOL.
KREEEEE-AAAA

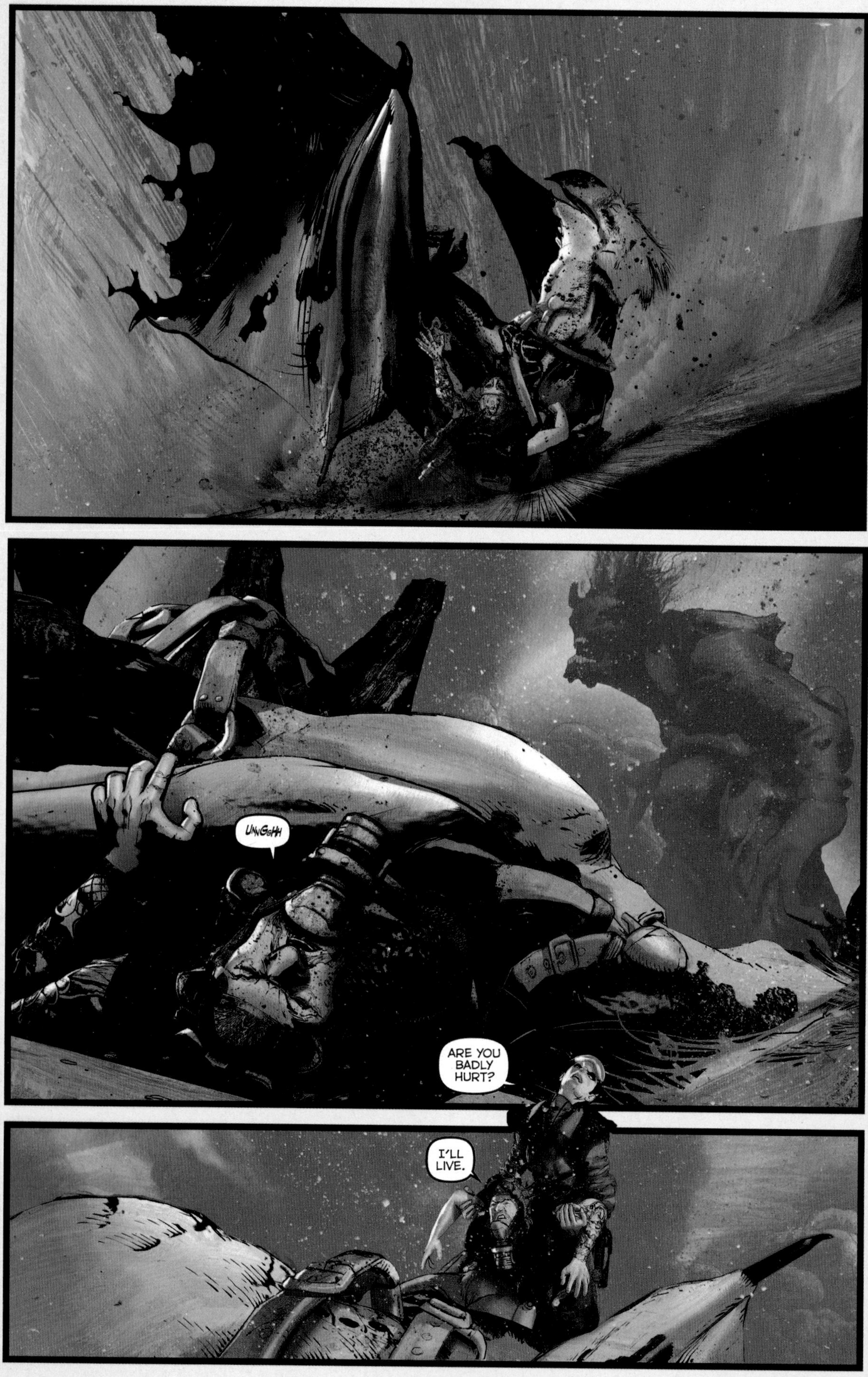
UNNGHH
ARE YOU BADLY HURT?
I'LL LIVE.

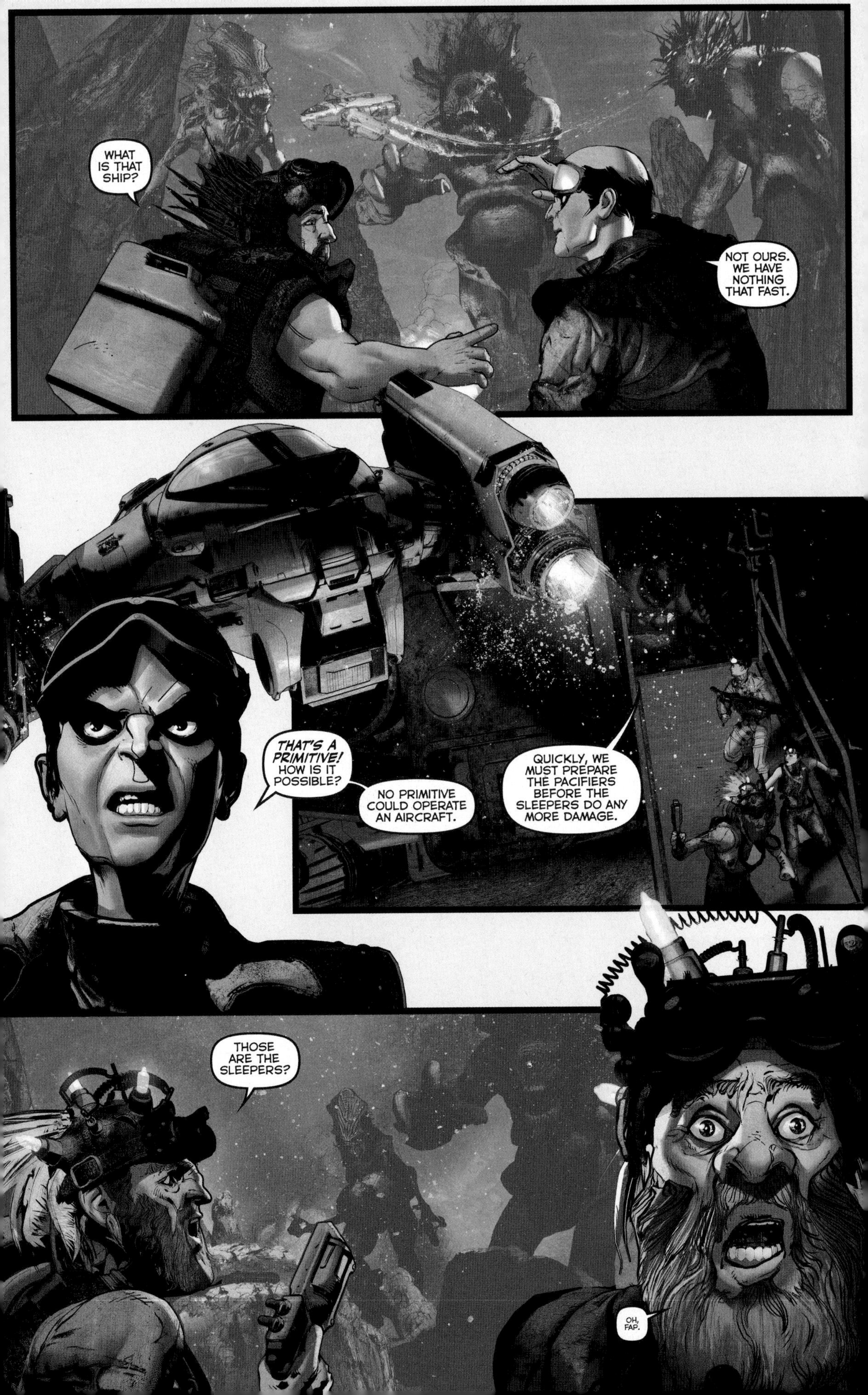
WHAT IS THAT SHIP?
NOT OURS. WE HAVE NOTHING THAT FAST.
THAT'S A *PRIMITIVE!* HOW IS IT POSSIBLE?
NO PRIMITIVE COULD OPERATE AN AIRCRAFT.
QUICKLY, WE MUST PREPARE THE PACIFIERS BEFORE THE SLEEPERS DO ANY MORE DAMAGE.
THOSE ARE THE SLEEPERS?
OH, FAP.

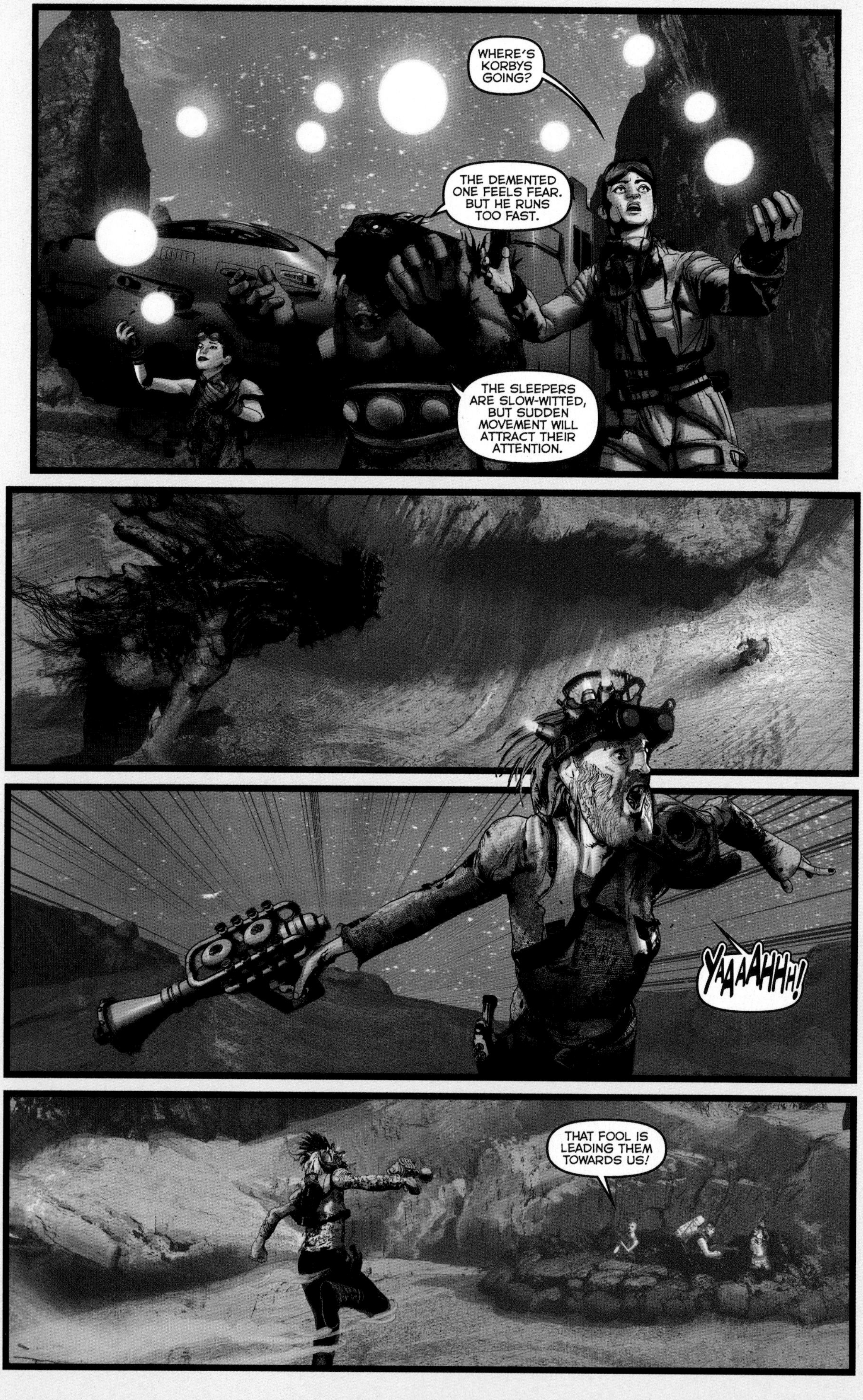
WHERE'S KORBYS GOING?
THE DEMENTED ONE FEELS FEAR. BUT HE RUNS TOO FAST.
THE SLEEPERS ARE SLOW-WITTED, BUT SUDDEN MOVEMENT WILL ATTRACT THEIR ATTENTION.
YAAAAHHH!
THAT FOOL IS LEADING THEM TOWARDS US!

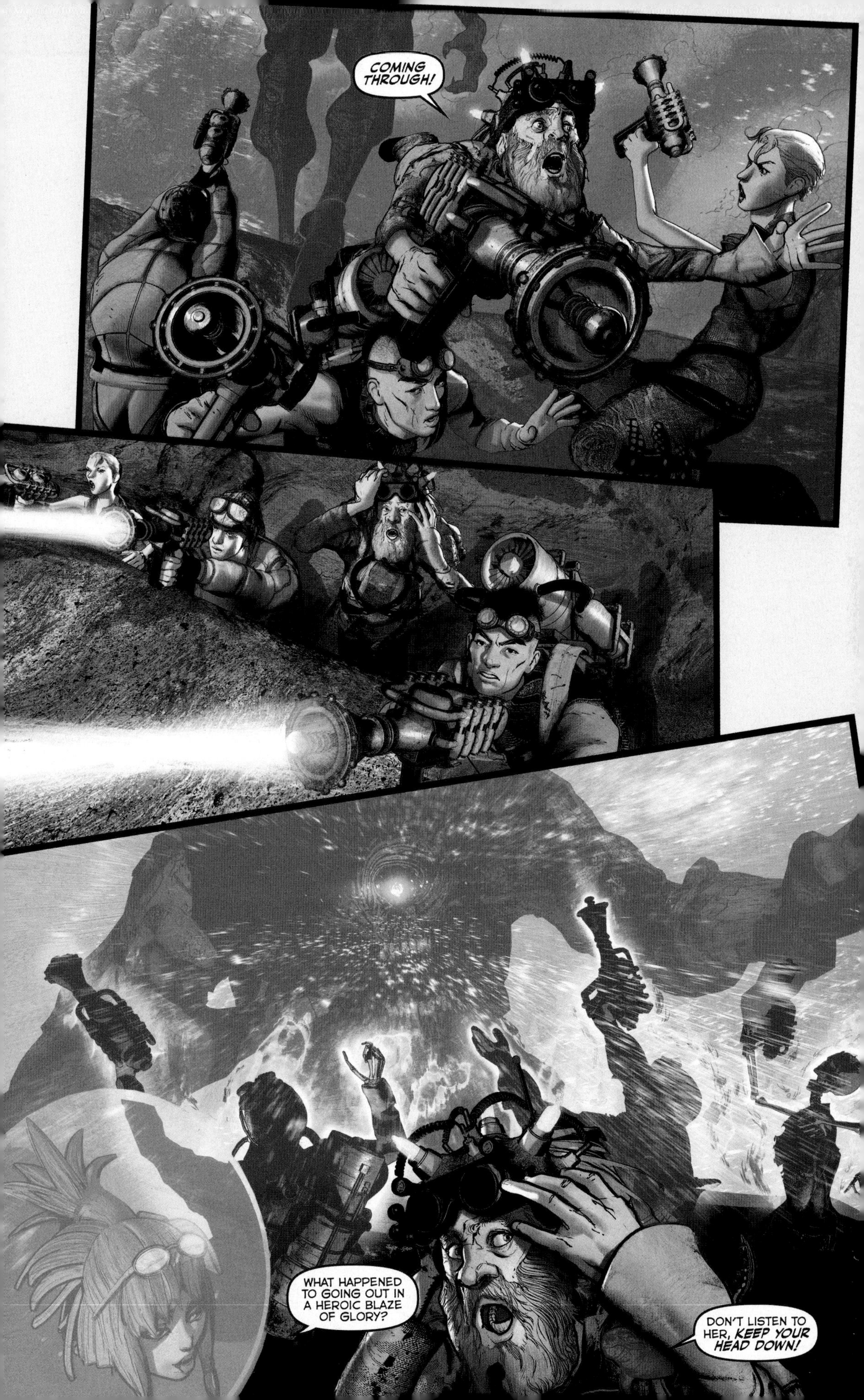
COMING THROUGH!
WHAT HAPPENED TO GOING OUT IN A HEROIC BLAZE OF GLORY?
DON'T LISTEN TO HER, *KEEP YOUR HEAD DOWN!*

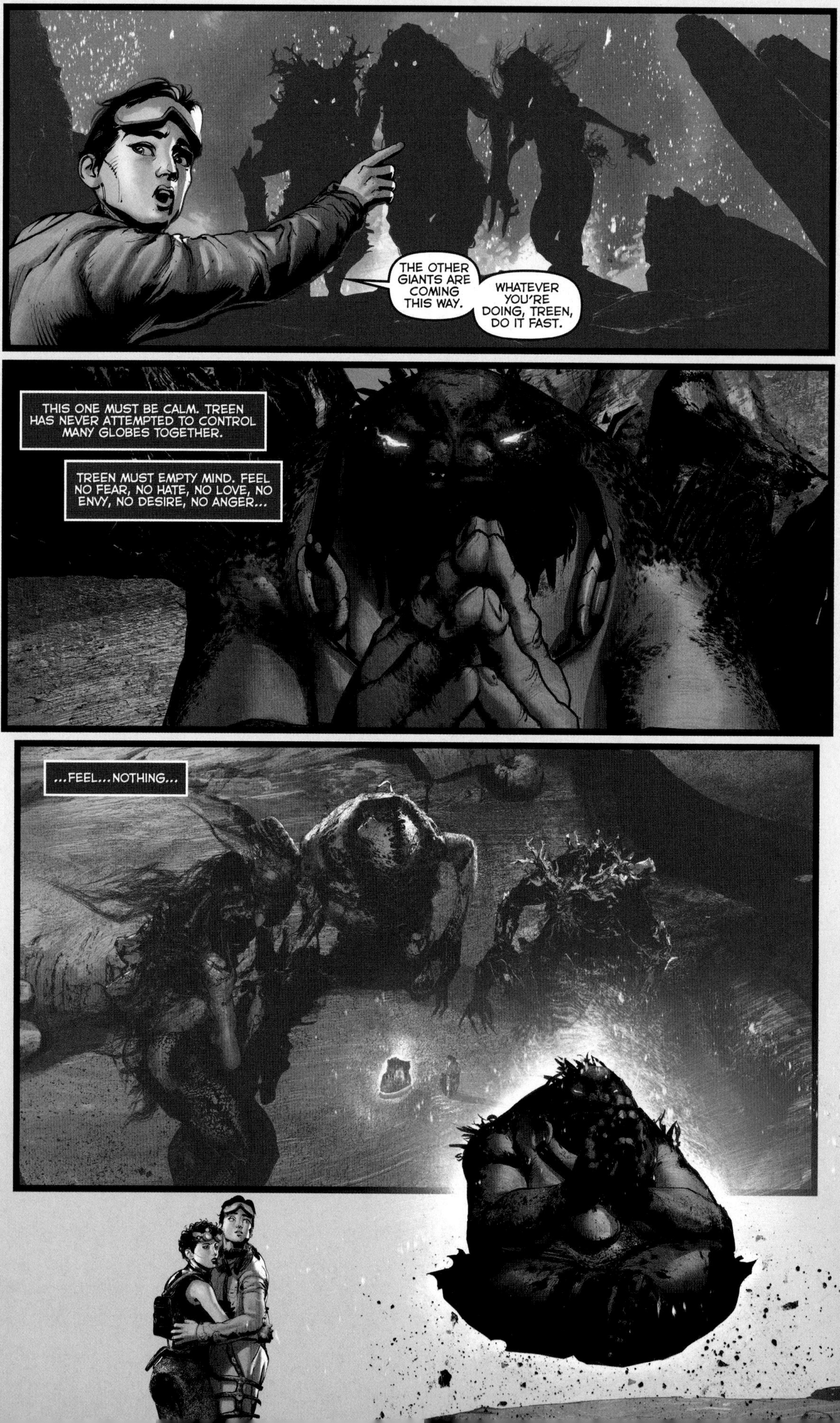

THE OTHER GIANTS ARE COMING THIS WAY.
WHATEVER YOU'RE DOING, TREEN, DO IT FAST.
THIS ONE MUST BE CALM. TREEN HAS NEVER ATTEMPTED TO CONTROL MANY GLOBES TOGETHER.
TREEN MUST EMPTY MIND. FEEL NO FEAR, NO HATE, NO LOVE, NO ENVY, NO DESIRE, NO ANGER...
...FEEL...NOTHING...

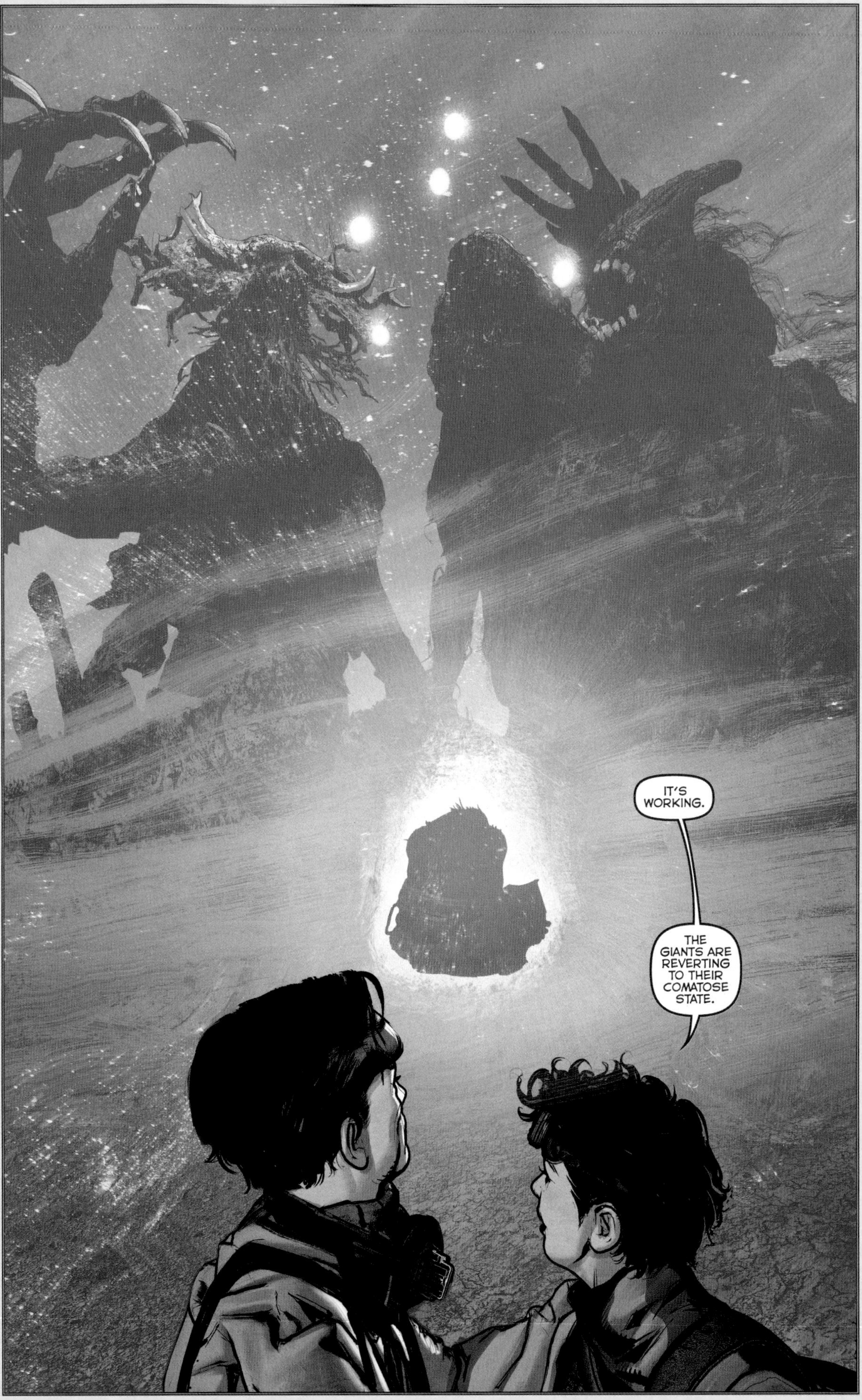
IT'S WORKING.
THE GIANTS ARE REVERTING TO THEIR COMATOSE STATE.

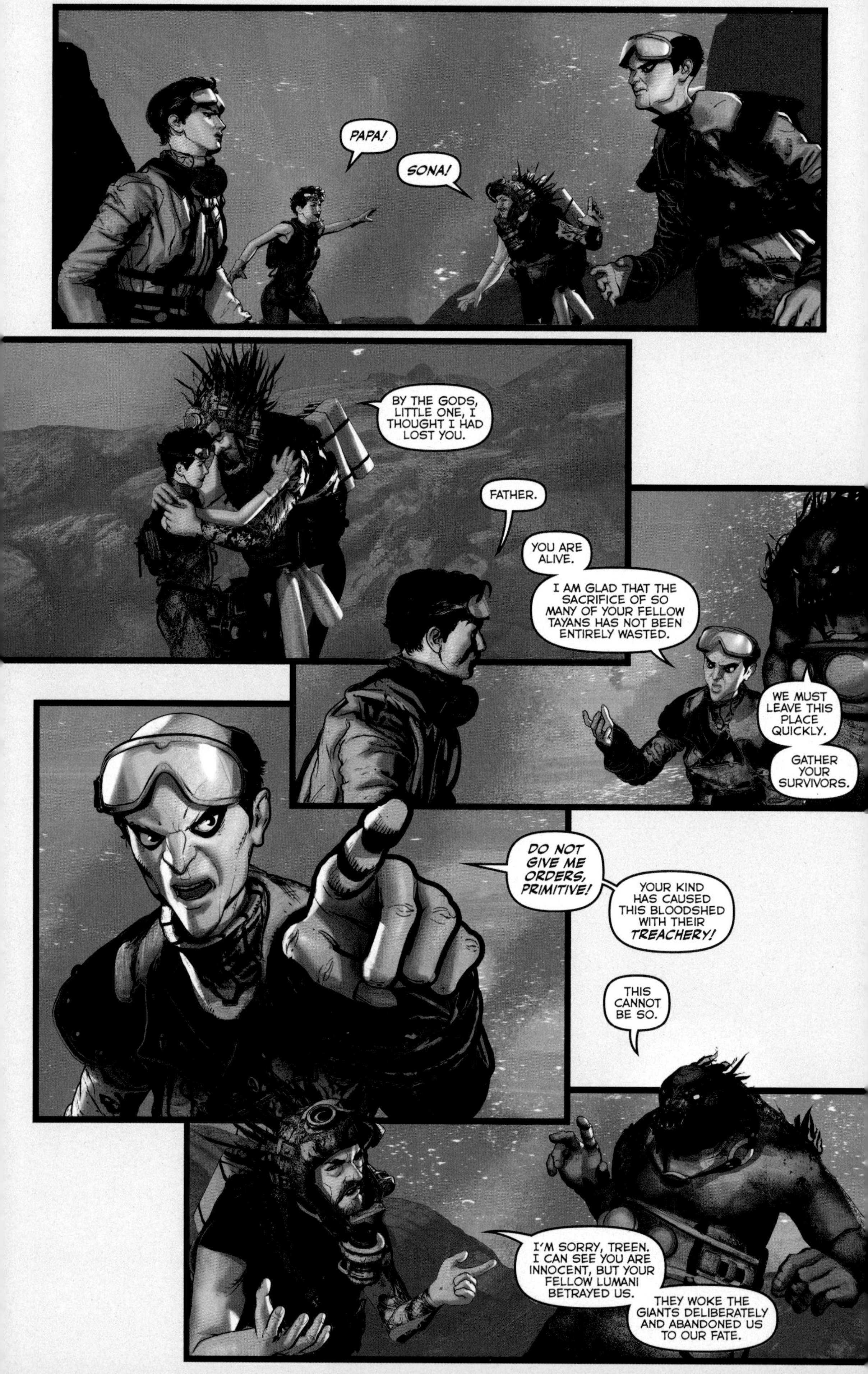
PAPA!
SONA!
BY THE GODS, LITTLE ONE, I THOUGHT I HAD LOST YOU.
FATHER.
YOU ARE ALIVE.
I AM GLAD THAT THE SACRIFICE OF SO MANY OF YOUR FELLOW TAYANS HAS NOT BEEN ENTIRELY WASTED.
WE MUST LEAVE THIS PLACE QUICKLY.
GATHER YOUR SURVIVORS.
DO NOT GIVE ME ORDERS, PRIMITIVE!
YOUR KIND HAS CAUSED THIS BLOODSHED WITH THEIR TREACHERY!
THIS CANNOT BE SO.
I'M SORRY, TREEN. I CAN SEE YOU ARE INNOCENT, BUT YOUR FELLOW LUMANI BETRAYED US.
THEY WOKE THE GIANTS DELIBERATELY AND ABANDONED US TO OUR FATE.

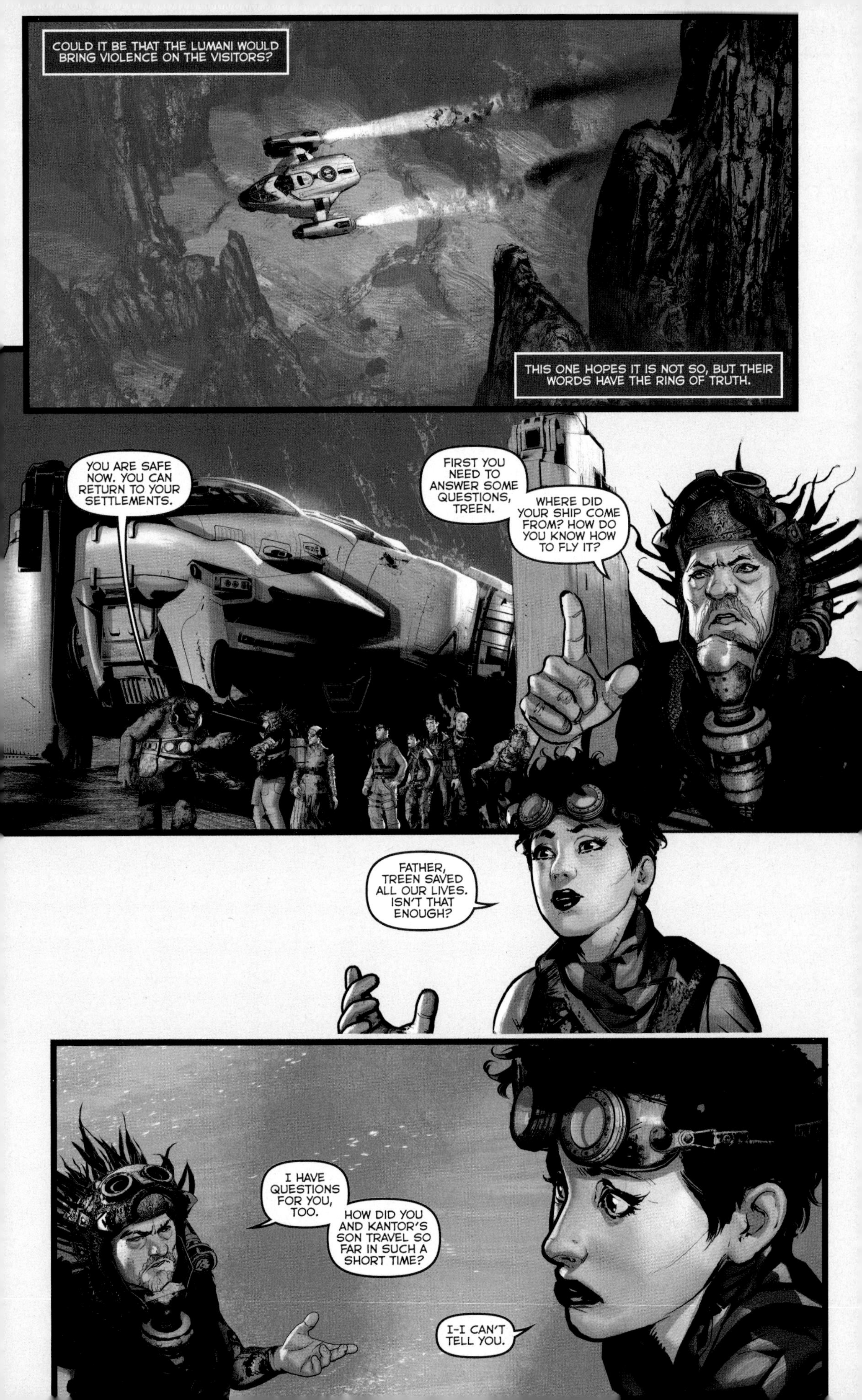
COULD IT BE THAT THE LUMANI WOULD BRING VIOLENCE ON THE VISITORS?
THIS ONE HOPES IT IS NOT SO, BUT THEIR WORDS HAVE THE RING OF TRUTH.
YOU ARE SAFE NOW. YOU CAN RETURN TO YOUR SETTLEMENTS.
FIRST YOU NEED TO ANSWER SOME QUESTIONS, TREEN.
WHERE DID YOUR SHIP COME FROM? HOW DO YOU KNOW HOW TO FLY IT?
FATHER, TREEN SAVED ALL OUR LIVES. ISN'T THAT ENOUGH?
I HAVE QUESTIONS FOR YOU, TOO.
HOW DID YOU AND KANTOR'S SON TRAVEL SO FAR IN SUCH A SHORT TIME?
I-I CAN'T TELL YOU.

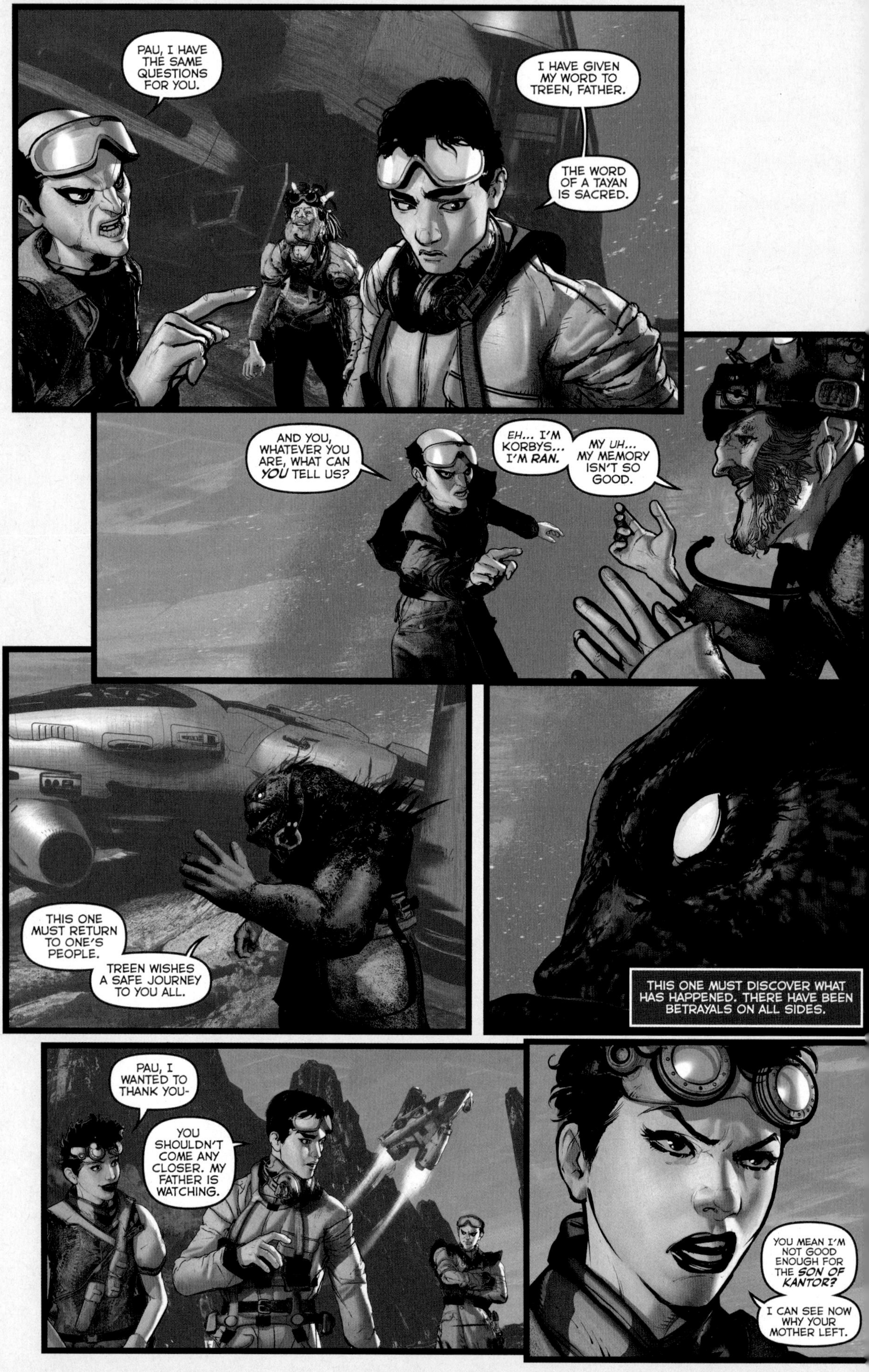
PAU, I HAVE THE SAME QUESTIONS FOR YOU.
I HAVE GIVEN MY WORD TO TREEN, FATHER.
THE WORD OF A TAYAN IS SACRED.
AND YOU, WHATEVER YOU ARE, WHAT CAN *YOU* TELL US?
EH... I'M KORBYS... I'M *RAN.*
MY UH... MY MEMORY ISN'T SO GOOD.
THIS ONE MUST RETURN TO ONE'S PEOPLE.
TREEN WISHES A SAFE JOURNEY TO YOU ALL.
THIS ONE MUST DISCOVER WHAT HAS HAPPENED. THERE HAVE BEEN BETRAYALS ON ALL SIDES.
PAU, I WANTED TO THANK YOU-
YOU SHOULDN'T COME ANY CLOSER. MY FATHER IS WATCHING.
YOU MEAN I'M NOT GOOD ENOUGH FOR THE *SON OF KANTOR?*
I CAN SEE NOW WHY YOUR MOTHER LEFT.

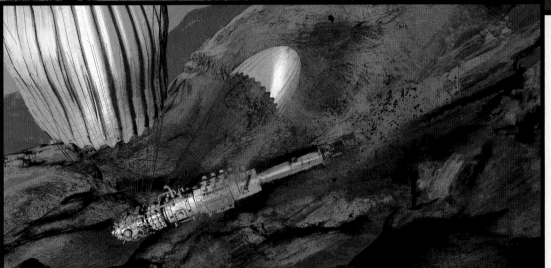

THE TAYAN SETTLEMENT
OF NEW VESPALA.

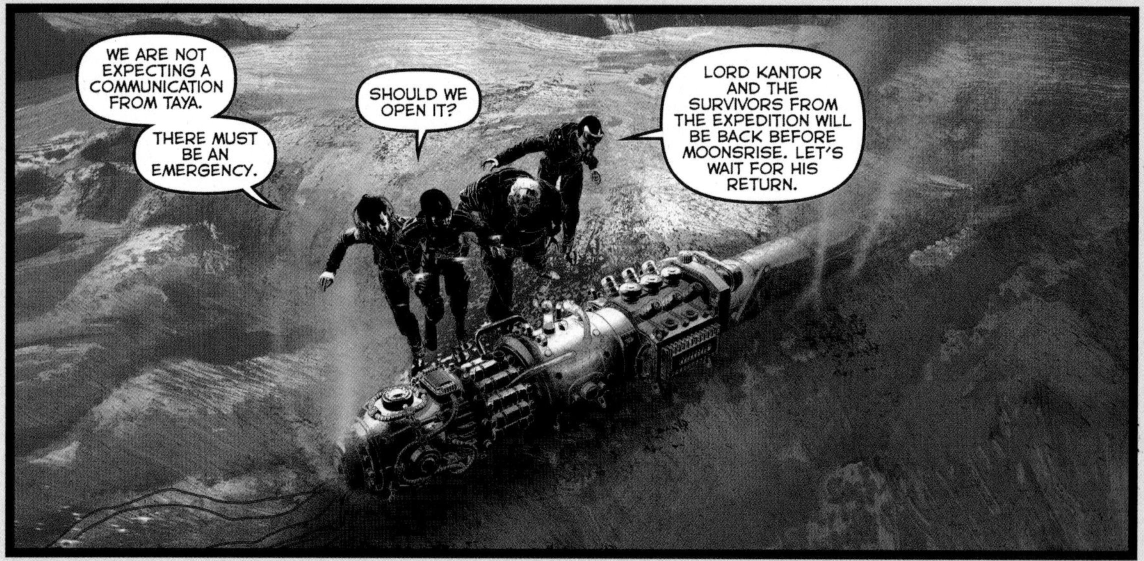
WE ARE NOT EXPECTING A COMMUNICATION FROM TAYA.
THERE MUST BE AN EMERGENCY.
SHOULD WE OPEN IT?
LORD KANTOR AND THE SURVIVORS FROM THE EXPEDITION WILL BE BACK BEFORE MOONSRISE. LET'S WAIT FOR HIS RETURN.

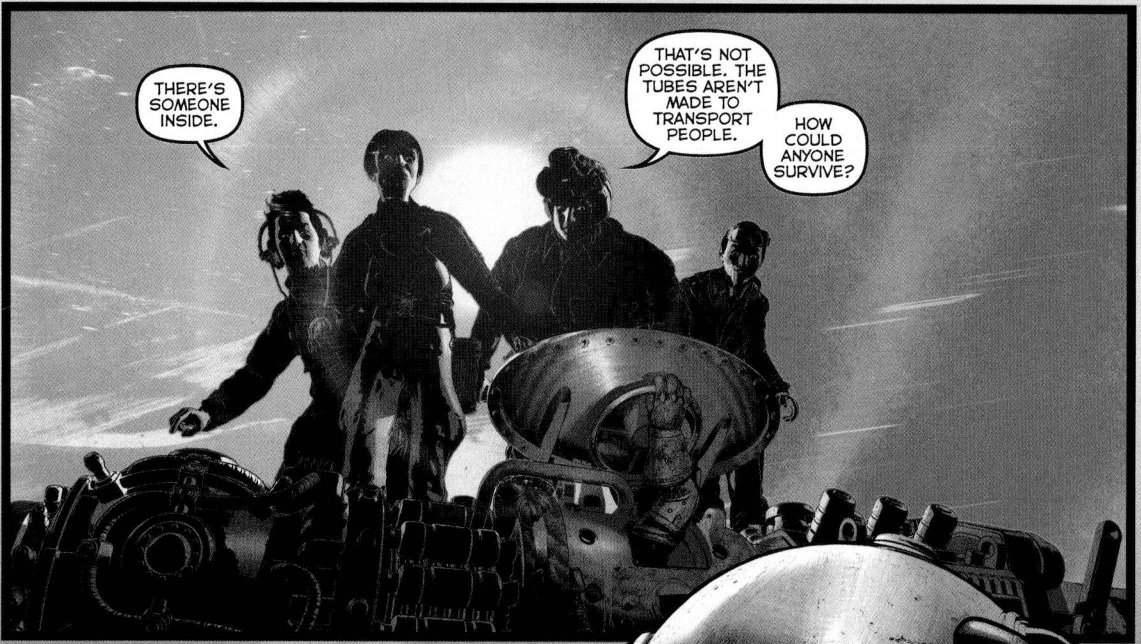
THERE'S SOMEONE INSIDE.
THAT'S NOT POSSIBLE. THE TUBES AREN'T MADE TO TRANSPORT PEOPLE.
HOW COULD ANYONE SURVIVE?

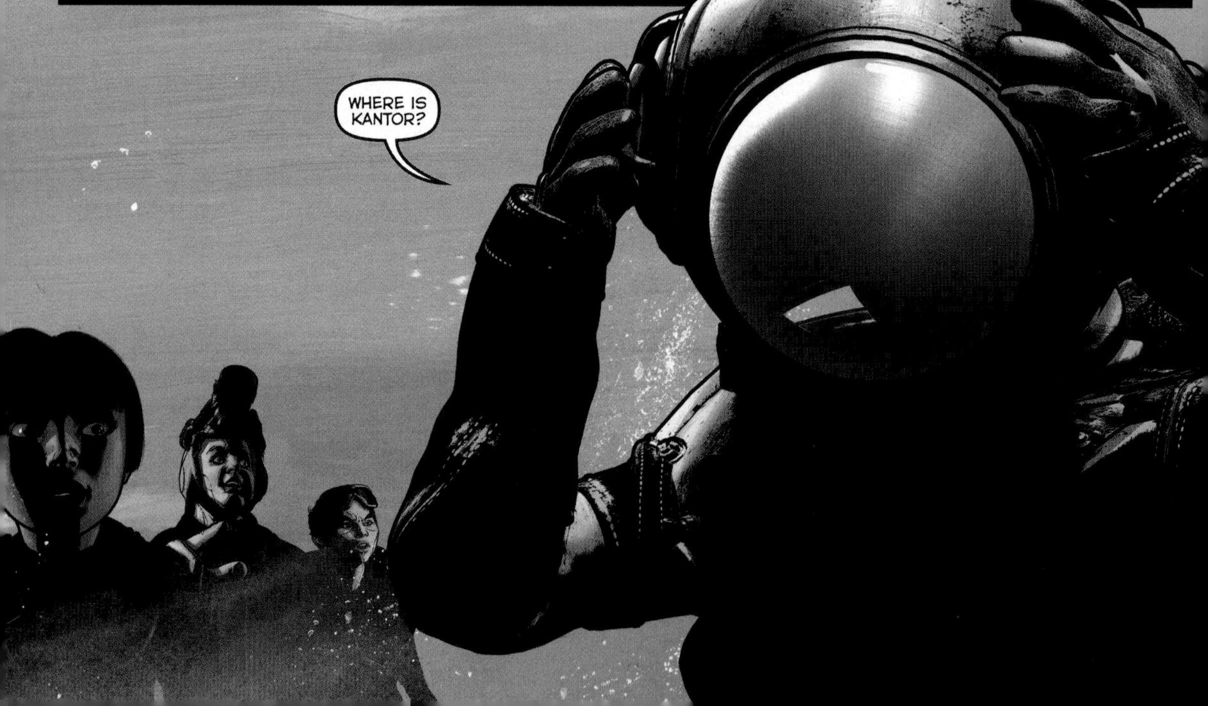
WHERE IS KANTOR?

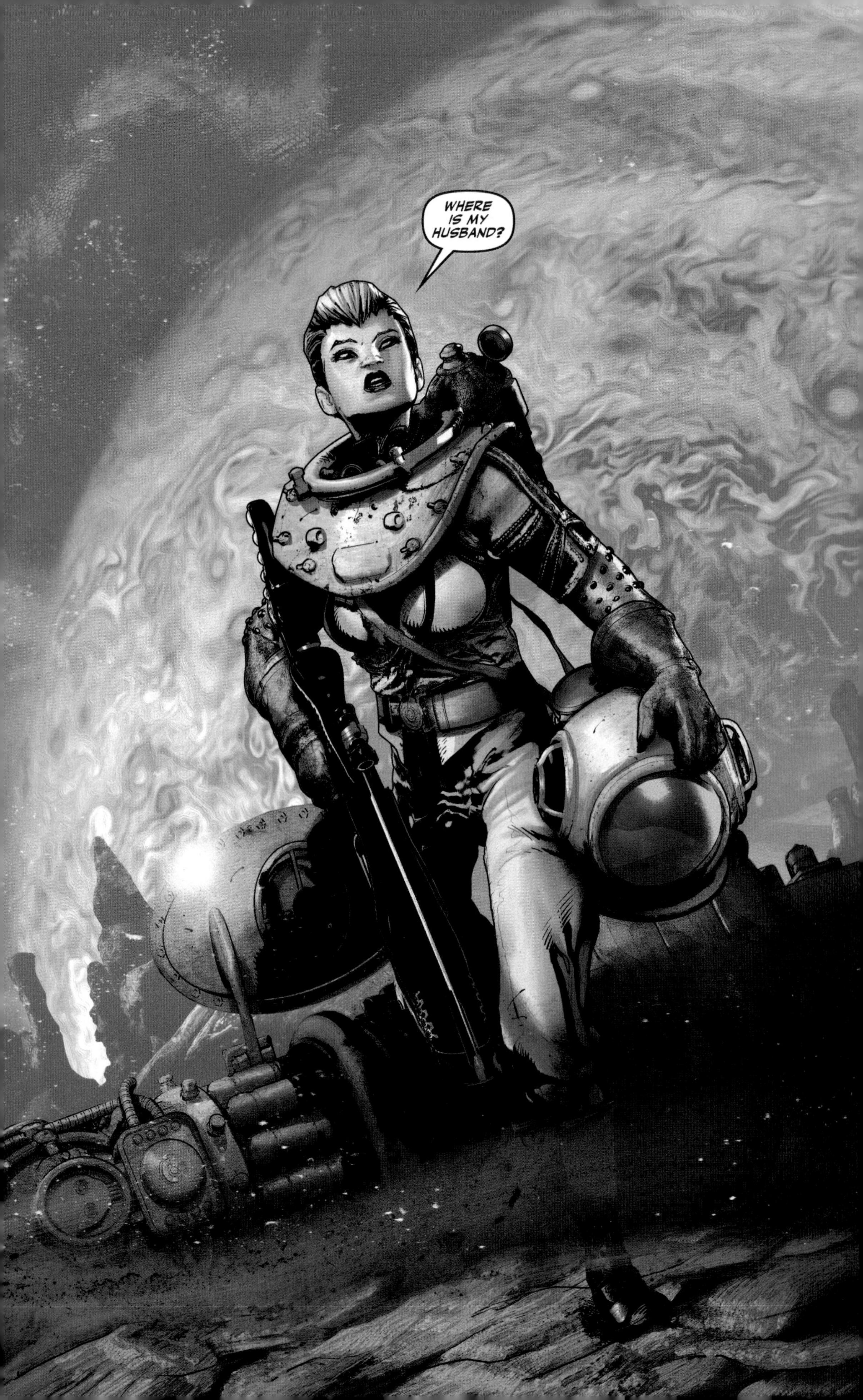
WHERE IS MY HUSBAND?

Issue #2 Second Printing Cover

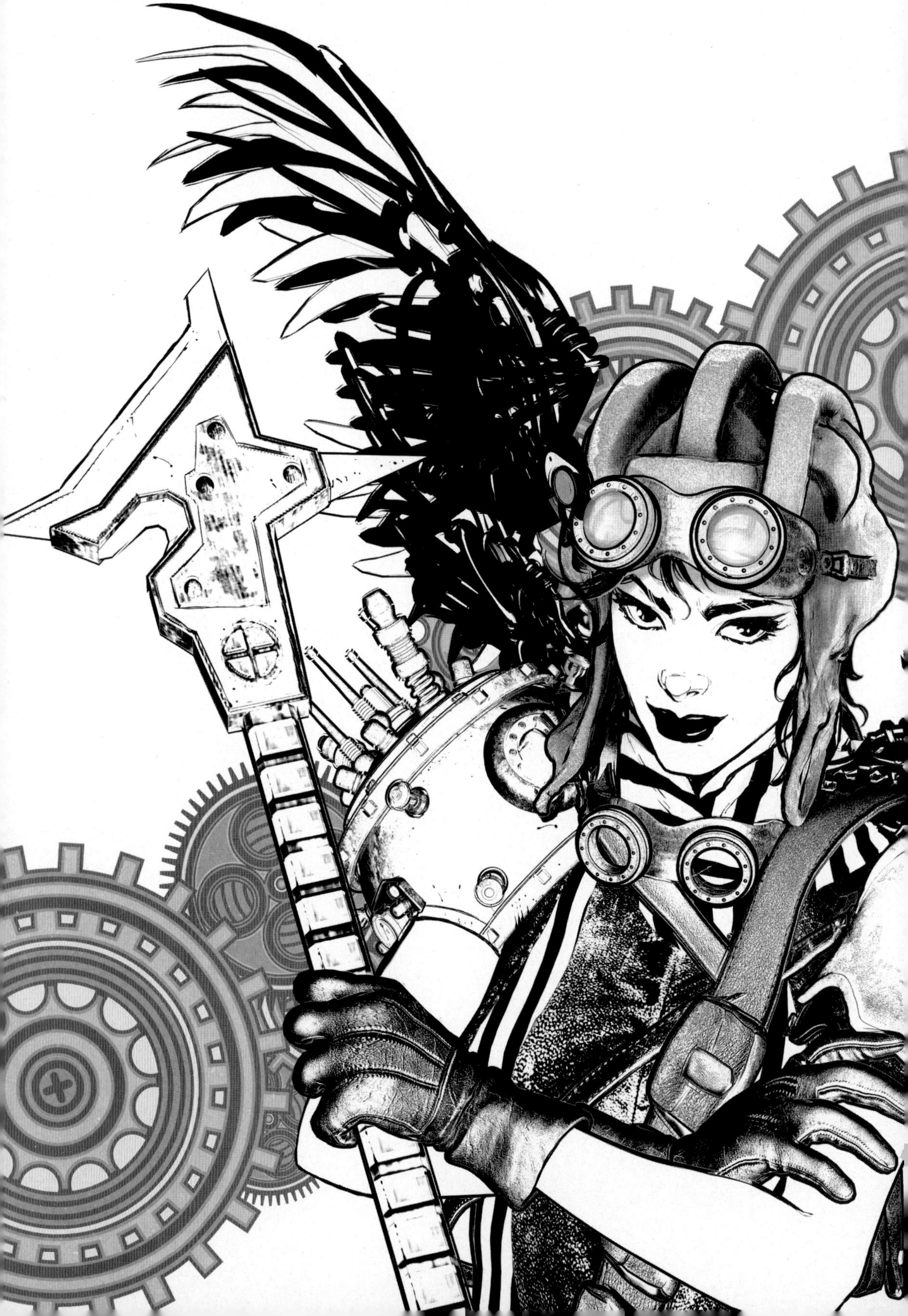

Issue #6 Cover A

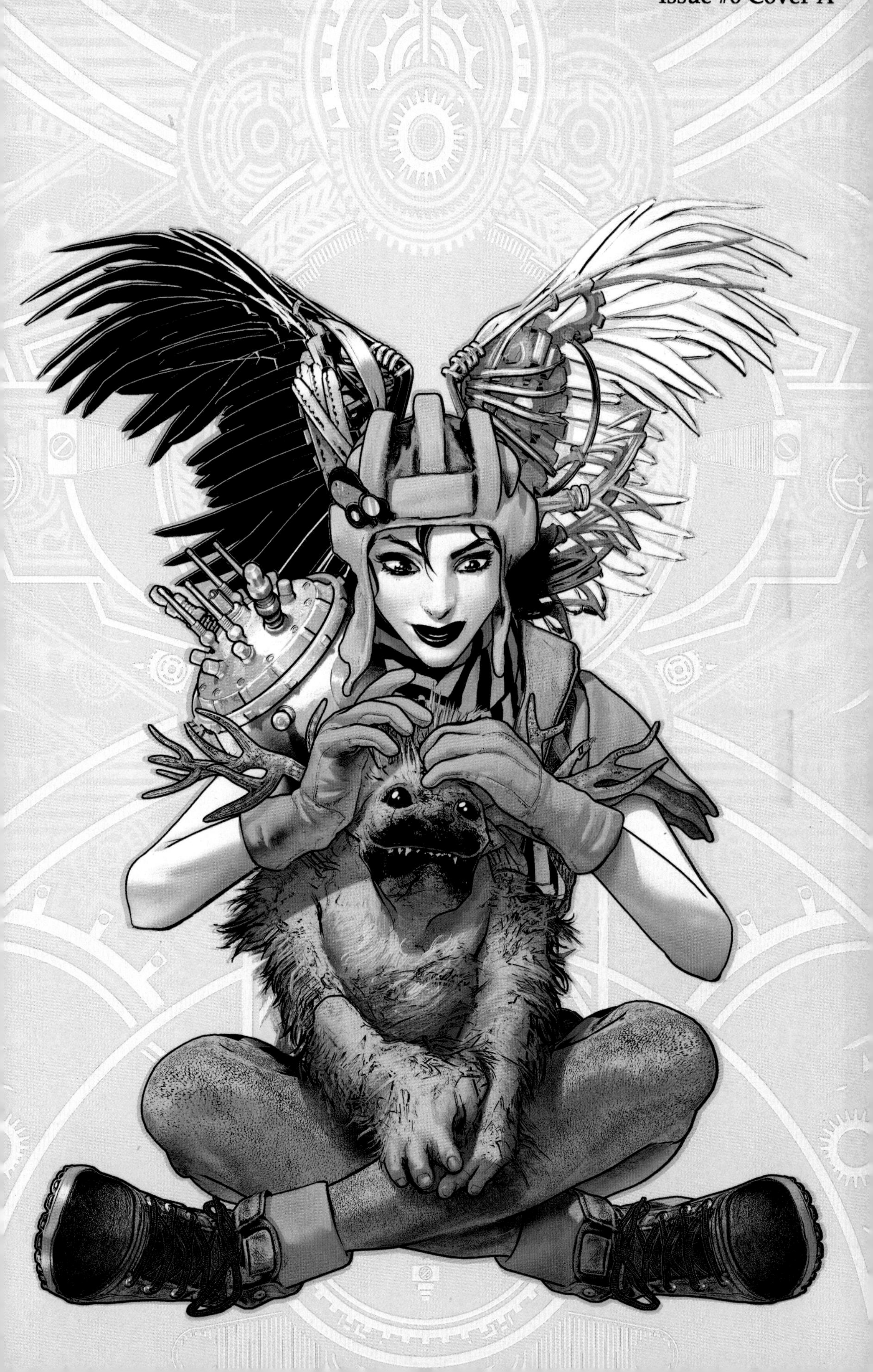

Issue #6 Cover B

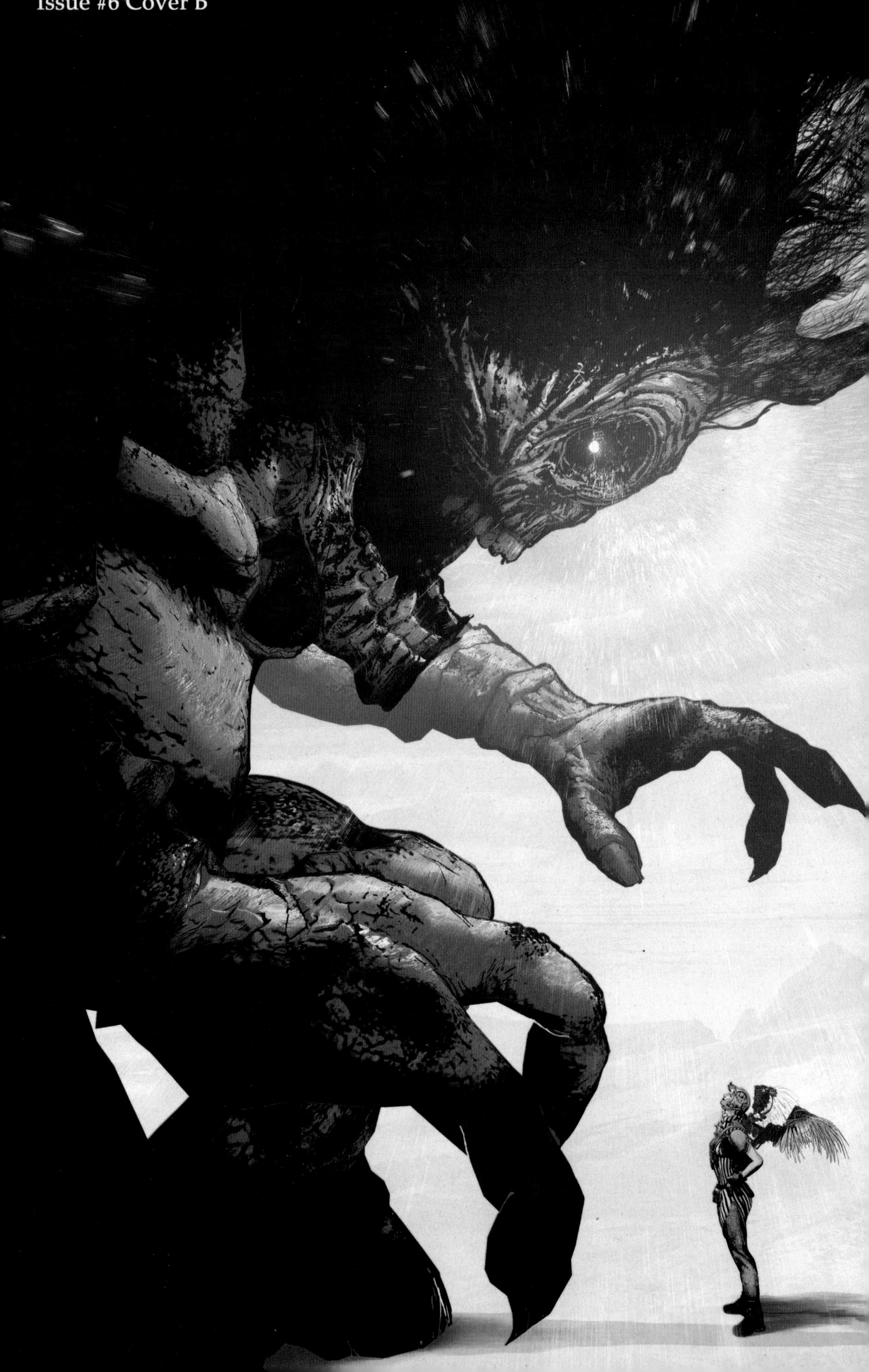

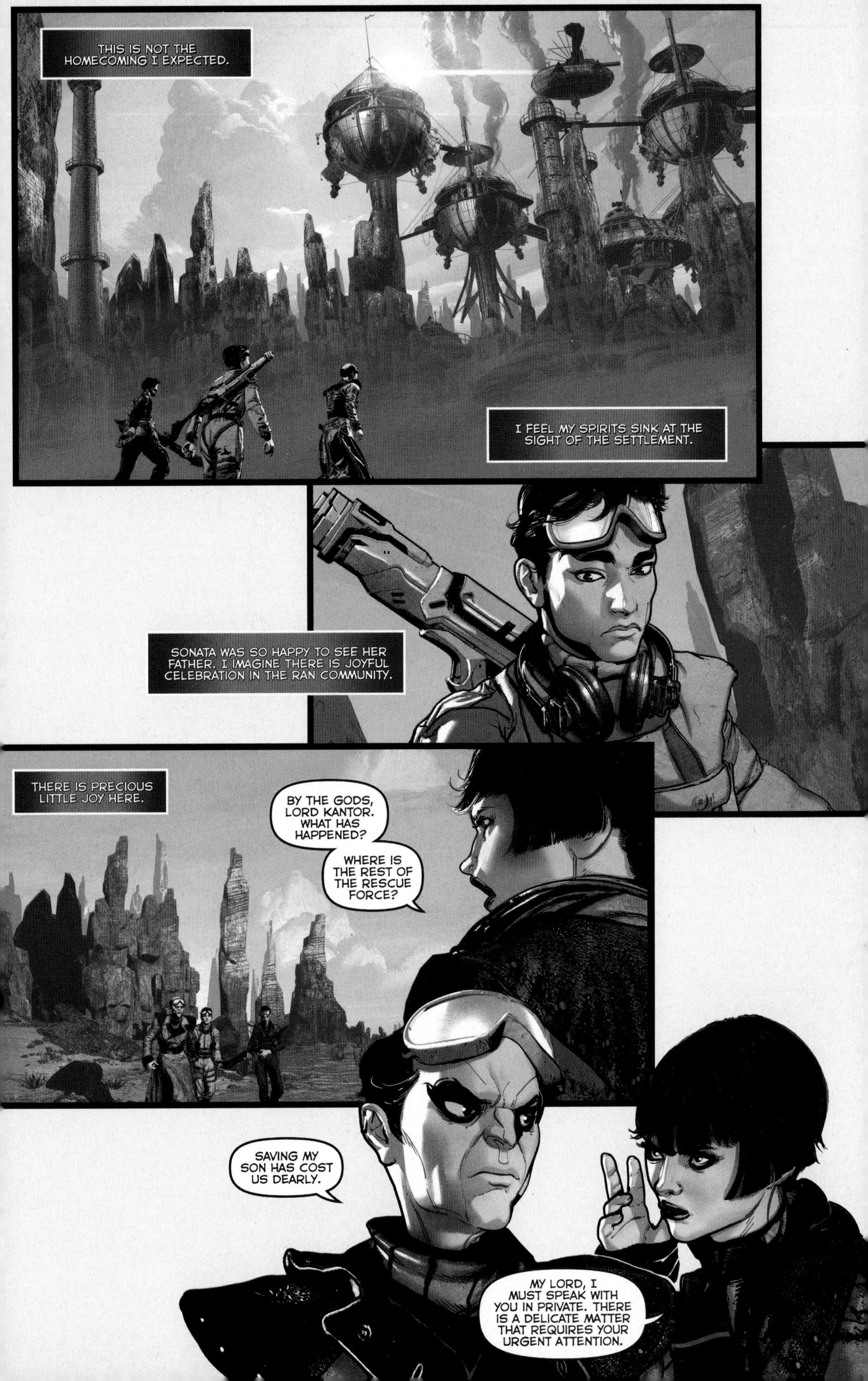
THIS IS NOT THE HOMECOMING I EXPECTED.
I FEEL MY SPIRITS SINK AT THE SIGHT OF THE SETTLEMENT.
SONATA WAS SO HAPPY TO SEE HER FATHER. I IMAGINE THERE IS JOYFUL CELEBRATION IN THE RAN COMMUNITY.
THERE IS PRECIOUS LITTLE JOY HERE.
BY THE GODS, LORD KANTOR. WHAT HAS HAPPENED?
WHERE IS THE REST OF THE RESCUE FORCE?
SAVING MY SON HAS COST US DEARLY.
MY LORD, I MUST SPEAK WITH YOU IN PRIVATE. THERE IS A DELICATE MATTER THAT REQUIRES YOUR URGENT ATTENTION.

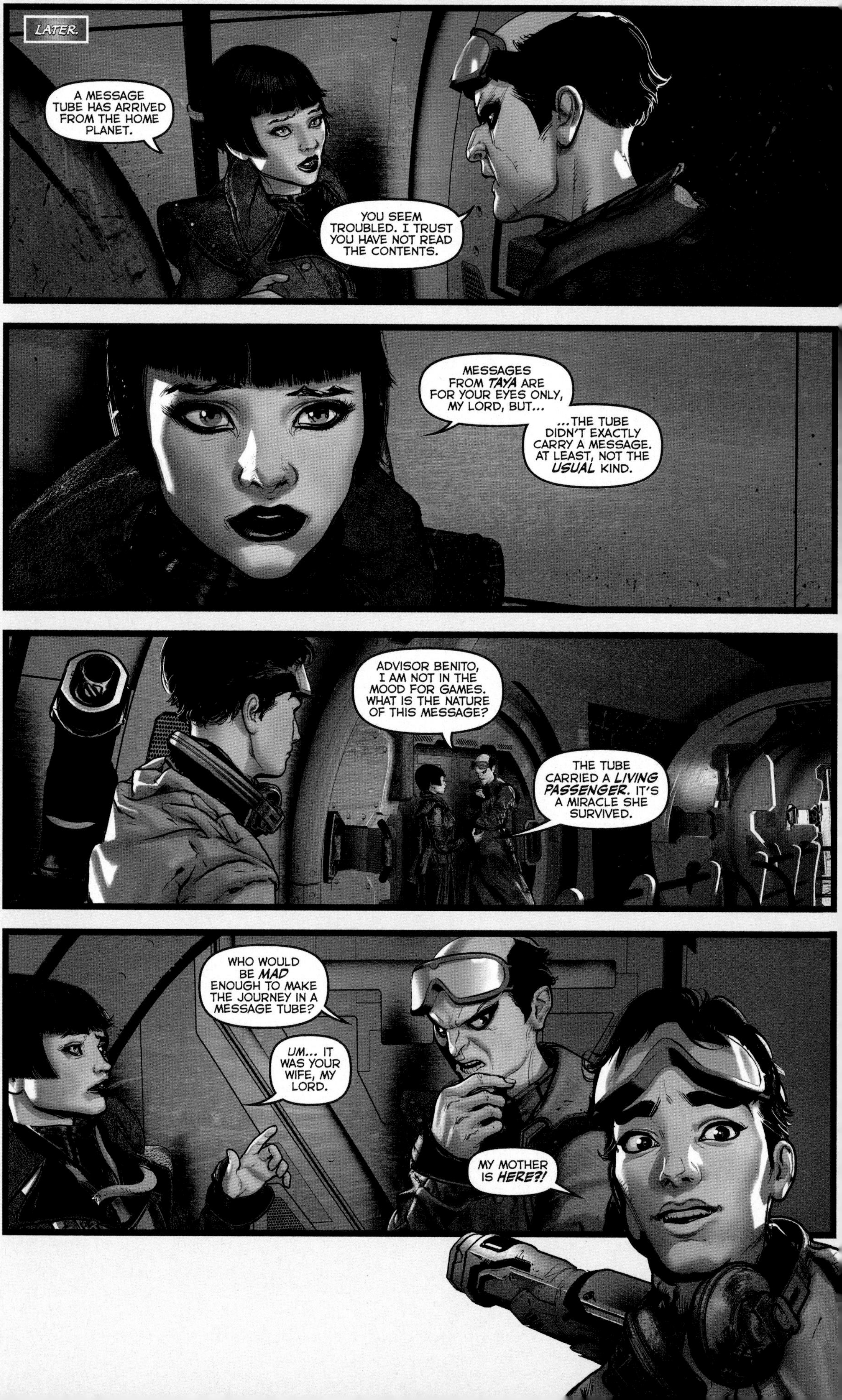
LATER.
A MESSAGE TUBE HAS ARRIVED FROM THE HOME PLANET.
YOU SEEM TROUBLED. I TRUST YOU HAVE NOT READ THE CONTENTS.
MESSAGES FROM TAYA ARE FOR YOUR EYES ONLY, MY LORD, BUT...
...THE TUBE DIDN'T EXACTLY CARRY A MESSAGE. AT LEAST, NOT THE USUAL KIND.
ADVISOR BENITO, I AM NOT IN THE MOOD FOR GAMES. WHAT IS THE NATURE OF THIS MESSAGE?
THE TUBE CARRIED A LIVING PASSENGER. IT'S A MIRACLE SHE SURVIVED.
WHO WOULD BE MAD ENOUGH TO MAKE THE JOURNEY IN A MESSAGE TUBE?
UM... IT WAS YOUR WIFE, MY LORD.
MY MOTHER IS HERE?!

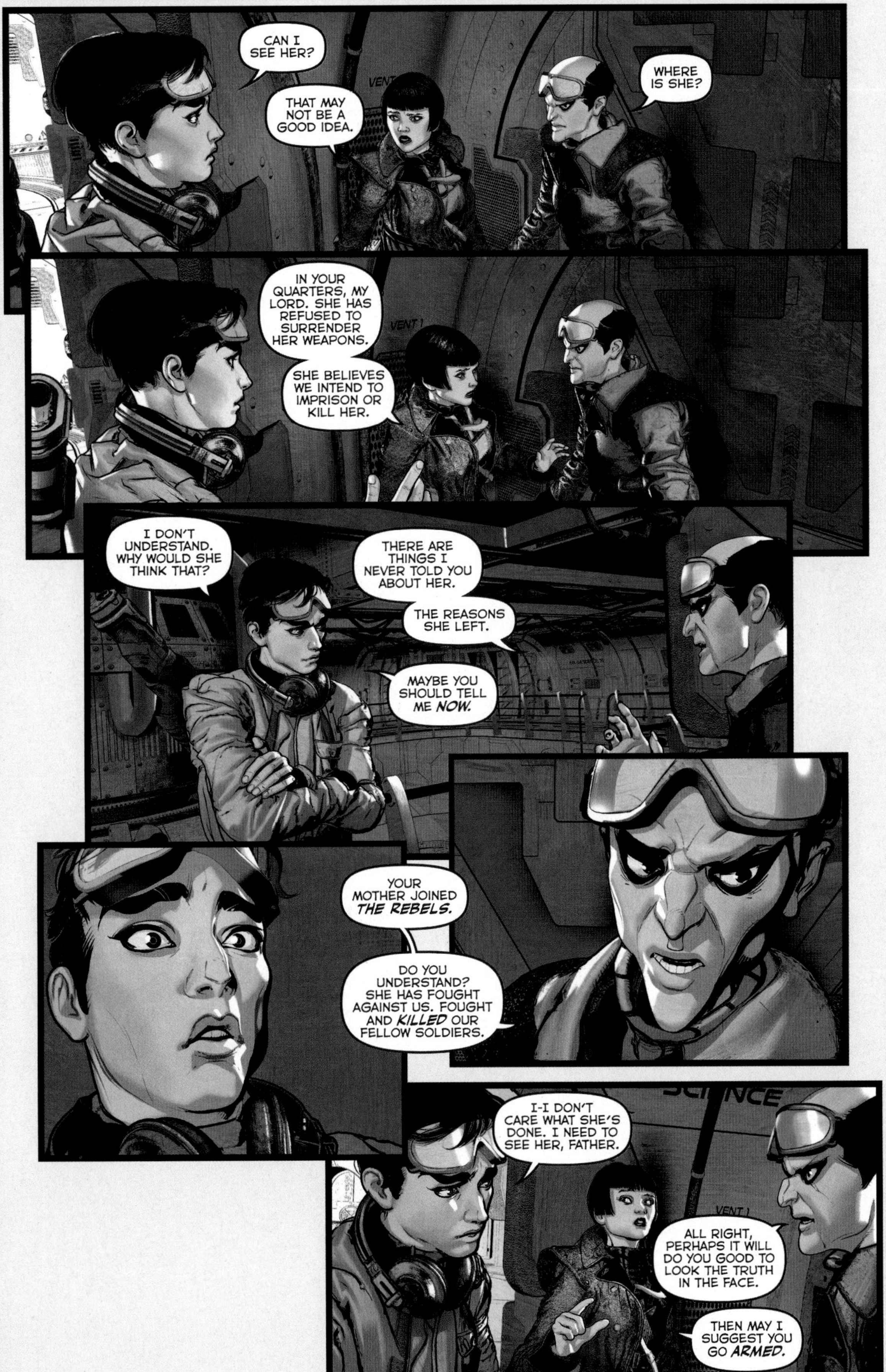
CAN I SEE HER?
THAT MAY NOT BE A GOOD IDEA.
WHERE IS SHE?
IN YOUR QUARTERS, MY LORD. SHE HAS REFUSED TO SURRENDER HER WEAPONS.
SHE BELIEVES WE INTEND TO IMPRISON OR KILL HER.
I DON'T UNDERSTAND. WHY WOULD SHE THINK THAT?
THERE ARE THINGS I NEVER TOLD YOU ABOUT HER.
THE REASONS SHE LEFT.
MAYBE YOU SHOULD TELL ME NOW.
YOUR MOTHER JOINED THE REBELS.
DO YOU UNDERSTAND? SHE HAS FOUGHT AGAINST US. FOUGHT AND KILLED OUR FELLOW SOLDIERS.
I-I DON'T CARE WHAT SHE'S DONE. I NEED TO SEE HER, FATHER.
ALL RIGHT, PERHAPS IT WILL DO YOU GOOD TO LOOK THE TRUTH IN THE FACE.
THEN MAY I SUGGEST YOU GO ARMED.

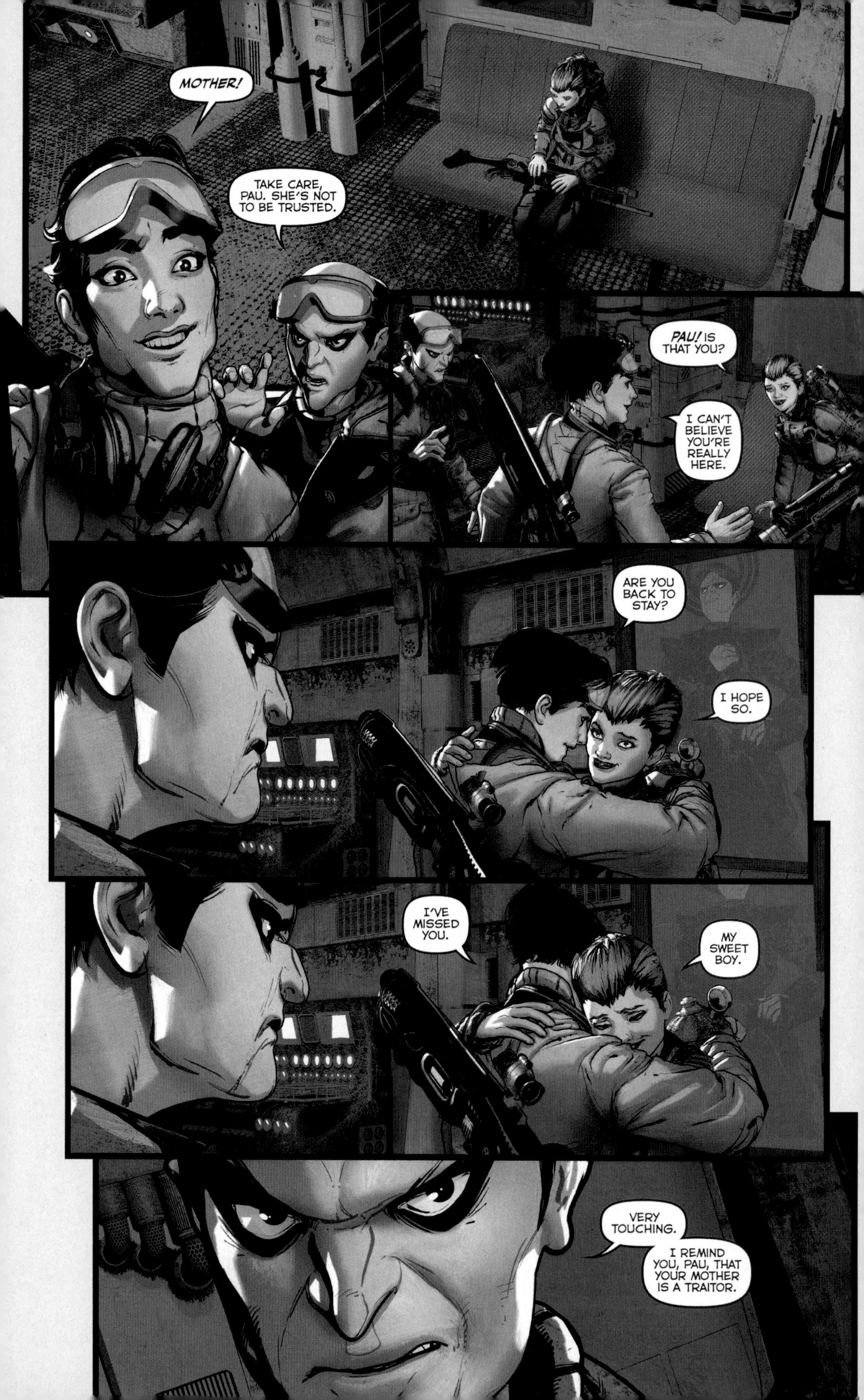
MOTHER!
TAKE CARE, PAU. SHE'S NOT TO BE TRUSTED.
PAU! IS THAT YOU?
I CAN'T BELIEVE YOU'RE REALLY HERE.
ARE YOU BACK TO STAY?
I HOPE SO.
I'VE MISSED YOU.
MY SWEET BOY.
VERY TOUCHING.
I REMIND YOU, PAU, THAT YOUR MOTHER IS A TRAITOR.

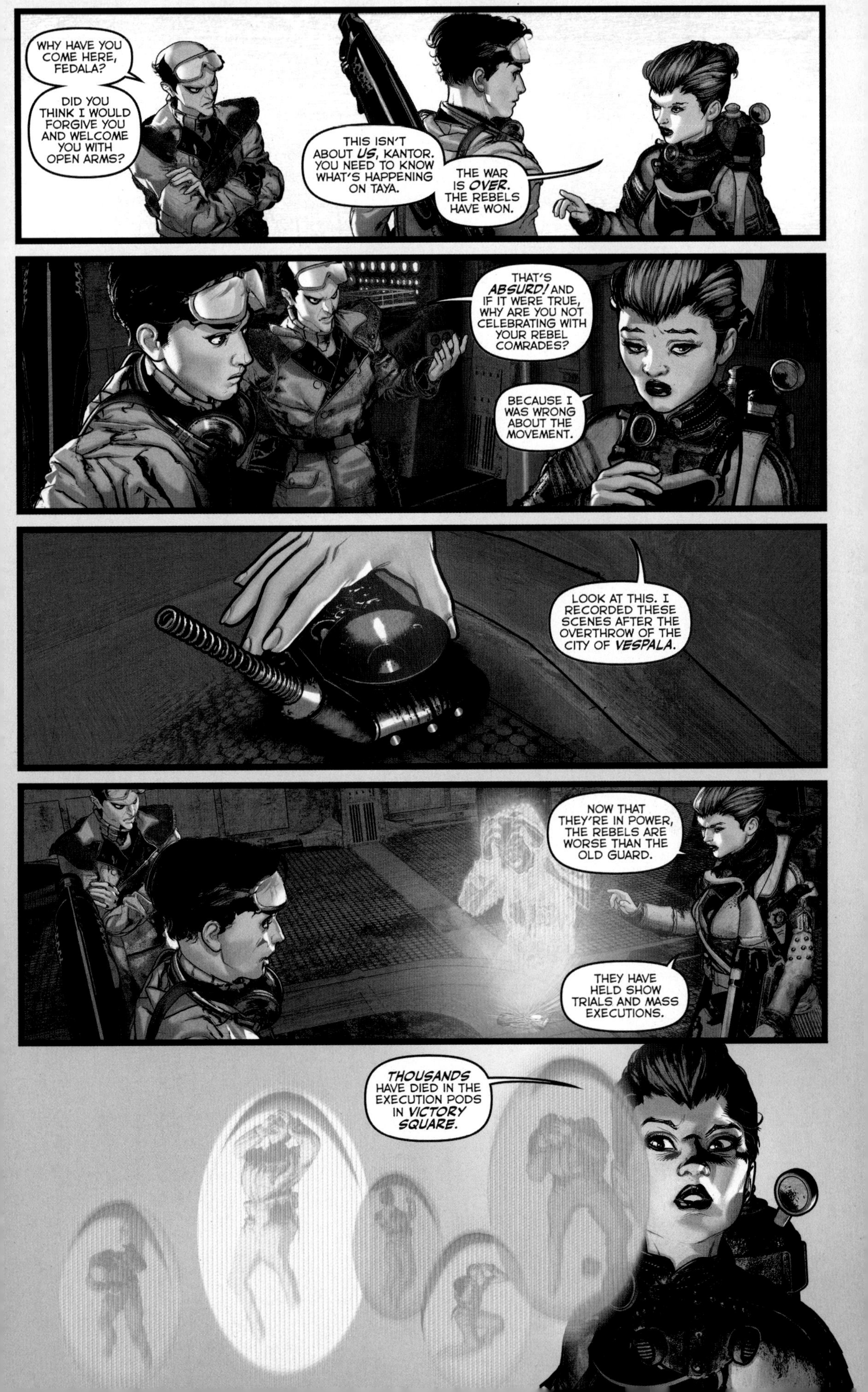
WHY HAVE YOU COME HERE, FEDALA?
DID YOU THINK I WOULD FORGIVE YOU AND WELCOME YOU WITH OPEN ARMS?
THIS ISN'T ABOUT US, KANTOR. YOU NEED TO KNOW WHAT'S HAPPENING ON TAYA.
THE WAR IS OVER. THE REBELS HAVE WON.
THAT'S ABSURD! AND IF IT WERE TRUE, WHY ARE YOU NOT CELEBRATING WITH YOUR REBEL COMRADES?
BECAUSE I WAS WRONG ABOUT THE MOVEMENT.
LOOK AT THIS. I RECORDED THESE SCENES AFTER THE OVERTHROW OF THE CITY OF VESPALA.
NOW THAT THEY'RE IN POWER, THE REBELS ARE WORSE THAN THE OLD GUARD.
THEY HAVE HELD SHOW TRIALS AND MASS EXECUTIONS.
THOUSANDS HAVE DIED IN THE EXECUTION PODS IN VICTORY SQUARE.

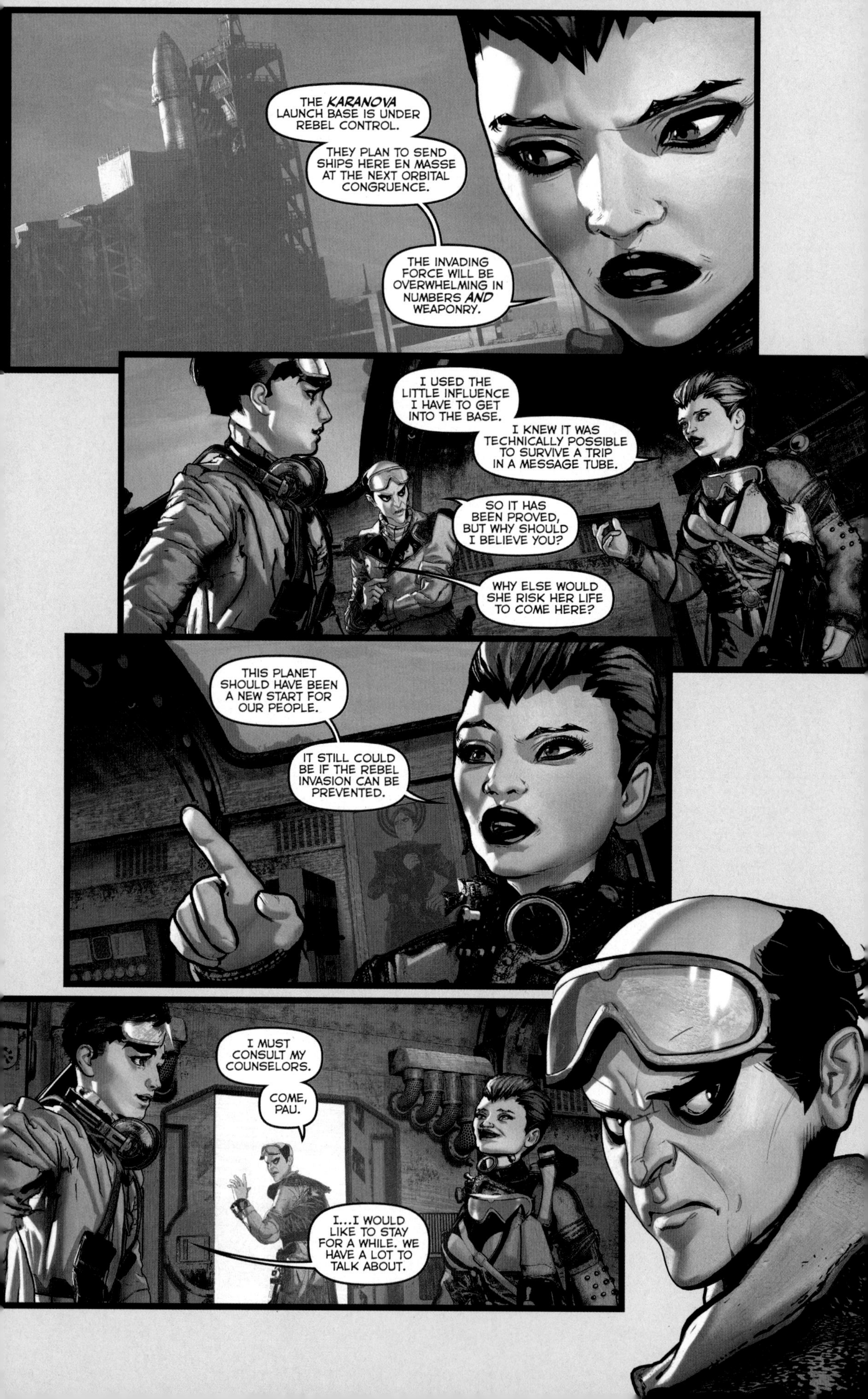

THE *KARANOVA* LAUNCH BASE IS UNDER REBEL CONTROL.
THEY PLAN TO SEND SHIPS HERE EN MASSE AT THE NEXT ORBITAL CONGRUENCE.
THE INVADING FORCE WILL BE OVERWHELMING IN NUMBERS *AND* WEAPONRY.
I USED THE LITTLE INFLUENCE I HAVE TO GET INTO THE BASE.
I KNEW IT WAS TECHNICALLY POSSIBLE TO SURVIVE A TRIP IN A MESSAGE TUBE.
SO IT HAS BEEN PROVED, BUT WHY SHOULD I BELIEVE YOU?
WHY ELSE WOULD SHE RISK HER LIFE TO COME HERE?
THIS PLANET SHOULD HAVE BEEN A NEW START FOR OUR PEOPLE.
IT STILL COULD BE IF THE REBEL INVASION CAN BE PREVENTED.
I MUST CONSULT MY COUNSELORS.
COME, PAU.
I...I WOULD LIKE TO STAY FOR A WHILE. WE HAVE A LOT TO TALK ABOUT.

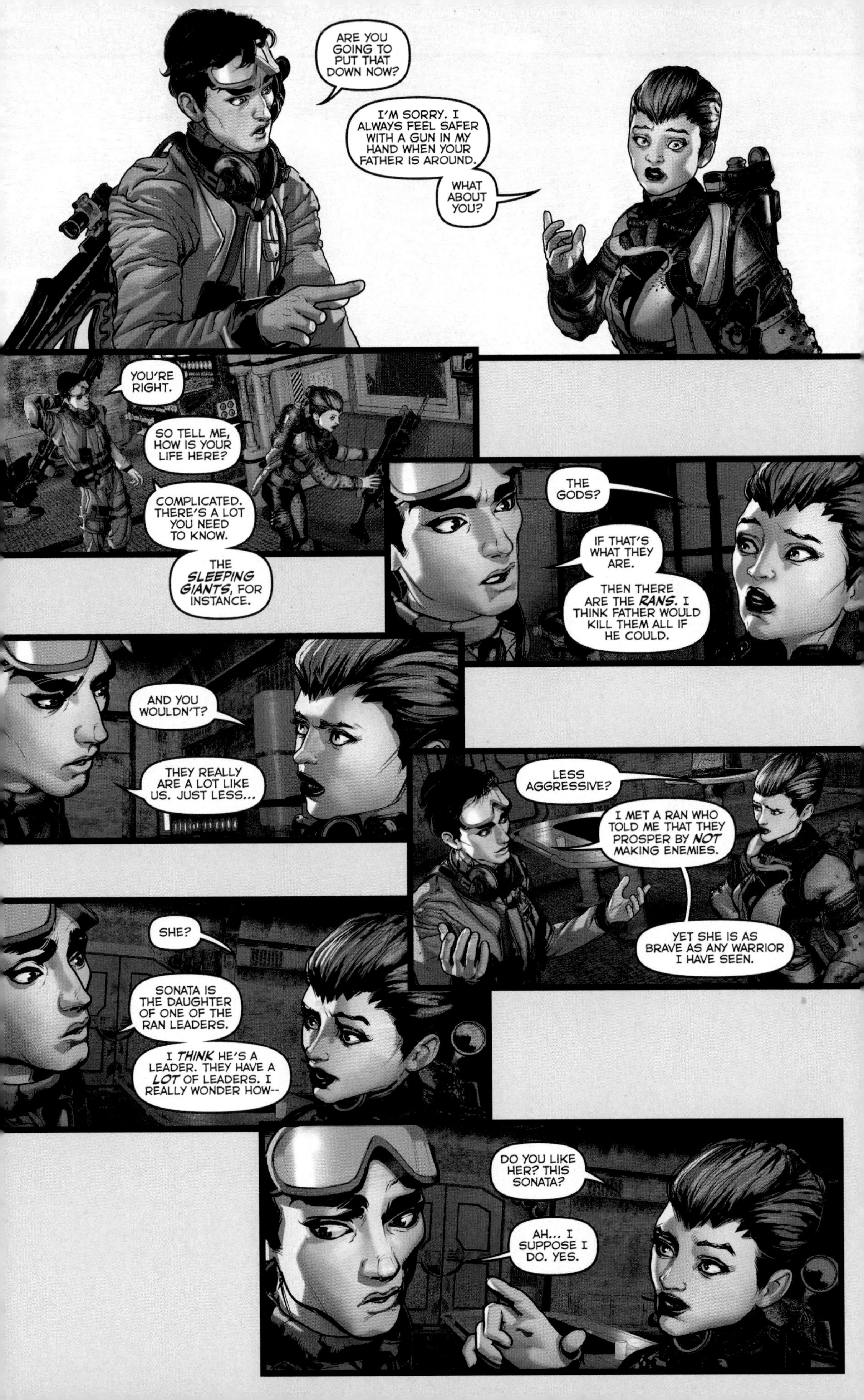
ARE YOU GOING TO PUT THAT DOWN NOW?
I'M SORRY. I ALWAYS FEEL SAFER WITH A GUN IN MY HAND WHEN YOUR FATHER IS AROUND.
WHAT ABOUT YOU?
YOU'RE RIGHT.
SO TELL ME, HOW IS YOUR LIFE HERE?
COMPLICATED. THERE'S A LOT YOU NEED TO KNOW.
THE SLEEPING GIANTS, FOR INSTANCE.
THE GODS?
IF THAT'S WHAT THEY ARE.
THEN THERE ARE THE RANS. I THINK FATHER WOULD KILL THEM ALL IF HE COULD.
AND YOU WOULDN'T?
THEY REALLY ARE A LOT LIKE US. JUST LESS...
LESS AGGRESSIVE?
I MET A RAN WHO TOLD ME THAT THEY PROSPER BY NOT MAKING ENEMIES.
YET SHE IS AS BRAVE AS ANY WARRIOR I HAVE SEEN.
SHE?
SONATA IS THE DAUGHTER OF ONE OF THE RAN LEADERS.
I THINK HE'S A LEADER. THEY HAVE A LOT OF LEADERS. I REALLY WONDER HOW--
DO YOU LIKE HER? THIS SONATA?
AH... I SUPPOSE I DO. YES.

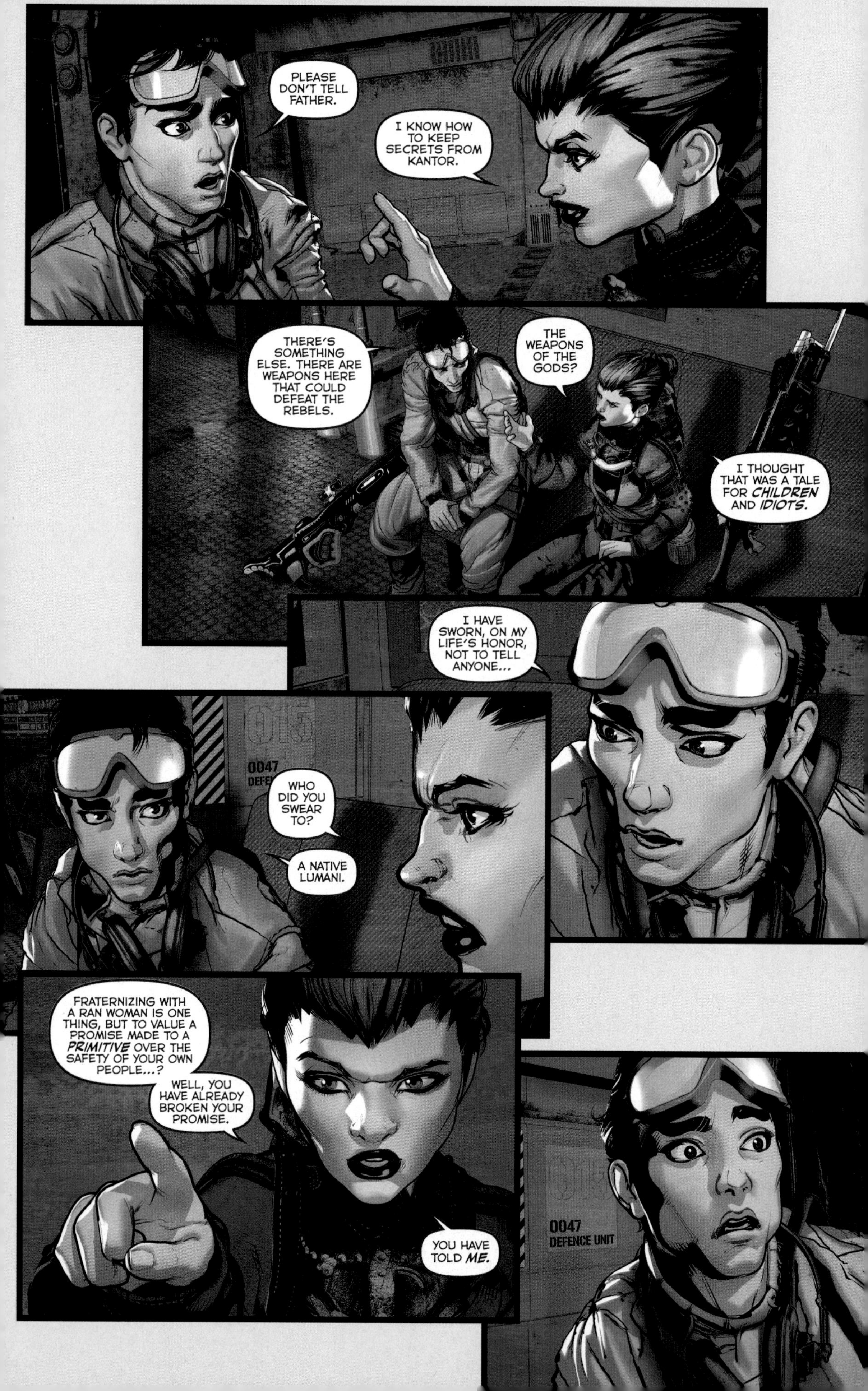
PLEASE DON'T TELL FATHER.
I KNOW HOW TO KEEP SECRETS FROM KANTOR.
THERE'S SOMETHING ELSE. THERE ARE WEAPONS HERE THAT COULD DEFEAT THE REBELS.
THE WEAPONS OF THE GODS?
I THOUGHT THAT WAS A TALE FOR CHILDREN AND IDIOTS.
I HAVE SWORN, ON MY LIFE'S HONOR, NOT TO TELL ANYONE...
0047
WHO DID YOU SWEAR TO?
A NATIVE LUMANI.
FRATERNIZING WITH A RAN WOMAN IS ONE THING, BUT TO VALUE A PROMISE MADE TO A PRIMITIVE OVER THE SAFETY OF YOUR OWN PEOPLE...?
WELL, YOU HAVE ALREADY BROKEN YOUR PROMISE.
YOU HAVE TOLD ME.
0047
DEFENCE UNIT

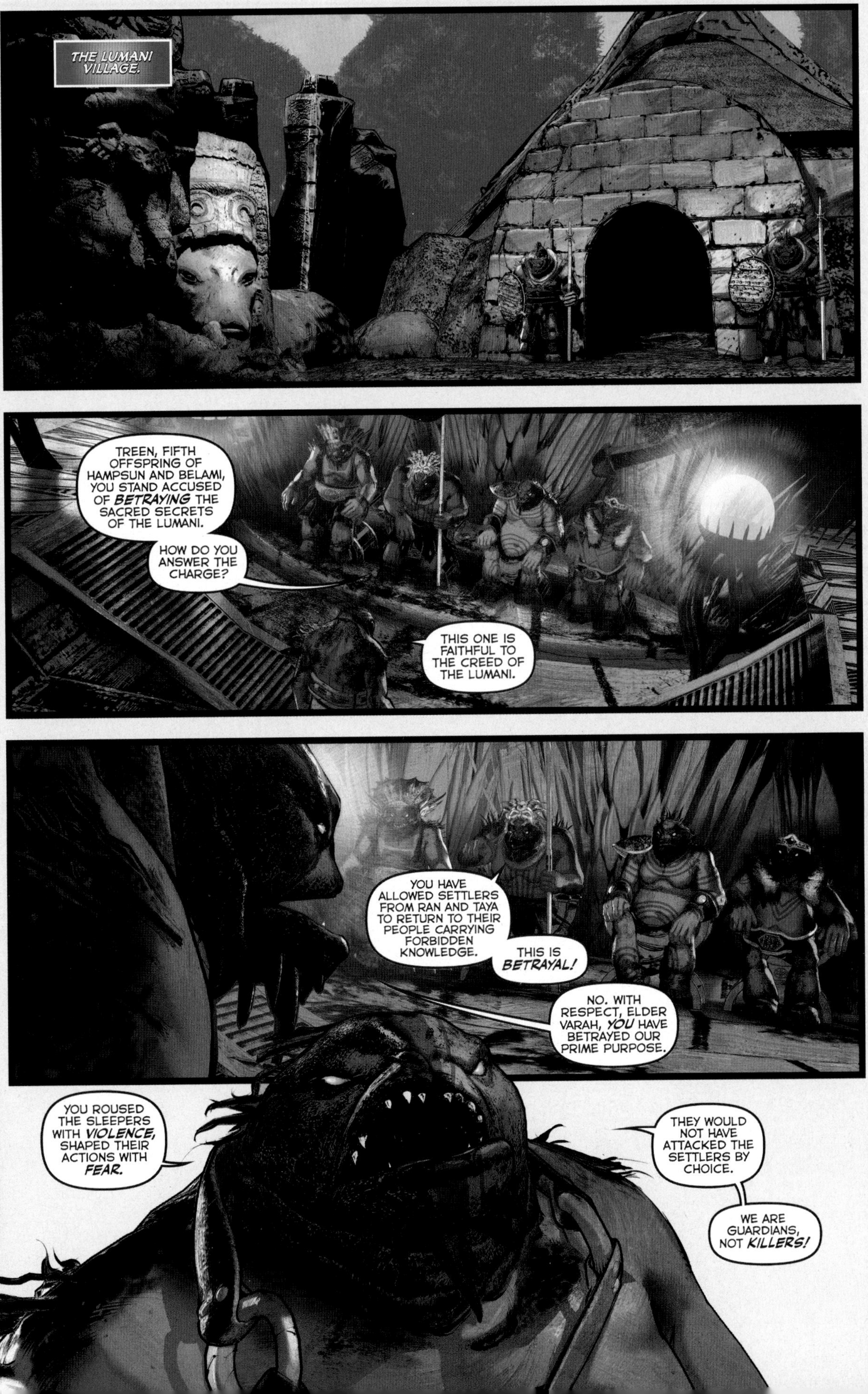
THE LUMANI VILLAGE.
TREEN, FIFTH OFFSPRING OF HAMPSUN AND BELAMI, YOU STAND ACCUSED OF BETRAYING THE SACRED SECRETS OF THE LUMANI.
HOW DO YOU ANSWER THE CHARGE?
THIS ONE IS FAITHFUL TO THE CREED OF THE LUMANI.
YOU HAVE ALLOWED SETTLERS FROM RAN AND TAYA TO RETURN TO THEIR PEOPLE CARRYING FORBIDDEN KNOWLEDGE.
THIS IS BETRAYAL!
NO. WITH RESPECT, ELDER VARAH, YOU HAVE BETRAYED OUR PRIME PURPOSE.
YOU ROUSED THE SLEEPERS WITH VIOLENCE, SHAPED THEIR ACTIONS WITH FEAR.
THEY WOULD NOT HAVE ATTACKED THE SETTLERS BY CHOICE.
WE ARE GUARDIANS, NOT KILLERS!

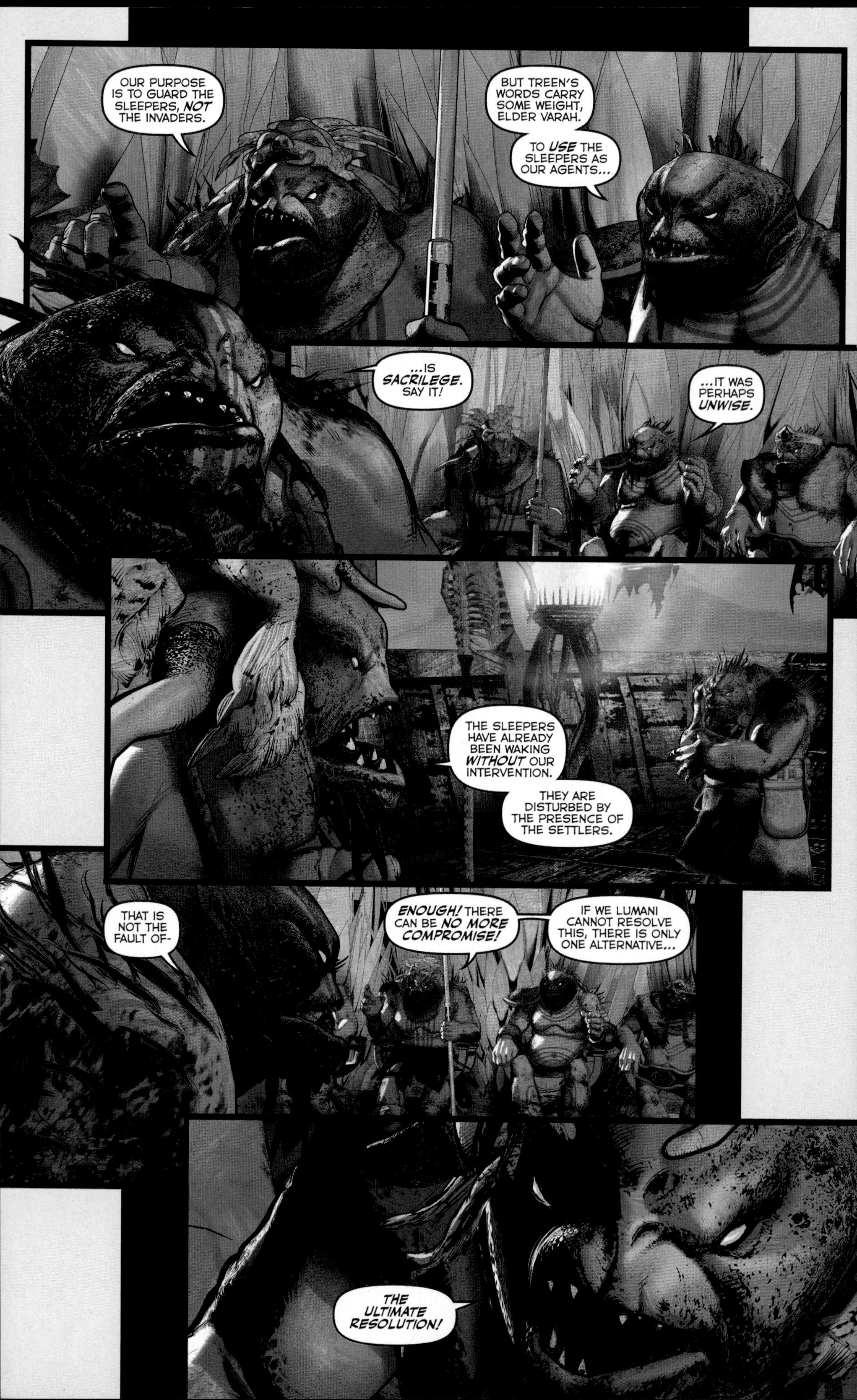

OUR PURPOSE IS TO GUARD THE SLEEPERS, NOT THE INVADERS.
BUT TREEN'S WORDS CARRY SOME WEIGHT, ELDER VARAH.
TO USE THE SLEEPERS AS OUR AGENTS...
...IS SACRILEGE. SAY IT!
...IT WAS PERHAPS UNWISE.
THE SLEEPERS HAVE ALREADY BEEN WAKING WITHOUT OUR INTERVENTION.
THEY ARE DISTURBED BY THE PRESENCE OF THE SETTLERS.
THAT IS NOT THE FAULT OF-
ENOUGH! THERE CAN BE NO MORE COMPROMISE!
IF WE LUMANI CANNOT RESOLVE THIS, THERE IS ONLY ONE ALTERNATIVE...
THE ULTIMATE RESOLUTION!

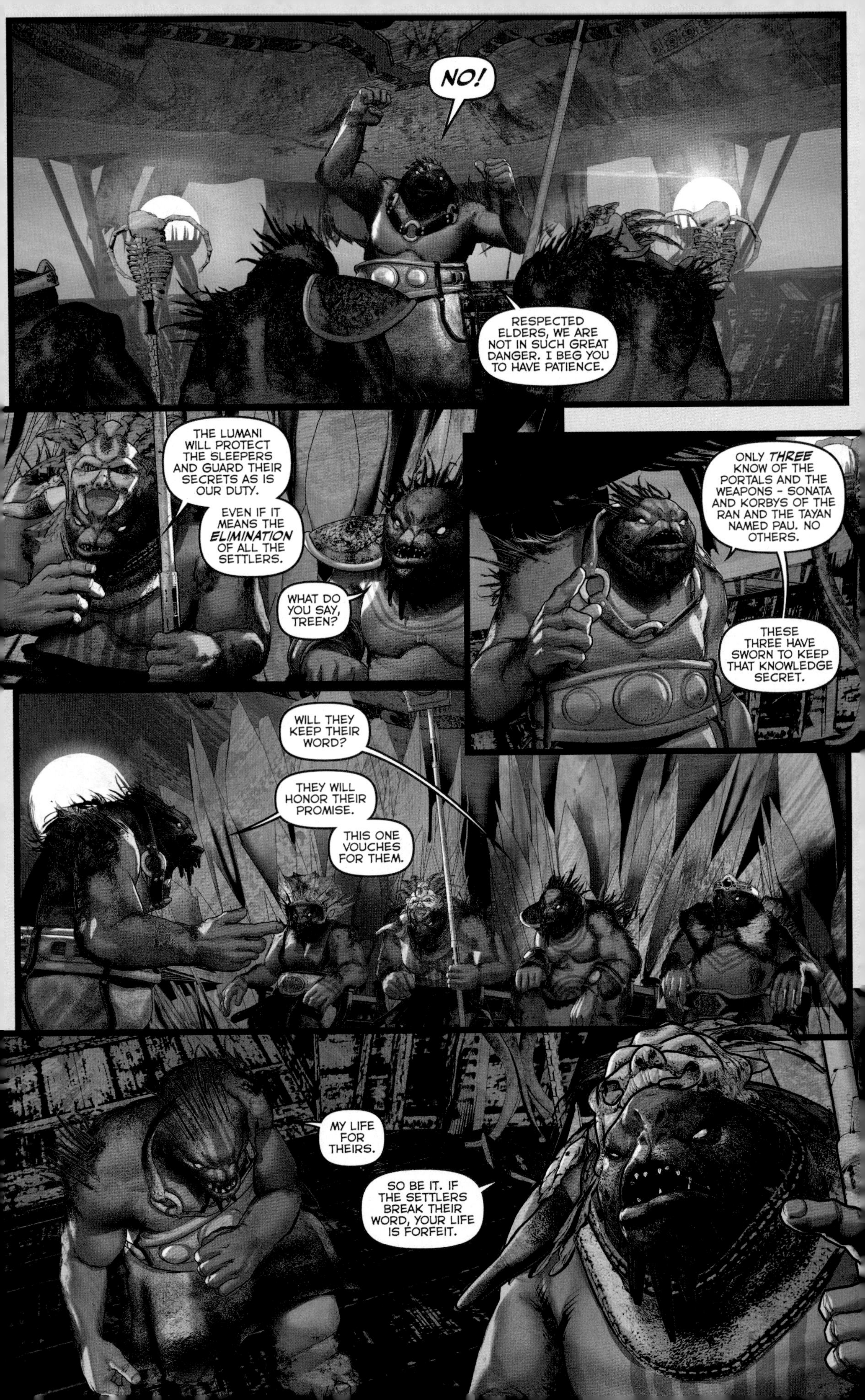
NO!
RESPECTED ELDERS, WE ARE NOT IN SUCH GREAT DANGER. I BEG YOU TO HAVE PATIENCE.
THE LUMANI WILL PROTECT THE SLEEPERS AND GUARD THEIR SECRETS AS IS OUR DUTY.
EVEN IF IT MEANS THE ELIMINATION OF ALL THE SETTLERS.
WHAT DO YOU SAY, TREEN?
ONLY THREE KNOW OF THE PORTALS AND THE WEAPONS - SONATA AND KORBYS OF THE RAN AND THE TAYAN NAMED PAU. NO OTHERS.
THESE THREE HAVE SWORN TO KEEP THAT KNOWLEDGE SECRET.
WILL THEY KEEP THEIR WORD?
THEY WILL HONOR THEIR PROMISE.
THIS ONE VOUCHES FOR THEM.
MY LIFE FOR THEIRS.
SO BE IT. IF THE SETTLERS BREAK THEIR WORD, YOUR LIFE IS FORFEIT.

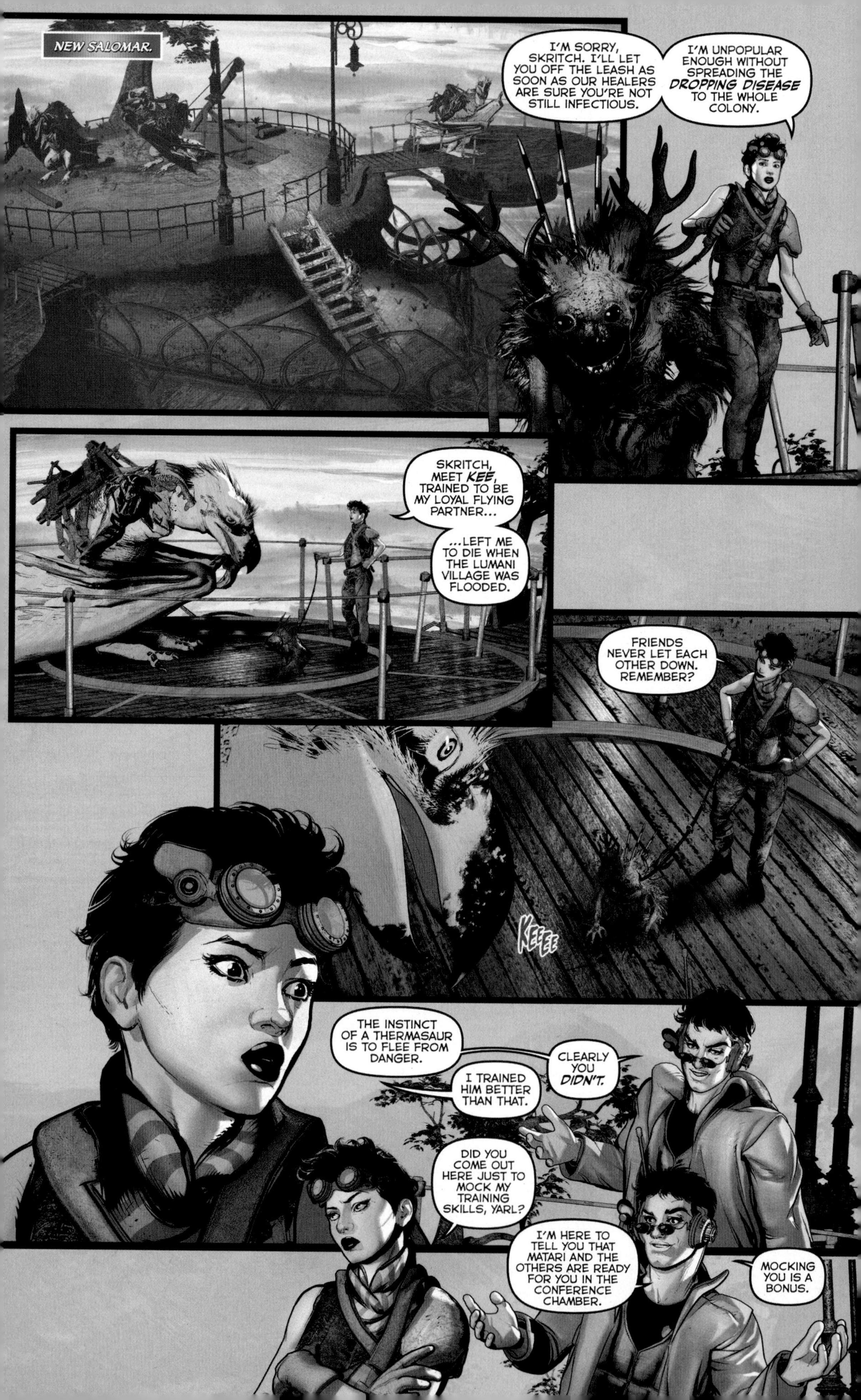
NEW SALOMAR.
I'M SORRY, SKRITCH. I'LL LET YOU OFF THE LEASH AS SOON AS OUR HEALERS ARE SURE YOU'RE NOT STILL INFECTIOUS.
I'M UNPOPULAR ENOUGH WITHOUT SPREADING THE DROPPING DISEASE TO THE WHOLE COLONY.
SKRITCH, MEET KEE, TRAINED TO BE MY LOYAL FLYING PARTNER...
...LEFT ME TO DIE WHEN THE LUMANI VILLAGE WAS FLOODED.
FRIENDS NEVER LET EACH OTHER DOWN. REMEMBER?
KEEEE
THE INSTINCT OF A THERMASAUR IS TO FLEE FROM DANGER.
I TRAINED HIM BETTER THAN THAT.
CLEARLY YOU DIDN'T.
DID YOU COME OUT HERE JUST TO MOCK MY TRAINING SKILLS, YARL?
I'M HERE TO TELL YOU THAT MATARI AND THE OTHERS ARE READY FOR YOU IN THE CONFERENCE CHAMBER.
MOCKING YOU IS A BONUS.

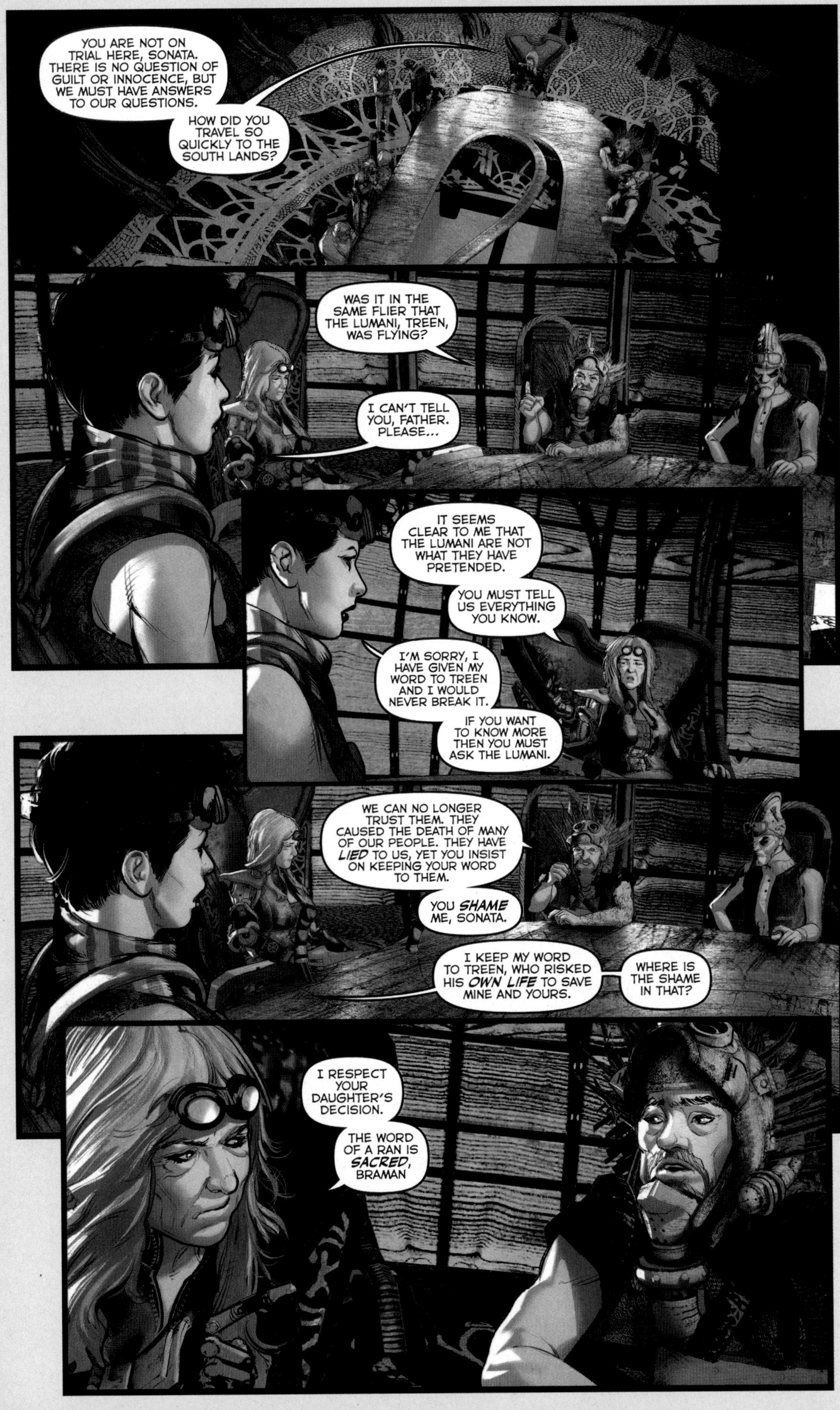
YOU ARE NOT ON TRIAL HERE, SONATA. THERE IS NO QUESTION OF GUILT OR INNOCENCE, BUT WE MUST HAVE ANSWERS TO OUR QUESTIONS.
HOW DID YOU TRAVEL SO QUICKLY TO THE SOUTH LANDS?
WAS IT IN THE SAME FLIER THAT THE LUMANI, TREEN, WAS FLYING?
I CAN'T TELL YOU, FATHER. PLEASE...
IT SEEMS CLEAR TO ME THAT THE LUMANI ARE NOT WHAT THEY HAVE PRETENDED.
YOU MUST TELL US EVERYTHING YOU KNOW.
I'M SORRY, I HAVE GIVEN MY WORD TO TREEN AND I WOULD NEVER BREAK IT.
IF YOU WANT TO KNOW MORE THEN YOU MUST ASK THE LUMANI.
WE CAN NO LONGER TRUST THEM. THEY CAUSED THE DEATH OF MANY OF OUR PEOPLE. THEY HAVE *LIED* TO US, YET YOU INSIST ON KEEPING YOUR WORD TO THEM.
YOU ***SHAME*** ME, SONATA.
I KEEP MY WORD TO TREEN, WHO RISKED HIS ***OWN LIFE*** TO SAVE MINE AND YOURS.
WHERE IS THE SHAME IN THAT?
I RESPECT YOUR DAUGHTER'S DECISION.
THE WORD OF A RAN IS ***SACRED***, BRAMAN

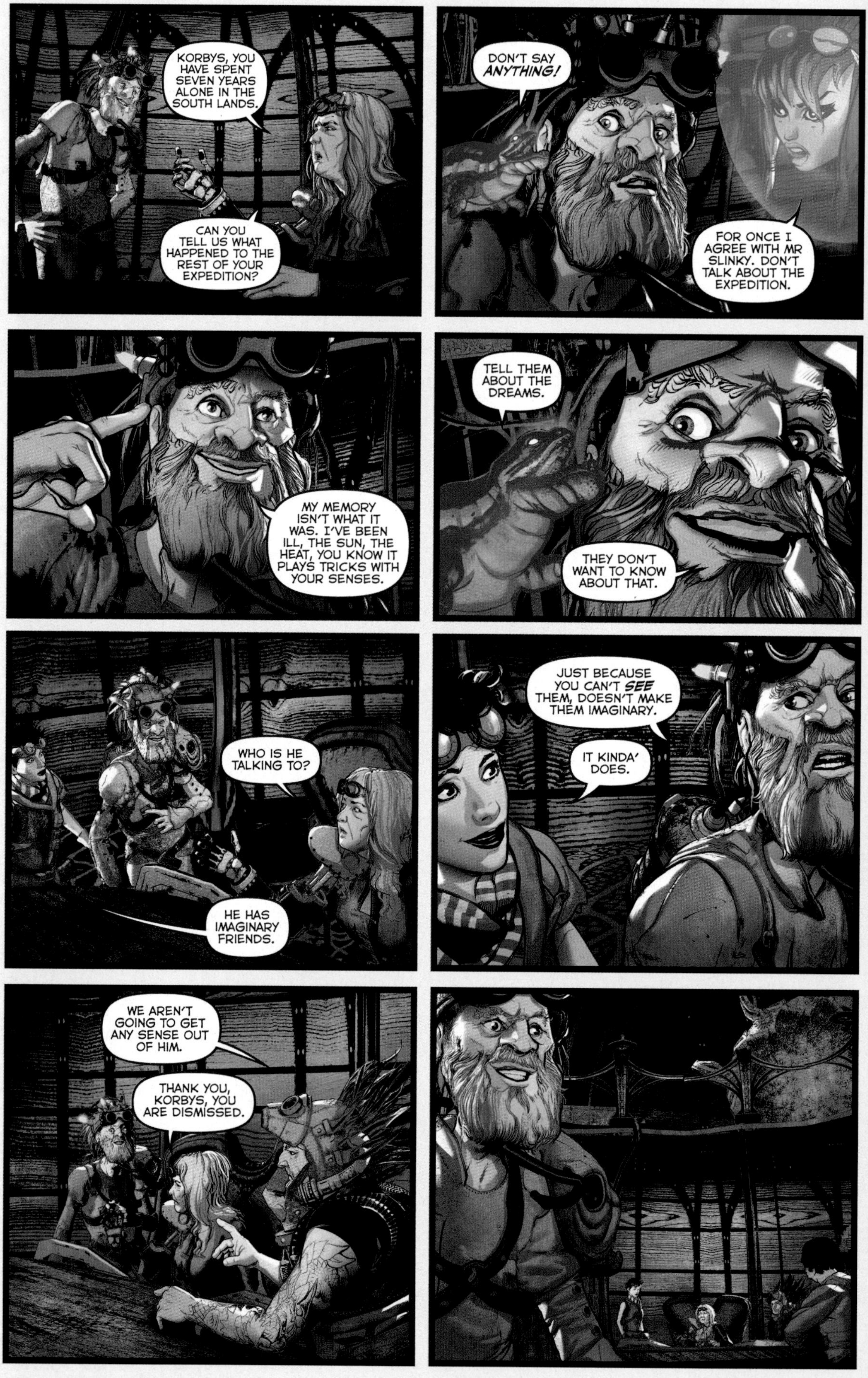

KORBYS, YOU HAVE SPENT SEVEN YEARS ALONE IN THE SOUTH LANDS.
CAN YOU TELL US WHAT HAPPENED TO THE REST OF YOUR EXPEDITION?
DON'T SAY *ANYTHING!*
FOR ONCE I AGREE WITH MR SLINKY. DON'T TALK ABOUT THE EXPEDITION.
MY MEMORY ISN'T WHAT IT WAS. I'VE BEEN ILL, THE SUN, THE HEAT, YOU KNOW IT PLAYS TRICKS WITH YOUR SENSES.
TELL THEM ABOUT THE DREAMS.
THEY DON'T WANT TO KNOW ABOUT THAT.
WHO IS HE TALKING TO?
HE HAS IMAGINARY FRIENDS.
JUST BECAUSE YOU CAN'T *SEE* THEM, DOESN'T MAKE THEM IMAGINARY.
IT KINDA' DOES.
WE AREN'T GOING TO GET ANY SENSE OUT OF HIM.
THANK YOU, KORBYS, YOU ARE DISMISSED.

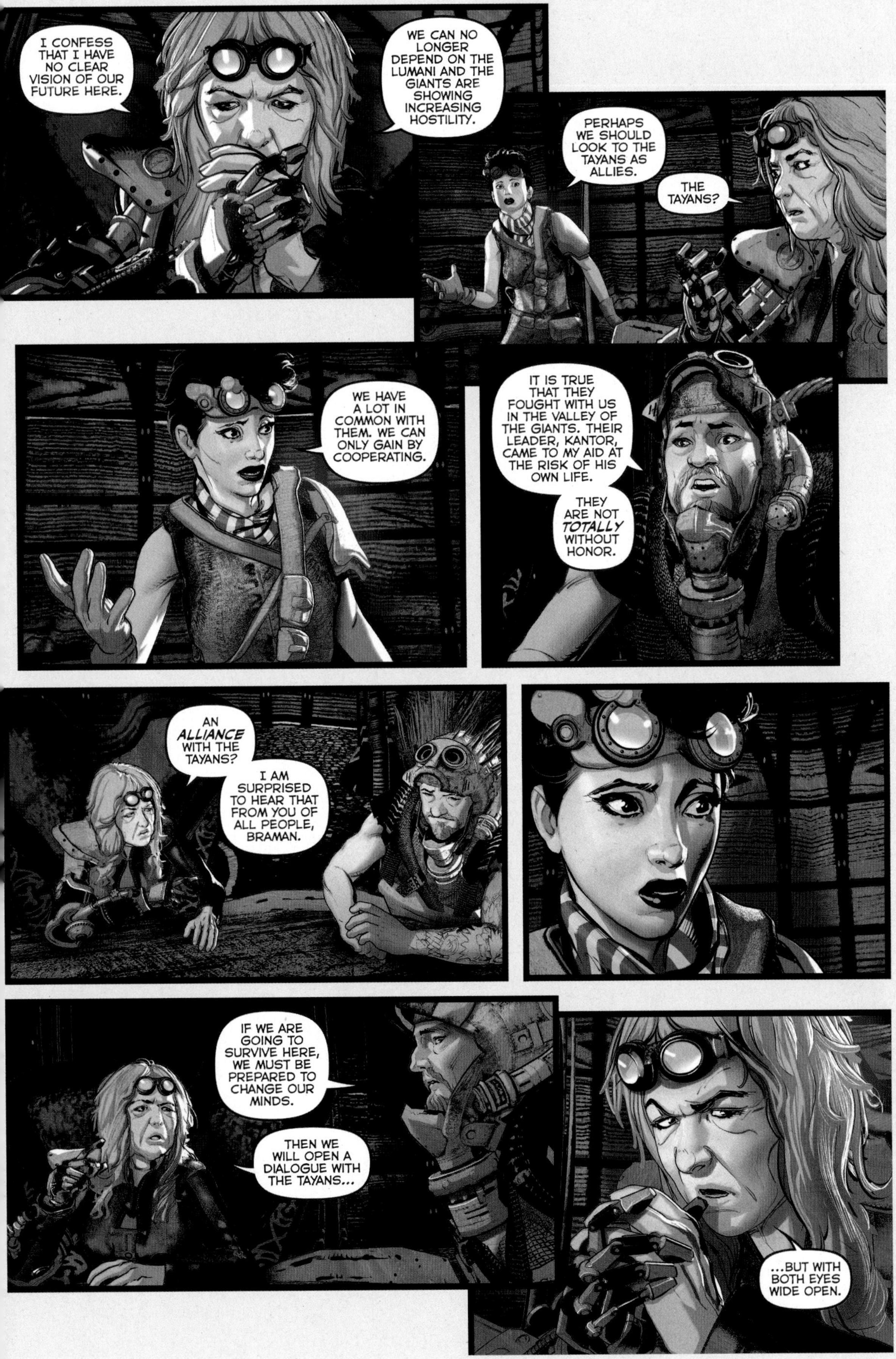
I CONFESS THAT I HAVE NO CLEAR VISION OF OUR FUTURE HERE.
WE CAN NO LONGER DEPEND ON THE LUMANI AND THE GIANTS ARE SHOWING INCREASING HOSTILITY.
PERHAPS WE SHOULD LOOK TO THE TAYANS AS ALLIES.
THE TAYANS?
WE HAVE A LOT IN COMMON WITH THEM. WE CAN ONLY GAIN BY COOPERATING.
IT IS TRUE THAT THEY FOUGHT WITH US IN THE VALLEY OF THE GIANTS. THEIR LEADER, KANTOR, CAME TO MY AID AT THE RISK OF HIS OWN LIFE.
THEY ARE NOT *TOTALLY* WITHOUT HONOR.
AN *ALLIANCE* WITH THE TAYANS?
I AM SURPRISED TO HEAR THAT FROM YOU OF ALL PEOPLE, BRAMAN.
IF WE ARE GOING TO SURVIVE HERE, WE MUST BE PREPARED TO CHANGE OUR MINDS.
THEN WE WILL OPEN A DIALOGUE WITH THE TAYANS...
...BUT WITH BOTH EYES WIDE OPEN.

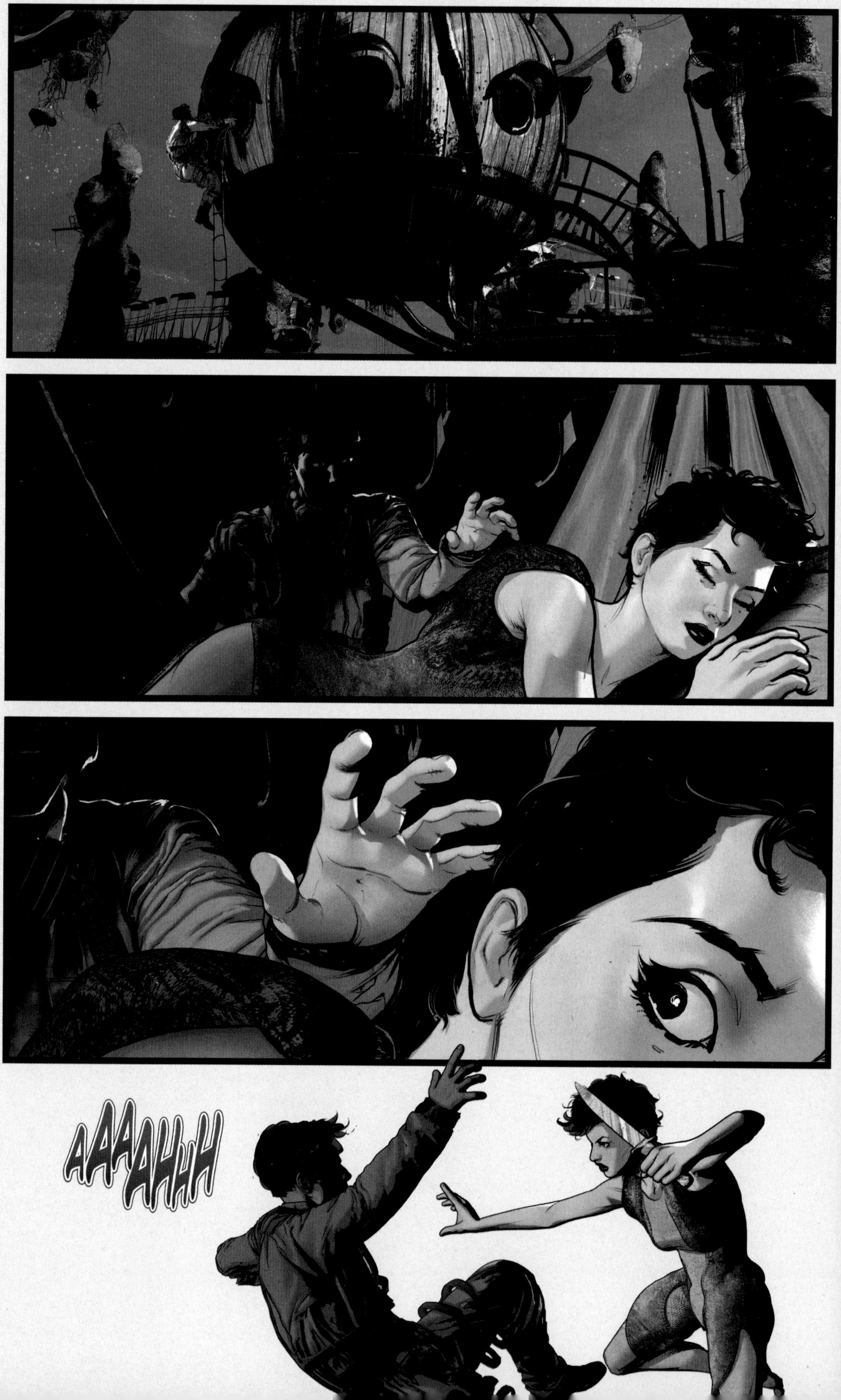
AAAAHHH

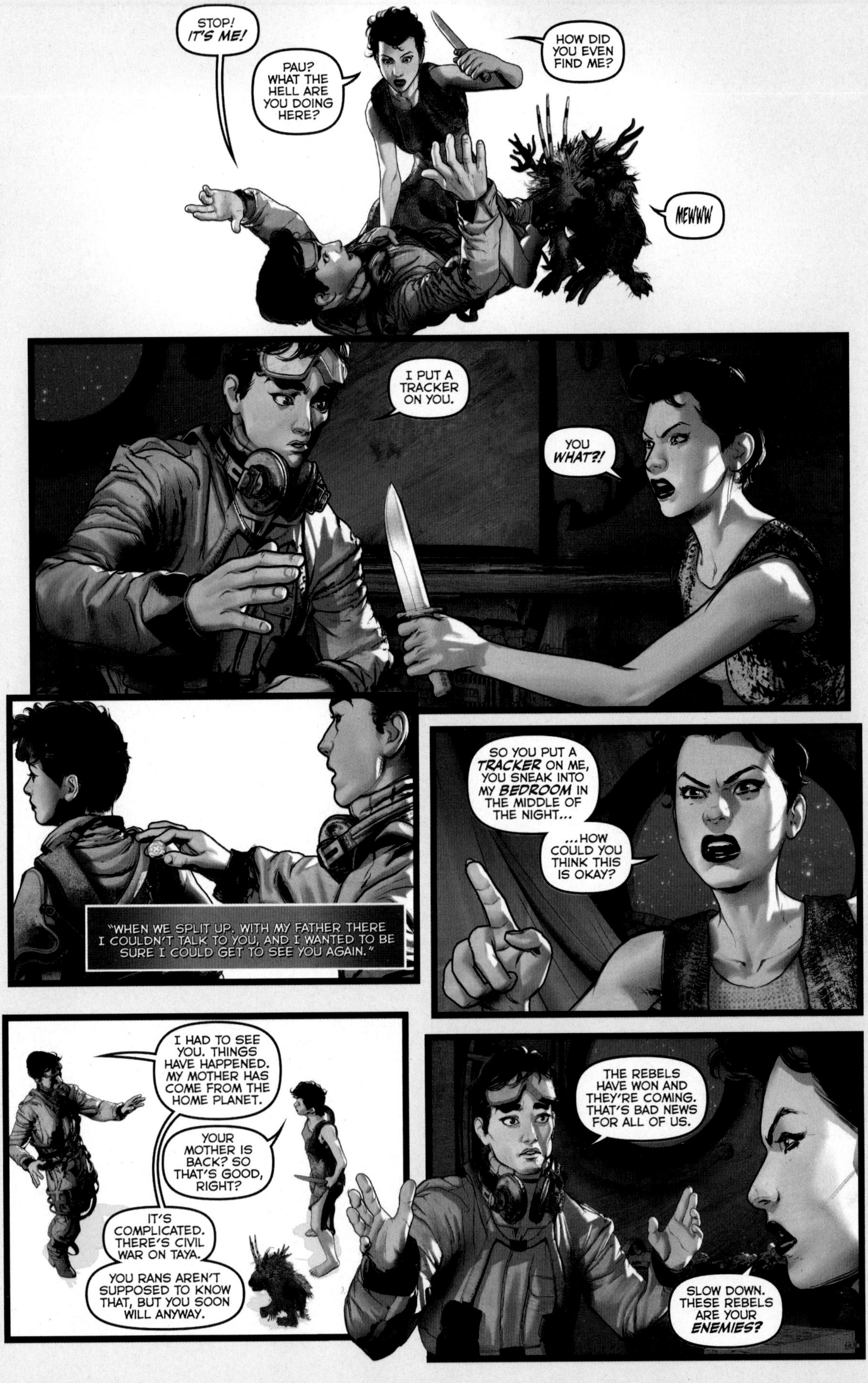
STOP! IT'S ME!
PAU? WHAT THE HELL ARE YOU DOING HERE?
HOW DID YOU EVEN FIND ME?
MEWWW
I PUT A TRACKER ON YOU.
YOU WHAT?!
"WHEN WE SPLIT UP. WITH MY FATHER THERE I COULDN'T TALK TO YOU, AND I WANTED TO BE SURE I COULD GET TO SEE YOU AGAIN."
SO YOU PUT A TRACKER ON ME, YOU SNEAK INTO MY BEDROOM IN THE MIDDLE OF THE NIGHT...
...HOW COULD YOU THINK THIS IS OKAY?
I HAD TO SEE YOU. THINGS HAVE HAPPENED. MY MOTHER HAS COME FROM THE HOME PLANET.
YOUR MOTHER IS BACK? SO THAT'S GOOD, RIGHT?
IT'S COMPLICATED. THERE'S CIVIL WAR ON TAYA.
YOU RANS AREN'T SUPPOSED TO KNOW THAT, BUT YOU SOON WILL ANYWAY.
THE REBELS HAVE WON AND THEY'RE COMING. THAT'S BAD NEWS FOR ALL OF US.
SLOW DOWN. THESE REBELS ARE YOUR ENEMIES?

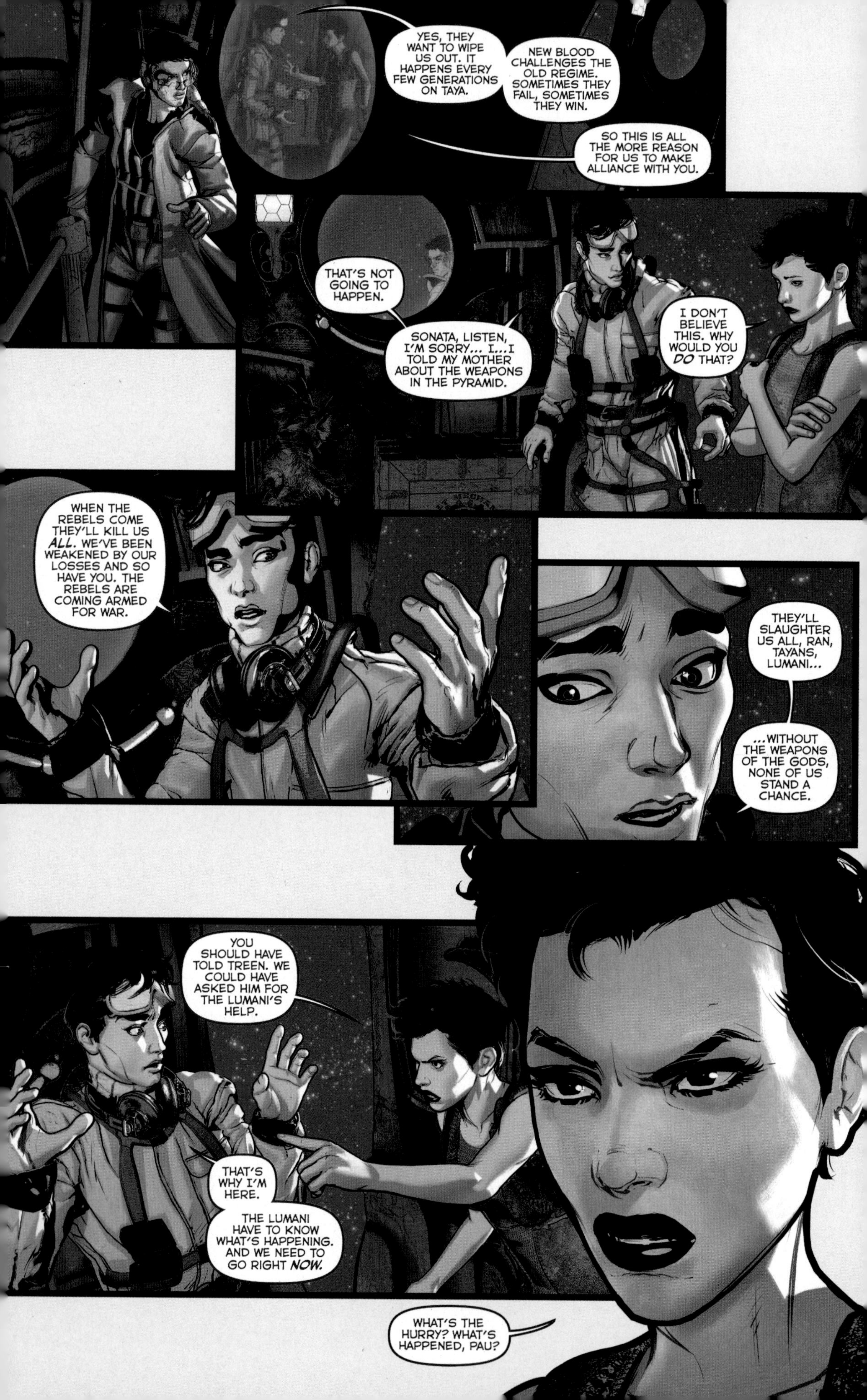
YES, THEY WANT TO WIPE US OUT. IT HAPPENS EVERY FEW GENERATIONS ON TAYA.
NEW BLOOD CHALLENGES THE OLD REGIME. SOMETIMES THEY FAIL, SOMETIMES THEY WIN.
SO THIS IS ALL THE MORE REASON FOR US TO MAKE ALLIANCE WITH YOU.
THAT'S NOT GOING TO HAPPEN.
SONATA, LISTEN, I'M SORRY... I...I TOLD MY MOTHER ABOUT THE WEAPONS IN THE PYRAMID.
I DON'T BELIEVE THIS. WHY WOULD YOU *DO* THAT?
WHEN THE REBELS COME THEY'LL KILL US *ALL*. WE'VE BEEN WEAKENED BY OUR LOSSES AND SO HAVE YOU. THE REBELS ARE COMING ARMED FOR WAR.
THEY'LL SLAUGHTER US ALL, RAN, TAYANS, LUMANI...
...WITHOUT THE WEAPONS OF THE GODS, NONE OF US STAND A CHANCE.
YOU SHOULD HAVE TOLD TREEN. WE COULD HAVE ASKED HIM FOR THE LUMANI'S HELP.
THAT'S WHY I'M HERE.
THE LUMANI HAVE TO KNOW WHAT'S HAPPENING. AND WE NEED TO GO RIGHT *NOW.*
WHAT'S THE HURRY? WHAT'S HAPPENED, PAU?

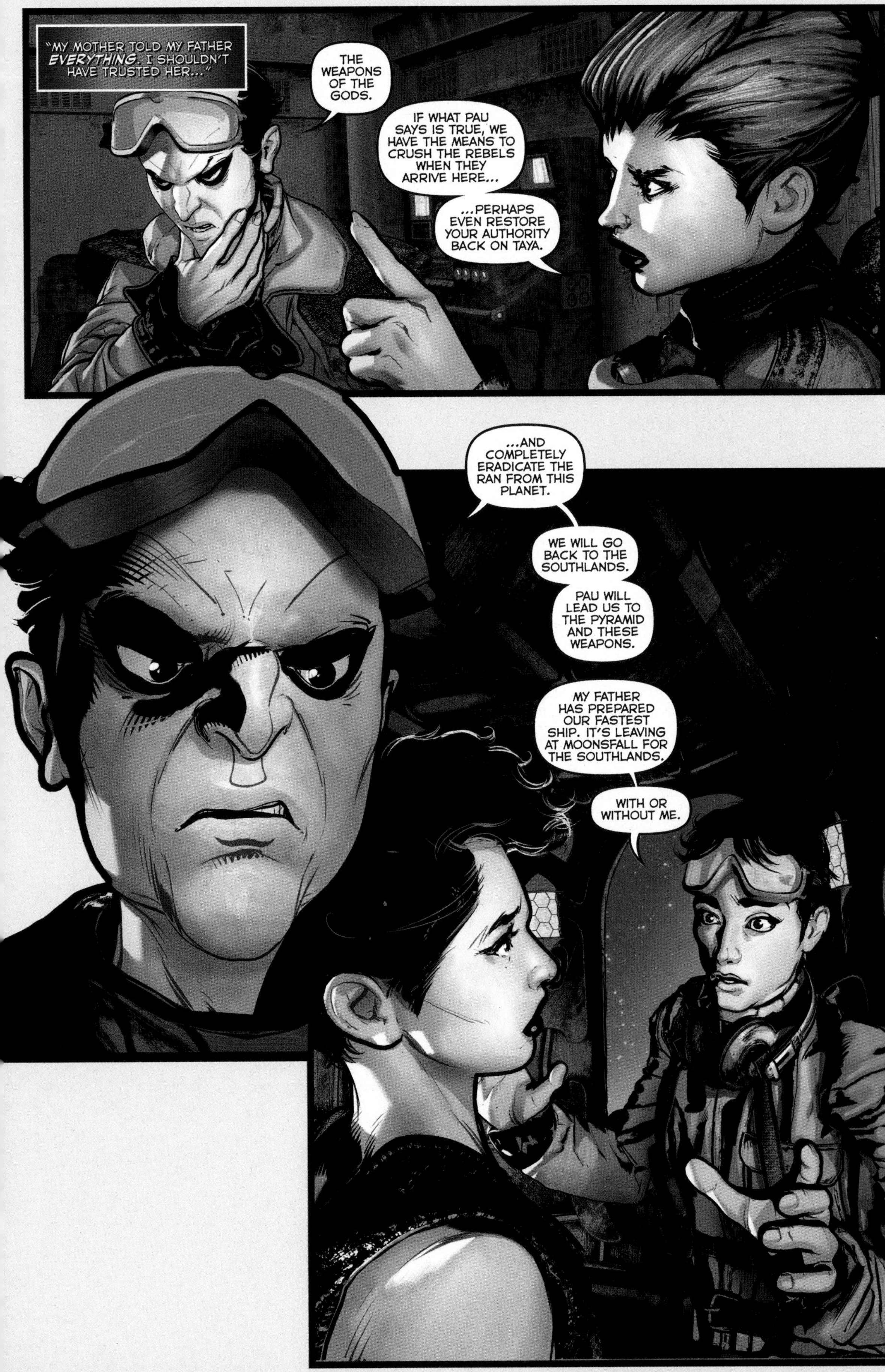
"MY MOTHER TOLD MY FATHER *EVERYTHING*. I SHOULDN'T HAVE TRUSTED HER..."
THE WEAPONS OF THE GODS.
IF WHAT PAU SAYS IS TRUE, WE HAVE THE MEANS TO CRUSH THE REBELS WHEN THEY ARRIVE HERE...
...PERHAPS EVEN RESTORE YOUR AUTHORITY BACK ON TAYA.
...AND COMPLETELY ERADICATE THE RAN FROM THIS PLANET.
WE WILL GO BACK TO THE SOUTHLANDS.
PAU WILL LEAD US TO THE PYRAMID AND THESE WEAPONS.
MY FATHER HAS PREPARED OUR FASTEST SHIP. IT'S LEAVING AT MOONSFALL FOR THE SOUTHLANDS.
WITH OR WITHOUT ME.

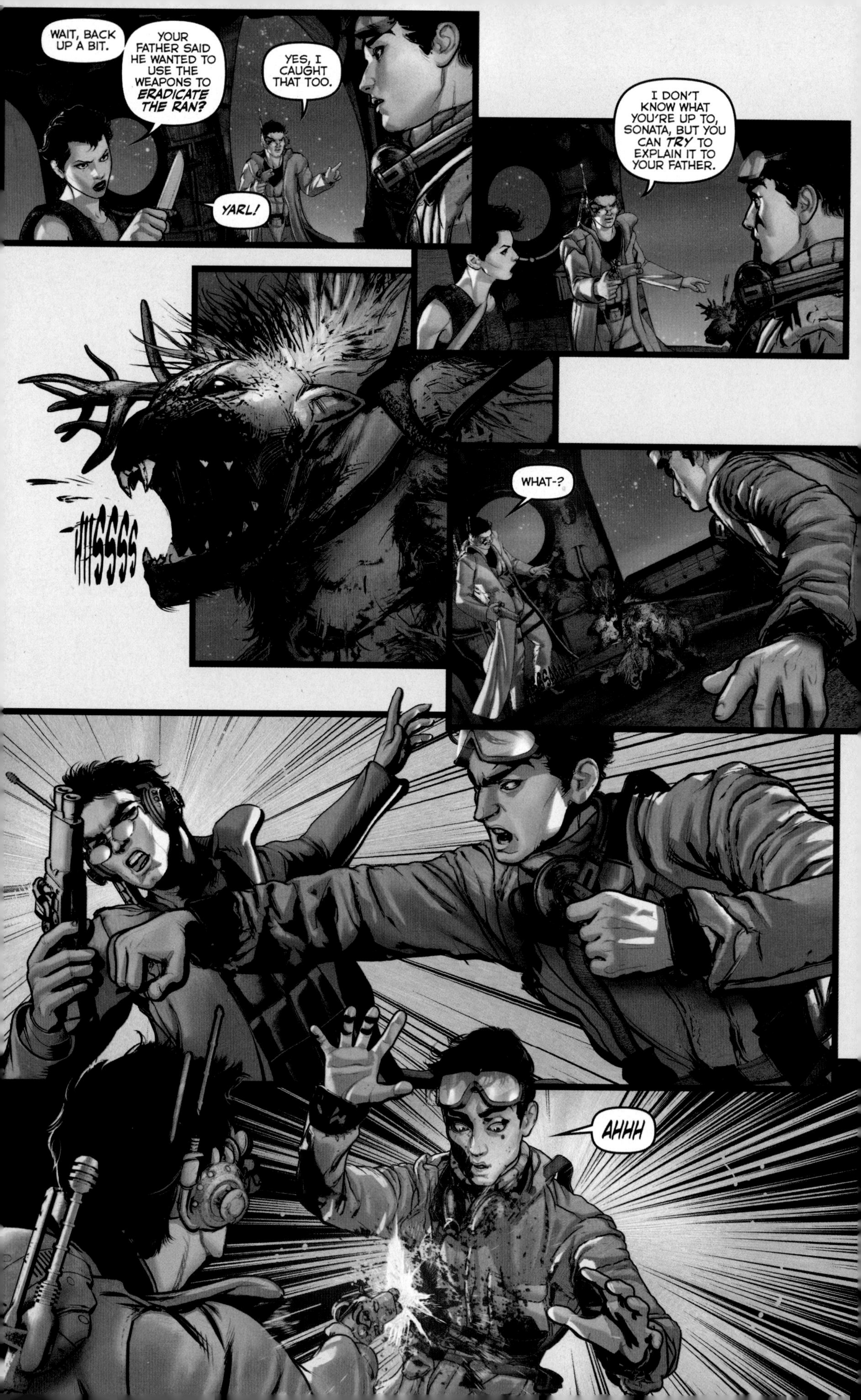
WAIT, BACK UP A BIT.
YOUR FATHER SAID HE WANTED TO USE THE WEAPONS TO *ERADICATE THE RAN?*
YES, I CAUGHT THAT TOO.
YARL!
I DON'T KNOW WHAT YOU'RE UP TO, SONATA, BUT YOU CAN *TRY* TO EXPLAIN IT TO YOUR FATHER.
HHSSSS
WHAT-?
AHHH

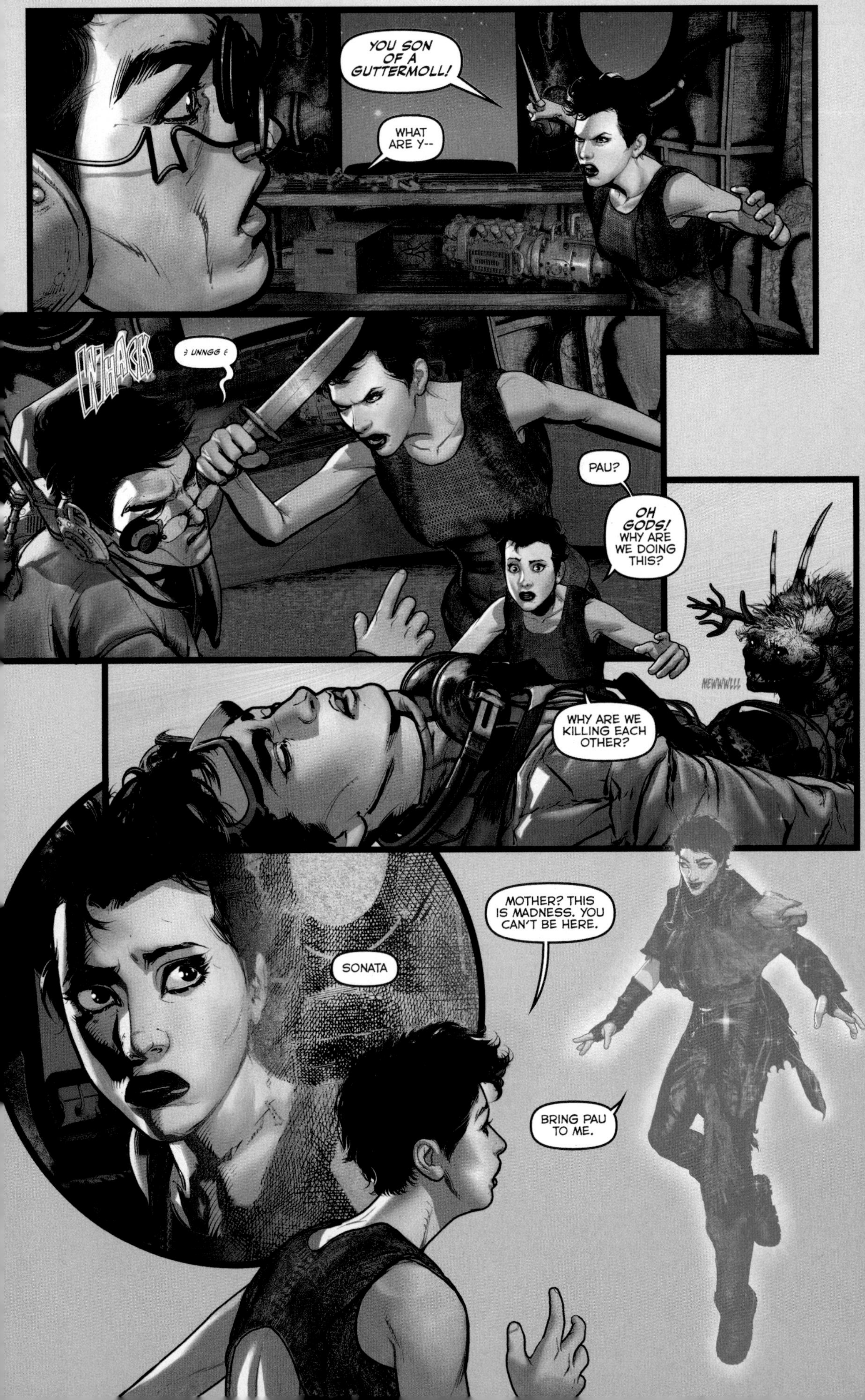
YOU SON OF A GUTTERMOLL!
WHAT ARE Y--
WHACK
UNNGG
PAU?
OH GODS! WHY ARE WE DOING THIS?
MEWWWLLL
WHY ARE WE KILLING EACH OTHER?
MOTHER? THIS IS MADNESS. YOU CAN'T BE HERE.
SONATA
BRING PAU TO ME.

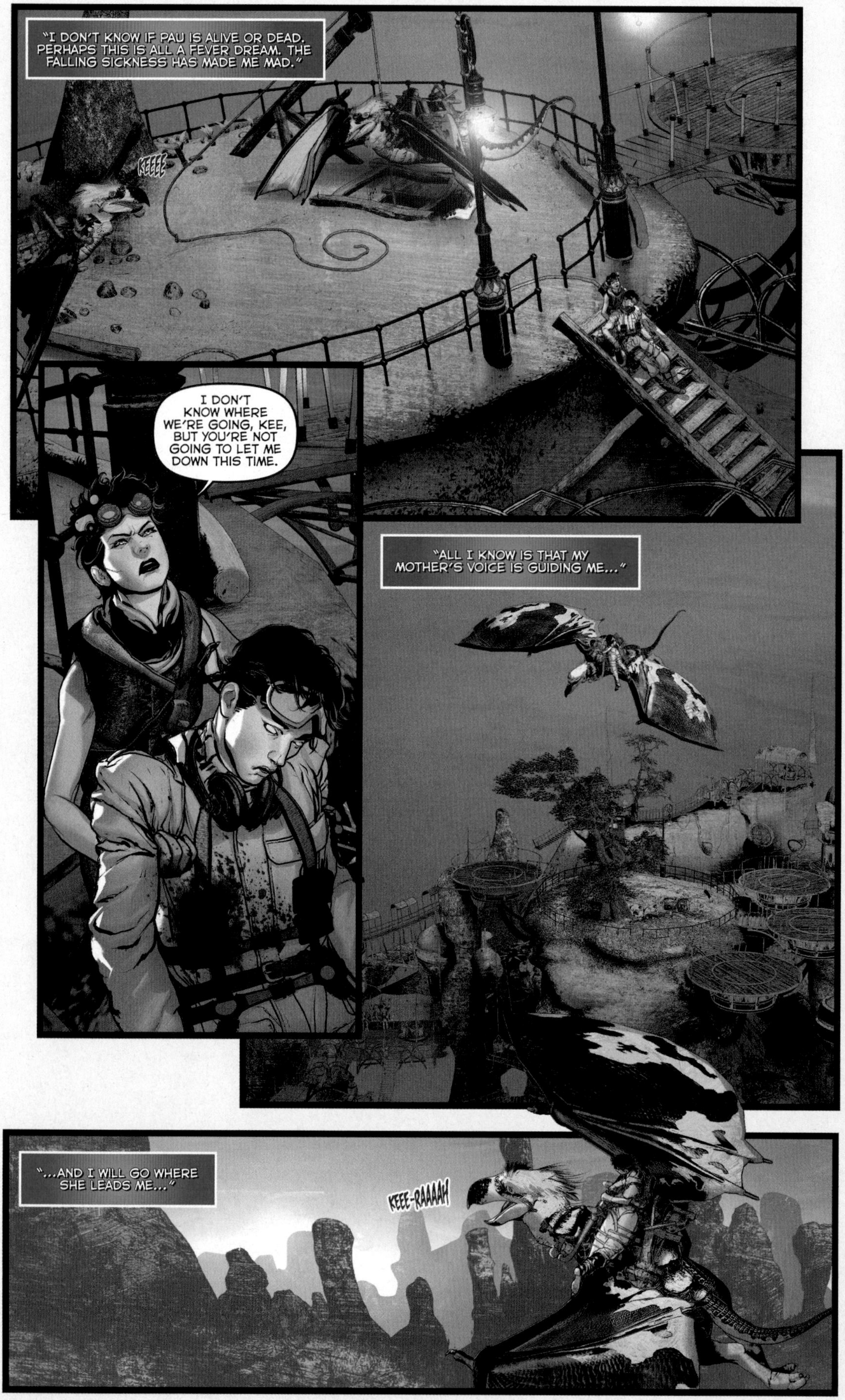
"I DON'T KNOW IF PAU IS ALIVE OR DEAD. PERHAPS THIS IS ALL A FEVER DREAM. THE FALLING SICKNESS HAS MADE ME MAD."
KEEEE
I DON'T KNOW WHERE WE'RE GOING, KEE, BUT YOU'RE NOT GOING TO LET ME DOWN THIS TIME.
"ALL I KNOW IS THAT MY MOTHER'S VOICE IS GUIDING ME..."
"...AND I WILL GO WHERE SHE LEADS ME..."
KEEE-RAAAAH

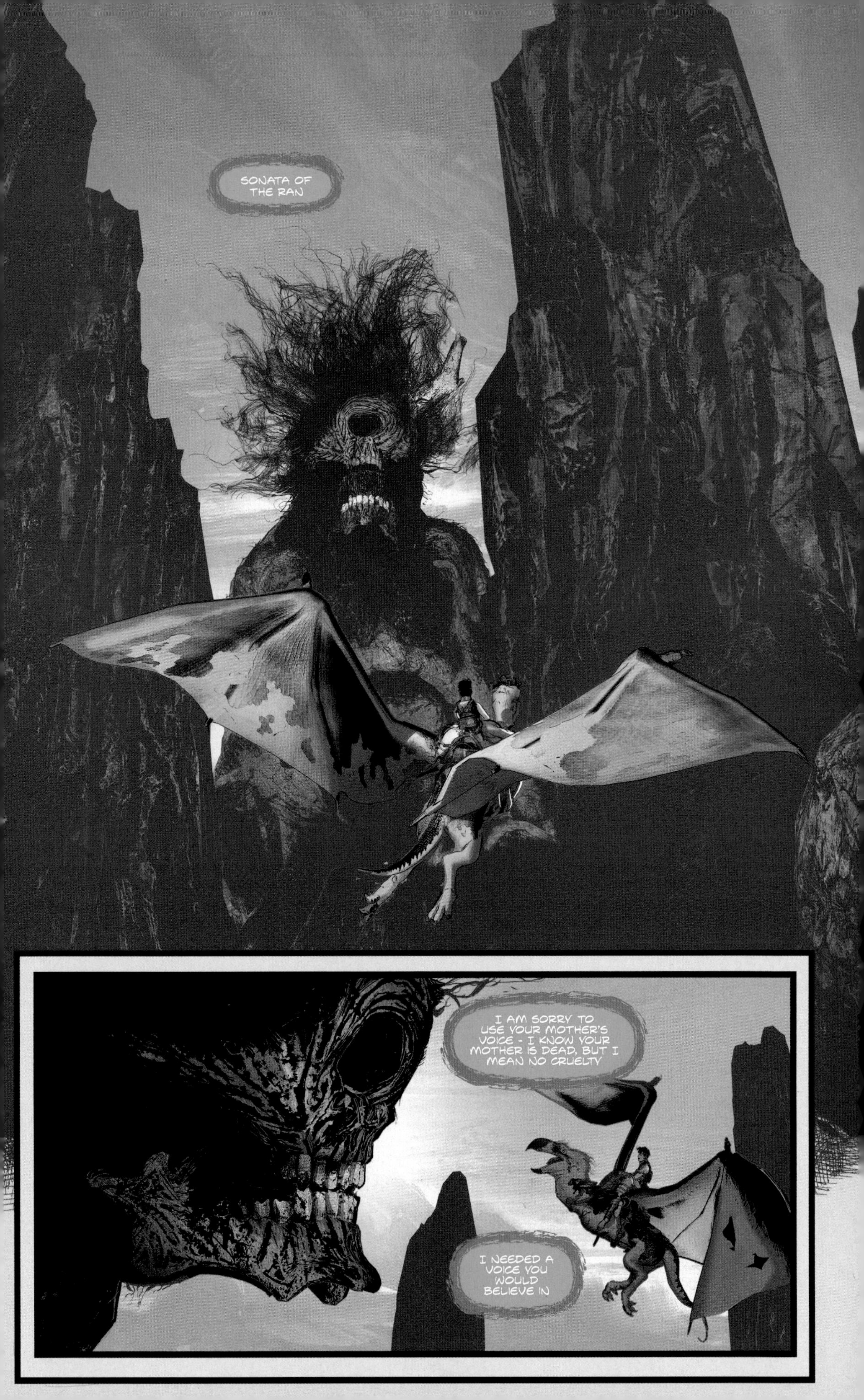
SONATA OF THE RAN
I AM SORRY TO USE YOUR MOTHER'S VOICE - I KNOW YOUR MOTHER IS DEAD, BUT I MEAN NO CRUELTY
I NEEDED A VOICE YOU WOULD BELIEVE IN

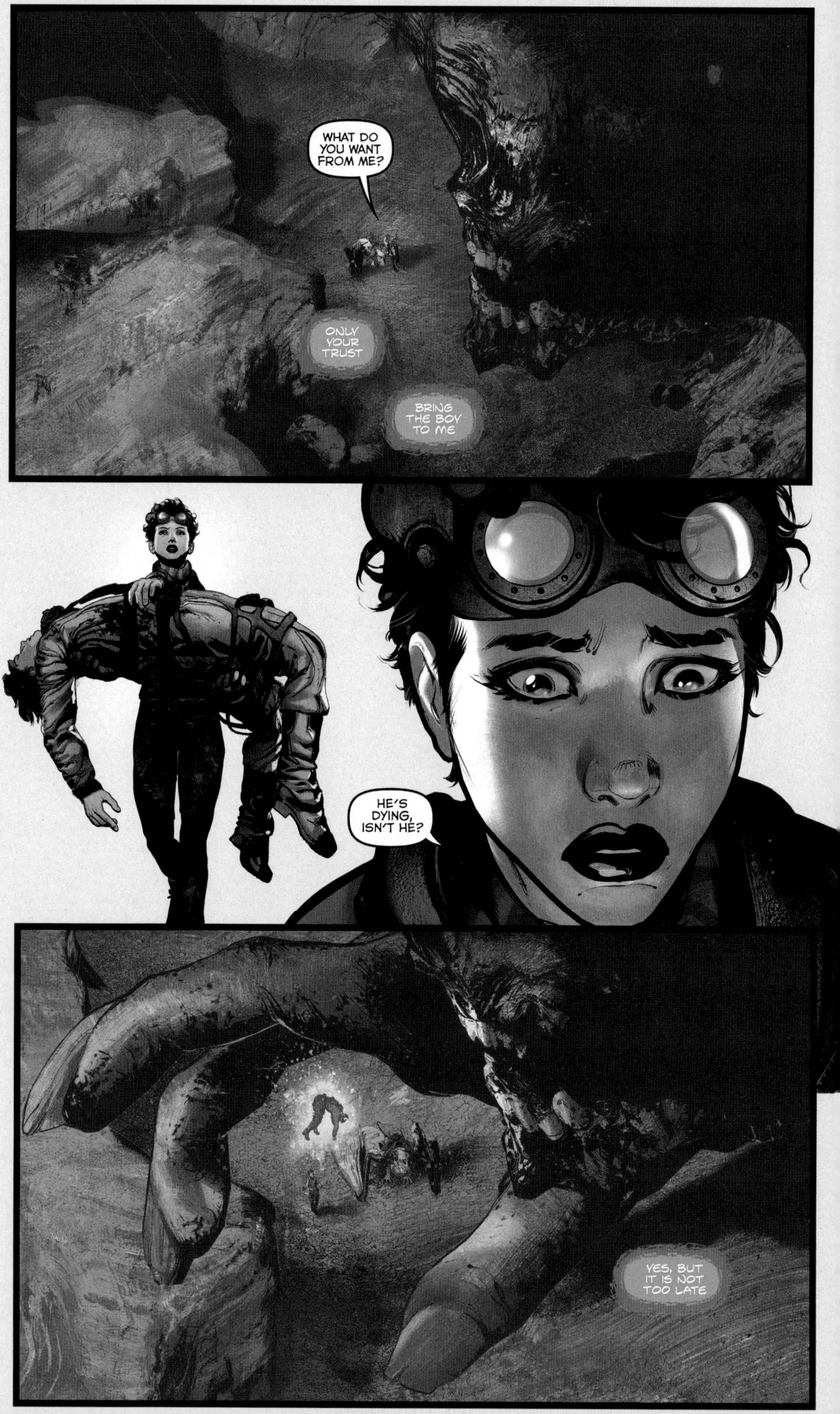
WHAT DO YOU WANT FROM ME?
ONLY YOUR TRUST
BRING THE BOY TO ME
HE'S DYING, ISN'T HE?
YES, BUT IT IS NOT TOO LATE

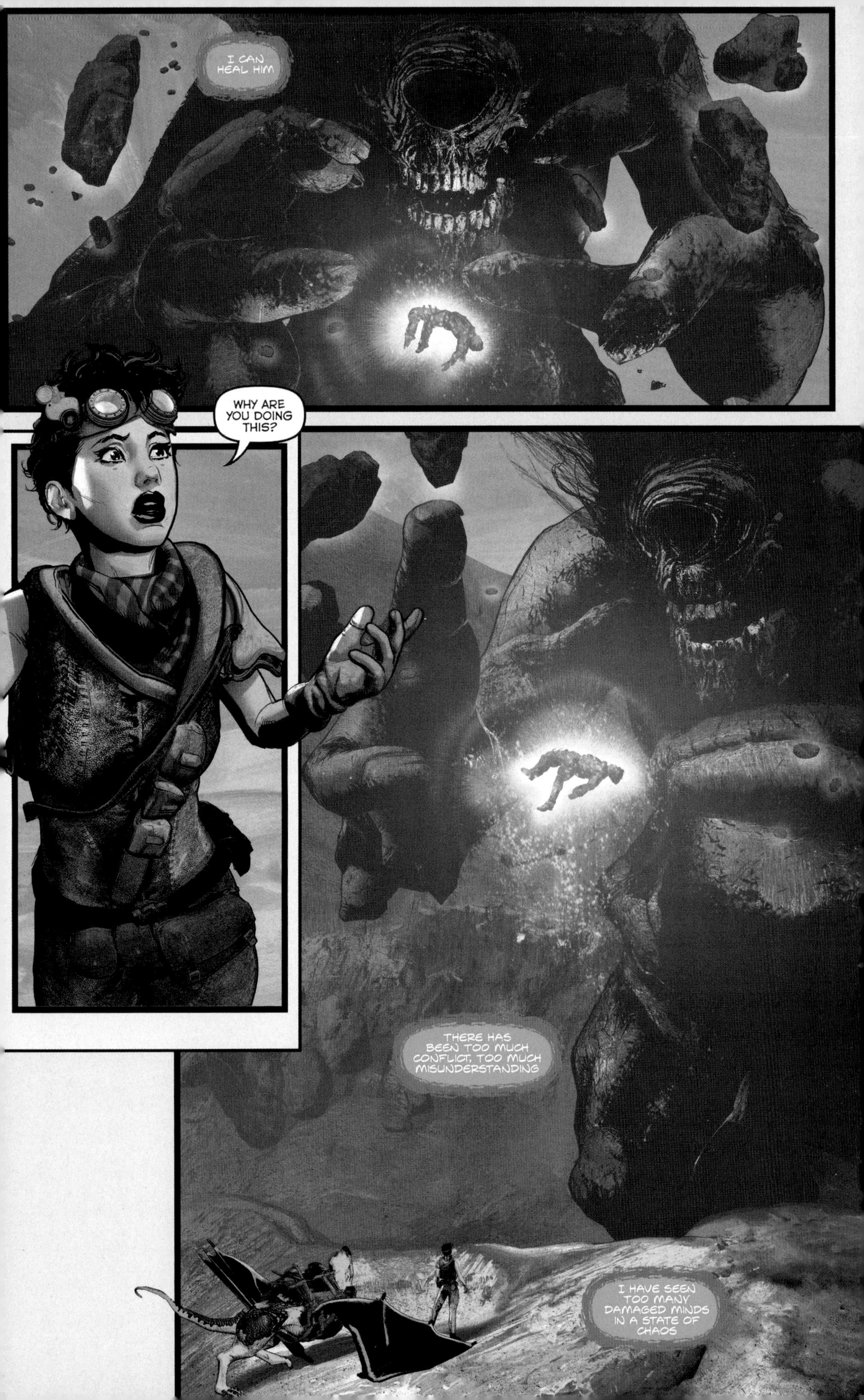
I CAN HEAL HIM
WHY ARE YOU DOING THIS?
THERE HAS BEEN TOO MUCH CONFLICT, TOO MUCH MISUNDERSTANDING
I HAVE SEEN TOO MANY DAMAGED MINDS IN A STATE OF CHAOS

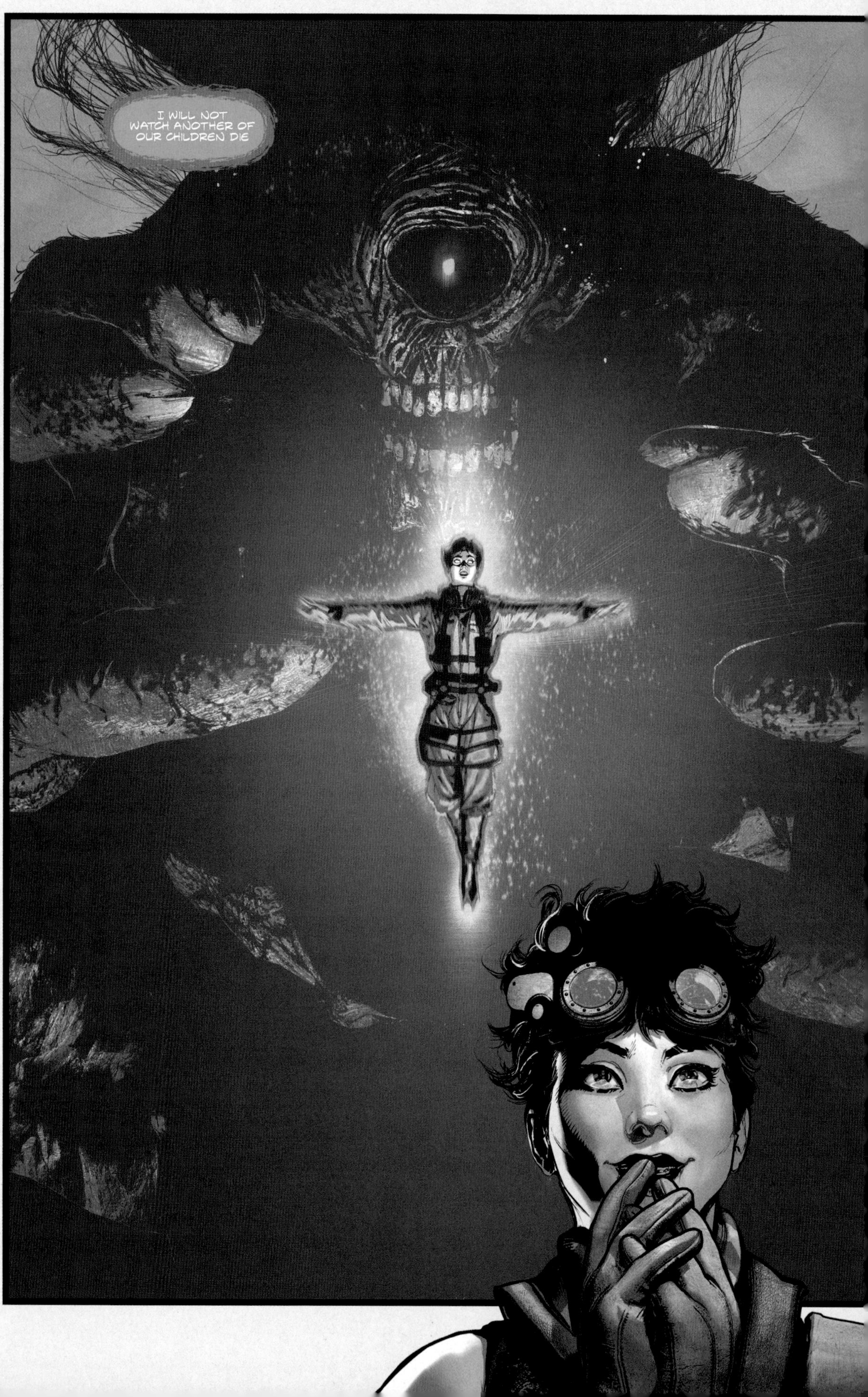
I WILL NOT WATCH ANOTHER OF OUR CHILDREN DIE

Issue #3 Second Printing Cover

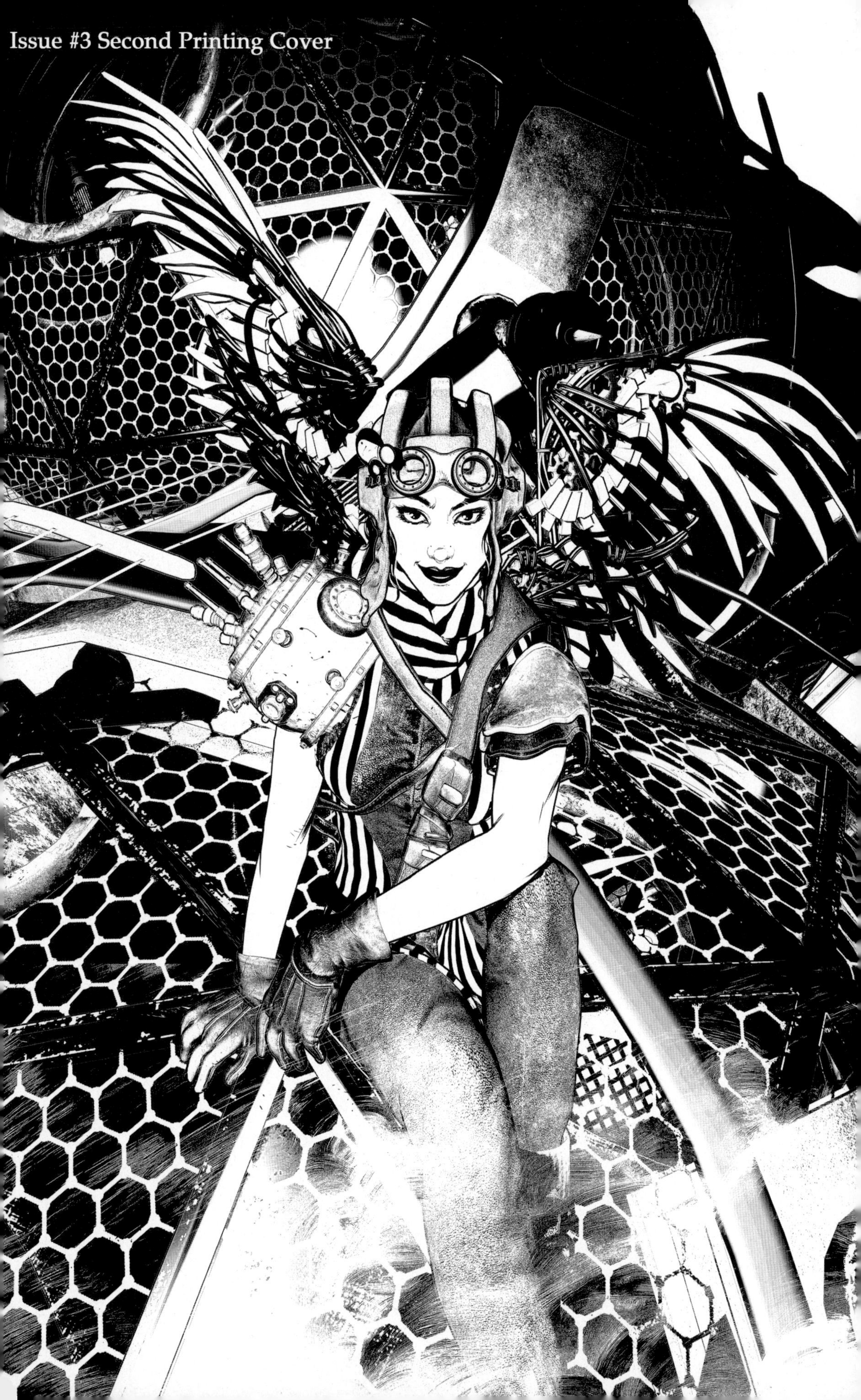

Vegas Summit Exclusive Cover

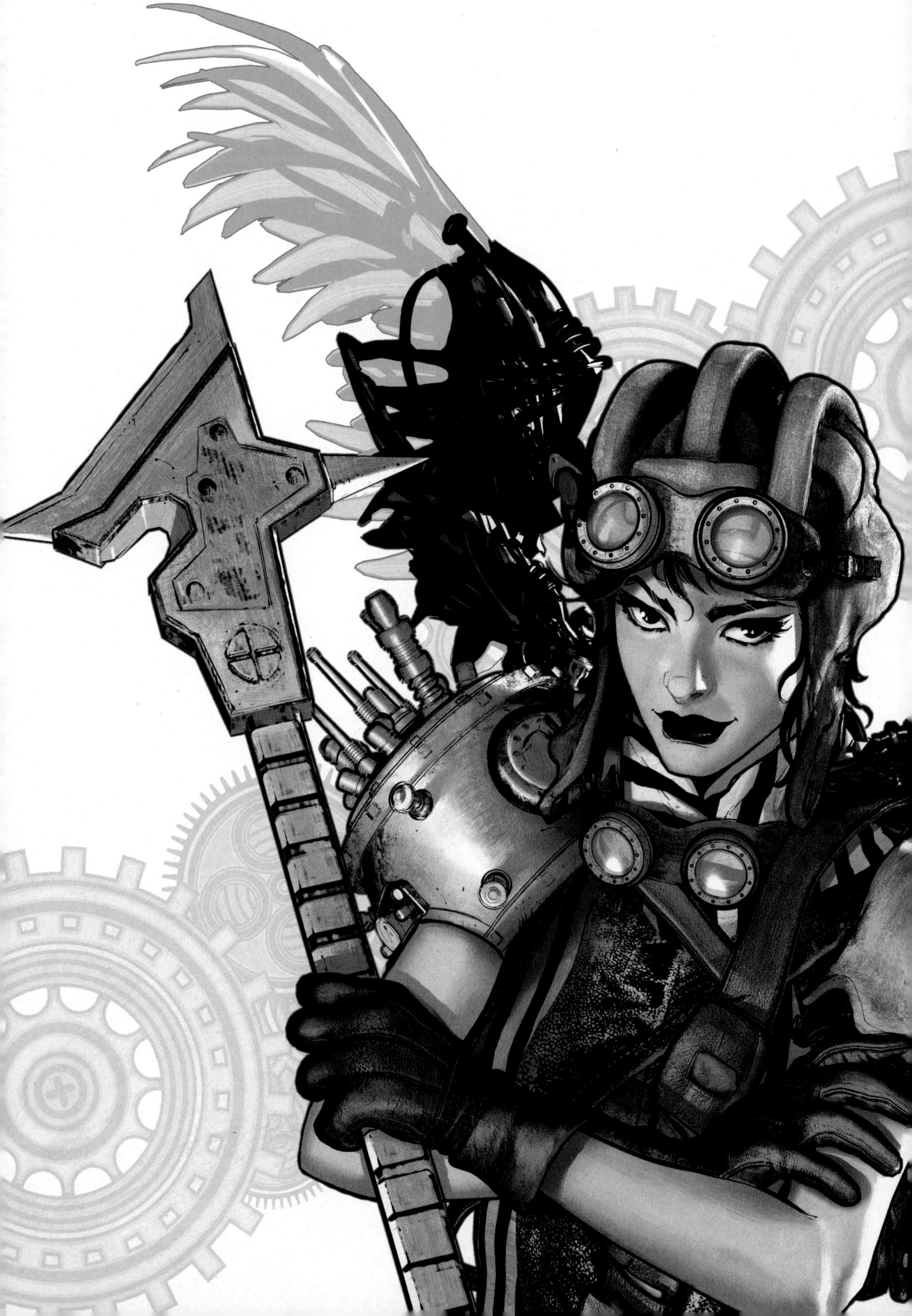

EARLY CONCEPT PAGES

with early version of Sonata

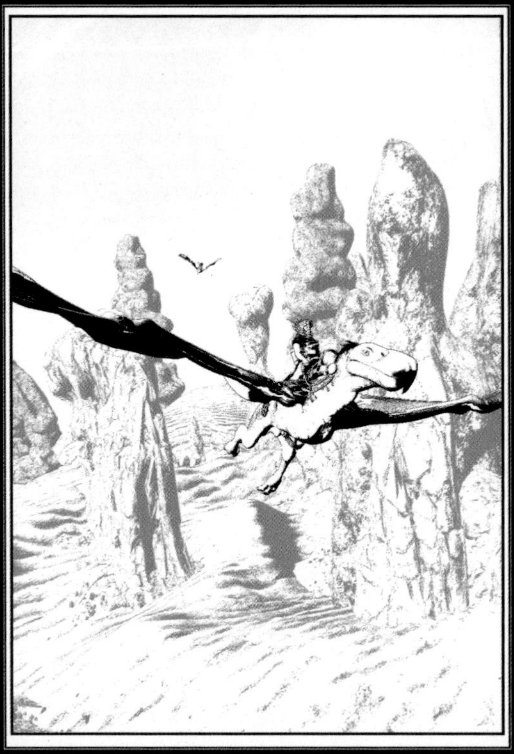

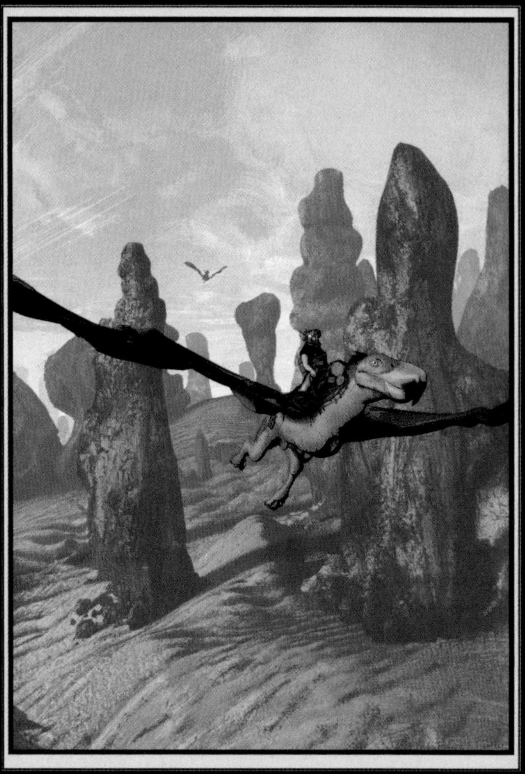

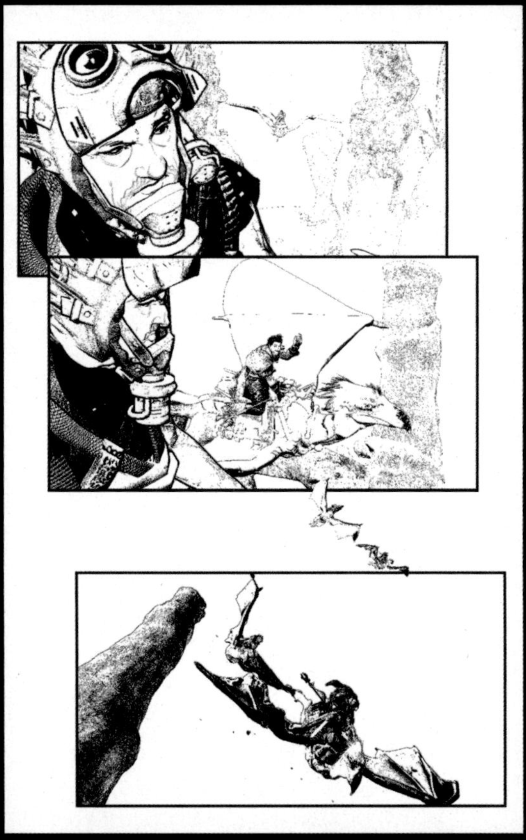

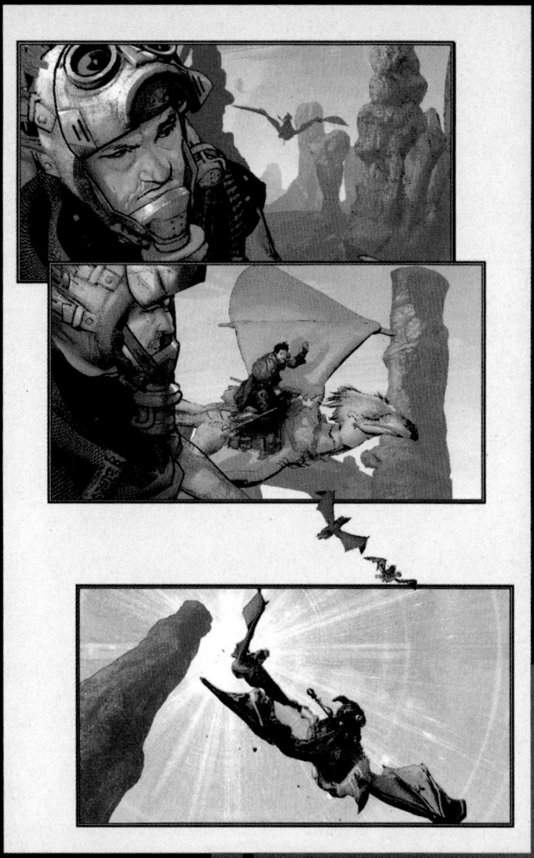

EARLY CONCEPT PAGES

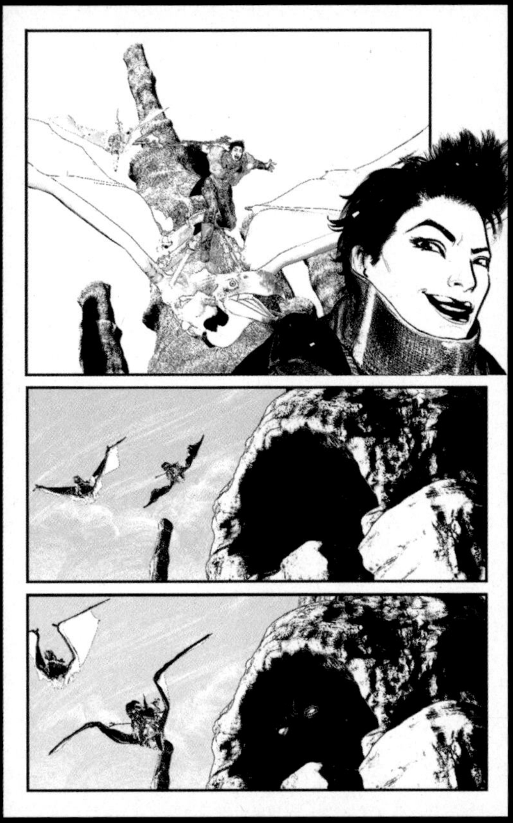

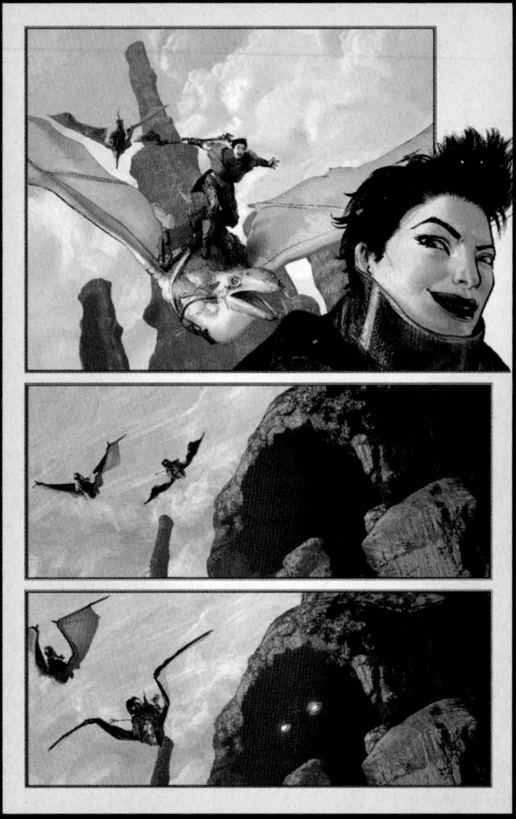

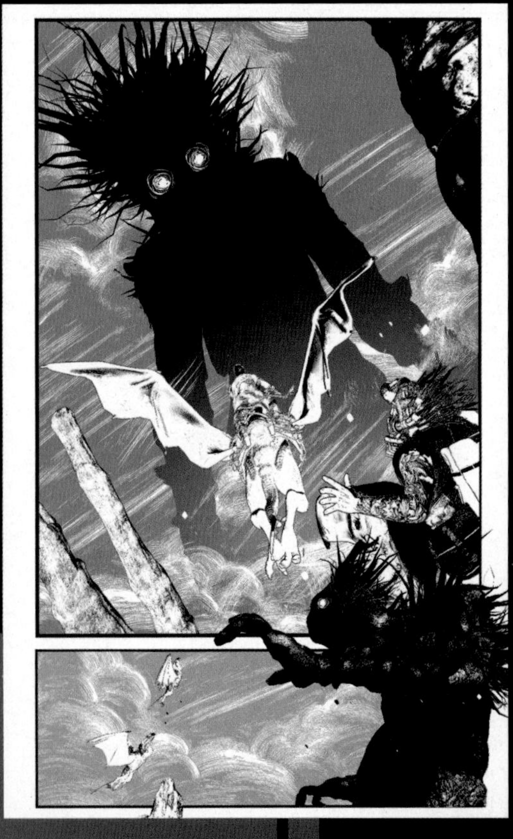

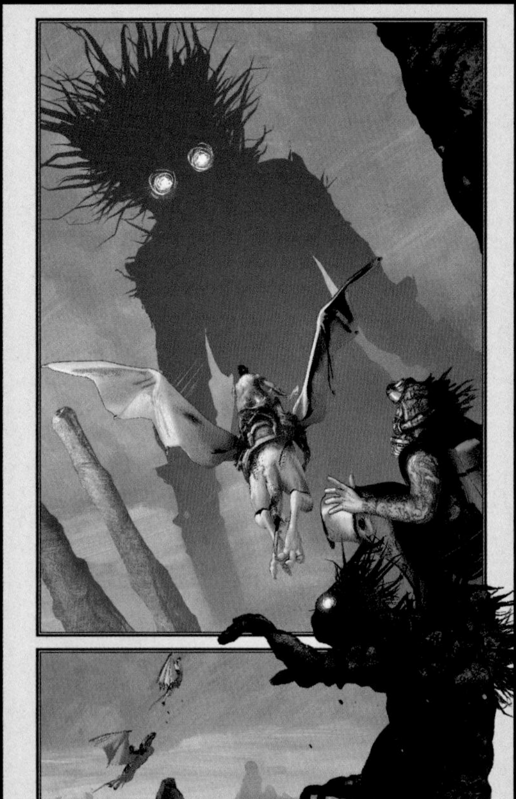

image® Shadowline®

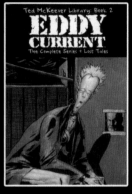

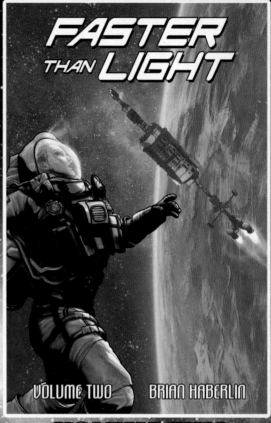